Danish Sword

Book 4 in the Danelaw Saga

by

Griff Hosker

Published by Sword Books Ltd 2023

A CIP catalogue record for this title is available from the British Library.

Contents

Real People used in the book

King Sweyn Forkbeard - King of Denmark
King Æthelred – King of England
Edmund Ironside- his son
Ælfheath – The Archbishop of Cantwareburh
Abbot Ælfmaer – Abbot of the Augustine monastery in Cantwareburh
Harald Sweynson – the eldest son of the King of Denmark.
Cnut Sweynson - second son of the King of Denmark
Eadric Streona – A Saxon leader mistrusted by all
Eiríkr Hákonarson – Eorl of Northumbria
Lady Ælfgifu – a Saxon noblewoman and later Queen of England
Lord Ælfhelm – her father
Thorkell the Tall – Jarl of the Jomsvikings
Hemingr – Thorkell's brother
Æthelstan, the son of King Æthelred
Oswy - the son-in-law of Eorledman Byrhtnoth
Thurbrand the Hold – A Northumbrian lord who controlled southern Northumbria
Thorkell the Tall – the leader of the Jomsvikings
Uhtred the Bold - A Northumbrian lord who controlled northern Northumbria
Ealdred – the eldest son of Uhtred
Findláech – Mormaer of Moray (the father of Shakespeare's Macbeth)

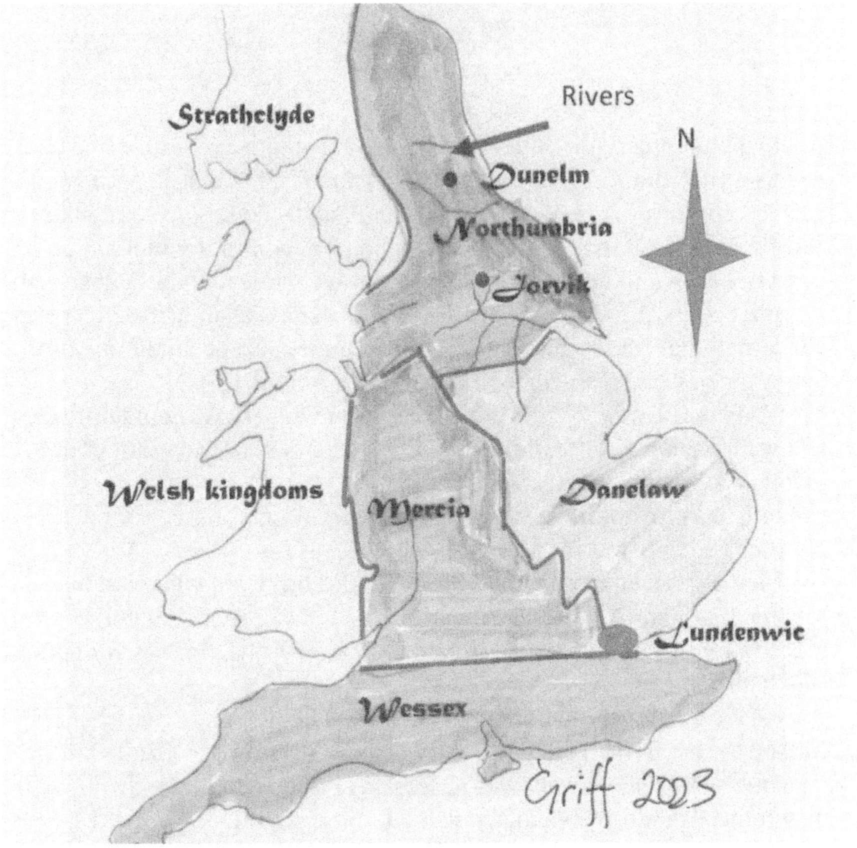

England at the start of the 11th Century

Prologue

I had but one night with Mary before I had to leave with Prince Cnut for the court of the new King Of Denmark, Haraldr. Prince Cnut's hearthweru now lay dead along the Trent and it would be Sven Saxon Sword and the Dragon Sword that would protect him. I would take my hearthweru. Although I had escaped from the battles largely unharmed, I did not count the cuts and knocks I had received as injuries, Mary was concerned that I was now in even more danger. As she lay in my arms on our one evening together she confided her fears to me.

"You and I are lucky. We have children who are without ailments and we have a good life. Give up the sword and become a farmer or a merchant. I will be content."

I kissed the top of her head, "You do not wish your manor in Norton?"

I felt her shake her head, "I thought I did but from what you have told me that part of the land of my birth is an even more dangerous place to live. With the Scots raiding and civil war rife I would rather stay here."

I stayed silent. I did not believe her for I knew that in her heart she wished to live in the land of her birth. She had said what she had to keep me safe. The journey was necessary. Prince Cnut intended to visit his brother Harald who had just named himself King of Denmark. I was still uncertain as to what Cnut's real intentions were. I did not trust Harald and I was certain that he had some involvement in the death of his father King Sweyn but as Cnut had squandered his father's army, we had no choice. We needed help if Cnut was going to claim what he saw as his birthright, England, but what was he willing to do to achieve that end? I had sworn an oath to protect Prince Cnut. I had said I would help him to gain the crown of England and I dared not risk the wrath of the Norns, but the oath threatened to shackle me to the prince for my whole life.

"When the meeting with the king is over then you will return here will you not? You have earned a rest and I deserve some time with my husband and my son."

"You deserve the truth, Mary, and the truth is that I know not. My thread is irrevocably bound with Cnut. I cannot escape my fate."

Her body shifted with the anger of her words, "Not those three witches again! Cnut is Christian, surely, he must know that they are a fiction."

I did not like her slandering the Norns. She said she did not believe in them but I did. "I have sworn an oath to him then, how about that?"

She snorted, "You did not swear on a Bible and so the oath is meaningless."

I sighed, "An oath on a sword such as mine is more binding than one on a Bible. The blood of the dead is within the blade. You cannot cleanse a sword of the dead. They are there and they watch." I hugged her, "I will go with Cnut tomorrow and my foster father will come too. We will see the king and when we return, we will have a better idea of what we face."

I was treating her as I had done with my children when they were younger, I was telling them a story. The truth was I knew that I would be going to war once more and Oathsword would be drawn again.

Chapter 1

The king and the prince

We did not travel as an army for that would provoke war. The brother of a new king could not travel in his own country with an army. The handful of his bodyguards who had survived the slaughter at Gegnesburh guarded Cnut while I had Dreng, Snorri, Faramir, Gandálfr and Steana with me. My foster father, Sweyn Skull Taker came with four of his hearthweru. There were just twenty of us who rode the road east to King Harald's stronghold. I rode with my foster father and Cnut protected by my four hearthweru while Steana, my son, rode behind leading the pack horse. The other bodyguards followed. Cnut might be the one who was of royal blood but that did not mean he had the best warriors surrounding him. The best lay dead at Gegnesburh. His survivors deferred to my men.

My foster father was a practical man and a wise one. It was he who cleared the air, "Before we meet with King Harald, prince, what is it that you hope for?" Cnut looked at Sweyn. "Do you wish the throne of Denmark?"

"My father did not name an heir. Why should I not claim the crown?"

There was a laugh in the voice of my wise foster father, "Because, princeling, your father left Harald in command of the country when he left. He took you to England and we all know that he intended you to be the King of England. More than that his army is untouched and whole; the bones of your army lie along the Trent."

Cnut smiled, "But as my father did not name an heir then I have every right to ask, quite reasonably, of course, if I might share the throne with my brother."

I saw my foster father nod appreciatively. He did not know Cnut as well as I did. Cnut liked to play stone wars with the little figures and he understood strategy. By asking what he did he invited his brother to help him to gain the English crown. Of course, if King Harald had been behind the plot to kill King Sweyn, then we might be inviting our own murder at his new palace.

"What of Thorkell the Tall?"

Thorkell the Tall, the leader of the Jomsvikings had, effectively, been the main reason why Cnut had lost England. The prince had been foolish but it had been the defection of the Jomsvikings to the Saxons that had ended all hopes of Prince Cnut being crowned King of England. My foster father's tone told me what he thought of that. He almost spat the words out. He hated betrayal in any form.

Cnut was more pragmatic, "He took the money from the Saxons. I can understand his motives. I do not approve of them but men have been seduced by smaller amounts of gold in the past. He was never my man. He betrayed my father. I have too few men as it is to reclaim my birthright without making an enemy of Thorkell." My foster father nodded. He understood his practicality. "How many fighting ships can I rely on, Sweyn Skull Taker?"

It was a vital question. A drekar could carry anywhere between thirty and sixty men. Although we could take as many in knarr, we needed fighting ships to ensure that we could land safely.

"Not enough. You have one drekar, Prince Cnut. My foster son has another. I have three and Einar the Fat has one. Even if we used my son's knarr then we could only muster four hundred warriors. Is that enough to take a kingdom? Even one led by one as poor as Æthelred?"

When we had been heading back from England I had had word of the king, "It is rumoured he is dying."

Cnut smiled, "I would rather he lived and continued to make such poor decisions."

"It is his second son, Edmund, that you should fear, Prince Cnut." They both looked at me. "When I went north to fight for Uhtred, I learned that Edmund, now that his elder brother is dead, is seen as a better prospect as king than his father. Uhtred supports him and as I helped the Northumbrian to wrest control of the north from the Scots then that means Edmund has control of the north of the land. He is the one we should fear. Æthelred just holds Lundenwic and Wessex."

As we rode east, I told them all that I had learned of the men we might have to fight. The Northumbrians had so much Viking blood in them that I felt they were almost equal to us. They fought as we did and having fought the Scots for so many years they had honed their skills. I did not underestimate them. If Uhtred and Thurbrand the Hold did not have such a bloody feud then they might already have taken back the land called Danelaw. As I spoke, I saw Prince Cnut taking it all in. He had asked me to be an adviser, to be his Karl Three Fingers and he heeded my words.

King Harald had built a new stronghold on the east coast of Denmark. It had ditches and palisades and would have been called a fortress if he had not made it so comfortable. He had garrisoned the stronghold with those loyal to him. I did not necessarily think that they were a martial threat to us, they had not fought in major wars and battles like the supporters of Prince Cnut but this was not time to take them on. We were viewed with suspicion as we sought entry.

Cnut was unruffled by their attitude, "Bersi Long Breeches, I come to tell my brother, the king, of our father's end. If you think he does not need to know then tell me and we will return west. It is your decision."

The commander of the watch was clearly undecided. My foster father said, "The king needs to know how his father met his death. There are rumours, are there not? Surely King Harald would wish to know the truth."

He nodded, "Only three of you may enter and without weapons too. The rest stay without."

"Of course."

He brought ten warriors to escort us. I smiled. Had we chosen to then the ten could have been slain in ten sword blows from the men we had with us. We were tempered steel and they were untried iron. There were more guards at the doors to the mead hall. It struck me that Harald was a fearful man.

"Your swords." Bersi held his hands out for the weapons.

I shook my head, "I do not give Oathsword to one I do not know, nor trust." My eyes met Bersi's and he looked away. "Here, my son, hold Oathsword and try not to frighten these watchmen with it." I was insulting them and it was deliberate. I needed them to know that we did not fear them and that I was using the reputation I had garnered to intimidate them. Bersi flushed but nodded. He feared to take me on. I saw my foster father smile as he also handed his sword to Steana. Cnut gave his to Olaf, one of the last of his bodyguards.

King Harald had either inherited a building begun by his father or had spent a fortune to have built such a magnificent mead hall in such a short space of time. King Sweyn had been a practical man and I saw the same attributes in his son. Denmark was Christian but the carvings in the hall were filled with dragons and creatures from our mythology. Crosses were featured but you had to seek them out. The king had a dais to raise him above the rest and he sat on a throne that was also well-carved. It was cleverly constructed so that it did make the king look bigger than he was and men had to look up at him. He had to have been warned of our arrival and I wondered if the delay in our admittance was to allow the king the time to make a more regal impression. If so it showed that he feared either his brother or the company he kept.

He had draped about his shoulders a bearskin. Many men wore the skin of a bear and some, Ulfheonar, fought in them but this one was white. It had come from the far north and the fiercest of bears. The king had not killed it and I wondered how many men had died in the killing.

He wore a crown upon his head and he had a sword across his lap. On his fingers were rings and around his neck were hung golden necklets. He had four men flanking him. Two were bodyguards and two patently advisers although all were armed with good swords. They were not as good as the one held outside by Steana but they had jewels in their pommels and showed that they had been designed by a Frankish weaponsmith. I recognised their work.

"Approach brother."

The king held out his hand so that Cnut could kiss the ring that was worn by the King of Denmark. We had taken it and the crown from King Sweyn's body and sent them back to Denmark before the disaster that was Gegnesburh. I wondered what would have happened had we retained them. Cnut dutifully bowed and kissed the ring. The obeisance done the king smiled and said, "Gorm, fetch a chair for my brother."

One of the bodyguards descended and brought a chair. He placed it at the foot of the dais so that Cnut had to look up at his brother. The king was demonstrating his power in a crude way. My foster father and I were left to stand.

"So, little brother, tell me how our father died."

We had all sworn an oath to keep the secret of the murder of King Sweyn. I believed that King Harald had hired the killers. There could be no proof of that for the killers had all died.

Cnut told the version that we had told the army. I kept my eye on the king as Cnut spoke, "He was tired and weary. It may have been that he ate some bad fish but whatever the reason he went to bed and died in his sleep. God took him."

I saw that Harald did not believe the story but there was relief in his eyes. I did not doubt that he had heard the story from those who had returned to Denmark after the disaster of Gegnesburh. He must have known, however, that Cnut knew the truth.

The king nodded, "And you were unlucky to be betrayed and lose the country that our father gave to you." He smiled, and there was relief in that smile, "So, brother, what is it that you wish?"

Cnut smiled too, "To rule Denmark at your side, brother. Between us, we can conquer Norway and the lands of the Wends. Who knows, we might be able to challenge the Empire."

He had avoided mentioning England. Cnut was far cleverer than I was. I was a good warrior and knew strategy but I was as a babe in arms compared with Cnut.

One of the advisers snorted and the king held up his hand, "Peace, Karl, what my brother asks is not unreasonable. Our father did not name an heir, although as he left me to rule Denmark in his stead it is clear that he saw me as King of Denmark and my brother as King of England. It is a pity that you have lost your kingdom, Cnut."

The fencing continued, "And yet, brother, together we are stronger. I have learned much in England, not least how to fight." He was challenging Harald who, so far as I knew, had no battle honours to his name.

"I think, little brother, that you have learned to lose."

His bodyguards and advisers laughed. I could not remain silent, "Prince Cnut was betrayed, King Harald, and many men might have been destroyed by such betrayal. Prince Cnut survived and he is now here. More, he has men and swords who are loyal to him."

Cnut did not look around but continued to sit with his hands folded together as though in prayer, looking at his brother. The king's eyes fixed on me and they were cold and reptilian. In that instant, I knew he had ordered the death of his own father, "Ah, yes, Sven Saxon Sword and his allegedly magic sword. Surely you, as a Danish lord, are loyal to Denmark."

"Of course, King Harald, but your father made me swear an oath to protect Prince Cnut. Surely you would not wish me to risk the wrath of the Norns and break such an oath."

His four men were Christians but they all wore Thor's hammer and their hands went to them. The smile left King Harald's face. It was my turn to smile.

The king nodded, "An oath, even a pagan one, is not to be ignored." He turned his attention back to his brother, "We appear to have a problem. I am not willing to share my throne with you." Cnut nodded, "Yet civil war would benefit no one, save our enemies. If the lies told by my enemies were true then I could have the three of you murdered here and end any threat to me." My eyes narrowed and the king went on hurriedly, "I do not threaten, Sven Saxon Sword, I am merely pointing out that I am an honourable man and my little brother deserves something. I am saying that it is not here in Denmark that he will find a crown but in England. In return for an oath not to threaten the crown of Denmark, I will find men and ships to help Cnut take back England. What say you, brother?"

He stood and walked up the three steps to the throne, I saw the four men put their hands on their sword hilts. The king waved an arm as though to calm them. He stood and embraced Cnut.

Cnut knelt, "So long as I am supported in my endeavours to take England, I will do nothing to jeopardise King Harald's throne."

I am not sure it was the oath that the king wanted but it was the only one he would get. The king nodded, "And I swear to use my power to build an army for you." Cnut stood and they embraced once more. "And now that is done then you have no need of these two lords for while you live in my home you are safe from any enemies and Oathsword can go back to Agerhøne and Ribe."

"Is that what you wish, Prince Cnut?" I was happy to challenge the king.

He turned, "I will be safe here for I know that if any assassin came to end my life, then the Dragon Sword would wreak its vengeance and there are none who can fight against that blade, are there?"

I bowed, "Of course, and you should know that when we return home my foster father and I will begin to recruit men to help you take back your kingdom. Treachery should not be rewarded."

We turned and left the hall.

The door closed and we donned our swords. "Olaf, the prince stays. The king has assured us that he will be safe but…"

"We will watch him, my lord. We owe it to those who are now in Valhalla."

We headed back to our horses. My foster father shook his head, "Not a particularly hospitable welcome." He looked up at the skies which threatened rain. "He did not like your words and he punishes us with a rough night."

I nodded, "Aye, we will have to find shelter this night but at least we get to our home sooner rather than later."

We stayed that night, just two miles from the king's hall, in the home of a hersir who had fought at Svolder. He was happy to give us beds in his hall and was honoured that he would be able to view the Dragon Sword. We were not able to speak openly but we enjoyed the old man's hospitality. His mead was a fine one.

The next day we spoke as we rode. "Will the king keep his word, Sven?"

I shrugged, "Why do you ask me? You are a wiser man than I am foster father and know the politics of Denmark better. I know Cnut but not his brother."

He laughed, "You have a mind as sharp as a bear trap and you read men like a volva reads the runes."

I sighed, "The king is not secure. What better way to make yourself secure than by sending your rival as far away across the sea as you can manage? He will procure men to follow Cnut but they will be those he feels are a threat. If Cnut wins then they will have homes in England and if he fails then he has removed a threat. Harald is indolent. He will wend his way through life like a lazy river. There will be many loops and twists just so long as he is safe. Did you not see the walls he has put around him? Heiða-býr was a sheepfold in comparison."

"I am not sure I wish land in England, Sven."

I shrugged, "Then do not take it. When Cnut wins you will be given lands. Just take the coins the land produces and make Ribe richer. If you do not wish to fight then…"

I got no further for Sweyn Skull Taker held up his hand and his voice stern, "I am not King Harald, Sven, I am still Sweyn Skull Taker and I shall not cease fighting until I am in Valhalla. Alf has given up war but my son and I will continue to be warriors."

On the last night before we reached our home, we stayed at one of my foster father's old oar brothers. Einar the Lame had been hamstrung in a battle. He now farmed a day's ride from Ribe. We were able to speak more freely in his home and he had news. We had left England and in that short time, the mood had shifted.

"King Æthelred has been restored to the throne of England."

"So, the people of that island have given him a second chance."

"What else do you know?"

"Little save that he is now married to the daughter of the Duke of Normandy, Emma."

That was disturbing news for the Normans had claimed part of Frankia and made it their own. Whilst not a kingdom they were a powerful force and a solid crutch for the weak English king. "Then he has a powerful ally. Perhaps that is why his people have taken him back. They may fear the Normans as much as they fear us."

We rode cautiously even though we were close to home. It was not ambush that greeted us, just a mile from Einar the Lame's farm, but a band of warriors intent on fighting. There were twelve of them and they were armed for war. We had ridden in mail too but these had dismounted and formed a line across our path. My foster father was jarl and he spoke.

"Who is it that bars the road to Jarl Skull Taker?"

"I am Sigismund, brother of Sigebert whom you slew at Gegnesburh."

"He died as a warrior, a treacherous snake of a warrior but a warrior nonetheless."

"He died killing a king on the orders of a prince. The lies you told are another reason why we will kill you here. You can run but we will come for you. We have sworn a blood oath to have vengeance for my brother."

I dismounted and donned my helmet, "Steana, stay with the horses." I drew Oathsword and pointed it at Sigismund. "He is a boy. Let him go." In truth, Steana was old enough to fight in the shield wall but I wanted him safe.

The others, including my foster father, dismounted and donned their own helmets.

Shaking his head Sigismund said, "He is to die with you."

That angered me beyond belief. We were outnumbered but I could not believe that the Norns would allow us all to die in such an attack. The sword had come to me for a purpose and until Cnut was on the throne then its task was unfulfilled.

My foster father and I were flanked by our hearthweru. Sweyn had not come with his father and the other four were all new men. I did not know them. I knew mine and their quality. The twelve who approached us had a mixture of axes and swords as weapons. The axes were all held one handed. They were a powerful weapon but with a weakness. Their heads were large and, in their swinging, often either unbalanced a warrior or made it difficult to respond to a sword thrust. For me, the more dangerous weapons were the swords. I would try to take out the axemen first. We had to even the odds as quickly as we could. I looked at their mail. Only eight wore mail. The leather byrnies would offer less protection. The other mail byrnies came down to the knees. Their shields were well decorated but ours had leather covering. The leather disguised the metal studs in the shield.

There is always one madman in any band of those who have made a blood oath. Perhaps they think themselves a berserker or, more likely, they are the youngest and intent upon impressing the leader. Whatever the reason the young warrior with the short mail byrnie and war axe who launched himself at me crying, "Death to Sven Saxon Sword!" precipitated the fight.

He obligingly ran straight at me and my men gave me room and also afforded me more protection from the side. The rest of the band did not run and they moved menacingly towards us confident that, as they outnumbered us, they would win. I held my shield before me and the temptation for the young axeman was too great. He swung his axe to smash into it and, he thought, break my arm. Even had he hit me the padding I used would have saved me. I pulled back the shield and the swinging head missed. I was already stepping forward and I brought Oathsword down to sever his arm. The axe fell and the spurting blood let all know that he had but moments to live. I was tempted to shout in triumph but it was too early for that. I stepped back so that we had a single line. The warrior had slumped to the ground and was trying to stem the bleeding. In his dying, he aided us as his blood puddled around him. Not only was his body an obstacle but he had sullied and muddied the ground there too. So long as we held our line then they would have to cross it.

One warrior almost slipped when they were just four feet from us. He looked down and Gandálfr did not hesitate. He stepped forward and smashed his sword into the helmet of the unfortunate warrior. He used the flat of the sword so as not to blunt it. The helmet dented and the man sank to the ground. He was either unconscious or dead and either way, he was out of the fight.

My foster father had no such barrier before him and I heard the clash of steel and the cries of warriors intent on killing their enemies. A blood oath is a powerful thing. Sigismund and his men would fight to the death. They would not retreat. Sigismund himself came for me. I took that as a compliment. Sweyn Skull Taker was the jarl but Sven Saxon Sword was the more famous warrior and when I died, he would have fame. He, too, had a sword but it was not a Dragon Sword. I balanced myself and waited for the first blow. He was a veteran. I saw scars on his face and arms and they were not the ones used by men to make themselves look tougher. They had been earned in battle. I had such scars. He was shorter than I was but broader. When he swung his sword sideways then I knew he intended to use his strength to weaken me. What he could not have known was that when Lodvir the Long had taken me under his wing to make me into a warrior he had made me carry heavy weights from the forest to the village and whilst I was not broad, I was strong. I braced myself for the blow and leaned into it, relying on my well-made shield. I also used my hand to lift the metal boss. It bore the brunt of the blow. I would need to replace the boss for it was now dented but it had done its job. His sword would be slightly blunted and I knew that the blow had jarred his arm from the look on his face.

His words confirmed what I had thought for he tried to intimidate me when I did not strike at him, "You are afraid to damage the precious Dragon Sword? Mine is a weapon used in many battles, boy." Thinking that he had distracted me with his words he swung his sword, as he said, 'battles', down towards my head. He was emulating Gandálfr. I had no intention of allowing him to strike and as it came down, I pirouetted away from the blow. I continued my swing and brought Oathsword to slam into his unprotected back. I broke links and he could not contain the cry of pain. As I stepped back into the line, I saw that two of my foster father's hearthweru were down. That meant he was outnumbered.

As I faced Sigismund, I saw the anger on his face and his determination to end this fight. Once more I did the unexpected. I lunged with the tip of my sword at his eye. It takes a brave man not to flinch and as he did so I punched with the dented boss of my shield. It smacked into his face and he began to overbalance. The dead wild axeman was his undoing. He fell backwards over the corpse. His natural reaction was to spread his arms to ease the fall. Stepping forward I slashed my sword across his throat.

I had no time to even think for Petr, another of my foster father's oathsworn fell. There were now four of them fighting two. I left my oathsworn and ran to the aid of my foster father. Even as I ran, Lief was struck and I knew that I would not reach my foster father before the Danish axe split open his skull. The stone which struck and killed the man surprised us all. I saw that Steana had used his slingshot well. I reacted first and drove Oathsword through the links of the assassin's mail and as I tore it out smashed my shield into another. Leif was wounded but not out of the battle and, from his knees, he drove his sword up through the body of the warrior who had just been about to end my foster father's life. The last man found three blades entering his body. I turned around as the last man fell and saw that my oathsworn had slain the rest.

Leif was bleeding heavily and I tore a piece of cloth from one of the dead men's kyrtles and tied it around his upper arm. "Light a fire, we need to seal this wound. Are you hurt, foster father?"

He shook his head and looked at the three dead hearthweru, "Only from within for I have lost more men that are dear to me." He suddenly looked at me, "Sigismund said that the king was killed. You said he died."

I held up the hilt of my sword, "I swore an oath, foster father. Prince Cnut commanded. I cannot say more."

He shook his head, "And you need not. You have not broken an oath and I will honour the dead by keeping silent. We were ambushed by bandits." We all nodded, "And you, Steana, son of Sven, I owe you a life."

My son shrugged, "I could not stand by while you were slain."

I was pleased with my son and his courage, "There is some good mail here, Steana, strip the bodies and take the best. It is time you were trained as a warrior. I can see that in trying to keep you safe I merely put you in danger. You are a warrior now and will be dressed and fight as a warrior."

We slung the bodies of the three dead bodyguards on the backs of their horses. When the fire was going, we sealed Leif's wound. We were not far from home and the volvas there would remedy our clumsiness. After taking the mail from the dead ambushers and their weapons and treasures, we put their shields and bodies on the fire. This was our land and we did not want to feed the carrion. We left when the flames were licking the bodies and the stink of burning flesh filled the air and followed us home. It was a reminder of how close we had come to death.

Chapter 2

Agerhøne 1014

We rode to Ribe first and stayed the night. Had we not been ambushed then we might have parted but we had a duty to Leif and my foster father. My cousin Sweyn One Eye sat with us in my foster father's hall and we told him of the decisions made by the king and of the ambush. With his one eye, many men called him Odin who had sacrificed one eye to gain knowledge. Such an idea was frowned upon by the Christians in our community but the warriors, even the ones who had taken the cross of the White Christ, liked the image.

"Already I like not this Harald but to go to the land of the Saxons and live there… I know not."

My foster father smiled, "Fear not my son for while I do not like King Harald, I will not live in the land they call England. There will be a home here."

I said nothing and my cousin, who knew me as well as any man alive said, "My cousin is not so sure, are you, Sven?"

"My wife comes from that island and she would be happy to return there. I have a farm in the north and, to speak honestly, I like the land. When I travelled north, I saw a fertile and verdant land. King Æthelred might have been the most incompetent king ever to have been anointed but even his disastrous decisions could not make the land poor. It is how he was able to buy our warriors off so many times. Cnut will make a good king. He has the skills to make the land a rich one, richer than poor Denmark. I will help him to win it." I smiled at Steana, "And over the next months it will be my job and my hearthweru to make you a warrior who can stand in a shield wall."

Lady Agnetha, Sweyn Skull Taker's wife, had heard and as she filled up our beakers with more mead she shook her head, "Your wife will not like that, Sven. She is a Christian and she likes not war."

"I know and I have the difficult task now of persuading her. However, in listening to her I almost lost my son. We were lucky today. You almost lost your husband and me, my son. It was a warning and the Norns were spinning. They have not spoken to me but I know their meaning. Steana and Bersi must become warriors. I have a name, a reputation and a sword. They cannot hide behind the cross of the White Christ. Sigismund made that clear today."

On the ride home I spoke with my hearthweru. They had sworn an oath to me but they had fulfilled it many times over, "I am committed to following Prince Cnut and that means the future of my family will be across the sea. I will understand if you no longer wish to be committed to a life beyond your homeland."

Faramir nodded, "The problem is, hersir, that we are threads in a spell of the Norns. If we cut one thread then our lives might be forfeit. Better to follow you and see where it takes us." He waved a hand at the others, "We have spoken of this and are all of the same mind. When we fought, yesterday, none of us suffered a wound, not a serious one at any rate. Leif will be lucky if he can go to war again and the other three all died. Were they poorer warriors than we? I do not think so for I could never best Petr at weapon practice. The sword protects us. I know not how but if we leave your side and serve another then we will all die. A man cannot fight fate. Our families know that. When your family settles in Prince Cnut's new kingdom then so shall we."

I saw from Steana's smile, that he was happy too.

Mary's smile was as broad as a sunset and she hugged me. We had decided not to mention the attack as it could do no good. My hearthweru whisked the horses and the mail away before she even noticed. She was more concerned that Steana and I were back home. I stank, of course. Riding horses always made me stink of horse and sweat. She also wrinkled her nose as she detected something else. She could not put her finger on it but I knew it was blood. Steana and I bathed as she had the house thralls wash our clothes.

That evening while we ate Steana and I told our family of the king's decision. Mary was relieved for she was a clever woman and knew that civil war had been a possibility. The relief, however, quickly turned to worry, when she realised the implications. "That means that when he has enough ships then Prince Cnut will sail west and you will go with him."

"And Steana."

"Steana! Why?"

My son answered, "Because, mother, I am a warrior." He nodded to Bersi, "My little brother will not be long behind me. He will learn to use a sling and fight behind the shield wall."

"And if I will not allow it?"

The rain had begun to fall outside. We could hear it. I smiled, "You might as well try to stop the rain, my love. Our young men go to war. Your father did not and he was a religious man. My sons and I are made from different stock. You cannot change our nature and if you try then you are doomed to a sad life. Embrace it for we are good at what we do and you and I both know that Cnut will make a better king than Æthelred."

I knew that my argument had worked for she was silent. She had been appalled at the massacre on St Brice's day and knew that it was a mistake, a stone that began a Danish avalanche. She said nothing but there was no smile.

The next day I set my weaponsmith to repair my shield and to make Steana one as good. We had coins from the dead assassins and my frugal wife did not need to know of the expense. Steana had taken Sigismund's sword. Whilst not as good as Oathsword, no sword could be, it was still a well-made Frankish blade and after it had been sharpened and the bindings on the hilt changed, we began to practise. Bersi joined the other boys who, knowing that someday they would be called upon to go to war, spent every day using slings and bows. Some would show enough skill to become archers while others would become spearmen in the shield wall. I also asked for a new helmet. I had seen, when we had fought in Northumbria, warriors fighting with a herkumbl on their helmets. It was a clan design. I wanted one on mine. I asked for the bird that was the symbol of our village, the partridge. I wanted its long tail to be the nasal and its wings to form the eyepieces. It was not just to make the helmet look better, it would strengthen those parts of my helmet.

Hastein, the weaponsmith nodded, "A good design but it could be improved. Why not have the bird's head reaching for a snake that would strengthen the top too."

"I am not sure. I like the practicality of it but partridges do not eat snakes."

He laughed, "When they attacked Agerhøne and Oathsword slew them was that not like the devouring of a reptile?"

He was right and so my new helmet was begun. He took a blank helmet and tried it on me. When he found one that was satisfactory, he took the rough, unpolished and unprepossessing pot and began to work his magic. When next I saw it, the helmet would be a finished, gleaming, beautiful and practical helmet for war.

All my warriors were at the practice together. Those like Bersi who were slingers watched us practise the shield walls. We used a simple three-line shield wall with a wall of wood and the spears we used jabbing over the top. Then there was the wedge with one or two men at the fore. The most complicated formation was the swynfylking. It combined the strength of the three-line shield wall with a series of small wedges along the front. The practice that amused the slingers was shield jumping. We formed two shield walls and one tried to break the other by having warriors run at the other shield wall and leap into the air. Often a warrior's weight could break the shield wall. Whilst hazardous it was not the act of a berserker. The shield jumper could roll along a narrow line of shields and roll off the back. Thus far we had not used the tactic but there might come a time when it would win a battle.

My cousin, Alf, had married well and Aksel, his father was a successful merchant with a fleet of knarrs. He was a mine of information. His captains reported back every piece of news they picked up whilst in foreign ports. It was they who had told us that Æthelred's eldest had died and that Æthelred had married Emma. We had been at home for a month when we heard that he had ordered the execution of the two leaders of the Danelaw whom he thought had aided us. Morcar and Sigeferth had made their peace with the Saxon king but it made no difference. They were executed and their lands in the north were confiscated. Æthelred's second son, Edmund, took them for his own. I knew it was a mistake to execute them for the king had made the whole of Danelaw into his enemies. With Thurbrand the Hold and Uhtred of Northumbria still unreliable allies he was treading a perilously dangerous path.

I wondered about Cnut during those months he stayed with his brother the king. For some reason, I did not fear for his life. The king had sworn an oath and if anything did happen to Cnut then oath or not, I would reveal to everyone that King Harald had come by his crown through treacherous means. I could only assume that no word had reached me because he was busy raising an army and, equally importantly, the means to deliver the army to England. For my part, I was busy not only training men but working my land. Crops did not grow without help and animals needed care. I visited with my farmers, including my old oar brother Siggi the Pig. It was good to speak to someone who had given up war. In addition, I had to man my ships. When we had sailed to England the last time, with King Sweyn, there had been five ships from Agerhøne. We had lost a couple on the Trent but we had rescued more than half of the warriors. What we had lost was their weapons and their mail not to mention the experience of the warriors. We had spare weapons, indeed, the ambush had given us some good ones but experience was something that had to be earned and the only way for that to happen was through war. We repaired the old drekar and had a new one built.

One day, after we had trained and while the men sharpened weapons and spoke of the day, I stood with my hearthweru and Steana, "Could we not raid, father? That will give the men experience."

I nodded, "And that is a good idea, except that we do not wish to raid the land of the Danelaw. We need those men to support Cnut when we sail. We could raid Northumbria but Thurbrand the Hold will be watching for us. I dare not risk losing the men we have. No, my son, we will wait for Prince Cnut to come, and come he will." Fighting for a kingdom was one thing but my warriors liked to line their own purses with coins taken in raids and to furnish their homes with objects taken from the richer English houses and halls.

Once more we had news from Aksel. The Witan in the Danelaw part of England wanted Cnut as their king. So long as Edmund, Thurbrand and Uhtred held the north while a dying Æthelred held the south it was something of a moot point but it showed that there would be support. The executions of Morcar and Sigeferth had angered the Danes and Norse who lived in England. It was also discovered that Edmund was minting his own coinage and styled himself, King Edmund Ætheling. He intended to claim the crown when his father died.

It was not long after the winter solstice that Prince Cnut arrived at the head of a hundred warriors. They were the nucleus of his army. Many of them were simply men who sought action and as King Harald showed little martial intent, they had sided with Cnut. Others were men who had served King Sweyn and seen more in Cnut that they liked. There were others too and they were fitting out ships. Cnut came to stay with me rather than my foster father. I knew that Sweyn would not take offence at that but my wife found the extra men a trial. They were warriors all and not prone to peaceful activities. My mead hall was noisy. I accepted that but Mary did not like it and I think that was the moment that she decided to throw her weight behind Cnut's attempt to retake his crown. She would rather live in England than have Danes bring chaos into her home.

Cnut and I spent each day in conference. He had not brought other generals with him and relied on my foster father and me for advice. "We have one hundred ships already committed to this enterprise. With the ten or so from this coast, we are almost in a position to attack."

Sweyn Skull Taker said, "But not yet. It is not that we do not have enough men although, in my view, we do not, we cannot fight the seas, the weather and the English."

Cnut smiled, "Of course. It will be summer when we sail. The English will be toiling in their fields."

I was happy that he was not being reckless, "And where do we attack? Do we land in the Danelaw?"

Cnut had grown and matured. His marriage to Ælfgifu had changed him and made him more mature. The young girl we had rescued had proved to be the making of the young prince. "We strike at Wessex, Æthelred's heartland. It is a ripe plum for the picking. I thank Aksel for his work but we also have our own spies and they tell me that there are many mints in Wessex. If we take the mints, we take the coins that Æthelred needs to keep an army in the field."

My foster father nodded, "And Edmund is in the north."

Cnut was clever and sensitive too. He picked up the implied criticism, "Are you suggesting that I am afraid of Edmund?"

My foster father, since the ambush, had been less belligerent. When I had spoken with him, and that was often, I had the impression that the deaths of his hearthweru had changed his mind about warring until he died. He had grandchildren and he had fought long and hard enough. He shook his head, "No, my prince, I think it is a wise decision. If we take the south then we have the richest part of England. We know the land better there for we raided it often. I was admiring your strategy. Edmund is untried in war. That is to our advantage."

Mollified the prince nodded, "My aim is to win a kingdom. My father took the line of least resistance. The Danelaw will support us. They do not need us to fight over their land. My father's action cost us two great lords and the land that they ruled. We will fight in the land of the English and not the land of the Danes."

I knew the skills that Cnut possessed. My foster father did not.

The element of the army given by King Harald that caused me concern was the mercenaries. The king had paid for pirate bands to follow Prince Cnut. There was no doubt that they were fierce warriors but they were used to following warlords and not princes. How reliable were they? Would they run at the first sign of trouble? As they formed half of the men brought by Prince Cnut there was a worry.

It was a month later as we were using the beach to strengthen the legs of the men when we saw the nine drekar off the coast. Cnut frowned, "It is too early for the fleet. Come, let us return to the port and arm the men."

We did not need to raise my men and fetch them from their fields. The one hundred warriors of Cnut were more than enough. They were all veterans, mailed and well-armed. When the ships turned to enter the port, I had the horn sound to let my people know that there might be a danger. When I recognised the ship of Thorkell the Tall I wondered if I should have summoned all my men.

Wisely, the turncoat came ashore alone and without a helmet. He prostrated himself before Cnut, "Forgive me, Prince Cnut. You have every right to have me thrown into a wolf pit but I beg you to hear me out."

The prince was practical. "Very well, Guthrum stay here with the men. Let none ashore until either I or Lord Sven speaks to you."

"Yes, my lord."

We said not a word until we entered my hall and I had it cleared of all once mead and bread and cheese were fetched.

Thorkell addressed me first, "Thank you for your hospitality, Sven Saxon Sword. I know you for an honourable man and felt sure that you would hear me out."

My words told him that I was not in a forgiving mood, "Your treachery, Thorkell the Tall, cost the lives of many good men. You are not forgiven, merely tolerated."

"Of course." He turned back to Cnut. "I have brought just nine boats and their crews but we have, in Wessex, another thirty. Their crews are loyal to you."

I snorted, "They have a strange way of showing it."

"Peace, Sven, go on Thorkell."

"We made a mistake in joining Æthelred. I see it now. The murder of the archbishop coloured my judgement. The land is ripe and ready to be plucked."

I was not convinced, "Prince Cnut, this has all the hallmarks of a Thorkell ploy. If we do as he suggests and invade now then I fear it will be a knife between our shoulder blades."

Thorkell began to grow angry, "What more can I say, Sven Saxon Sword? I will swear on a Bible if you will."

I drew Oathsword and placed it between us on the table, "Swear on this and I might believe you."

"I am a Christian now. This is pagan."

"And you are a Jomsviking. If you do not believe in the sword then what harm is there in an oath upon it?"

Cnut smiled, "A good point, Sven."

I saw that despite his attestations that he was a Christian through and through it was not true. He knew that an oath on Oathsword would be binding.

He put his hand forward and it hovered over the hilt. He looked at me and I held his gaze. He nodded. Grasping the sword he said, "I swear that I will follow faithfully Prince Cnut and help him to recover his kingdom." He stopped and was about to put it down when I shook my head. He sighed, "And if I do not may I be condemned to Hel with the others who are foresworn."

I took his hand and squeezed it about the blade. His palm was cut and his blood was on the blade. Taking the sword back I smiled, "And now I am satisfied." It was now a blood oath and Thorkell knew it.

The prince was also satisfied, "And how do we contact your ships, the wolves in sheep's clothing?"

"I will send back eight of my ships and stay here as a hostage to my true intentions. My men will wait at Wiht and we can use that as a base to attack."

Prince Cnut nodded, "This might well work. We can use your ships to disguise the arrival of our fleet. And what do you wish, in return for your ships?"

"In return, my prince?"

Cnut laughed, "You are a Jomsviking and you are doing this for some reason."

He nodded, "A title and land of my own."

"Very well although until England is conquered there will be no reward."

"Of course."

Thorkell returned to his ships, his bandaged hand physical evidence of the oath. They would need water and supplies but then they could return to England and be the wolves in the sheepfold. After he had gone, we spoke together. "You still do not trust him, even though he swore an oath."

I nodded, "He is a great warlord and the forty ships he brings will be the best that there are but you are right I do not trust him and when we go to battle against the English, I will have my men closer to you than he. I would also suggest that you put the Jomsvikings at the fore of any battle. It is harder to run away if you are locking swords with an enemy."

"I will and until we sail, he will be close to me. This is good news, is it not, Sven?"

"It is but it is not the news we can boast of for it must be secret. If we told men that Thorkell the Tall and his Jomsvikings were with us then men would flock to our banner."

In the end, men did flock to my banner but they came for plunder and to some extent, to be fighting alongside the Dragon Sword. Warriors came from Norway and the land of the Rus to join us. Some of them came in knarrs and some in drekar. A few even came in snekke although they would not sail across the seas in such ships. Cnut hired ships and boats from Aksel's fleet to transport warriors. The Swede did not mind for a profit was a profit and sailing with armed warriors lessened the likelihood of pirates.

The speed of our departure alarmed Mary for there would only be our daughter, Gunhild, left at home. It did not help that Bersi and Steana were desperate to leave. Bersi would be a ship's boy on the ***'Falcon'*** and Steana would have an oar. He had enjoyed a growth spurt over the winter and now looked like a man, a young man but a man nonetheless. He would have an easier time than my first voyage. My cousin Sweyn would also command a drekar and its crew but Alf, his little brother, would merely captain one of his father-in-law's ships, drop men off and return home. Since his aerial exploits at Svolder, he had ceased to be a warrior and had become a merchant. *Wyrd.*

The night before we left Mary lay in my arms and hugged me, "It is not just you who go to war but all the men in my family and I fear for them."

I sighed, "You say your prayers?"

"Of course."

"And your god listens to them?"

I felt her clutch her cross, "He does."

"Then God will watch over the boys and my sword shall protect me." She was silent and I felt guilty for having used her own religion against her. "I believe that until Cnut is crowned King of England then my work is not done. Once he rules the land across the water we shall move to Norton and you will be amongst your own people once more."

Her voice was small as she said, "I will not know them I have been away so long."

I chuckled, "Not as long as you think." I kissed the top of her head, "I know that you fear for me but I am confident that our plan is a good one. We will send messages when we can."

"Just come back safely with my boys, Sven, and come back whole."

I whispered in her ear, "Yet a wound would guarantee that I sailed away no more."

"Come back whole."

The ships began to arrive in greater numbers the next day and were marshalled into some sort of order. The great longships, like Cnut's, given to him by his brother and those of men like my foster father were at the fore and on the flanks. They would be the sheepdogs guarding the weaker vessels in the centre. This time the plan was to sail down the Danish and the Frisian coast until we reached the narrowest part of the channel that separated Frankia from England. Cnut wanted the English to have no warning of the fleet about to descend upon them. Once we reached Cent, we might be seen but the plan was to sail that part of the journey at night. It was a risk but we knew the waters well and if we arrived at Wiht just after dawn then we would have a complete surprise.

The prince's ship was crewed by his new hearthweru. They were the best warriors in Cnut's army and they were all loyal to Cnut and had been chosen by him, They were not the mercenaries sent by Harald. Thorkell would be with Cnut and as much as I mistrusted him, I knew he was our best chance to reach Wessex unseen. He would guide Cnut's ship along the Wessex coast. When the order was given to lower the sails, it was as though the whole fleet sighed as the wind filled the sails and we began to move. It would not be a swift voyage. The tubby knarrs could carry many men but they were not sleek longships. We would be perilously close to hunger when we reached Wessex. The Jomsvikings, we were told, would have supplies waiting for us on their island base. I hoped so.

I stood with Lars, our helmsman, at the steering board. He was no warrior and I was no navigator. He could fight and I could steer but our skills lay in other areas. It made us a good team. When he was not steering my drekar, Lars and his sons fished. He was successful at what he did for unlike many of the fishermen he was not afraid to sail well out to sea and take from the rich fishing grounds that lay halfway between Denmark and the Holderness. The fisherman leaned easily against the gunwale, "It will be a slow voyage, hersir. Those knarrs of Aksel wallow like milk cows." He chuckled, "The men aboard them will not have an easy time."

"They will endure for when we succeed there will be a great profit."

He gave me a shrewd look, "And yours will be land."

"It has been given already but the English are rich. I want no slaves but this war with Æthelred has cost me men and families, fathers. I would have weregeld for those families. The English will pay."

"When you live in England, I shall be sad."

"Sad, why?"

"For you are a good man. The people of Agerhøne know that you do not take more than is due, sometimes less, and that you will defend them. What will happen when you leave?"

I had discussed this with Sweyn Skull Taker and my cousin Sweyn as well as Cnut. Prince Cnut wanted me in England but when I moved to England then Sweyn would be hersir. He was happy to do so knowing that he would be Jarl of Ribe in time and by then his son would be able to be trained as a hersir.

"There are plans, Lars, but we have yet to conquer this land. Do not tempt the Norns by making prophecies. That is what the Norns do."

He clutched his hammer of Thor, "You are right. They are still spinning those threads, are they not?" I nodded.

Steana was disappointed that he did not have to row. Bersi had to scamper up sheets and shrouds to adjust the sails to Lars' satisfaction but Steana's hands did not need the salve his mother had sent. "Think yourself lucky, my son. When Siggi and I went to sea we had to row the whole way. My hands and buttocks knew that they had endured a journey. If you do have to row it will not be a hard one as we have to keep pace with the slower knarrs. Save your energy for battle."

He nodded, "I will not let you down, father."

"Just emerge from the battle whole. I will not care if your spear is without blood for battle in the shield wall is hard. You will not be in the front rank or the second. If you are called upon to fight then many men will have died."

"You will be in the front rank."

"Of course for men follow Oathsword, even if it is sheathed." I saw the worry on his face, "Fear not, Dreng, Snorri, Faramir, and Gandálfr are the best of hearthweru. Even those who guard Prince Cnut do not have their skill. When we were ambushed, they were whole at the end. Remember that. Some men sport battle bracelets and wounds as signs that they are great warriors. Real warriors need no such adornments. The fact that they are whole and others are not, tells its own story."

The winds came from the west and while that did not slow us yet, if they continued to do so then Steana would have to row when we neared Cent. That was still some days away. We sailed at night too. The leading ships, ours included, hung a light from the stern. It was as though stars had fallen from the sky as their blinking lights guided the slower ships south down the coast. Each morning we saw our progress was being followed by the Frisians and Franks. They could only hope that we intended to attack England and not raid their coast. Horsemen followed us as we slowly headed south.

The winds did change but they turned, briefly, against us. As we reached the narrowest part of the channel, they turned from the north and west to blow from the south and west. We reefed the sails and Steana got his wish. We rowed.

We sang the song of Svolder. Sweyn the Skald had made the words and it was a popular song in the mead halls. Even the ship's boys could join in and it helped to shift the drekar across the narrow waters.

The king did call and his men they came
Each one a warrior and a Dane
The mighty fleet left our home in the west
To sail to Svolder with the best of the best
Swedes and Norse were gathered as one

To fight King Olaf Tryggvasson
Mighty ships and brave warriors' blades
The memory of Svolder never fades
The Norse abandoned their faithless king
Aboard Long Serpent their swords did bring
The Norse made a bridge of all their ships
Determined that King Sweyn they would eclipse
Brave Jarl Harald and all his crew
Felt the full force of a ship that was new
Mighty ships and brave warriors' blades
The memory of Svolder never fades
None could get close to the Norwegian King
To his perilous crown he did cling
Until Skull Taker and his hearthweru
Attacked the side of the ship that was new
Swooping Hawk leapt through the sky
To land like a warrior born to fly
Mighty ships and brave warriors' blades
The memory of Svolder never fades
With such great deeds the clan would sing
They cleared the drekar next to the king
Facing Olaf were the jarl and Sven
Agerhøne and Oathsword joined again
Mighty ships and brave warriors' blades
The memory of Svolder never fades
The bodyguards of the King of Norway
Fought like wolves in a savage way
It mattered not for the Dragon Sword won
Stabbing and slaying everyone
The king chose the sea as his way of death
And Long Serpent was his funeral wreath
Mighty ships and brave warriors' blades
The memory of Svolder never fades
Mighty ships and brave warriors' blades
The memory of Svolder never fades
Sweyn Skull Taker was a great lord
Sailing from Agerhøne with his sons aboard
Sea Serpent sailed and ruled the waves
Taking Franks and Saxons slaves
When King Sweyn took him west
He had with him the men that were best
Griotard the Grim Lodvir the Long

Made the crew whole and strong
From Frankia where the clan took gold
To Wessex where they were strong and bold
The clan obeyed the wishes of the king
But it was of Skull Taker that they sing
With the Dragon Sword to fight for the clan
All sailed to war, every man
The cunning king who faced our blades
Showed us he was not afraid
Trapped by the sea and by walls of stone
Sweyn Skull Taker fought as if alone
The clan prevailed Skull Taker hit
Saved by the sword which slashed and slit
From Frankia where the clan took gold
To Wessex where they were strong and bold
The clan obeyed the wishes of the king
But it was of Skull Taker that they sing
And when they returned to Agerhøne
The clan was stronger through the wounds they had borne
With higher walls and home much stronger
They are ready to fight for Sweyn Skull Taker
From Frankia where the clan took gold
To Wessex where they were strong and bold
The clan obeyed the wishes of the king
But it was of Skull Taker that they sing

As the sun began to set, I saw, in the distance, the coast of Cent. The chant would be carried astern of us but I knew that, as we began to pass the land those ashore might hear a ghostly moan from the sea. Those with long memories would clutch their crosses and bar their doors for they would know what the strange noises meant. We changed rowers regularly and even I took a turn at the oar. In the darkness, we could not see where the water ended and the land began. We were in the hands of Thorkell the Tall and the helmsmen. The chanting helped as it was a link to the warriors of the past.

When dawn broke, we found that Thorkell had taken us further south and the coast of Wessex was just a faint line to the north. When Cnut's mighty longship made the turn to sail north and west, we were able to store the oars on the mast fish and let the wind take us. We headed for Shamblord on the island base of the Jomsvikings and the home of the Jomsvikings. When we saw the forty drekar waiting and not a fleet of Saxon ships then I knew that our venture was not over before it started. Thorkell had not betrayed us… yet.

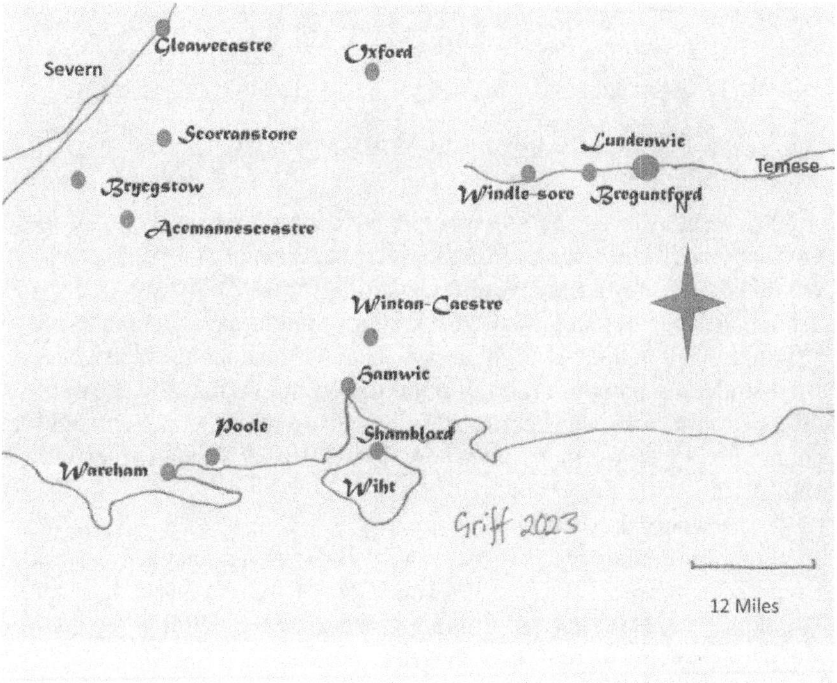
Gleawecastre
Oxford
Severn
Scorranstone
Lundenwic
Temese
Brycgstow
Windle-sore
Breguntford
Acemannesceastre
N
Wintan-Caestre
Hamwic
Poole
Shamblord
Wareham
Wiht
Griff 2023
12 Miles

Chapter 3

The taking of Wareham 1015

We went ashore. That we would have been seen from Wessex could not be helped. The eorls and lords would be raising the fyrd. The burhs would be barred and they would be waiting for us. As we stepped ashore and men began to cook the first hot food in days, Steana asked, "Should we not attack straight away? They will be behind their walls."

I smiled at my son. I did not mind the questions for they showed a curious mind. That was healthy. "They know that a fleet is here and that cannot bode well for them but where do we attack? Wintan-Caestre? Hamwic?"

"And where do we attack?"

I pointed to the west, "Just along the coast at Wareham. It has not been raided for more than twenty years. There are two mints there and although it is a burh, we have enough men to take it. While they guard their other towns, we will take this rich jewel. Prince Cnut knows his business, my son."

I was now an adviser to the prince and that meant I was held in greater esteem than my foster father. When Cnut held his council of war, I was on one side and Thorkell the Tall on the other. Cnut, for one so young, was very patient. He explained how we would land on the Wessex coast as close to Wareham as we could. He had obviously consulted with Thorkell before he spoke to the council for he knew that while some of the defences had been improved with stone, there were still wooden palisades on the south side of the burh and that was where the river flowed. The anchorage which stretched from Wareham to Poole was the largest, so Cnut said, in the world. I had been there when we had raided before and it was impressive. Our plan was a simple one. We would use the drekar we had as a bridge over their ditches and assault the walls directly. It was a good plan and I began to think better of Thorkell the Tall for he had clearly scouted out the defences and come up with a plan that might save lives.

We left at noon the next day. The direct route was fifty miles but Cnut had taken into account the slower knarr and the fact that we wanted to arrive soon after dawn. We headed south and, as the sun set, turned and used the oars to row to the enormous harbour. This time it was Thorkell's ships that followed Cnut's. We headed southwest before turning to sail towards the sun as it grew lower in the sky. It was a steady row and as night fell, we turned north and entered the harbour. We were in Thorkell's hands and I could see that he had thought this through and scouted thoroughly. I had learned from some of those who stayed at Shamblord, that one of the reasons Thorkell had defected back to Cnut was that the English king had failed to pay him some promised gold. It was yet another example of the foolishness of the man descended from the great Alfred.

The men were rowing in their mail. It would not be comfortable and for Steana, in particular, it would be a real trial. We stopped in the middle of the harbour and that allowed men to make water, eat and drink ale from the barrels. We had refilled at Shamblord. Our weapons needed no attention for they were sharpened already and every man in the huge fleet was ready for war. The treachery of Gegnesburh needed an outlet for our fury and Wareham would suffer. Some men slept, they were the veterans while the young and those who had yet to fight did not. Steana was not the only one on his first raid. My crew had eight others. Every ship that had sailed from Ribe and Agerhøne had a similar number of new warriors. I was not as worried as I might have been had we been facing a Saxon shield wall.

When we saw the first false dawn the crews resumed their seats and ship by ship, we rowed in four lines towards the burh. The line to the north, we were twelfth in line, would be made up of the ships that would turn and become the bridge over the ditch. The other three would make a longphort to allow men to cross the ships like an enormous bridge.

The town knew we were coming. We had been as silent as we could but noise would travel at night. Perhaps they thought that we might raid Poole or even land and ravage the hinterland. They manned their walls and as we neared the wooden palisade, we heard the sound of the church bells tolling their warning. They would carry across the harbour and soon every Saxon who could hear the bells would be armed and defending their walls. As my crew sculled us in a long line of longships towards the ditch and rampart, I stood with my hearthweru. We had the gangplank we used in port and my intention was to cross that. My shield was across my back but I could swing it around when I needed it and, in my hand, I held my long ash spear, Saxon Slayer. It had been the first weapon I had named and while I used my sword more often this would be a time for the spear. Its length would protect me as much as my shield. My hearthweru had tried to dissuade me from being the first across the narrow bridge but I was adamant. It was not just our crew, many of whom were new, but the rest of the fleet who needed to see that Sven Saxon Slayer led the attack. My name was known and like it or not I knew that it inspired men

The wooden palisade bristled with men but I knew that not all would be warriors. Most would be the townsfolk who had a variety of weapons and the training after church as their only experience of battle. I saw consternation and knew why. They had men on every wall and they needed to bolster those on the river wall, the weak one. Arrows flew at us and stones were hurled. It was not a shower for they just released when they were ready and, as such, we were able to avoid them. I was confident that my helmet and mail would protect me and it would put fear in the hearts of the defenders if they saw that the Danes who attacked did not fear their weapons. When an arrow slammed into the gangplank before me, Faramir said, “Enough is enough, Sven, use your shield.”

Gandálfr added, “We will soon be landing in any case.”

He was right and I swung my shield around. In a perfect world, every drekar would have ground ashore at the same time but we lived in a world where Loki played tricks and the Norns spun. Some ships struck before others. As an arrow smacked into my shield, I braced myself for the impact. The drekar’s bow slid up the rampart and then settled. We slid the gangplank across to the top of the palisade. The ship’s boys used their bows and slings to discourage those who tried to hurl it down. Bersi was trying to kill men for the first time. I hauled myself up and with Saxon Slayer held before me ran across it. I kicked the arrow that had hit the gangplank to the side and looked for my first enemy. The gangplank was at a slight angle and it was not an easy run but I saw that the stones and arrows had made the defenders take shelter. I leapt, not as high as Alf had at Svolder but high enough so that when I landed on the fighting platform, I had left enough space for my hearthweru to follow. Even as I was landing, I thrust my spear at the nearest Saxon and it drove into his side. I flicked his body from the fighting platform and it crashed into the men who were trying to climb the ladder and reinforce the wall.

A mailed warrior had organised the men closest to us and he led a knot of them towards us. Dreng and Faramir had flanked me. Faramir was dangerously close to the edge of the fighting platform. Dreng, however, had the advantage that the man he would be fighting would have the palisade to his right and would struggle to use his spear. I pulled my shield tight so that just my eyes were exposed and we marched towards them. I was confident that we would march in time for we had often practised. The Saxons, in contrast, did not move as one and while our three shields had no gaps, theirs did. I watched the mailed warrior's spear and as he thrust at me, I thrust too. The difference was that he was watching where his spear went and I was not. He had aimed, foolishly in my view, at my head. I lifted my shield slightly and it was enough to deflect the spear head up to scrape across my new helmet. I had new leather straps and the helmet held. I had thrust Saxon Slayer at his thigh. I had sharpened the tip and it penetrated the mail byrnie and with little to slow it, the spear drove into the Saxon's thigh. I twisted and then felt the head grind against the bone. The Saxon grimaced and when I pulled out the spear blood spurted. I punched with my shield and he reeled. He was losing blood quickly. The two men next to him had no mail and Dreng and Faramir both stabbed with their spears at the same time. The mailed warrior was weakening but he was still standing and I pulled back Saxon Slayer as his shield dropped and speared him in the stomach. He fell from the fighting platform and the three of us stepped into the gap.

All along the fighting platform, the remains of the Saxon defenders were being assaulted on all sides by Danes with superior weapons, armour and, most importantly, skills. Thorkell's Jomsvikings had last fought fellow Vikings and the chance to slaughter Saxons was too much. The fighting platform was quickly cleared and I raised Saxon Slayer, "Agerhøne, with me!"

So far as I could tell we had lost not a warrior from my drekar. I was relieved to see that Steana had not yet crossed the gangplank. The fighting platform was just eight feet above the ground. There were bodies littering the ground and so rather than risk turning my back to descend the wooden ladder I jumped. I almost tumbled but managed to retain my balance and I pulled up my shield and held my spear before me as I waited for my men to follow. When my hearthweru joined me, we took three steps forward. Out training would now tell.

"Wedge!"

As Saxons ran towards us my men began to form a wedge behind us. The three of us at the front easily dealt with the first Saxons and, as we felt shields pushed into our backs and spears were thrust over our heads, we took a step further forward. Leif Long Leg commanded the rest of my men and when he shouted, "Agerhøne!" then I knew we had a wedge. We had practised this manoeuvre but there were men in the middle who, like Steana, were new and had never done it in combat. If we were to drive into Wareham we had to do so as one.

I began to chant and I picked the simplest one and the most relevant to our clan.

We are the bird you cannot find

With feathers grey and black behind
Seek us if you can my friend
Our clan will beat you in the end.
Where is the bird? In the snake.
The serpent comes your gold to take.
We are the bird you cannot find
With feathers grey and black behind
Seek us if you can my friend
Our clan will beat you in the end.
Where is the bird? In the snake.
The serpent comes your gold to take.

The raising of Saxon Slayer was the signal to march and we all stepped onto our sword legs. There was little need to even swing my spear for we were like a huge hedgehog that prickled with spikes. Shields protected our heads and we heard the clatter of stones and arrows as they fell. One arrow even hit my helmet but it did no damage. The Saxons simply ran into our spears in a desperate attempt to slow us. There were too many sharp spearheads to avoid and the hardest part was in stepping over the bodies of the dead. As we did our mailed line rippled but the chant helped us to hold formation and we neared the town proper. I knew that the wedge would not be able to function as well in the narrow streets of Wareham. I had experienced warriors behind me and while it would not affect the front four ranks, the rest would have to narrow. I relied on Leif Long Leg and my other veterans to marshal the men. I was confident in the twelve who were at the fore.

The chant helped us not only to keep step but to drown out the screams and cries and the clash of battle in the town, as two thousand men hacked and slashed their way into Wareham. The town was doomed. Men and families might escape for the gates to the north, east and west were not being attacked but the warriors who tried to slow our advance would all die. The end, when it came, was dramatic. We must have slain their best warriors for the ones before us suddenly turned and ran. They escaped for we could not follow in the narrow streets of Wareham.

I raised Saxon Slayer and yelled, "Agerhøne!" The cry was repeated by the men behind me. As luck would have it, we were outside a huge building and I shouted, "Let us see what treasure the Saxons have left for us."

The door was barred but we easily burst in using the axes of the men who preferred that weapon. The four terrified men abased themselves before us, begging for mercy.

"What is this place?"

One raised his head and said, "Lord, it is the mint."

I looked up and saw that there were sacks of coins already pressed and disks waiting to be made into coins for the king. I smiled and said, "What is your name?"

"Æthelgar, lord, the moneyer."

"Then stay close to this building. Prince Cnut will have need of your services when he becomes king."

I saw that Æthelgar was a pragmatist when he bowed and said, "Yes, my lord."

I turned to Leif Long Leg, "Have four men guard this for the prince. For the rest, you have earned the right to plunder the dead. The town is ours." I knew that the majority of women and children would have fled along with the fat merchants who had saved their own skins and no, doubt, their treasure while the young warriors had died. My men would all gain treasure, swords, helmets and, perhaps mail. Even a poor helmet could be reused. We wasted nothing. I took a bag of silver blanks and handed it to Steana, "Take this back aboard the ship and place it in my chest. You can fetch Bersi back."

"Yes, father."

As he ran off, I nodded to Dreng who followed him. The only men I truly trusted were the men of Ribe and Agerhøne.

Outside bodies and houses were being plundered. Being a burh Wareham was a rich town. The walls gave an illusion of security to merchants and lords alike. It was why the mint had been moved from Old Sarum. Its loss would hurt the English king. My three hearthweru followed me as I headed towards the centre of the town. Cnut and Thorkell were there already. Both had bloody byrnies and swords. They had fought.

"That was easy enough, Sven. I hope that the rest of the invasion goes as well."

Thorkell said, "It will my prince. Edmund is in the north and he and Eadric Streona neither get on nor trust each other. So long as we are in Wessex then it will be easy."

I hoped that Thorkell was right but I still did not trust him.

We ate well that night. The voyage from Denmark had seen us suffering cold rations but now we dined well. We and my foster father ate in the mint. The prince had appointed Æthelgar as his moneyer and the diligent maker of coins had made an account of the gold and silver. It felt good, however, to be in the most solid building in Wareham and eating, surrounded by gold and silver. Our men had all profited well and been lucky. The handful of wounds suffered would merely be badges of honour when we returned home. Sweyn One Eye began to compose a saga about the battle although none of us felt as though we had been stretched. Bersi, being the son of the hersir did not have to stay aboard the drekar and he dined with us. His eyes widened as he heard the songs and listened to the tales. He would want to be a warrior, no matter what his mother wished.

Einar, one of Cnut's hearthweru, sought me out just as we were finishing the food. I was taken to the stronghold in the centre of the town. It had not been defended. Thorkell and Cnut awaited me.

"We have made a good start, Cnut, but that is all it is, a start. I have men seeking horses and when we have them then I will send to the five Boroughs summoning the leaders. I would hold a Witan here."

We held 'Things', and the English held Witans.

"And if they do not come?"

"Then Sven Saxon Sword, I know that I do not have their support and when I am king then they will suffer." Cnut was becoming as ruthless as his father had been. Blood will out. "Until they arrive, I will stay here behind these walls. I intend to raid this part of Wessex to both feed my army and remove any opposition. I will send the ships loaned to me by my brother to take and hold Poole. Thorkell will take his Jomsvikings west to raid and I want you to take the men of Ribe and Agerhøne, along with the men who follow Einar the Fat, to raid the north."

I did a quick calculation in my head, "You will be left with just a quarter of the army here." He nodded. The men he was keeping were his own hearthweru and those who had sworn loyalty to him. It was a clever move.

"We will defend this burh better than its previous owners."

"And our ships, now that we no longer need the longphort?"

"They will anchor in the harbour."

Thorkell asked, "And the booty we take? Is it ours to keep?"

Cnut smiled, "You are a warlord, Thorkell the Tall, but you serve me and one day I will be king. I will send one man with each of you and one-third of all that is taken shall be my due. Does that seem fair?"

Thorkell smiled, "More than generous, my prince."

At least Thorkell was being a little more honest than I had expected.

I returned to my men with the news that we were to raid as we saw fit. We had done this before and the prize that we sought, apart from gold and silver would be the animals. Siggi the Pig had benefitted from my first raid and his herds were the best in Agerhøne.

Bersi looked a little downcast, "I am to stay with the fleet?"

"Would you wish to come with us?"

"Aye."

I saw the eagerness in his eyes and heard it in his voice. His mother would not be happy but I nodded, "Then you shall. Steana, find him a leather helmet and byrnie. See if there is a short sword or seax for him. Perhaps a march around Wessex may let him know how well off he is on the ship."

Chapter 4

The burh and mint at Brycgstow

There would not be enough horses for us and so we marched and we did so without spears. This would be sword and axe work. Spears were what we used to break a shield wall and there would be none on our route. Before we left I questioned Æthelgar about the land to the north. There were, it seemed, no burhs and, in addition, there was a newly built mint on the coast, about forty miles away. The town was called Brycgstow and I planned on marching there, taking the villages we found along the way. I worked out that we could reach it in six days of raiding. If we rested there then we could use captured horses to make an easy journey back. There would be no hurry for the leaders who were coming to the Witan would take far longer to reach Wareham from the east.

My conversations with the moneyer had already told me that there were no burhs to the north of us. Even Thorkell would have an easy time until he came to Exeter. We had destroyed that burh once and I knew that Thorkell would overcome it easily. While I did not expect to find serious opposition, I knew that men would fight us, it was in their nature. We headed towards Shepton Mallet and took farm after farm. We slept in villages and ate well. I gave orders and the only ones slain were those who fought against us. Prince Cnut wanted to make Wessex his and we wanted no resentful Saxons who would make life harder for us. We took their horses and their treasure. While Prince Cnut was Christian, we were more ambivalent. We stripped the churches and religious houses of their gold and fine cloth. We endured the curses of the priests, monks and nuns. The religious houses had wagons and carts. We used them and as we had more than enough men to deal with any opposition, I was able to send armed convoys back to Wareham where our booty would be taken to my ships. It made our progress north easier. When we reached Acemannesceastre, we headed west for their walls were spear lined. The burh had been laid out by Alfred and there were stone walls. We might have taken it but it might have cost men and I was anxious to get to the mint. If we had a bigger army, I might have risked it but there would be time. This would not be a short war.

The greatest opposition we faced was at Brycgstow. The small port was newly constructed and had been used by Eadric Streona when he had gathered a fleet to oppose us the last time that we had raided this coast. There was a ditch, a rampart, and a palisade. Many who had fled from us on our northern raid had taken refuge there and there were enough warriors to mean we had to fight.

With the town surrounded and an ox we had taken roasting, I sat with my foster father, Einar the Fat and Sweyn One Eye and we drank the pillaged cider from the last farm. "I have no wish to build siege engines. We will do this the old-fashioned way."

Einar the Fat nodded, "We attack the walls and gate."

"Aye, but we do so simultaneously. We will take the doors and gates from the farms we have captured and use them as bridges. Axemen will assault the walls and the gate while our slingers and bowmen keep their heads down. This is a new port and the wood will not yet have taken root. If Eadric Streona built it then you can guess that it was thrown up in a hurry. We need the mint. This time we keep two-thirds of what we take. This one raid will make us all rich men. No matter what happens in the rest of the war those men who wish to return to Denmark will have heavy purses."

I knew that not all would want to do as I intended and remain in England. More than half of the men who had come with us had done so for profit. When Cnut became king then they would have to find other places to raid.

"We will attack in groups made up of the crews of our drekar. I will use the men of Agerhøne to attack the gate. Einar, you will take the north wall and Sweyn Skull Taker the south. I would intimidate them. We will make a shield wall around the town so that when they wake, they see us. I will shout 'Oathsword' and then every warrior will bang his shield and chant until I sound the horn once. Then all will stop. I want a sudden silence that will be louder than any battle cry. When the horn is sounded twice, we attack, as one."

I had come a long way from the diffident youth who ran with Siggi the Pig into a maelstrom of war he did not understand. I had fought in enough battles to know what made men afraid. My tactic might not work against Danes, Normans or Norsemen but it would frighten the men of Wessex who had taken refuge behind the wooden walls of Brycgstow.

That done I sat with Bersi and Steana, "Bersi, tomorrow you will be under the command of Bergil the Black. He may have lost a hand but he can still command. You need to throw as many stones as you can. Even when you are exhausted and think that you cannot raise your arm once more you will be able to. Steana, your task will be to hold your shield over the heads of the men before you. Lean your body into their backs and when they advance then you follow."

"Where will you be, father?"

"Where every good leader should be, Steana, at the front leading his men." I saw fear cloud the face of my youngest son, "Bersi, I have the best mail, a padded jacket to protect me from hard blows. My byrnie goes below my knees and I wear the finest of boots. On my head, I have an arming cap, a mailed coif and a new helmet with a fine design made by the greatest of weaponsmiths, Hastein. It will take a mighty warrior to defeat Oathsword and I do not think that such a man would have fled to Brycgstow. I will have harder tests in the future but this skirmish is not one."

Although I spoke with confidence, I knew that accidents could happen. The Norns could spin and weave just to amuse themselves but as I had told Mary, the sword had come to me for a purpose and the taking of the mint at Brycgstow was not important enough for the Norns to cut my thread. When they did so it would be at a momentous time.

We had eaten well and we slept well. I was awake well before dawn and had made water and dressed by the time the camp was roused. As I ate cold beef, I walked around my men. This was an important time. The veterans would appreciate a word from me while the younger, newer warriors would be worried about what faced them. They would not worry about death for it was not in our nature. Their fear, for I remembered it well, was of failure. A warrior feared letting down his oar brothers, his family, and his clan. The sentries I had spoken to as I walked among the men told me that the walls of Brycgstow had been manned all night. They had feared a night assault. They would be tired and, as the sight that would greet them when the sun rose behind us was of serried ranks of warriors then they would be hungry too. They would hear us moving and suspect an attack. That was confirmed when I heard a bell toll and a horn sound. More faces appeared behind the palisade.

Dreng had the horn and my hearthweru flanked me. The rest of our men shuffled into position. I did not turn for men like Lief Long Leg and Hakon the Fearless would ensure that they were in three ranks and that the archers and slingers were close enough to shower the walls.

The sun came up behind us and we stood in silence. It was so quiet that I could hear the gulls out to sea, the dead sailors calling to us. I heard the murmur of conversation from those on the walls as they discussed what we planned but my men obeyed my order. It gave me the chance to view our target, the gate. It was new, I could see that and there were two small towers on either side. They were not roofed and the handful of men within them would soon die. The fighting platform looked to be wide enough for three men. I saw that from the huddle of mailed men with good helmets who were over the gate. The ditch was an obstacle but the wood we had taken from the farms would give us a bridge and prevent us from breaking ankles.

We waited for a good while and, when I deemed the time right, I drew the Dragon Sword. I could feel the tension from my men as it slid from its scabbard and I raised it. Light from the sun flashed on the polished steel and the words, '***Melchior made me***'. I lifted it high and roared, "Oathsword!"

As one the whole of my army began to bang the pommels of the swords against their shields. It sounded like thunder. I had not named the chant but Sweyn One Eye was the master of words and he began the song. He used one that he knew the warriors would all know. The song of Sweyn Skulltaker.

Sweyn Skull Taker was a great lord
Sailing from Agerhøne with his sons aboard
Sea Serpent sailed and ruled the waves
Taking Franks and Saxons slaves
When King Sweyn took him west
He had with him the men that were best
Griotard the Grim Lodvir the Long
Made the crew whole and strong
From Frankia where the clan took gold
To Wessex where they were strong and bold
The clan obeyed the wishes of the king
But it was of Skull Taker that they sing
With the Dragon Sword to fight for the clan
All sailed to war, every man
The cunning king who faced our blades
Showed us he was not afraid
Trapped by the sea and by walls of stone
Sweyn Skull Taker fought as if alone
The clan prevailed Skull Taker hit
Saved by the sword which slashed and slit
From Frankia where the clan took gold
To Wessex where they were strong and bold
The clan obeyed the wishes of the king
But it was of Skull Taker that they sing
And when they returned to Agerhøne
The clan was stronger through the wounds they had borne
With higher walls and home much stronger
They are ready to fight for Sweyn Skull Taker
From Frankia where the clan took gold

To Wessex where they were strong and bold
The clan obeyed the wishes of the king
But it was of Skull Taker that they sing

We sang it ten times and the booming of the banging shields rolled around the wall threatening with every thunderous crash, "Dreng, the horn."

It sounded and every man obeyed. Gulls still screeched and, in the distance, we heard the sound of wind on the water of the channel but that was all. Silence wrapped my men like a blanket. I could feel the tension for we knew what we were about to do but those within the walls had no idea.

"The horn."

As it sounded twice every warrior began to step forward. Bergil the Black shouted, "Loose!" Arrows and stones flew over our heads. We had stunned the defenders for we had taken ten steps before a ragged volley of arrows hurtled towards us. My shield protected my face. I took solace from the fact that they aimed mainly at me and my hearthweru. Arrows and stones clattered and crashed into our helmets, mail and shields but we had the best that our weaponsmiths could make. A few of the stones hurt, but a bruise was nothing. It meant that those who were standing behind, without mail, would be safer and when the torrent slowed, I knew that Bergil the Black had rid the walls of the danger.

When we were ten feet from the ditch I shouted, "Halt!" We opened our ranks and men darted forward carrying the wooden bridges. Four were hit by missiles sent from the walls but the archers and slingers who felled them died. Once the bridge carriers were back in line, I pointed my sword at the gate. We had to go in single file to cross the bridges and I was first across. I stood eight feet from the gate and looked up, over the rim of my shield at the walls. They would have men with rocks ready to hurl them down but I saw no smoke and that meant they were not heating oil, water, or sand. That had been my only fear.

My hearthweru and I had no axes and we stood back as our axemen ran at the walls to begin to hack and slash at them. Those who wielded the axes were experts. Back in Agerhøne, they used one every day. Some were skilled men who could carve strakes from a single tree. Others were those who felled the trees. They began to demolish the gates and the walls. The archers and slingers had progressed behind us and were so close now as to make a miss almost impossible. Had anyone in the town had the wit then they would have duelled with them but their greatest fear was the axe.

The gates, supposedly the strongest part of the burh, were the first to yield. The axemen had hacked at the gap between them and hacked through the bar that bound them. Karl Red Hair shouted, "It is almost time, lord."

I raised my sword and men formed a wedge behind me. When Karl and the axemen stood aside, I pointed my sword at the gates and we ran, a block of twenty men with shields held before them. We struck the almost wrecked gates and they sprang open. They had tried to brace them but twenty mailed warriors are a heavy weight and they shattered like kindling. We had no spears to encumber us and swords and axes are easier to wield. The defence of Brycgstow lasted just the killing of eight Saxons. The rest realised the futility of defiance and, perhaps emboldened by the news that we had not slaughtered thus far, the warriors surrendered.

I raced with my band of warriors through the town to the port. Men were loading ships with the ones who had fled first. That delay ensured the ships failed to sail for my men leapt aboard and took the steering boards. Had they abandoned the last refugees when they saw us then they might have escaped. As it was my men boarded the merchant ships and there was a collective wail. The ones on the ships feared the worst. I did not want a panicked populace and so I shouted, "You will neither be enslaved nor slain. Prince Cnut offers you friendship." I recognised the irony in my words but I had to calm them. "I am Sven Saxon Sword and I give my word that all those who cooperate will not be harmed."

My oath worked and I ensured that none of the men I led disobeyed me.

I turned to Faramir, "Remove the crews and man them with our fishermen. We will send the treasure back to Wareham by sea. We can send the wounded too."

Dreng laughed, "That is less than a dozen, lord. This has been a mighty victory."

"We will decide that when we have found the mint." However, I knew that the capture of the six ships was a great victory. We were a sea-faring people and ships were as valuable as gold, even poorly made Saxon ones.

We found a mint which, although not as big as Wareham, gave us sacks of gold and silver. We loaded them on the ships. They did not take up too much space and we managed to load the riches of Brycgstow aboard as well. We over-crewed the ships in case there were pirates and sent them back. We did not destroy the walls of Brycgstow, they had barely held us and it would have taken time to do so. I was increasingly convinced that we had a toehold in England and that Cnut would rule this part of it. Better to leave a people slightly less resentful than they would be if we destroyed their town. We left for Wareham with wagons and carts as well as horses. What we learned, as we headed south, was that illness had taken a hold of King Æthelred and he was unlikely to recover. He had gone to Lundenwic where his ailments could be tended to by his healers and priests. The people there still liked the English king for they had suffered less than the rest of the country. They would support the king until the end. An English Witan had made Edmund, now named Ironside, his heir. We had every reason to get back to Wareham as quickly as we could.

Our numbers were depleted compared with those that had headed north. Many had returned on the Saxon ships and we had sent others back with wagons and animals.

Eorl Thyrcetel had raised the fyrd in East Wessex and we were confronted by a ragtag army at Acemannesceastre. He had watched us pass to the northwest and now thought, as we were depleted in numbers, he would risk coming from behind his walls and fighting us beard to beard. My men had taken spears and weapons from Brycgstow and we took them from the wagons. I had the wagons made into an improvised fort and had the slingers and the archers guard it. Bersi would be safer. We then arrayed ourselves in our usual three lines. The spears were used by the men in the front rank. I just used Oathsword and Norse Gutter. I had no intention of initiating the fight. The eorl had decided to battle and I would let him begin. I relied on the unreliability of the fyrd and the strength of my shield wall.

We watched their priests come and bless the army. Then we saw Thyrcetel ride his horse along their ranks, no doubt exhorting them to great deeds for England and the dying Æthelred. Einar the Fat nodded at the eorl, "He looks ancient, lord and the men he leads are a mixture of fat merchants and skinny farmers."

Sweyn Skull Taker said, "Do not let them fool you, Einar. I can count at least one hundred housecarls as well as another two hundred who wear mail. They will outnumber us and provide us with a better challenge than Brycgstow."

Einar shrugged, "We fight whatever they bring. Perhaps they think that the taking of Brycgstow cost us men."

"I hope for overconfidence. We let them shatter their spears on our shields and when I sound the horn we attack." I turned, "Sweyn One Eye, take command of the rear rank and when the horn sounds then surround the enemy and end this battle."

My cousin grinned as he and his hearthweru left the front rank, "Thank you, cuz, I shall have the opportunity to compose a song about me and my nephew, Steana."

I had forgotten that my son was in the third rank. *Wyrd.* Today he would be blooded, one way or another.

"Bergil, rain death as soon as you can. You shall be the rocks on which they break."

"Aye, lord. You heard Sven Saxon Sword, throw and release as fast as you can."

We waited but there was no fear amongst the men I led. We had yet to be defeated and the mob, large though it was, that advanced upon us, did not frighten us. The eorl dismounted and after the priest had anointed him with what I can only assume was holy water, he took his place at the front of the largest wedge and they advanced. The fyrd formed two other wedges on either side but they only had the front three ranks mailed and the rest were armed with spears, improvised weapons and wearing only helmets. They were there to bolster numbers and it was the housecarls that followed the eorl that were the threat.

"Loose!" Bergil had been a good warrior before losing his hand. He was still relatively young and had a quick mind. He must have ordered the slingers and the archers to target the two wing wedges. The initial result was more than we could have hoped. Many of the fyrd had no shields and the arrows and stone reaped a fine harvest. The men closed together for mutual protection and that slowed them down. The eorl and the housecarls were not as practised as we were and their gait was more uneven. The eorl held a spear as did the housecarls although I could see that the ones at the front had the long two handed Danish axe strapped to their backs. I smiled. They would not be able to use such a weapon in a wedge.

The two wing wedges were shrinking not only because of the rain of missiles but also because some men left to slink back to the safety of Acemannesceastre and its walls. When the wedge was just forty feet from us, I saw the spear of the eorl rise and knew what they intended. They would run and rely on the weight of mail and men to knock us back.

"Brace!" Spears appeared over the shoulders of the front rank. There were not huge numbers but the ones that there were protected the point at which the wedge would strike me. I felt shields pushing in our backs and I placed my right leg behind me. The old man at the front could not run as fast as the younger housecarls around and the single point became a flatter three. The three men thrust as one and each spear found the metal on our shields. I hacked down with my sword and chopped through the ash spear of Eorl Thyrcetel. I had quick hands and even as the old warrior was pushed closer to me by the press of men behind, I backhanded the Dragon Sword up. It was to prevent the sword from being trapped but the result was I caught his helmet and his old straps broke. The helmet fell from his head. I was pushed back a handspan before the shields behind held me. There was always a danger in such a melee of being lifted from your feet and I squatted lower. The eorl had a broken shaft in his hand and he could not move his right hand, nor could those next to him. I took my chance and brought the pommel of my sword down onto the head of the old man. I hurt him and so I struck again and again until his eyes closed and he began to sink to the ground. A spear from behind me jabbed into the face of a surprised housecarl who had been staring into the back of the eorl's head. Its head pierced the eye and killed him instantly. He fell and in that falling exposed the housecarl next to him. I had just enough room to stab at the side of his head. He wore no coif and my sword entered his skull and he died. A wedge functions best when it has integrity. Three men at the fore had fallen and as I punched with my shield I stepped over the bodies. The housecarls' spears were less effective in such a fight. Their shields were locked and as a spear scraped along my helmet, I slid Oathsword between two men and into the side of one of them. I broke links and when I felt the metal resistance cease, I pushed harder and my sword slid into vital organs.

We now had momentum. My hearthweru had killed the bodyguards of the eorl and we were now a sort of wedge ourselves. This time Dreng did not have the horn but his younger brother Thorstein who was in the third rank. "Thorstein, sound the horn."

Our front two ranks now knew that we would be briefly under pressure and they redoubled their efforts. We now had space and I was able to swing my sword. Some of the more experienced housecarls dropped their spears and tried to grab their axes. A man cannot hold a shield and defend himself whilst reaching for an axe. I slew two men as they tried to do so and my hearthweru, keen to emulate me were right next to me doing the same.

Both formations were now broken and it was warrior against warrior. When I heard a wail from the flanks then I knew that my cousin had fallen on the two weaker formations. Even my third rank would be more than a match for farmers with bill hooks and sharpened hoes. One of the Saxon housecarls had managed to swing his shield to his back and held his axe two handed. He began to swing and move towards me. It suited my men for it naturally cleared all the Saxons around him. I waited for my opening. I was watching his swing and calculating when I should strike. It was clear to me that he was coming for my head. He moved steadily and was clearly trying to intimidate me. I feinted with my shield and he reacted. Even as the axe came at me, I held my shield above my head and then swung my sword hard at his leg. I struck below the skirt of his byrnie and felt the edge, still sharp, slice through flesh and crack bone. He began to try to move back and I stood, bringing the metal rim of my shield under his chin. The combination of strikes made him flounder like a fish and I ended his life by driving my sword into his throat.

As I looked for my next enemy, I saw that the fyrd had fled and behind the housecarls were Sweyn and my men. "Saxons you are lost. Your eorl lies dead. Surrender and I will allow you to walk away."

What I was doing was risky. These men were good warriors and one day we might have to fight them again but that had to be balanced against our losses if they fought to the death.

A bloodied warrior with a good sword faced me and said, "Is that the Oathsword? The gift of a king to a Dane?"

"It is." All fighting had ceased and the two sets of foes faced each other. They were ready to continue the fight but awaiting the outcome of our words.

He nodded and sheathed his sword, "Then there is no dishonour in surrender to Sven Saxon Sword. What are your terms?"

"Take your arms and march east. Go to Wintan-ceastre and tell whoever rules there now that Prince Cnut has come to claim his birthright. Meet us in battle and it can be settled by warriors."

"I am Edwy of Gleawecastre and as all those above me are now dead I will accept your terms." He turned to his men and said, "Follow me and we will take the news to the king that he has lost a fine warrior." They sheathed their weapons and marched off. They did not head to Acemannesceastre whose gates gaped wide but south and east on the main road to the capital of Wessex.

As they did, I shouted, "Sweyn, take the town!"

He and the untried warriors raced to obey. I saw Steana close to his uncle and was relieved. Both would be happy.

We stayed in Acemannesceastre for four days. We had lost men and they were buried. The Saxons begged me to allow their own dead to be buried and I complied for we were busy stripping all of value from the burh. It too had a mint. I reflected that we had gathered more gold on this one raid than every raid I had ever been on added together. I knew then that England would fall. They could not afford to lose so much treasure, not to mention men of the quality of the housecarls we had slain. With nothing left to take in Acemannesceastre, we headed back to Wareham.

Bersi and Steana marched with me and both were ebullient. Steana had killed more than ten men and while only one was what you might truly term a warrior, he had covered himself in glory. Bersi too had seen men, for the first time, fall to his sling and having taken a shield and a sword from the dead he was more determined than ever to be like his big brother.

Chapter 5

The Wareham Witan 1015

When we reached Wareham, we were just in time for the Witan. The Danes who lived in Wessex, Mercia and the Danelaw had all come to choose their own king. There were also Saxons there who could not support Edmund and were being practical. They would side with the winners. The prince was pleased with our success. I did not interrupt the meeting to tell him but waited until there was a lull for drinks.

"The loss of two such important mints will hurt Edmund." He smiled, "Thorkell has enjoyed success too but not in the form of gold. You and your men will be rich, Sven."

I nodded, "And, given that, I would like to send a couple of knarrs back to Agerhøne with what we have taken thus far. If we are to conquer Wessex and Mercia then we will be away for a long time. My men would like to send animals home."

He frowned. "We will need every warrior we can muster."

"They would only be away for three weeks at the most and it will take a month for us to be ready to march, will it not?"

"You are right."

"And how goes the talking?" I was a man of action and not words. I would have hated to sit through a debate.

"They will name me as king. It is just a matter of who gets what that concerns them."

"And will they fight with us?"

"The disaster at Gegnesburh means that the men of the Danelaw are reluctant to risk the wrath of Edmund if we lose and with Thurbrand, Uhtred and Edmund so close to them they will leave their swords sheathed. We have more support from Mercia and that is where we shall begin our taking of the land. You and Thorkell have secured the west and north of Wessex. We take the east and then move into Mercia."

A messenger came over, "Prince Cnut, you are sought."

He nodded, "You may send some knarr over and see if the gold you send enlists the support of more warriors."

"Yes, Prince Cnut."

I had Lars take the largest two knarrs that we had brought and he choose his crew. Some men had been wounded and I gave them the chance to return home. Five chose to do so and another five volunteered to be extra crew. Lars loaded the treasure and the animals while I waved over Steana and Bersi. "I would have one of you go with the knarr to our home. Your mother would appreciate the visit, however short, and you can give her the message that all is well here."

They looked at each other and Bersi nodded, "I am the ship's boy, for the moment, and I can learn from Lars. Steana is the warrior. I will go." It was what I had hoped and showed that my son was growing both within and without.

The delegates from the Witan departed two days after the knarr. Cnut was named as king of England. Of course, it meant nothing until Edmund and his father were defeated but it was more than we could have hoped for. Half the land supported us and we just needed to defeat the other half. In preparation for the attack, Cnut had us moved from Wareham itself to the island in the middle of the harbour. There we had the protection of a wooden wall of ships and the island was more than big enough to accommodate us all. We spent the winter month when the days were shortest there. We ate well and with captured cider, ale and mead we drank well. As winter camps go it was better than most. The proximity of the water kept an even temperature and there was no snow. Each night I sat with Cnut and Thorkell and the most important jarls and we planned our attack.

Thorkell knew the land. While he had served the English king, he had been invited to many halls to speak to their leading lords. He knew them, their strengths and their weaknesses. Eadric Streona was the unpredictable one. He had managed to change sides so often that I wondered why any would trust him but they did. Thurbrand the Hold and Uhtred the Bold were the leaders of two powerful warbands but their enmity for each other negated that influence. The best general that the English had appeared to be the man we had already fought, Ulfcetel Snilling. As for Edmund himself? He was an unknown factor. Even Thorkell knew little about him.

"I knew his elder brother and he was a good warrior. He was nothing like his father. Edmund? He was rarely at court." He drank some of the ale and wiped the foam from his beard, "If I were to speak truthfully, my lord I would say that he was the reason the English reneged on their payments to me. Before you arrived with this army, we heard that he had used the new lands he had been given to build an army that will fight just as ours does."

That, too, made sense for the north of the land had as much Viking blood as Saxon blood. Such a hybrid army would be more of a threat than one led by Æthelred.

Cnut nodded, "Then my plan to secure Wessex and Mercia first would seem to be the most sensible. We tempt Edmund and the two squabbling lords to leave their heartland and fight in a land that does not support them."

Cnut had come of age. He had stepped out of the shadow of his father and now wielded power as well as I did Oathsword.

I spent the days with Steana and my men. He now had oar brothers. He slept not in the tent with me but with those alongside whom he fought in battle. Steana had a byrnie and now that we had defeated a Saxon army his oar brothers did too. They spent each day honing the skills that they would need when we fought Edmund. There were ten of them and all were young men from Agerhøne. They had grown up together and gone to war together. They reminded me of when Siggi and I had gone to sea and become so close. The bad apples in Agerhøne had been discarded and that was better for the clan. I felt happier that when we faced the English shield wall then Steana would have as much chance as any of surviving. In war and in battle, there were no guarantees of survival.

Lars and the two knarrs were later back than we expected. While we had enjoyed a benign solstice, they had suffered a storm on the way back. Lars told me that had the storm been on the homeward leg then they might have lost the animals. As it was, he had extra crewmen, as another ten men came back with him and they were able to save the two knarrs. He patted Bersi on the head, "And this one showed great courage, my lord. He is a natural sailor and when our knarr was almost put on her beam he did not panic but obeyed orders. He has steel within him."

Later Bersi told Steana and me that he had been terrified. "I will go to sea again, father, but Lars is wrong. I am no sailor. I will learn my trade and join the shield wall."

"Good. And your mother and sister?"

"They are well and made a fuss of me. They fed me up and wept when I left."

"As they always will."

Mary had sent us all knitted caps, ostensibly to keep us warm but also as added protection from the clash of battle. I smiled as I fingered mine. Mary would hate the idea but she was being like a volva who spun, wove and knitted threads to make spells. I knew that when she had woven the hats. she had been thinking of us and praying for our safety. She had been doing what the Norse and Danish women had done for centuries. *Wyrd.*

Our ships ferried our army to the north shore of the harbour. Every village, farm and town for twenty miles around the harbour had been looted and pillaged. It was winter but we had plenty of food and we headed towards Wintan-Caestre. We met no opposition until we reached the burh that had been Alfred's capital. Edmund was still in the north and my battle with Thyrcetel had robbed Wessex of the one leader who might have rallied the Saxons to defend the walls. Such was the size of our army that we completely surrounded the city. We had Saxons fighting alongside us and it must have sucked the heart from the inhabitants of Wintan-Caestre. We raided the land around the burh and the Saxon leaders debated for three days about what to do. We had no need to assault the walls and the burh had clearly not laid in supplies for on the fourth day they sued for peace and asked Prince Cnut for terms. He knew how to negotiate and in return for leaving Wintan-Caestre untouched, he demanded that they swear allegiance to him. The swearing meant little, despite the fact that it was sworn on a Bible, for if Edmund came south then the gates would be barred to us. If that happened then Prince Cnut would raze the burh and sell the inhabitants into a life of slavery.

We headed north into a land that had been untouched by war for some time and was ripe for the plucking. We surrounded the burhs and waited for surrender. We were well fed and they began to starve. Gradually we took the whole of Wessex and neared Mercia. In many ways, Mercia was even easier than Wessex had been. The Mercians had lost their independence when the granddaughter of Alfred the Great, Ælfwynn, had her land taken from her by her uncle, King Edward the Elder. The Mercians resented their Wessex overlords and we were seen as the lesser of two evils.

However, the closer we came to the north the more opposition we found. Men defended towns and villages. They did not stop us but slowed us and we began to lose men for the first time. My raid had been the only one with anything like a battle but now we left the graves of warriors killed in battle to mark our progress. Cnut began to become frustrated that we could not bring Edmund to battle.

It became slightly easier once we entered Mercia. They had not been attacked for some time and it showed. Still, we were losing men. It was a Saxon traitor that finally helped us. Eadric Streona, who was known to be a treacherous man having betrayed the king before, came to speak with us, Mercia was his and I knew that he would be bargaining with Cnut for land when the two of them spoke alone. Thorkell and I knew the nature of the snake and we ensured that he was searched and every weapon removed before he was allowed to speak with the prince. The Mercian was outraged while Cnut just smiled. Gegnesburh had put steel into the prince and I knew that he kept two daggers with him at all times.

Thorkell and I spoke as we waited outside the hall where they spoke. Cnut had made a point of using the largest hall in every town we took as his base. It made a statement that only the best was good enough for him.

"You know the English better than I do, Thorkell, can we trust this eorledman, Eadric Streona?"

He shook his head and gave a sardonic laugh, "Not in the sense that you mean, Sven. He serves only himself. He was the one who executed Sigeferth and Morcar. I think that even Æthelred came to recognise his treachery and made him execute the men to keep him loyal. If you mean, can we use him, then the answer is yes. We have enjoyed greater success in Mercia than Wessex and he wants us out of Mercia and the only way he can do that is if he suggests another target that is easier to raid. He will give us intelligence that even I do not have. He has come from the court of Edmund. He is a snake but a clever one. What I know of him tells me that he will not be seen to openly support our efforts and he will keep a conversation going with Edmund. Whoever becomes the king of England will have Eadric Streona close by their side."

When the two emerged the Mercian left us and went back to his men. Cnut looked pensive. "We have allies in Mercia." He saw Thorkell's face and nodded, "Aye, we cannot trust him but I want the word spread amongst our men that Eadric Streona, Eorledman of Mercia is our ally."

Thorkell smiled, "You are sending a message to Edmund."

"I am. The Mercian has given us some information. Thurbrand the Hold is willing to join us and as Uhtred the Bold is away raiding with Edmund then we can take Northumbria. We have plundered Wessex and Mercia. Let us take Northumbria."

I was doubtful, "Prince Cnut, we have still to bring Edmund to battle."

"And what is the alternative, Sven? Do we squat like toads and wait for him to come to us? I know that more than half of the men we brought are here for plunder." Thorkell looked away, "I am not a fool, Thorkell the Tall. You switched sides when the English stopped paying you. Many of the warriors, mercenaries, sent by my brother wish just for gold. We have to continue to give them what they need until we can bring Edmund to battle. Tomorrow, we head north and east. Sven, I want you to return to Wareham and fetch the fleet. You can leave the knarr and just bring the longships. You know the waters along the east coast better than any. Meet us at the Humber. The men of the Danelaw may well be willing to give us their support. We will be taking back the lands of Sigeferth and Morcar."

Thorkell said, "Who were executed by our new ally Eadric Streona."

The prince sighed, "I have learned much, Thorkell the Tall, since I began this journey. I have planned this game to a conclusion. Judge me at the end of it and not at the start." He saw the doubt on my face, "Sven, the Eorledman told me that Edmund is heading to London. We will not battle him yet and I do not expect opposition that would necessitate the Dragon Sword being needed. I can trust you to use your men to crew the ships and bring them safely to anchor in the Humber close to where it meets the Trent. When we fled it was from there. Let us have vengeance on the man who tricked and betrayed my father. Uhtred the Bold has many sins for which to answer." I nodded, "And there is something else, Sven. I do not trust Eadric but one thing he said which rang true concerned a sword." My hand went to the hilt of Oathsword. I could not stop it. The prince smiled, "Aye, swords again. King Offa, the mighty king of the Mercians had a sword. Eadric believes it is a Dragon Sword. It was in the possession of Æthelstan the Ætheling and when he died, he bequeathed it to his brother. Streona believes that it should be wielded by a Mercian and not a warrior of Wessex. So you see that your three sisters are weaving still. That sword hangs from the baldric of Prince Edmund…" he shrugged.

"I will do as you say, my prince but I beg you not to …" I paused for I was about to say, 'throw away an army as you did at Gegnesburh'.

He shook his head. We knew each other well, "I am not the same fool who feasted at Gegnesburh when he should have been building walls. Uhtred's treachery cut me to the quick. Fear not, my friend and mentor."

We left at dawn and marched through a land we had pillaged. It was a cold, wet and hungry march. When we reached the harbour, we feasted for we had left food there. I gathered the crews of the drekar and explained what we would be doing. "Every drekar will have a crew to row who come from Ribe and Agerhøne and I know that will not be enough. We need the aid of the wind and the gods. I will lead. We sail east and then follow the coast. I do not intend to lose sight of the land. Prince Cnut will need every ship he can if he is to transport his army north."

That night I dined with Einar, my foster father and my cousin. My foster father looked weary, "I tire of this, Sven. I never thought that I would but I do."

"And you wish to return to Ribe."

"I have grandchildren I wish to spoil and I have hawks and hounds I wish to use for hunting. It is not too much to ask, is it, for a man who has given his life to war and buried too many friends? Griotard the Grim and Lodvir the Long feel the same. They are here not because of Cnut, Sven, but because of you and the sword. I am too."

I nodded, "And the threads that bind us need something special to cut them." I leaned in and told them of King Offa's sword. "It is my belief that my sword and that which is wielded by Edmund must meet in battle. Stay until the two swords have clashed and then go home. I know here," I patted my heart, "it will be within the year."

That night I prayed that we would have favourable winds and the next morning made a blót to ask Njörðr for his help. The Christian priests left in the camp frowned on our actions but not a man amongst those who sailed did. Many wore the cross of the White Christ but they still believed in the old ways. Adverse winds would mean rowing with a skeletal crew. We could do it but it would leave us in no condition to fight the Northumbrians. The blót worked for the winds came from the south and west. They were perfect to take us to the Humber and, had we chosen, then we could have been in Agerhøne in a matter of days.

I rarely thought of vengeance. It was not in my nature but as we headed along the Saxon coast it filled my head. I had been betrayed by Uhtred and his son Ealdred. Warriors I had known well had died as a result of that betrayal and I was more than happy to lead my warriors in a battle that would see him defeated and, I hoped, executed. That decision would be Cnut's and I knew that he was a far-sighted prince. If it suited his purpose then he would forbid me to slay the deceiver and I would have to obey. I was oathsworn.

When we entered the estuary of the Humber, we were met by the fleet of ships commanded by Thurbrand the Hold. Neither fleet had shields along the sides of their ships and that meant both of us had peaceful intentions but I kept my hand on the hilt of Oathsword as we left the ships to speak on the southern bank of the river.

Thurbrand and I had a history. I had taken Cnut's bride-to-be from his home and he had tried to pursue me and failed. When we had met at Gegnesburh he had appeared to have forgiven me and, to be fair to him, he had pointedly remained neutral when Uhtred had deceived us.

"Sven Saxon Sword, welcome."

"Thank you, Thurbrand the Hold." I pointed to the northern shore, "You could have asked us to meet on the north shore, in your land, Holderness."

He nodded, "And that thought crossed my mind but I chose to meet here so that you would know of my intentions and that, despite our history, I am a friend." He pointed to the path that led along the river, "Come, you and I need to talk."

We both waved to our bodyguards to stay where they were. For my part, I knew that I could take the warrior any time I chose. I had Oathsword to protect me.

"Your prince comes north." I cocked an eye and he smiled, "It is like a hunt. The smaller animals have fled already before the mighty army he leads and word has spread. I am a warlord, like you, and if this was just your warband that came north then I would fight you, but Cnut brings more warriors than we can fight. I would fight alongside Cnut but I would like a reward."

"And I do not have the power to grant that reward for I think that you mean land."

"I do and I know that while you do not have the power, Prince Cnut trusts you. Your word and support would go a long way to granting me what I wish."

"And that is?"

"All the land between the Humber and the Tees."

"That is half of Northumbria. Jorvik is a mighty city and a powerful one. The command of that city is not a gift to be given away lightly. Uhtred the Bold would not approve."

"And Uhtred the Bold is with Edmund in Cheshire, capturing the lands of Eadric Streona. He has chosen his side and it is Edmund. If Cnut is to defeat Edmund, then he must destroy Uhtred. We both know that."

We stopped and I rubbed my chin. All that Thurbrand had said made sense to me but I did not trust him, not completely. "Your idea has merit and I will speak with Prince Cnut when he comes but know that I cannot guarantee he will grant your request."

"And I will be equally honest with you and say that if he does not then Thurbrand the Hold will huddle with his men in Holderness and see which of the wolves emerges victoriously. If there is nothing in it for me and my people then why should we fight?"

We returned to our ships and I headed for the confluence of the Trent and the Humber. Thurbrand and his ships followed us but when we tied up on the southern shore, he and his ships chose the north. It was symbolic.

Chapter 6

The march to Northumbria

We had made such good time that Cnut and our army did not reach us for another week. They arrived with men from the Danelaw and food taken from the Saxons. I was summoned to his side as soon as he arrived at the defended camp we had made.

I could see that he was eager to discover the importance of Thurbrand's proximity. I told him. Thorkell, of course, was present as was Eadric Streona. The attacks on his home had driven him to openly declare for Cnut and Edmund and Uhtred now ruled Mercia. "We have had no battles on our way here, skirmishes only. Edmund and Uhtred seemed intent on making Cheshire their own." He turned to the Saxon, "What would your advice be, Eadric Streona?"

He smiled and it was an evil one, "Slay Uhtred, my lord. He is a treacherous man."

I looked at Thorkell and though no words were spoken we were thinking the same thought. The snake was telling us that there was a snake as treacherous as he was.

"And the gift that Thurbrand seeks?"

Eadric shrugged, "You could promise him, my lord. His warband would swell your numbers and guarantee victory, afterwards…"

"Eorledman Streona, if I say one thing and do another then will men trust me? I seek a kingdom. This is not a raid to tear the treasure from this land. It is a war to take that which is, I believe, my birthright."

I knew there were many Saxons who would dispute that. King Sweyn had gifted the land to Cnut and he had not conquered it fully; it was not really his to give. His murder had created a situation that was like the fog. It made things that should have been clear, indistinct instead.

Cnut nodded, "Thorkell and Eadric, leave us. I would speak with Sven Saxon Sword alone." Eadric did not like the command but he obeyed. Thorkell knew me and, I think, trusted me. "What are your thoughts, Sven, for I trust you."

"Northumbria is a barrier that prevents the Scots from raiding and pillaging. You need a strong hand to rule it. I agree with Eadric, and that is strange for I do not trust the Mercian." Cnut smiled. "Uhtred needs to die but I do not think that Thurbrand is the man to rule Northumbria. It is a moot point in any case as we still have to bring

Uhtred to battle. Dunelm and Bebbanburgh are strong burhs and we would lose many men if we tried to take them."

He leaned forward, "You should know, Sven, that I have not been idle. When I was with my brother, I sent word to Eiríkr Hákonarson."

The surprise showed on my face. The Norwegian had fought alongside us at Svolder and as a reward, King Sweyn had made him Jarl of Norway. "A mighty warrior, Prince Cnut, and an excellent addition to our leaders."

"And I think that he would make a good Eorl of Northumbria. He and his ships are waiting in the estuary of the Tees. I had already decided that Uhtred will be removed but it will be Eiríkr Hákonarson who has Northumbria. We can give Thurbrand the bone that is Holderness and the land up to Jorvik. Eiríkr Hákonarson can tether him. If he does not like that then he shall be crushed." The treachery at Gegnesburh had changed Cnut and made him more ruthless.

The next day he sent for Thurbrand and the two of them spoke without witnesses for some time. He agreed to the compromise. He was a practical man. He would rule a greater land than before and he would not have to bow the knee to Uhtred. I saw as he left us that he would be plotting how to become the eorl. To do that he would have to outwit Cnut and I could not see that happening.

Two days later we left for Jorvik. The fleet was swollen by Thurbrand's ships and the ships from the Five Boroughs. We had a triumphal entry into the city, sailing our fleet into the heart of it, and they immediately swore allegiance to Cnut. Had Uhtred been close we might have had to fight for it. His absence meant that we took that jewel without shedding blood.

The return to the sea was quicker and we headed up the coast of Thurbrand's new domain. There, waiting for us in the mouth of the Tees were the twenty ships of Eiríkr Hákonarson. We headed north to the Tyne. Cnut could have sailed to the far north but he wanted the jewel that was Dunelm and the cathedral that held the bones of St Cuthbert in his grasp. We now had enough men to besiege and take the mighty fortress. Leaving our ships guarded by half of Eiríkr Hákonarson's men we marched south. Such was the speed of our march that we reached it within a long day and had it surrounded before the defenders even knew that we were there. We arrived at night and our campfires told them that they were surrounded and ensured that no one could flee and take word to Uhtred.

After we had breakfasted, Cnut, along with Eiríkr Hákonarson, Thorkell the Tall, Thurbrand the Hold, Eadric Streona and I marched to the bridge over the Wear. We wore no helmets but we were all arrayed with the regalia of office and our banners were carried by our hearthweru. Cnut's Raven banner was the most ancient and special of them. I was the most underdressed and I doubted if the men on the walls had any idea who I was.

"I am Prince Cnut and I am here to ask for the surrender of this fortress. I have been appointed king by a Witan of lords."

"But not by us, Prince Cnut. We owe our allegiance to Eorl Uhtred and Prince Edmund." There was no mention of the king.

"Then prepare yourselves for battle. We have a mighty army and we will take your walls."

We retreated back to our camp. A council of war took place, "We could starve them out, Prince Cnut."

The prince shook his head, "Eorledman Streona, if we do that then we may find ourselves both hungry and attacked by Uhtred and Edmund. This is not a good place to defend."

"Then trickery, my lord."

We all looked at Thorkell. He pointed at the walls. "The bridge to the city is guarded by towers and the walls themselves. It is narrow and an assault would cost us men but the river loops around the city and we could fashion rafts and send men across at night. We have all climbed greater obstacles. As I remember Exeter had high walls. We send bands of some of our best men to scale the walls. We only need one of them to succeed and to open the gates."

Cnut nodded and I could see that the idea appealed, "And who would be these men?"

"A band chosen from mine, one led by Sven, a third led by Thurbrand and a fourth made up of the men who were sent by your brother."

Thorkell the Tall was a cunning warrior. By choosing the two of us first he was showing both our loyalty and our courage but by including Thurbrand and King Harald's mercenaries he was seeking a commitment from them.

"And when would we do this?"

Thorkell smiled, "Why tonight, of course. The days and nights are equally long and there is no moon this night. They will await an attack on their walls in the morning. Tonight their sentries will not be as alert as they would have been had we showered them with arrows and stones."

Prince Cnut looked at me and I nodded. In my head I had already chosen the men I would lead. "Thurbrand?"

The warlord looked uncomfortable. He sought land and power. To gain it he had to show commitment. "Of course, my lord."

Cnut turned to Olaf Bloodaxe, the leader of the mercenaries, "And you shall choose men from my warband. Thorkell, assign the walls. It would not do to have any misunderstandings."

That Thorkell had planned it well was clear from his instructions. He gave each of us a section of the wall. Mine was to the west. He also gave us the time to attack. It did not need to be precise, for if one band attacked earlier then that would simply draw defenders to that part of the wall. We would all be in place at roughly the same time in any case.

I returned to our camp and chose the men from my drekar to be the ones who would attack. I had arguments from Einar the Fat, and Sweyn One Eye, but not my foster father. I dismissed them. "I need men to follow me who need no words but know my mind. What I need the rest of you to do is to hew trees to make rafts."

As the afternoon wore on, I gathered my men around me. "We need not mail for this. Swords and shields along with ropes will do. Once we have crossed the river then we use shields and lithe young men to scale the walls." I saw Steana and his oar brothers brighten at my words. I was risking my son but if I did not do so then how could I expect others to follow my orders? I had to trust in his skill. If Mary discovered what I had done then my life would be made a misery. "We make for the gates. There will be three other bands doing the same and one should succeed. Eiríkr Hákonarson will lead the rest of the army to take the fortress."

No one argued. My inclusion of my son ensured that they would accept my plan.

Bersi was disappointed that he would not be coming with us. I smiled at him, "Your task will be to have a fine breakfast ready for us when we return. Others will have to secure the fortress and we will be able to enjoy food and ale."

I was not sure that he believed me but I had thrown him a bone and he nodded.

We had to wait until dark to carry the raft made by the ones not attacking, around to the place we would launch it. Olaf Bloodaxe and the mercenaries had the longest walk. Mine was the smallest band that would cross the river. I had chosen my men deliberately. The more men we took the greater the risk of discovery. I gave Olaf and his men enough time to get into position and then we paddled the raft across the river. The steering was awkward and the current did not help but the river was not wide and we only missed our mark by ten paces. We kept watch as we paddled. I had our four best archers with bows ready to strike at any curious sentry but Thorkell had been right. They had concentrated their eyes on the main gate. We saw sentries as they walked the fighting platform but they were not expecting an attack. We disembarked without dragging the raft over stones that might alert the defenders. If the raft floated away then so be it. Without mail and with swords in scabbards our approach to the walls was silent. Using shields we boosted the eight young warriors halfway up the wall. They used the stones as handholds and climbed like spiders towards the top. The four archers stood with bows ready to slay any Northumbrian head that peered over the walls but none came.

I watched Steana as he climbed and my heart was in my mouth. He was not the first up, that was Beorn. Beorn had always been a good climber. When he had been a ship's boy with Steana he was always the first up the mast. I saw the flash of his dagger as he slipped it out and clambered over the top. The eight disappeared and we waited. When we heard the cry of alarm it came from the distance. Either Thurbrand or Olaf had been discovered. The ropes, when they were hurled down, told me that the sentries had been disposed of and our men were undiscovered. Climbing up the ropes we heard the bells in the fortress sound the alarm and men would be racing to the walls. They would, of course, go to the walls where the alarm had sounded and that gave us time, not much but enough.

I reached the top and slid my shield around from my back. Drawing Oathsword I led the young warriors and my oathsworn along the fighting platform towards the gate. Thorkell had arranged it so that we two were the ones that would be closest to the gate. The other two warbands were simply bait. The three sentries all lay dead but men still raced to the walls. We appeared like wraiths and the first man to step onto the fighting platform was greeted by Oathsword. I hacked across his unprotected neck and mortally wounded him, he fell down the steps, crashing into the next two warriors behind him. I leapt down the steps and landed on the dying man. His body and that of his two companions softened the blow and I slew one while Faramir disposed of the other. My decision to choose a smaller group of men that I knew well was vindicated when my other three hearthweru led the other warriors to run for the main gate. Of course, the noise and the alarm had sent more men to the gate than anywhere else but they were not expecting to be attacked from behind by my warriors.

We were more evenly matched than one might have expected as they wore no mail either. The battle would be a test of skills. Mail armour allowed a warrior to make mistakes and still survive. Wearing no mail meant a mistake would cost a life. I ran to join my hearthweru and our blades were wielded as wildly as the Northumbrians. We aimed for places that had no protection. The tops of the shoulders were normally well protected and the Northumbrians forgot that, holding their shields and swords before them. Six fell before a Northumbrian voice ordered them to make a shield wall. It was too late for just as they were forming it Thorkell the Tall led his Jomsvikings to fall upon their unprotected rear. It was a massacre and ended the battle in moments. We opened the gates and Eiríkr Hákonarson led his Norsemen, hungry for blood, into Dunelm. We stood to the side to allow them to pass. When the army had entered, the last two to do so were Cnut and the Mercian eorledman, I clasped arms with Thorkell, "That was well done, Thorkell. Did you lose any men?"

"Just two, and you?"

I looked around and Leif Long Leg shook his head, "Just one, lord, one of your son's oar brothers, Lars Redshield was slain." He shrugged, "He slipped on a pool of blood and the Northumbrian hacked into his back. The Northumbrian is dead."

"Then bring his body and we shall honour him."

We left the fortress. Behind us, we heard the screams of death and the pleas for mercy. Cnut was not a fool and he would soon stop the bloodshed. He would allow just enough to satiate the warriors and to make Dunelm fear our wrath and no more.

We found a suitable place to bury Lars. It was close to the stream that fed into the Wear. He had died with a sword in his hand and would be in Valhalla but we liked to bury men close to the water for all water flows to the sea. It was a sombre funeral and sobering for the ones like Steana who had trained and fought with Lars. They now knew the cost.

We smelled the food as we neared our camp and found that Bersi had found some ham and was frying thickly cut slices on a skillet. Steana took the other young warriors to help him and I sat with my hearthweru.

"I cannot think of an easier fight, my lord."

"You are right, Dreng, and it is due to Thorkell's mind that we did so. I would not have thought of this and I do not think that the prince would either. We have all much to learn from each other."

By the time dawn broke, we had eaten well and we made our way into the stronghold. The warriors had all been slain but the people and monks were spared. Cnut was a Christian prince and the first thing he did, once we had secured the gates, was to go into the church and pray at the shrine of St Cuthbert. The gesture seemed to appease the priests.

My men and I found chambers to use, for the ones who had been spared, apart from the priests and monks, were ejected from the castle. The bulk of the army camped between the Cathedral, the monk's refectory and the mead hall. Cnut and his oathsworn would sleep in the hall.

I did not get to speak to him until the bells rang from the cathedral at noon, called Sext by the monks. He had not enjoyed the breakfast that we had and was devouring food. He waved me to sit next to him on the bench. "You and Thorkell did well." He glanced down the table at the men his brother had sent. He lowered his voice as he said, "The men led by Olaf Bloodaxe were clumsy and had alerted the defenders. He lost five men." Their response had been a vicious one and the only non-warriors who were killed were slaughtered by Bloodaxe's men.

"And now what, my lord?"

He smiled and, in that smile, I saw the clever mind of Cnut at work. "We need not move from here. Uhtred is far to the south and his son will be filling his breeks in Bebbanburgh. Uhtred cannot afford to lose the banner of St Cuthbert. He will either have to come and fight, which I doubt, or come and sue for peace. Either way, we have Northumbria and we can sail south and take Lundenwic. We wait until Uhtred comes before we move. His departure will weaken Edmund."

Chapter 7

The treachery of Thurbrand the Hold

It did not take long for messengers to arrive and tell us that Uhtred was on the move. He had with him forty men and that told us that he was either heading for the north to raise an army or he was coming to sue for peace.

I was sent with my men to greet him and escort him into the stronghold. I took just forty men, the same as Uhtred and we used horses we found in the walls. Faramir asked, "Why has Prince Cnut sent us, lord?"

I had wondered that myself, "I think that he would not trust Eadric Streona. He and Thurbrand are avowed enemies and it would be beneath his position for Eiríkr Hákonarson to come."

"But he knows that we are Uhtred's enemies."

"I know, Dreng, but he also knows that I am a man of my word and that must count for something." At the back of my mind was a nagging doubt that there was another reason. Had this been Cnut's father I would have feared I was being used as a sacrifice but Cnut was not like that. He was, however, very clever and would have his own reason for sending me. We could have simply waited at Dunelm. I did not mind the ride. Dunelm was very crowded and I did not like the mercenaries that had been sent by King Harald. They were replacing far better men who had died at Gegnesburh.

We met four miles south of Dunelm on the road which led from the moors road and Appleby. My men wore no helmets but we had our shields on our backs and we were ready to use our swords. We warily approached each other. As we neared, I held up my hand and my men waited. I rode forward. Uhtred halted his men and came to meet me.

"So the Prince has sent Sven Saxon Sword to greet me. Is this a threat? Do we fight here to settle the bad blood between us?"

I shook my head, "Prince Cnut sent me because he trusts me and he needed to know your intent."

He laughed and shook his head, "You must have had word that I led just forty men. Does he think I am arrogant enough to try to take Dunelm with just forty men?"

"No, but he might think that you are cunning enough to inveigle your way into the walls and to do harm."

His eyes narrowed, "I did not enjoy fooling you, Sven Saxon Sword, and we, in the north, are grateful for what you did. If it is any consolation to you, I am deeply sorry to have tricked you." I nodded and accepted his apology. "I know how many men Prince Cnut has. If I used every man who lives in Northumbria, I could not put enough in the field to have half your number. No, I have come back to stop any further privations. I do not wish my people to suffer and with an army of Danes loose in the north then they would pay the price." He waved a hand to the south. "My warband follows, led by my son. I come to ask for terms from Prince Cnut."

I wheeled my horse around, "Then I will escort you there so that you will not come to harm."

He laughed as he rode next to me and waved his men forward, "This is Northumbria, this is my land."

"It was your land but now it is part of Danelaw. You should know and accept that. You know that a Witan made him King of England."

"And that Witan was not an English one. The king lives still."

"But he is not only a poor king but I hear a poorly one and close to death."

"Perhaps but you should know, Sven Saxon Sword, that Edmund has taken the whole of Cheshire and Mercia. Streona is at your side for he has no lands left. Edmund is a good leader."

"Yet you are willing to leave his side and follow, I assume, Prince Cnut."

"Pure practicality, Sven, he has my lands and my people. I have to bow the knee."

I was not convinced. Uhtred was merely being pragmatic, "And that is a poor argument."

"What would you do?"

I was stumped for an answer, "In truth, I know not. I follow Prince Cnut and our threads have been tied for many years. I stood by him after Gegnesburh and had his brother chosen war, then I would have fought for him."

"You are lucky then. I was fated to be born in the time of a king who did not deserve the title. Alfred would have driven you from his land."

"Yet it was Alfred who gave half of the land to the Danes."

"To be ruled by an English king."

I patted my sword, "Then, perhaps, that is why the sword called to me and found me. It was the sword given by a Saxon to a Dane. It has a purpose."

My words silenced him and we rode in silence until we reached the walls. He reined in at the bridge, "Sven, you and I have fought but I trust you. Put your hand on your sword and tell me the truth. Why am I being allowed within Dunelm's walls?"

I put my hand on my sword and spoke truthfully, "I was asked to bring you and your men safely within the walls of St Cuthbert's city. I do not think that you will rule Northumbria alone but that is all I know. There will be a feast and, perhaps there, you will learn the truth."

He had looked into my eyes when I spoke and he nodded, "I looked into your head, Sven, and there was no lie. Let us go and I will bow the knee to the boy."

I put my hand on his reins, "Do not make the mistake of using such words close to the prince. He will take offence."

"And fear not, Sven Saxon Sword, I know how to put on a face to meet kings and princes. I have lived long enough to learn such skills."

We entered the city and rode up the hill to the burh. The walls were lined with Bloodaxe's men and the Norse brought by the jarl. Cnut was keeping Thurbrand away. When we entered the open ground before the cathedral, the camp and the hall we saw Cnut. He was flanked by Eiríkr Hákonarson, Eadric Streona and Thurbrand the Hold. I frowned. Had he wished peace he would not have taunted Uhtred with the presence of two of his enemies. As we dismounted the Northumbrian said, quietly, "A pair of vipers, Sven, do not trust either of them. At least Eiríkr Hákonarson is known to be an honourable man." He sighed, "And now I will play the penitent. Always remember, Sven, that a leader owes as much to his people as they do to him."

He walked alone to the four men and kneeling took off his sword. He held it before him, his head hanging down, "You have taken my land, Price Cnut, take my sword and allow me to use it in your service."

Taking it the prince handed it to Eiríkr Hákonarson. He smiled and took Uhtred's hands in his, "Rise, friend, for I accept your offer. The men of Northumbria will go to war with the men of the Danelaw and make this land of England as great as when Alfred ruled. Come, we have a feast planned."

I was ignored. I took the animals to the stables and when the Northumbrians had seen to their horses, I led them to the hall. There was a rule that no weapons were allowed within the walls of the hall at Dunelm and as I entered, Olaf Bloodaxe held out his hands, "Your sword, Sven Saxon Sword."

I took the sword and scabbard and handed them to him, "Have your men guard it with their lives for if anything were to happen to it then the Norns would not be happy."

The warrior and his men were all, purportedly, Christian yet their hands went to their Thor's Hammers.

"We will treat it with all due reverence." He then looked up at the Northumbrians, "Your swords too. You may keep your daggers with which to eat."

Having seen me give up the fabled sword they obeyed, albeit reluctantly. When we entered the hall, I saw that there was one long table and at the two ends were long tables that led from it. I saw that Cnut was at the head table and Eiríkr Hákonarson was on one side. There was a space next to him and Eadric Streona was on the other side of Eiríkr Hákonarson. The rest of the table was filled with the leading Norse warriors. On one of the other two tables sat Thurbrand the Hold and his warriors. Uhtred the Bold sat a lonely figure, on the other. I wondered at the arrangement. It was sensible to separate the two sets of warriors but why invite Thurbrand's men at all? The rest of the warriors, the mercenaries included, had not been invited. I went to my seat and Uhtred's men joined their leader. Thorkell the Tall was next to me. Servants brought ales and filled their horns. The doors were closed and Olaf Bloodaxe walked to take his place behind Prince Cnut. As Cnut's man, he wore his sword.

When they were all seated, the bishop who was pointedly seated at the far end of the table close to Uhtred, rose and said, in Latin, what I took to be grace and he blessed every warrior. The obvious Christians, Cnut included, made the sign of the cross. I noticed that Uhtred did too and I could not help but smile. He was a wily old warrior and knew how to play the game.

Prince Cnut rose and spoke, "Warriors, we are gathered here tonight to welcome Uhtred and the men of Northumbria who have seen the error of their ways and chosen to follow my banner." He held two arms out to the two groups of warriors. "The men of Northumbria can now break bread together to show that old enmities are forgotten. Tonight we feast and tomorrow we hold a council of war and plan how to defeat Edmund Ætheling."

The food was fetched in. There were pike and salmon to begin and the ale flowed freely. Prince Cnut was close enough to Uhtred for them to exchange pleasantries. I remained silent for something did not seem right but I could not work out what it was. Perhaps it was Eadric Streona's obvious good humour or the fact that Cnut ate and drank sparingly. The food, the wine and the ale were of the finest quality. A pair of cooked wild pigs were brought in and the warriors all cheered. I saw Uhtred relaxing and he said to me, for I too was close enough to talk, "Had I known the food would be this good I would have left

Edmund's side long ago." He held out his goblet to have more wine poured.

I smiled, "It must be in your honour, Uhtred, for up until now we have eaten warrior's rations." Even as I said the words I wondered if Uhtred was being fattened up. I had heard whispered conversations as we had marched from the Tyne to Durham about Eiríkr Hákonarson becoming the new eorl. I wondered how Uhtred might take that news. On our road north, he had only expressed doubts about Thurbrand and Streona but I knew it would be humiliating to no longer be the eorl.

Thorkell the Tall liked his food and he hacked a huge chunk from the pig and ensured he had the crispy, greasy crackling too, "The spoils of war Sven, eh? This is what it should always be like. Victory and then food. I shall enjoy myself this night."

Prince Cnut was engrossed in conversation with the Norse jarl and Eadric Streona was also animated. I looked over to the table where Thurbrand and his men were eating. The table headed by Uhtred was far livelier. The warriors, who had been fighting and campaigning in Cheshire, seemed happy to be feted. The men of Holderness, in contrast, appeared to be subdued and I wondered if they resented the honour being heaped upon their enemy.

Prince Cnut turned to me, "You seem distracted, Sven. Are the food and ale not to your taste?"

"They are both excellent, my prince, but I wonder at this lavish feast for one who was an enemy." I nodded to Thurbrand and his men, "Certainly they do not seem happy about it."

He smiled but it was with his mouth and not his eyes, "I know that despite being married to a devout Christian you are not one. If you were then you would know of the parable of the prodigal son who returns to his father penniless and is rewarded for his return. So it is with Uhtred. I need a Northumbria I can leave safely guarded when I go south to fight Edmund. As well as news of Uhtred's return Eorledman Streona also had word that Edmund has taken his army south to retake Wessex."

"Then all we fought for we have lost."

He shook his head, "We emptied the mints and damaged their burhs. Let him take solace from the recapture of that which we allowed him to take. I plan ahead. He will take men from his fields to fight us. When the crops they should have sown do not grow then his people will starve and we shall use that hunger to win."

I could not fault his argument. Ships had taken our treasure back to Denmark and our fleet ensured that we need not march like the Saxons, we could sail wherever we wished and know we had the means to escape if we had to."

The jarl asked him something and he turned. I saw two of Uhtred's men fall from their bench. They were drunk and Uhtred laughed, "Eardwulf and Wulfhun, you are embarrassing me! Can you not hold your drink?"

One of his oathsworn stood to help them back to the bench, "We are not used, my lord, to this heady wine." The two men were helped back to their bench and I noticed then that there were another six who were lying face down in their food. The servants brought in the sweet dishes, and the puddings to finish off the meal. They would soak up some of the drink but would be too late for some of the Northumbrians. When the servants left the doors were closed. The servants would only return when it was time to clear the tables and by then it might be dawn.

Uhtred liked his food and I watched him devour a whole pudding. Thorkell had also eaten and drunk well. He had bantered with Uhtred and the two of them seemed to get on. In contrast, I ate sparingly. I did not like heavy food at night. I began to wonder when I could leave and go back to my men and my bed.

Men had been rising and leaving the hall to make water all evening and it was no surprise when Thurbrand the Hold and four of his men rose unsteadily to pass Uhtred and his men and go to make water in the pots in the corner. I had drunk the least and was the soberest. I spied swords in their hands. I began to rise and felt a blade against my throat. Olaf Bloodaxe who had appeared from nowhere, hissed in my ear, "Stay in your seat and you shall live. Move and even though Prince Cnut forbade it I will slit your throat."

I felt a tendril of blood slipping down my neck. I was helpless. Thorkell, next to me, seemed to suddenly sober up. I saw him shrug. He understood that there was little I could do about it. Uhtred caught sight of me from the corner of his eye and he began to rise. He started to reach for his dagger and to shout but it was too late. Thurbrand reached him before it was out of its sheath and Uhtred the Bold was slashed across the neck by the sword of Thurbrand the Hold. I think he was dying even as he began to fall but he was a warrior and his blade caught Thurbrand across the arm. The other four who had risen with Thurbrand hacked and slashed at men who were drunk or too stunned to react. The rest of Thurbrand's men drew their secreted swords and raced over and joined in the frenzy of bloodletting. The warriors with Uhtred had been the best of his men, his chiefs and his leaders. They did not die quietly and six of Thurbrand's men suffered mortal wounds before the hall was still.

Olaf relaxed his grip and I stood and faced him, "This is not over Olaf Bloodaxe."

The mercenary grinned and held out his hand, "No hard feelings eh, Sven? I was obeying the orders of Prince Cnut."

I swiped it away and shook my head, "There are more than hard feelings. You and I will cross swords."

Cnut stood, "Stop! Olaf was following my orders. I told him I wanted no interference in this."

I whirled to face him, "You ordered this?"

He lowered his voice, "Be careful how you speak to me. I have done what was needed to secure my throne. You still want Norton, do you not?"

"Not at this price."

I turned and headed for the door. "Stop, I command you."

Reaching the door I opened it, "I do not follow a murderer. Uhtred was not my friend but he deserved to die with a sword in his hand and not be butchered by some nithing like Thurbrand the Hold." I spat the words out and he came towards me. "You would kill another unarmed man?" I whipped out Norse Gutter. "This time it will not be a drunk you try to kill."

"Thurbrand, sheathe your weapon. Sven, go outside and cool off."

"I am cool enough, Cnut." I gave him no title. "Tomorrow I will take my men and go with the men of Ribe and Agerhøne. I will breathe cleaner air in Denmark." I stepped outside and grabbed Oathsword from its rack.

The sounds of clashing steel and the cries of the dead and dying men had reached the camp and my foster father, Sweyn One Eye and Einar the Fat were all there, along with my hearth weru. Their weapons were drawn.

"What has happened Sven?"

When I spoke I did so loudly enough for others in the camp to hear me, "What has happened? I will tell you and every warrior in this camp. This night Prince Cnut condoned the murder of Uhtred the Bold and all his men. They were unarmed and Thurbrand the Hold and his men had swords." I pulled down the collar of my tunic to show the scar. "Olaf Bloodaxe held a blade to my neck so that I would not interfere. Tomorrow, we leave for home."

Sweyn Skull Taker nodded, "And tonight we stand guard in case there is more treachery. I have done with this Danish princeling. I thought he had honour but he is worse than his father."

I heard other men muttering the same. Cnut's army was disintegrating. I went to my tent and Faramir and my hearthweru came with me to tend to my wound and don their mail. As they washed it with vinegar and then applied honey I reflected on my actions. I could not nor would I undo them. I had said what needed to be said but it meant I had lost any chance of gaining Norton. So be it. It was *Wyrd.*

I woke early because I had not enjoyed a good night of sleep. It may have been the excess of rich food but it was more likely to have been the haunting sight of Uhtred's butchered body. I saw that it was Faramir who stood guarding my tent but that the other three lay around me along with Bersi and Steana. Nodding to Faramir I went to make water. He followed. The events of the previous night had made us all mistrustful. When we returned to the tent Faramir roused the others. Bersi rubbed the sleep from his eyes. "I will cook some food."

"Simple for me, my son, I ate well last night."

Steana stretched, "I will rouse the rest of the men. After you retired, they were still angry and are keen to depart."

My hearthweru helped me to dress. The leaving of Dunelm would be a ceremonial event. A large portion of the army of Cnut was deserting him and I knew that there would be objections. I did not enjoy the thought that I would be abandoning the young man I had nurtured to manhood and then followed to the brink of victory in England. I was not arrogant but I doubted that he would succeed without the aid of my sword and, more importantly, my men. Thorkell and his Jomsvikings still remained but they would be almost alone. The mercenaries could not be relied on and I doubted if Thurbrand the Hold would leave his lands for fear of vengeance from Uhtred's sons. Eiríkr Hákonarson and his Norsemen would be needed to hold the north. Cnut's dream was over.

We had the horses we would use to take our booty back to the river ready to load when we spied some of Prince Cnut's men dragging an old wagon from the side of the cathedral. Such was the atmosphere that I saw men don helmets and reach for weapons. I held up my hands, "Peace. There is nothing to concern us. Continue packing the horses."

The gates of the hall opened and Cnut, flanked by Eiríkr Hákonarson and Thorkell the Tall strode from the hall. Behind them came Eadric Streona, Thurbrand the Hold and Olaf Bloodaxe. The last three were now my enemies. Had they not been there then my face might have not been etched in stone. Cnut climbed onto the wagon. I noticed that the bishop, who had been present at the slaughter, was absent. What did that portend?

Cnut's bodyguards came to form a barrier before the other five leaders who now stood before the wagon. Cnut was dressed in his finest armour and his father's sword hung from his side. One of his men carried the Raven Banner. The morning light and his elevated position seemed to make an aura around him. He smiled and waved us forward, "Come, my friends, I would speak to you and ease your minds."

We began to shuffle forward but I looked around at the walls. I was seeking bowmen who might shower us with arrows when we were helpless. Such was the suspicion engendered by the murders. There were none save the handful of sentries. I found myself at the fore but I was surrounded by not only my hearthweru but my foster father, cousin and sons. They were protecting me.

Cnut looked down at me and I held his gaze. He nodded. Perhaps he knew what that meant but I did not. The prince then raised his head and began to speak, "Friends, for I think I might call you that, I know that there is bad feeling about the events of last night. I have heard that some of you are thinking of breaking your oath and returning home. I cannot stop that but I am disappointed." He looked down again at me. "There are warriors here who have been with me since I was a boy. I ask for you to hear my words and reconsider your actions." He raised his head and spread his arms. He looked, for all the world like a White Christ on a cross. "What I did was necessary. Uhtred the Bold was the reason why we lost so many men at Gegnesburh. Do you not remember how he tricked us and drew Sven Saxon Sword north? The wielder of the Dragon Sword might have died there, killed by an evil man and his son. Thurbrand the Hold had also many reasons to hate Uhtred the Bold. What happened last night was necessary. Could we have travelled south to fight Edmund knowing that we had left a viper to rouse our enemies in the north and undo all that we achieved?"

I had endured enough and I shouted, "I do not say that Uhtred the Bold should have been spared but if Thurbrand the Hold had any honour then he would have fought him man to man and not murder a man armed only with a dagger."

I was looking at the warrior as I spoke.

"Take back those words!" The Northumbrian did not sound convincing.

"Or what, Thurbrand the Hold? I am armed and I will fight you here and now. What say you? If your honour has been besmirched then let us fight while Prince Cnut's army watches. I trust that I will be victorious, do you?"

His eyes gave me the answer I wanted. He looked down and he would not fight. I heard murmurs behind me of 'coward', 'nithing' and the like. Thurbrand the Hold seemed to shrink.

Cnut said, "Has there not been enough bloodshed? We are a mighty army and we can sail south and take the crown from the king and his son. Uhtred is one man."

Einar the Fat shouted, "And how can we fight for you, Prince Cnut, when we know not if we might upset you and your mercenaries will slit our throats? Last night destroyed any trust there might have been."

I saw Olaf Bloodaxe colour. His hand went to the hilt of his sword. Einar the Fat cared not.

Cnut nodded, "You may be right, Einar the Fat. How can I restore that trust?"

"Swear on your father's sword that you will never seek to end the life of the warriors who follow you. Do that and it will go some way to repairing the damage. Then tell us what will be our reward for risking our lives to give you a crown."

I could have said those words but it was good that it was Einar who did so for he was a doughty veteran who had fought at Svolder.

Cnut nodded, "The first part is easy." He drew the sword and held it like a cross. He kissed the crosspiece, "I swear by my father's sword, God and St Cuthbert that none who fight for me shall die by my hand." He sheathed the sword. "As for your rewards, every leader shall be given an English manor. The income from those manors shall be theirs. Any treasure we take in this war shall belong to you, my warriors." He smiled and spread his arms like a supplicant, "If I can do more then tell me."

I did not need to look around to know that his promises had persuaded the vast majority to follow him. His words about the need for Uhtred's death were well chosen. Indeed, it was just the manner of the death which had upset us all.

My foster father, standing next to me, shook his head, "Your words and promises are persuasive, Prince Cnut and I know that many will have been swayed. I tire of war. I might have followed you to the end of this journey but for the murder of an unarmed man. I will take my ship home. I order no man to come with me. If it is just my hearthweru that sails my ship then I am content but I will be leaving still."

I knew that the objection from one man would not worry Prince Cnut but he wanted me and the sword at his side. He looked down at me and his eyes pleaded with me as he said, "And you, Sven Saxon Sword, Sweyn Skull Taker's foster son, will you desert me?"

I pointed an angry hand at Thurbrand, "I cannot fight alongside a murderer and the treacherous men he leads."

Cnut nodded and admitted defeat, "And I can see I made a mistake in allowing Eorledman Streona and Thurbrand the Hold to persuade me to this course of action. Thurbrand, I command you to guard the mouth of the Humber."

Cnut was a clever man. He had identified the two men responsible for the murders and, in doing so, won over most of the rest of the men who harboured doubts. The two men nodded. In Streona's case, there was some relief that he would not have fought against his king. He was a treacherous man who would change his allegiance as easily as most of us changed our breeks.

"There, Sven, does that satisfy you?"

I shook my head, "Not quite. Olaf Bloodaxe held a blade to my neck and for that, I would have him abase himself before me and beg for my forgiveness." Since Cnut had been speaking, I had been planning this. I did not trust the leader of the mercenaries. He had been sent by King Harald. If I did nothing then I knew that, at some time, Olaf would slit Cnut's throat. My words ensured that I would fight the mercenary.

"Abase myself before you, Sven Saxon Sword? You have an ill-deserved reputation and I will take your head."

Cnut shouted as men made space for us to fight, "This helps no one except for Edmund. I command you to clasp arms and become friends."

It was too late for that and the prince's words went unheeded. My shield was fetched and my helmet. Olaf had his shield and axe already. One of his men brought him his helmet. There was a huge circle around us and Prince Cnut had the prime position to watch us. Every man around us was armed and if there was any treachery then there would be a bloodbath that would end Cnut's attempts to gain the crown of England.

Olaf was bigger than I was but he was older. His axe, which he wielded easily, was longer than my sword. I kissed the hilt of the Dragon Sword and whispered, "Odin, guide my hand." I would have to use guile and agility if I was to survive.

Olaf was confident and he slipped his shield around his back so that he could use the axe two handed. He swung it in an easy figure of eight and advanced towards me. He intended to bully me into defeat. I had already established that the ground was reasonably even behind me but the grass was still a little slippery and men walking on it had made it slick in places. He kept coming towards me and he was driving me towards Eiríkr Hákonarson's Norsemen who held their shields before them. They would not move and if I was backed against the wall of wood then I would die. I took the offensive and I timed the punch with my shield when Olaf had finished one swing of his axe. I hit the back of his right hand with the boss of my shield but, more importantly, gave myself the chance to dance way, back towards the middle.

"You can run, little man, but Blood Drinker, my axe, shall drink your blood and she will become even stronger. Your sword has not the magic to defeat me."

It was the wrong thing to say. I saw men clutch their hammers. He was inviting the wrath not only of the Norns but the gods themselves. We might have been fighting before one of the holiest of Christian churches but what we did was pagan. He came towards me as he had before. This time instead of retreating before his axe I spun. Had this been a battle then it would have been the wrong thing to do but his arms could not react quickly enough to bring the axe to hack into my back. I, on the other hand, was able to slice Oathsword into the back of his legs. His byrnie went to his knees but I slashed his calf. His leather boots merely slowed the blade.

"Trickster! Stand and fight."

He whirled around but I darted with my sword before he could swing his axe. The tip sliced across his cheek and came perilously close to taking his eye. He screamed, not in pain, but in anger and as he raised his axe above his head, I punched him in the face with the boss of my shield. He reeled and swung his own shield around. I now had a slight advantage for he was tiring already and using the axe onehanded would be harder. I saw the sweat mixing with the blood on his cheek. He punched at me with his shield. He was trying to put me on the defensive once more. His axe was above his head and so I rammed my shield up under his chin. The metal rim hit him and the raised axe made him fall back a little so that the swinging head, when it came down, was easy to avoid. I brought my sword down to hack at his hand. I did not slice as deeply as I had hoped but deep enough to make more blood flow. He now had three bleeding wounds and losing blood weakens a man but he was still dangerous. He was like a cornered bear and he suddenly launched himself at me. I slipped, ironically, on some of his blood and fell to the ground, with the Dane on top of me. Oathsword was trapped beneath me and I saw him open his mouth. He was such a big man that I could not shift him. "I will rip your throat out with my teeth, little man."

I was fighting for my life. I had made the mistake of sensing victory. I could not move my sword hand but the shield allowed me to push him up and keep his blackened, stinking teeth away from my throat briefly. My fingers found Norse Gutter's hilt and I grasped it. His teeth were almost at my throat. I pushed as hard as I could with my shield and when I forced his body up, just a little I was able to ram my wickedly sharp blade into his byrnie, through his padded kyrtle and into his body. His teeth were at my throat and he thought he had me. I saw his eyes widen as the blade slid over his ribs. The pain made him raise his head and allowed me to make the last push. My dagger found his heart and life left his eyes. I pushed, with some difficulty, his body from me and stood.

Raising my sword I shouted, "Oathsword!"

With the exception of the mercenaries, every warrior raised their swords and echoed my words. I had won but come very close to death.

Chapter 8

Lundenwic 1015

The body of the mercenary was whisked away by his glowering warriors but any thoughts of revenge on their part would be fruitless for I had so many men around me that saw them shrink away. The ones who harboured such thoughts quickly disappeared after they had buried their leader. They deserted and were no loss to Prince Cnut's army. Sweyn Skull Taker came to speak with me, "I shall still be travelling home. Come with me for you owe Cnut nothing."

I nodded, "I know but he is right, I did swear an oath and his offer of treasure will tempt many men. Will you have enough to sail home?"

"Aye, for the older warriors want nothing more to do with a prince who does what Cnut has done." He leaned in, "And watch yourself. Thurbrand will harbour a grudge."

"I know and I will."

We were left alone by the prince and his advisers although Eiríkr Hákonarson did come to speak with me, "That was bravely done, Sven, and you were right to make the stand but when men throw the bones to win a kingdom then, sometimes, they have to make compromises. Cnut is a good man. Do not hold this action against him. Uhtred had to die and while you and I might not be happy about the manner the death was necessary. He needs both you and your sword at his side. Fear not, I will guard the north but this crown will be won in the south."

I knew the old warrior was right. A week after the fight we left for the Tyne. Thurbrand and his men had left almost immediately after the battle to return to Holderness. I was glad for my fingers itched to strike a blow. My foster father had already left when we sailed and would already be at home in Denmark before we even reached the sea. My cousin had stayed with us because he wanted the riches it might bring and, I think, out of loyalty to me. As we marched north, he told me that as I would be living in England, I could manage any manor he was given. Sweyn, for all that he was a skald, could be very practical when he chose.

It was as we were waiting to board that a ship arrived in the river from the south. She was a Saxon and, I think, would have fled had we not had so many ships surrounded her. Her captain was brought to Cnut and I was summoned. I had not spoken to him since the fight and the atmosphere was strained but he needed me for I was one of his leaders, a warlord.

The captain brought us the news that King Æthelred had died. Apparently, it had been on a saints' day, St George, and that was seen as propitious. The ship's captain had been sent with the news that a Witan had crowned Edmund as King of England. That meant that word had not yet reached Lundenwic telling them Uhtred the Bold was dead. The north was a foreign country and many days from Edmund's heartland. The furthest north that he knew was Cheshire and the northern borders of Mercia.

We held a council of war to decide what we ought to do. I think that Cnut knew all along what he planned but after the strained relations following the death of Uhtred, it was difficult for him. The twenty mercenaries who had deserted us had not been a major loss but they were a loss and we could not afford any more. It was the lack of numbers that worried Thorkell, "Edmund is in the south and has the whole of the fyrd to call to arms. If we are defeated then this whole venture is lost."

"Why talk of defeat, Thorkell?" The strained atmosphere told in Cnut's tone.

It was difficult for Thorkell but he showed courage, "When you were defeated at Gegnesburh you had to flee England. If you did so again then there would be no return."

Cnut's eyes narrowed, "As I recall it was you who caused that defeat."

"I know and I am sorry but we cannot unravel the threads of the past, can we Prince Cnut?"

I sighed, "For my part, Prince Cnut, I would rather go to meet King Edmund and fight him. If it is meant to be we will win and if not then I get to return to my family."

"An honest answer, Sven, and it confirms my own belief that we sail to Essex and use the men of East Anglia and the Danelaw to bolster our army." He turned to Eiríkr Hákonarson, "Do you need all your Norse to hold the north?"

The old warrior nodded, "Thurbrand is unreliable and we know not yet how Uhtred's son will react to his father's death."

It made sense and we could not afford to lose Northumbria. "Then we sail south and land in Essex. I will send a ship to Gegnesburh to summon the Danes of England to fight under my banner."

We sailed south, far fewer than when we had headed north. Our army would have to fight hard just to survive. As we sailed, I watched Bersi clambering up and down the shrouds as though he had not a care in the world. Had I made a mistake in not sending him home with my foster father? Only time would tell.

While I was distracted for a whole host of reasons the rest of the crews of my ships were in good humour. I had fought and slain a renowned Danish warrior and they had been promised a small fortune by Prince Cnut. We had yet to be defeated and so long as that state of affairs remained, they would be optimistic. Of course, what would happen when we suffered a defeat might change things. We sailed past Gippeswic and landed on the Crouch. While we made a longphort and a defensive camp riders were sent to our allies and we waited for them to arrive. While we waited, we hunted, fished and raided the Saxon settlements nearby.

Cnut sent for me just days after we landed, “Sven, we are blind until we know where Edmund is. Thorkell believes that he is in Lundenwic as do I. We need someone to go inside the walls as a spy to see if Edmund is there and ascertain the numbers of men.”

I thought, when he said it, that it was a good idea and then it came to me. He was not just asking my opinion, he wished me to be the spy. “Me, Prince Cnut, you wish me to be your spy?”

He nodded as though it was the most natural of requests to make, “Thorkell is too well known and if you leave behind Oathsword then you would be anonymous. Thanks to your wife you speak Saxon and with a northern accent. Take your son Bersi for that will add the shade of innocence to your disguise and he, too, speaks Saxon. You need not even spend a night there. Just go to the city and wander the streets. We cannot wait here, blind to Edmund’s intent. We have to know where he is and judge the mood n the city. If we can hold Lundenwic then we have England.”

I did not want to take my son but I knew that I could not refuse to obey the prince. His arguments made sense. It had to be a senior leader who went and it was clear that Thorkell was too well known. “I will go alone, my prince.”

He shrugged, “Very well but it adds risk. We have, I believe, Saxon clothes and a sword that we took. I will have them sent to your tent.”

I was delayed on my way back because some of the Danish mercenaries accosted me. My hand was ready to go to my sword but I did not think, from their faces, that they intended any harm. The one who spoke, Danner Liefson, was an older warrior and he had a scar running down his cheek. He had fought and been wounded at some time, “Lord, we come to you for we know that you have a low opinion of us and we would remedy that. We did not agree with the murder of Uhtred the Bold. The warriors who did agree with it fled when Olaf was dead. We are mercenaries, it is true, but we are good warriors. You are one of Prince Cnut's leaders and we would not be relegated to watching the baggage or guarding the horses. We swear that we will be good warriors who will fight alongside you with honour."

I saw the honesty in his eyes and I nodded. I held out my hand, "Then I give you, Danner Liefson, the warrior's clasp. I was wrong to judge you based upon a false leader." Their smiles told me that I had made the right decision.

When I reached my tent, I saw that Thorkell was there with the Saxon clothes and sword. I also saw that he was speaking to Bersi, Steana and Sweyn One Eye. Thorkell the Tall looked a little shame-faced as I neared them. "Here is the gear that we promised."

Bersi burst out, "And I will come with you, father, as the prince suggested. It makes sense and you will be safer," he looked into my eyes, "unless you do not trust me."

"Of course I trust you but what I do is dangerous." I turned angrily and faced Thorkell, "This should not have been mentioned."

Thorkell shrugged, "I am sorry, Sven, I thought a warrior as honest as you would have told your son of the prince's plan in any case."

"You! What does a treacherous man like you know of honesty? Quit my camp."

His eyes narrowed but I knew he would not risk a fight. He had seen me defeat Olaf Bloodaxe and Thorkell was an older man. He left.

Steana came and said, "This is *wyrd*, father. Give Bersi a chance to show what he can do. I would give all to be the one but they are right, a boy will act as a better disguise for you. He is ready for this challenge and it will make him a good warrior."

Sweyn One Eye said, "It is a good plan, cuz. Having Bersi with you would give the illusion that you were a father and son seeking work. A warrior alone might invite more questions. From what Thorkell said it is just one day of danger.

"That is the prince's natural optimism. It is more than a day to get to Lundenwic and enter." I turned to Gandálfr, "We will take horses and you and my hearthweru can come with us." He looked pleased, "You will wait outside the walls, hidden, for our return." He nodded. "We leave in the morning and Bersi and I will be at the gates when they are opened." The joy on my son's face told me that he was deliriously happy.

I spent the rest of the day speaking Saxon to Bersi and correcting any errors he made. We ensured that we both had weapons. I had the Saxon sword, a seax and Norse Gutter while Bersi had a dagger in his boot and a seax. He wore on his head, not the bjorr hat he normally wore but a simple woven one we had taken from a Saxon. That night I prayed to Odin to watch over my son. The prince's debt to me was growing day by day. The threads of the Norns were strong and I now saw that they had trapped my family too.

We rode without mail and without helmets. We took quiet greenways until we reached the wood just a mile from Cripplegate. Had we used the Bishopsgate then they might have been more suspicious as they would have known that the Danes were in Essex. Cripplegate suggested that we had come from the north.

We had a cold camp and, at dawn, with a freshly cut ash staff my son and I left the woods and headed west to find the main road to Lundenwic. My hearthweru could camp in the woods and keep watch for us.

"From now on we speak nothing but Saxon. Think Saxon and we might survive. It would appear normal if you were to look about you in wonder for Lundewic was a great city once."

"I will not let you down, father and I thank you for the trust you have shown."

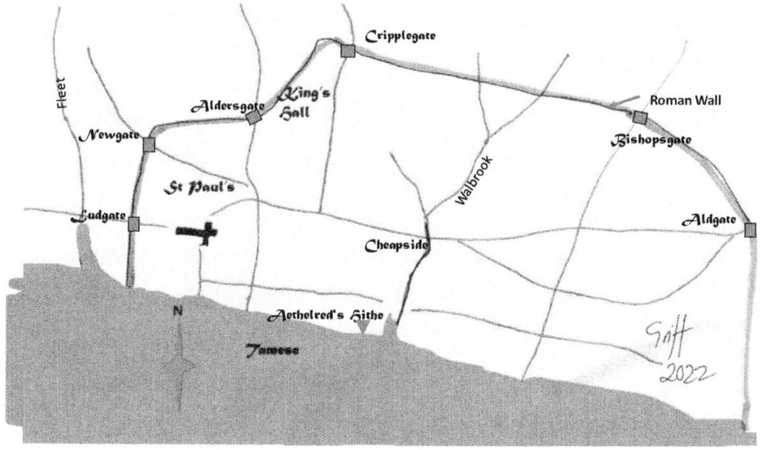

By the time the sun broke behind us, we were on the road and we caught up with a carter who was urging his horse and cart down the road. It was laden with produce from his smallholding. The Roman Road had not been repaired of late and the cart lurched over each displaced stone. Every time it did a vegetable fell from the cart. When he saw us approach, having stopped to pick up another cabbage, he looked worried. When he saw that Bersi was a boy he relaxed. Sweyn had been right.

"Heading to Lundenwic?"

I nodded, and, as he took his whip to his weary horse, added, "How far is it?"

"Another two miles." He shook his head, "I overloaded the cart else I would have been there when the gates opened. Still, I may be able to charge more when I reach the market at the Chepe. I am Edgar." He held out his hand.

"And I am Ælfred. This is my son, also called Ælfred."

"Named after a great king yet you are not from around here."

I shook my head. I had practised my story and this would give me the opportunity to see if it worked or not, "We lived in the north. The Danes came and the boy and I fled. We have got as far away from them as we can."

He made the sign of the cross, "Aye, they are the very devil. It is good that King Edmund is in Lundenwic and now raises an army. He is a good king and will lead us to victory. You will be safe there. I hear that they are to the east but if they come then I will join the rest of our village and flee to the safety of Lundenwic's walls. There we will be protected by King Edmund and his men. I am just glad that they did not come by the river."

I knew that I could, if I wished, return to Prince Cnut with the news he wanted. Edmund was in Lundenwic but the warrior in me knew that if I did so then I would not have the news that the prince needed. Bersi and I helped to pull the cart and Bersi collected the fallen produce ensuring that we did not need to stop. The old horse took an age to get going again once it had stopped and we made better progress. We spoke of farming and famine for both went together. Edgar, it seemed, only came to market when he had a surplus. The coins he took were to help his family survive when he had poorer crops. He was typical of the farmers in this part of the world. Their fields were fertile but one never knew what the future held.

Gradually more people appeared on the roads and we were forced to slow down as we closed with the city. As we neared the walls, I saw that they had been repaired lately. I looked at them with a warrior's eye, seeking weaknesses. The ditch, built by King Alfred's men, had been cleared of rubbish and the sides sharpened to make them ankle breakers. The walls also had wooden palisades added atop the stoutly built Roman stone. The gates were new and guarded by two warriors. Both wore helmets and had spears and simple shields. They smiled when they saw the age of the horse and one said, "You need a better horse, friend."

"Then I can only hope that the prices are higher this visit."

The man nodded, "They are for the city is filling with warriors." He saw my sword and said, "You could find employment for that blade, too."

"I thank you. We are just glad for the safety of the walls."

With that, we were in. We left Edgar at the Chepe, the market in Cheapside. He tried to press food on us but I shook my head, "The Danes did not get my treasure, friend, and we can afford to buy food until I find work. The coins you make will feed your family. Farewell."

I headed directly for the bridge. As we wound our way through the busy city, we heard the name of Edmund Ironside spoken. It was as though he was a hero from legend who would come and strike the head from the Danish worm. It took some time to reach the newly built bridge. My heart sank when I neared it. Both ends of the wooden bridge were fortified and they had used stone to strengthen it. There looked to be a hundred men there and they had fires and shelter. Even if the southern end was taken arrows sent from the northern bank would clear any attacker from the narrow entrance to the city. Before we could be viewed with suspicion we went first to the east end of the city where there were equally large numbers and then to the western side. The west had fewer warriors guarding it but it was the busiest. We drank some ale from a street vendor and watched as warrior after warrior marched through. They were the men of Wessex and King Edmund was bolstering his defences. The ones we saw had a determined look about them which I could understand for we had run wild in their land and taken all of their gold. They had been badly led but they were warriors who would fight. We followed them across the city. I was anxious to see where they went. They ended up at a huge mead hall and were greeted by Edmund himself. I did not recognise him but when the men of Wessex saw him, they hailed, "King Edmund!" The cheers and cries rang out. Women tried to kiss the hem of his cloak. He was popular and that had never been the case with King Æthelred. More than that his people believed that he could win. Prince Cnut would have a fight on his hand.

We were about to leave for I saw that the king was taking his new warriors inside when I heard a furore as men approached down the road from the Cripplegate. It was a joyful noise and when I saw a lord leading fifty men I knew why. It was Ulfcetel Snilling. The man who had almost beaten us once before had arrived with his oathsworn to bolster the defences of Lundenwic. The odds were now stacked even more in the favour of the English. I did not think he would recognise me but it would have been foolish to take any chances and I kept my head hidden in the cowl of my cloak.

Ulfcetel's greeting was warm, "Hail King Edmund! Now that King Offa's sword leads us then we cannot but fail to drive these Danes from our land."

He nodded but his voice was humbler than it might have been, "And words spoken by a great warrior such as you encourage me to believe that if every man takes up a weapon then with you by my side and God in our hearts we might well succeed." The roars that greeted his words were confirmation that the English had a leader and this would not be an easy task.

We continued west to the Aldgate. The guards looked at us curiously as we headed out of the city, "Did you not wish to see the great Eorledman Snilling?"

I shook my head and pointed ahead, "I have seen him before but I have never seen the Roman fortress. I thought to show it to my son."

He nodded and waved us through, "The work that has been done recently has made it much stronger but do not approach the ditch the sentries there will not like it."

I was not foolish and I said, "I just want to see the walls upon which the Danes will die."

Bersi and I stood with our backs to the walls of the city. I could see that originally, they had been continuous but a section had been breached and the river had reclaimed some of the ditch making it secure on two sides. I also saw the fresh masonry, presumably started in the reign of Alfred. It was now whole and the towers had timbers on the top to protect the archers who would fight from there. It was a formidable fortress and a last refuge for the king should we ever take his city.

I had seen enough and we headed back into the city, "You are right, friend, and I am glad that we are safe within these walls."

"Not that safe. I have heard that there are over two hundred Danish ships heading for us and they have the magical Danish Blade with them. We will have to fight."

His companion said, "But King Edmund Ironside is made of stronger metal than his father. God rest his soul. This will be like Gegnesburh all over again."

As we headed back to the Chepe I thought again about Uhtred. I still did not like the manner of his death but his treachery had enabled our enemies to defeat us and I was now glad that he was dead.

By the time we reached the market, the traders and farmers were packing up and leaving. It would have looked odd if we had travelled back with the carter we had seen and so I waited until he had hitched his tired old horse and was walking out before we followed. I joined a group that had not had wagons and managed to sell most of their goods.

We walked just behind them and, at the gate were given barely a second glance. We had to walk slowly so as not to overtake the carter and it was dark when we reached the woods. As we neared them, I said, "Well, Bersi, you have had your first real adventure but know this, we were lucky."

He shook his head, "Father, I am young but I can recognise skill when I see it. You handled it all well. They will not know that they could have had the adviser to the prince in their hands and we have learned much."

I looked at him with new eyes for my son had surprised me, "What have we learned?"

"That this will be a harder place to take than the others think and that their leaders are worthy men."

He was right but when we had been at the west gate, where we had seen the men of Wessex enter the city, I had spied hope. The trouble was my idea would only work if luck was on our side and if we could use the water to our advantage.

We were seen well before we spied Dreng and Faramir appeared behind us, "You were so long in Lundenwic we began to worry, lord, if we should come to seek you out."

"No, Faramir, but my stomach thinks my throat has been cut and I could eat a horse… with the skin on."

He laughed, "Gandálfr thought you might be hungry. We hunted and a small deer is cooking. He thought it was a risk worth taking as the only warriors we have seen this day were heading for Lundenwic and not seeking enemies hiding in woods."

Chapter 9

The Lundenwic longphort

"So, Edmund is in Lundenwic?"

"Aye as is Ulfcetel and the men of Wessex."

"The defences are strong?"

"They are. Freshly cleaned ditches, masonry repaired and a Roman fort that is made of stone. Add to that the air of optimism with two good leaders and I would say we will have to fight hard to take it."

Thorkell rubbed his beard, "If we sail to Grenewic we can block the river and stop help coming from Cent and the sea."

I shook my head, "They can cross the bridge and it would be hard to take. It could be done but it would take many days and the lives of warriors we can ill afford to lose."

Cnut knew me well and smiled, "You have spied some hope."

I nodded, "To the west is a wooden small abbey and an old warrior hall. They both lie outside the walls of the city. If we could take them then we could enjoy a wall we could defend, a roof and we could surround the city."

"But how would we get there?"

"In the same way that the Rus sailed to Miklagård. We dig a channel and float some ships on the water. We only need forty or so and we could drag them. We have many threttanessa and it could be done. We then besiege them."

I saw Cnut debating. None of us had ever done this but it would be possible. We could, of course, simply destroy the bridge. It had been done before. King Alfred had built this new bridge. I could almost see Cnut working that out. "We will do as our adviser suggests and sail for the Temese." He smiled, "We can raid the Isle of Sheep on the way and take our own food with us."

The Isle of Sheep lay on the south bank of the Temese in Cent. I liked the idea that we could keep the sheep alive and eat them throughout the siege.

The men were all happy to be doing something and we broke camp and headed for our ships in good humour. The exceptions were Eadric Streona and his men. The Mercians had yet to draw a sword for Prince Cnut and as they had no ships of their own were simply passengers who did not even have to take an oar. If this state of affairs remained then the bad blood that was there would boil over into violence. Our numbers were depleted enough as it was. I put those thoughts from my head as I led my small fleet to follow Cnut and Thorkell the Tall.

It was not a long journey and we surprised the shepherds on the island. Leaving their sheep they fled in small boats back to the mainland and we filled every drekar with as many sheep as we could capture. Their bleating and their stink were annoying as we rowed up the Temese but we endured them knowing that we had a good supply of fresh meat.

While we had been in Essex Sweyn had not been idle and he had composed a song about the duel in Dunelm.

The feasting hall in Cuthbert's town
Was filled with warriors brave
Cnut's Danish band, they had grown
And yet to take a slave
Uhtred the Bold he bent the knee
And submitted to the Danes
The throne was there for one to own
Prince Cnut and the English crown
The throne was there for one to own
Prince Cnut and the English crown
No swords allowed in the feasting hall
The warriors drank and ate
But anger burned in Thurbrand's heart
And filled his mind with hate
When he drew his spiteful sword
And hewed Uhtred in twain
The throne was there for one to own
Prince Cnut and the English crown
The throne was there for one to own
Prince Cnut and the English crown
Sven Saxon Sword held his ground
And threatened he would leave
The prince asked for the oath that was bound
And swore he was deceived
Bloodaxe would not back down
And weapons they were brought
The throne was there for one to own
Prince Cnut and the English crown
The throne was there for one to own
Prince Cnut and the English crown
In the shadow of Cuthbert's church
A bloody battle it was fought

Between Oathsword and the axe
Odin looked down, as did the Lord
As blades clashed and cracked
He chose Lord Sven and his Saxon Sword
Into Bloodaxe's body they hacked
The throne was there for one to own
Prince Cnut and the English crown
The throne was there for one to own
Prince Cnut and the English crown
Then there was peace amongst the band
And enmity set aside
Right had won and peace regained
Thanks to the Saxon Sword
Thanks to the Saxon Sword.

Even as we sang it, whilst towing up the Temese, I reflected that posterity would not know the truth. Sweyn had made Cnut innocent of the murder yet I knew his hands were bloody.

The voyage up the Temese was slow and those in Lundewic knew that we were coming. It could not be helped. We reached Grenewic and the hall there was abandoned long before we reached it. The thegn who lived there would have added his retinue to the defence of the city. We had a roof and walls that we could defend. We made a longphort so that we bridged the river and men were sent to man the northern defences. Eventually, we would surround the city but first, we had work to do. The first thing we did, to let the English know who had come, was to unfurl the Raven banner. The banner was all white but when the wind made it flutter a black raven appeared. The hearthweru who held it was charged with making sure it just showed white until Cnut appeared and the raven was unfurled. It appeared magical.

I went with Cnut, our bodyguards and the other leaders to view the bridge. Some thought that I had exaggerated the defences there. I had not and if anything, they were stronger than when Bersi and I had spied.

Thorkell turned to me, "You are right, Sven Saxon Sword, and your doubters proved wrong. I can see where we could dig. We need two sets of diggers and two sets of warriors to protect them. We dig two channels, one upstream and one downstream. When we break through and join them, we will have your channel."

Thorstein Hakkensson asked, "And we are supposed to sail threttanessa along this narrow channel?"

He explained, as to a child, "Sven's idea is a clever one. We do not dig a deep channel, just one with water in it so that we can drag our drekar over it and pass the bridge. We relaunch them and make a second longphort to the west of the city. Then we can surround it and cut it off."

It was clear that the best warriors, even including the Danish mercenaries were the Jomsvikings and my men. We formed the two bands of protectors. The next day, well before dawn had broken, we marched south and then split up. Thorkell began digging his ditch closer to the east end of the bridge while I took my warriors and my diggers to the west of the bridge. We found a place that was already low and somewhat swampy and our men began to dig. They piled the earth on two sides of a channel wide enough for a drekar with sixteen oars on each side. We stood to with shields and spears. They did not breach the bank at first. Instead, we dug a snekke's length from the river. We had fifty men, stripped to the waist to dig. Ship's boys firmed up the banks of the channel. We used Einar, one of my ship's boys as a human measuring stick. When the channel was the same depth as his height we were satisfied. When we dragged the drekar they would be empty. We would even take the ballast from the keel and with every man pulling we would make them slide over the water like a hot knife over butter.

We could hear the church bells of Lundenwic marking time and it took until terce before the defenders of the city realised what we were doing and reacted. We were too far from the walls for arrows and so they sent warriors across their bridge. One hundred came for us. They came as a wedge and as soon as I spied them, I ordered the diggers to stop and for my defenders to bar the progress of the wedge. We met them in a swynfylking formation. The English would have the weight of numbers but we would have three points of our own wedge. The tip of each point was a leader. Einar, Sweyn and I would have our mailed hearthweru and I doubted that Edmund would send his best warriors. As they marched and chanted, using the name of the White Christ, I saw that I was right. The front six warriors wore byrnies but the rest, although they were warriors, wore studded byrnies.

I hefted Saxon Slayer; I had not used the weapon yet and the sharpened blade was ready to tear into flesh. I held it before me and Dreng and Faramir thrust their spears over my shoulder. I pulled my shield tightly to me so that only my eyes could be seen. The Saxon wedge came on. This was not the best ground for such a formation as the ground was slippery in places and uneven. It meant they could not run hard and knock us back. It was why I had chosen the swynfylking. I was confident that I could hold them and when the leather-armoured men struck Sweyn and Einar they would be easily stopped.

Their steady approach allowed me to study the leader. He had a helmet with a mask on and at the top of the helmet was a small bird. His byrnie reached below his knee. His shield also had a bird upon it. That was *wyrd* for our symbol and my herkumbl was also a bird. His lower arms were bare and I saw he had a fine scabbard on his sword. A man did not use a poor scabbard for a fine sword. His mask meant I could not work out his age. Perhaps I was becoming arrogant but I did not fear him. I had fought enough single combats and won to believe that I could best any enemy.

The leader shouted, "Charge!" and launched the attack when they were just fifteen feet from us. It was just enough room to gain some momentum but nowhere near enough to break us.

I timed it right and shouted, "Brace!" just as the Saxons pulled back their spears to thrust. My command was also a command for my men to stab with their spears. For any warrior, this was a nerve-wracking time. I trusted to my skill and did not look where I had thrust. Instead, I watched the spear as it came for my head. I merely ducked my face behind my shield as the spear scratched and scraped over the rim of my shield and across the top of my helmet. My spear struck his byrnie below his shield while Dreng's drove towards his eye making him flinch. It was the flinch which detracted from the Saxon push and we were easily able to hold them. That was the point where Einar and Sweyn's smaller wedges came into their own. They struck men without mail and some died.

We had our own battle to fight and I pulled back Saxon Slayer. I saw that there was blood on the tip. I had cut him. This time Faramir and I drove our spears together at the same time and it was Faramir's that found his eye hole. He pulled his head back and screamed as the tip entered the orb. I punched with my shield and roared, "Push!"

Those behind me put their shields into my back and the whole line pushed an already disorganised wedge backwards. The thegn who had led the wedge had not been mortally wounded but losing an eye affects a warrior and his spear flailed wildly before him. His lack of balance meant that his shield was not held where it would offer any protection and Saxon Slayer drove into his middle. As soon as I felt flesh, I twisted and then pulled. He attempted to move back and in doing so exacerbated the wound. He began to fall and I lunged at the man behind. He was not expecting the blow and I skewered him. It was Einar and Sweyn who broke the Saxons. The ones at the front of the wedge had expected a hard fight but the ones at the back hoped that they were just there to push and when men fell all around them they broke and ran back to the bridge. Their shouts and the noise from the bridge told those fighting Thorkell of the disaster and both attacks failed.

We had not lost a single man and fifteen Saxons lay dead before us.

"Back to work. Strip the bodies and throw them in the river."

I knew that the bodies who have a demoralising effect on those at the bridge. Naked warriors with bloodied bodies passing beneath them would be a clear sign that they had lost.

By the end of the day, we had a channel twenty paces long. There was still some way to go but it was a start. We left sentries on the work we had done. The last thing we needed was to have our work undone.

When we returned to our camp at Grenewic Thorkell and I spoke with Cnut. "Prince Cnut, if you could have your Danes attack the bridge tomorrow it will keep the defenders occupied and we can work without interruption."

"Thorkell, I do not wish to lose warriors in a failed attack."

I shook my head, "Are you saying, Prince Cnut, that it is alright for Thorkell and me to lose men but your mercenaries must be spared? We were lucky today and that is down to our skill. Do not waste good warriors while you have swords for hire idly sitting by."

Since Dunelm, I had been less than patient with the prince. Thorkell was more of a diplomat, "Prince Cnut, they need not prosecute the attack. Just make a shield wall and stop them from leaving the bridge."

"Very well." His posture made him look petulant and I had to remember that he was still a young man.

He did as we asked and the next day there were no attacks. The mere presence of more than forty mailed warriors was enough to deter them. We were able to work faster and after four days the two channels had been joined. The breaching of the earth walls was a trickier situation. At my end, I had men on the side with ropes tied around their waists and six ropes on each side were attached to the two men who volunteered to breach what was, in effect, an earth dam. They would work at the bottom and once they saw water seeping through, they would be hauled to safety and we would let the river do the hard and dangerous part of the work. The two were not too far down and I hoped that having six men to pull each digger would save them. The clay was hard to dig and it took longer than I expected. It was Sweyn whose one eye proved more effective than ours, "Water!"

The tiny trickle looked harmless but I took no chances, "Pull them out now." We pulled them to safety and I began to doubt myself for the trickle did not appear to grow. I was about to order them back in when I saw a crack in the clay above the water. Suddenly, a torrent poured through and the river almost took us by surprise. It crashed through the banks, widening the hole. We had to scurry back to safety as the earth banks we had made began to slip into the river. I hoped Thorkell had also been farsighted for the wall of water that hurtled downstream would have taken men with it.

My men all cheered. It had been hard work but we could now drag our ships from one side of the bridge to the other. Within a few days, the city would be surrounded and Cnut would have his siege.

The chosen ships and their crews boarded their drekar. The stone ballast lay on the banks of the river near our camp and would have to be ferried down later. Our drekar needed the ballast. We had half of the army with ropes to pull them through. The masts were stepped and the oars would only be used to punt the ships through. Once we reached the far side then we would construct a second longphort and we would have two bridges across the Temese. The ones who were pulling upstream on the steerboard side of the ships would only be able to pull up to the channel.

I led the men on the riverside. We went mailed with shields upon our backs as the Saxons, seeing what we were doing, had boats brought out to rain arrows upon us. As soon as I saw them I ordered the ships' boys to join the helmsmen on the drekar to send our own arrows and stones back. Danner Liefson had taken charge of the Danes sent by King Harald and that included the smaller number of mercenaries who remained. He formed them as a shield wall and stood between the new channel and the bridge. The defenders of the bridge would be close enough to send arrows at the ships too. We began to pull. I knew it would be hard for we were pulling against the current and the drekar, shallow draughted though they were, might still bottom on the channel.

We chanted as we went. As I was leading my men, we used the clan chant to give us the rhythm.

We are the bird you cannot find
With feathers grey and black behind
Seek us if you can my friend
Our clan will beat you in the end.
Where is the bird? In the snake.
The serpent comes your gold to take.
We are the bird you cannot find
With feathers grey and black behind
Seek us if you can my friend
Our clan will beat you in the end.
Where is the bird? In the snake.
The serpent comes your gold to take.

Once we got the ship moving then progress was steady rather than spectacular. Arrows and stones showered us but they only bruised us. When we neared the end of the channel my muscles burned but, instead of returning to the start we stayed and helped the others pull the next drekar. The result was that the first ship was the slowest but all the rest, with many more men pulling, made a faster passage and by dark, all the ships were on the south bank of the Temese. The next day would see us form the longphort. That night, under cover of darkness, the drekar were refilled with their ballast. They became warships again.

The men I led made a camp opposite the small abbey. As my men buried stakes and made shelters, I saw that there were horses there and many armed and mailed men. If they were fortifying the hall then we might have to take that first. It made sense to me as that would give them two strongholds we had to overcome before we could take the city walls. Half of my men were on guard that night, along with me. Until we constructed the longphort then we were vulnerable to attack on our ships. I slept aboard the outboard drekar. It was an uncomfortable night of sleep but no one came.

Thorkell brought his Jomsvikings the next day. Danner Liefson would lead his men across the downstream longphort and when he had established his camp then Eadric Streona would join him with his Mercians. Haraldr of Gippeswic would lead the men from the Danelaw and East Anglia to join up the two ends of the siege works. I knew that as the mead hall was now occupied that it would be Thorkell and me that would have the harder task.

Saxon horsemen and mailed men waited on the northern side of the river. When we neared them we might have a battle and so I ensured that our longphort was securely constructed. We built the longphort much as a child might build a pile of rocks on the beach. We already had four ships secured to one shore and we moved another three to join to them. After tying them together we placed planks across them to make a good bridge. Then we added another three. Each time we attached a drekar we moved more men onto the ship so that there was a wall of ninety warriors ready to fend off any attack. The next three ships saw us more than halfway across. I stood on the prow of ***'Snow Dragon'***, one of the Norse ships and held on to the forestay. I shaded my eyes to look at the riders for I saw that many had mounted their horses and I wondered if they were about to attack us. Even as the thought came into my head I dismissed it for there were just fifty riders and they could do nothing. When I saw that one of them was King Edmund and another, Ulfcetel Snilling, then I knew there would be no attack. They were evaluating our strategy. Even as we put the next three ships in place, I saw the column of riders spur their horses and head west. The king was leaving. We would have the city surrounded but the prize that Prince Cnut wanted would not be there.

It did not slow our progress and when the last four ships were put in place, Thorkell and I lead three hundred of our best warriors to race ashore to take the hall. The building had been abandoned and all that remained were the priests in the church. Cnut was a Christian and we left them unharmed. While my men and I dug our first ditch, Thorkell took his men to the north side of the city and cut it off. The horse had left the stable but we still needed to surround the city Edmund Ironside had abandoned.

Chapter 10

The siege of Lundenwic 1015

It took three days to surround the city and dig ditches but any euphoria we might have felt had evaporated with my news that the king had fled. That he had taken with him the most effective English leader I had fought against, Ulfcetel Snilling, was an even more depressing thought. As soon as the encirclement was complete Prince Cnut called a council of war. By now we were familiar with one another. Danner Liefson had taken the place of Olaf Bloodaxe although he did not act as a bodyguard. Thorkell and I worked well together and it was only the presence of Eadric Streona that brought any discord to the councils. We waited for him in the old hall. It was a large mead hall and needed a good fire to heat it but the high ceiling made it less smoky. We occupied one end while our hearthweru ate in the rest. They seemed to get on.

As food was fetched by the slaves we had taken, Cnut drank some of the ale and said, irritably, "Where is Streona? The sooner we reduce Lundenwic the better." He waved over Hastein, one of his hearthweru, "Go to the camp of the Mercians and discover what delays the eorledman."

"Yes, Prince Cnut."

Danner was still to be comfortable in our presence and he remained silent. Thorkell was in good humour, "Let us use the flight of the king to our advantage. He has abandoned his people and they will lose heart soon."

I shook my head, "He is no King Æthelred. For a start the people like him. When I was in Lundewic the people sang his praises and Ulfcetel is seen as the man who almost took your father, Prince Cnut. They will be happy to squat behind their walls while they wait for the return of their king. He will fetch more men from the west."

Cnut nodded, "Then we starve them out. I would have a third of the army raid Cent and Essex to feed us." He looked up as the great doors opened but it was not Streona. It was a hearthweru who had been outside to make water. "This Mercian seeks to embarrass me. He thinks that he is more important than he is."

Thorkell knew England better than we and he shook his head, "We need Mercia, my prince, for with that land and Northumbria secure we know where our enemy lies. The last thing that we need is to fear a Mercian knife in our backs." Thorkell was the diplomat.

We ate the food. Mutton, slowly cooked was delicious and we drank the ale which was not to our taste. I knew that we would have to brew our own. Men would suffer short rations but not bad beer.

When the door next opened it was Hastein and he ran to the side of the prince and knelt, "Prince Cnut, the Mercians have fled. They have deserted the camp. There is a gap in our defences. They have all fled."

Cnut stood, "The treacherous dog. He will have run to Edmund."

I said, "Danner, your men are close to the Mercian camp, send a messenger to have them occupy the space they left. The last thing we need is for the city to be reinforced through the gap."

Aye." He strode over to his men.

The three of us faced each other. Cnut now looked as though he had the weight of the world upon his shoulders. Thorkell was ever practical. "This changes all. We have to worry about any army coming from the northwest as well as the west to attack our siege lines."

I said, "Thorkell, you tempted the Norns."

"What?"

"You said that the last thing we needed was a Mercian knife in the back."

He laughed, "You are still a pagan, Sven."

"Perhaps but I know better than to annoy the Three Sisters."

Danner returned, "We still have more than enough men to contain the city, my prince."

I could see that Cnut had been thinking about the betrayal and it was almost as though he had not heard our words, "Streona will not go to Mercia, he will go to the king and abase himself. That gives us time. King Edmund will be at Wintan-Ceastre to gather an army and that takes time. We will go and fight him while he has still to gather a sizeable army."

Thorkell shook his head, "You cannot abandon the siege, Prince Cnut."

"And I will not. I did hear Danner's words. There are enough men to hold the city. I will take the men of Ribe and Agerhøne along with Danner and my Danes. Thorkell, you will stay here and prosecute the siege with your Jomsvikings and the men of the Danelaw."

Thorkell was far from happy, "Prince Cnut, you are taking a mighty risk."

"I know but I am throwing the bones to win a mighty kingdom. This land is rich. We have seen that already. Look at the food they have." He looked into Thorkell's eyes, "I must be the one who is there when

Edmund is taken. Thorkell, you will dress as me and I will dress as you. Our men will know the truth but the English will be confused. In confusion lies victory. I will leave the Raven Banner with you and it will add to the illusion." He picked up a mutton bone and threw it to one of the hunting hounds, "We will leave before dawn. Sven, Danner, go and tell your men that we leave. Thorkell, you will need to move your men under cover of darkness. Perhaps we can make them think we attack."

"My prince, this is not a council of war for you ask not our opinions."

Cnut's smile was a thin one. It was the same smile I had seen when Uhtred had been executed, "Thorkell, I heard your words and know your opinion. Sven and Danner are silent." He turned to us, "Does that mean that they agree with Thorkell the Tall and think that I make a mistake?"

I looked at the Dane who deferred to me, "Prince Cnut, we are committed to a siege but my men would be happier going to war to bring, through battle, this strife to an end. You may be right and King Edmund has just a seedling army. Better to fight it now than when it becomes an oak. Besides even if we do not defeat him, we can weaken him."

Danner nodded, "I am of the same mind as the Oathsword. Sitting around a city's walls is not war. There will be discord and when it becomes cold there will be hunger. Once desertions begin, they are hard to stop."

I could see that the prince was delighted, "Then it is decided."

I hurried to my camp and gathered the hersir around me. As I had expected they were happy to be leaving the soggy camp that would soon become pestilential. They went off to organise their men and it was then that Bersi and Steana came to speak to me, "Father, you will take Bersi will you not?"

"We will need to leave some men here to guard the drekar."

Bersi said, "There are others who can do that, father. I did not let you down in Lundenwic did I?" I shook my head, "Steana and I are your sons. That makes us different from all the rest of the men you lead. Some day Steana will lead men as will I. I am young and I cannot fight in a shield wall but I can watch and I can learn. I can use my slingshot and draw my bow. I need to come so that I can become a warrior like Steana."

He was right. I nodded, "You know that I cannot give you the attention that your mother might wish?"

He nodded, "And I need it not. I know you care for us, father, but that does not mean you need to wipe my nose or worry that I am hungry. I will be a warrior."

It was decided. We took horses, not to ride but to carry our war gear. I knew that Steana would find the march hard for he now had a mail byrnie and it was many miles to Wintan-Ceastre and who knew how far west Edmund had ridden to gather his army. At least Streona would be in the same position as we were. He might be able to ride to Edmund's side but his Mercians would have to march.

As some of Thorkell's men joined us so we sent men to the western Roman Road, the one they had called the Portway. It led to Dorchestershire but I doubted that Edmund would be there. Scouts would have to be used to find them. We rested just two miles from the siege lines and awaited the others. The Danes had the furthest to march and Cnut arrived before they did. He had his own hearthweru now and two of them, Lief and Einar, had lived in the land of the Danelaw. They spoke Saxon well and knew a little of the land to the west. They took off their mail and mounted two horses. Prince Cnut sent them off to find the trail.

By the time dawn came, we had marched five miles to the west of Lundenwic. We knew where their burhs lay and they would be avoided. We ate and rested for an hour before pushing on. We had to outrun the news that a Danish army was following Edmund Ironside.

One thing I had ensured before we left Agerhøne, was that the three of us had good boots. I had paid for seal skins boots and a spare pair to be made for each of us. That investment now yielded results. While some men suffered from blisters and bleeding feet, we were comfortable. Mary had made us good socks which we oiled. The horses we took carried our sleeping gear but Steana and I were like the rest of the army and carried our helmets on the end of our spears. We camped that first night in Egeham. Chertsey Abbey was close by and many of the Danes wanted to use it as a camp but Cnut did not want to anger the church. We were exhausted and retired earlier than might have been expected. I was woken by one of Cnut's hearthweru. I went to the hut commandeered by the prince and found his scouts, Lief and Einar, speaking with the prince.

"They have found the Mercians. They are just a few miles ahead at Sunninghill. Streona and his bodyguards have raced on."

"You wish to attack them?"

"Aye, but the men are tired."

Danner arrived and yawned, "The Mercians?"

I pointed, "They are a few miles up the road. We are too late to attack them now but if we get an early start, we can get ahead of them and ambush them."

Prince Cnut nodded, "When you are rested, Leif and Einar, I want you to take fresh horses and find us a place to ambush them. Only one of you needs to return here."

I saw the weariness on their faces but they were hearthweru and they nodded.

I returned to my bed and slept but it was only a fitful sleep. I was already planning the ambush. That it would be my decision was clear. If Thorkell had been present then there might have been some debate. I had to trust that Lief and Einar would have the wit to choose a place where we would be hidden and could surprise them. We had slingers and bowmen and they could do great damage to men on the march. It would be our spears which would win the battle.

I woke first and even though it was still dark I woke the men. The bells of Chertsey Abbey sounded Lauds and I knew that our men had not had enough sleep. I had the fires rekindled and hot food prepared. Food was as good as sleep and the monks had given us food. It was a way of ensuring that we did not take more than food from them.

While they were eating, I gathered the slingers and bowmen. Bergil the Black still led them.

"Bergil, we are going to ambush the Mercians. I want the slingers and bowmen divided into two groups. One will strike at the head of the Mercians and the other at the rear. I want the Mercians grouped in the middle so that we can attack and slaughter them."

"Aye, lord, we can do that and it is an honour to be chosen."

I saw Bersi looking determined. His small leather byrnie afforded him more protection than the other slingers as did his leather cap but it was still not enough.

We set off down the road and Danner and I led. Einar rode to meet us two hours after we had begun our march. A thin sun had appeared but the low cloud made it feel darker somehow. "Lord, we have found somewhere, The Mercians are just a mile ahead. They rose late. Three miles from here there is a small wood on one side of the road. It lies on a slight slope and across the road are tended fields that lead down to marshy ground. The wood is to the south of the road."

It sounded perfect, "Then lead us there."

We left the road and headed south and west. We did not run but it was a faster march than the previous day. The thought of battle woke the men up and they were eager to close with the Mercians. There had been ill feeling in the camp as the Mercians had enjoyed all the rewards of the campaign but had yet to draw a sword. Having deserted us our men wanted vengeance. In many ways, it was easier to move through scrubland, thin woods and over tended fields for we could move more like a warband. The Roman Roads were fine for an organised army but we simply spread out like a flock of starlings. We saw the wood ahead and Bergil waving to us.

We entered the wood and the birds took to the skies. Danner and I began to organise our men as Bergil the Black personally placed his archers and slingers. We spread out in a double line in the trees and I was at the fore next to Bergil and half of the slingers and bowmen. As we were using the cover of the trees to disguise our presence, we were not a solid line but that did not matter. I hoped that, like us, they would march with their shields across their backs. If they marched with the shields on their left arms then they would have some protection from our initial attack. We waited, as still as we could and the birds returned to the trees. They would only take to the air when we moved. The Mercians would, if everyone obeyed my instructions, only be aware of us when we attacked. We held our shields on our left arms and our spears rested on the ground. With donned helmets we were ready.

We heard them long before they reached us. It was not just the sound of jingling metal but the laughter and banter of men who had not a care in the world and did not suspect that they were about to be ambushed. They were led by Ecgfrith of Yarpole. I had often seen him for he was close to Streona and I did not like him. He was a lazy man and not a good warrior but he owned land and Eadric Streona thought well of him. He rode the only horse and I suspect was enjoying the glory of leading four hundred Mercian warriors. Had he been better thought of then he would have been with Eadric. He rode ten paces ahead of the rest of the Mercians. His bodyguards, the better armed and armoured, followed him. There were just twenty of them and they carried spears over their shoulders and, as we had done when we marched, had their helmets hanging from their spearheads. The rest lumbered on behind and were dressed in a mixture of metal studied byrnies and short mail. We were still and they looked straight ahead or at each other. They had not had scouts out and that showed their lack of quality.

I relied on the skill of Bergil the Black to initiate the attack and he did not let me down. He waved his spear and the arrows and stones flew. He then ran from cover and rammed his spear up, under the arm of Ecgfrith of Yarpole. The warrior fell, taking the spear with him. It was such a sudden attack that Bergil had time to grab the thegn's horse and lead him back into the woods before his hearthweru knew what had happened. Even as the stones and arrows fell, we moved forward and, as we cleared the trees, locked shields and drove our spears into Ecgfrith's hearthweru. The first warrior I slew was in the act of pulling around his shield when Saxon Slayer drove through the links of his byrnie, through his ribs and into the man's heart. I pulled out and thrust again before the next warrior had brought his shield around. The next file had managed to swing around their shields but their spears were still a heartbeat behind. It meant that my men all had the first strike with their spears and even those who managed to block the spears could not bring their own to bear. The best that they managed was not to die. That death was only delayed by a few moments for we had killed their best in that first attack and we turned, having destroyed the head of the metal snake to fall upon the rest. It was a slaughter and had been brought about thanks to the careless leadership of Ecgfrith of Yarpole.

When the last man had been killed, my men stripped the bodies of weapons and armour as well as any coins that they might have had. It was not simply greed, we needed to reduce the chance of weapons being used against us. They might have been poor warriors but they had good weapons. We also took their pack horses with the food that they had brought and by noon were heading down the road once more. We had no need of a fast pace for we knew we had more than sixty miles to go before we reached the west.

It was at the village of Ferneberga that we learned whither Edmund had gone. Terrified that the army of Danes would destroy their settlement the headman happily cooperated with us. King Edmund Ironside was not heading for Wintan-Caestre. He was heading deeper into Wessex. He was in Sumorsǣte far to the west. Within its ancient boundaries lay the old royal palace of Cheddar. It was where King Alfred had fled and hidden from Guthrum. *Wyrd.* I found myself clutching the sword that linked the two men. It was a land that suited the English. It was full of fens and swamps. There were many places where the English could hide and, more importantly, there had been little fighting there since I had raided after we had taken Wareham. Edmund was using the men of the west to fight for him much as his grandsire, Alfred had done. It gave us our direction and the distance we would have to march. We had more than fifty miles to travel.

Chapter 11

The Battle of Scorranstone 1016

The further west we went the more nervous we all became. We were a warband and not an army. Our night camp had a third of the men on sentry duty. We did not wish to be ambushed by a Saxon king who showed that he knew what he was doing. If this was a trap then we had many miles to march before we would reach our friends. To the south of us was Wareham but the fleet had long ago left there. I had raided Shepton Mallet and Brycgstow but we had not slaughtered those whom we had defeated. I wondered if my kindness would come back to haunt us. We moved cautiously and having taken more horses, were able to send out more scouts. We discovered the whereabouts of Edmund and his army. They were waiting for us at Penn in Selwood. They were protected by hills and, more importantly, were rested while we would have marched a hundred miles from Lundenwic.

We made a defensive camp a mile from the English. We had good sentries but I was confident that the English would not attack. They were waiting for us and would have prepared well. This would be the first time that we fought Edmund Ironside and would be a good measure of the man's skill.

With just three of us as leaders, the council of war was an easy one. Danner was happy to go along with the plans that Cnut and I conjured. Einar had told us that the English were camped on a slight slope and that suggested they would wait for us to attack. Cnut was pessimistic about our chances of advancing up an uneven slope against an enemy who was well prepared. "We do not even know their numbers, Sven."

I sighed, "Prince Cnut, we have marched far from our base. If you do not wish to fight then let us scurry back to Lundenwic with our tails between our legs. If we do that then we give the English a bloodless victory. We put heart in their men and suck the confidence from ours. Do you wish that?"

He shook his head, "Yet I do not want to give Edmund an easy victory."

I looked at Danner, "Streona will be with Edmund." He nodded, "He will know of the fight between Bloodaxe and me."

The Dane laughed, "The whole of Danelaw will know that."

"He will also believe that there is bad feeling between the Danes you lead and the rest of the army." He did not like the words but he could not escape their truth. He nodded. “Then let us use that. Tomorrow I will hide half of my men on the flanks and you will lead the rest, led by your Danes. The archers and slingers will advance before you and shower the English. You will advance only until their archers and slingers try to kill you. Then you flee down the slope.”

Far from being insulted the veteran grinned and nodded, “They will think that we are afraid and our flight means we are deserting. They will follow us to make their victory complete.”

“They will be desperate, especially after my raids at Brycgstow, to have vengeance. When they pass me and my men, we will fall upon them. You will turn and we will have them trapped.”

“A good plan.”

Cnut shook his head, “They will be looking for you. Edmund is no fool and he will hold back his men until he knows where you are.”

“And he will see me where he expects to see me. Standing with your banner, your hearthweru and the baggage.”

Danner frowned, “Are you a galdramenn or an aelfe? Can you be in two places at once?”

“I will be with my men. My son will wear my mail and helmet and carry my shield. He has grown and Edmund has never seen me. Men will have described my armour and he will know my banner. He will come if only to get me and to slay you, Prince Cnut.”

“You will use your prince as bait?”

I sighed, “I am using my own flesh and blood as bait. It is not arrogance but I think that Edmund will be just as keen to get me in his clutches as you, Prince Cnut.”

Once he swallowed his pride, he saw the sense in what I said and, after he nodded his approval, we planned the details.

I spent time with Steana explaining what he needed to do. He had a mixture of emotions. He was proud that he had been selected but a little disappointed that he would not have the chance to fight.

“But you will be guarding Prince Cnut, along with his hearthweru. What more honour could you wish? If my plan fails then it will be up to you to save the future King of England. His eyes brightened at the thought.

We did not march until the mid-morning. We wanted them to have to wait for us and for them to think we feared facing them. Einar and Leif had done a good job and told us that the English waited between two woods. That suited my plan and Einar the Fat and Sweyn led half of our men to the right where, like us, they could approach without being seen. Danner and Prince Cnut made a great show of marching and then arranging their lines. They banged their shields and shouted insults at the serried ranks of Saxons. It allowed us to move ahead of the main body and lie down to wait. The hardest part for me was knowing that Bersi would be advancing before the army and whilst I hid, he would be in danger.

When Danner was ready, he and his men knelt while a priest blessed them. Danner was like me, a pagan, but Cnut had to be assuaged and Danner and his men played their part. We heard the chanting of Edmund's priests as they did the same. That done a Danish horn sounded and the archers and slingers advanced before the shield wall. I could not see the English army but I could see my son and the others armed with missiles as they advanced up the slope. When they stopped, almost level with us, then that told me where Edmund waited. Arrows and stones flew. More arrows and stones came back and I saw men fall. Bersi was not one of them. I saw Bergil wave them back and then Danner led his Danes up the slope. They were being arrogantly noisy and would confirm the eorledman's words to the king. I heard the clatter of arrows and stones on shields and then the clash of steel on steel. Danner and his men had the tricky task of extricating themselves from battle without losing too many men. Only half were his men and the other half were mine and Prince Cnut's. It was Danner and his mercenaries that were in the front rank and when I heard his cry, "Back! We are undone!" Then I ordered my men to their feet. We locked shields as our army turned and ran down the slope. It looked like a wild flight but they were pacing themselves and encouraging, we hoped, the English to follow closely.

I heard a cheer and the English army tumbled down the slope after Danner. The lightly armed and armoured men were able to run faster than the mailed warriors and I waited until the mailed men were level with us before I led my men into the attack. We had forty paces to cover and the English were oblivious to our presence. The first they knew was when an English voice from the top of the hill shouted, "It is a trap. Fall back!"

It was, of course, too late. Danner and his men had turned and Einar and Sweyn were leading their men into the far flank. The slope meant our attack was not as effective as it might have been had we stood on flatter ground but we were in a line and the English were milling around. Some had gone too far to turn and were being slain by Danner's men. My slingers and archers had free rein to strike at men who had no defence against their missiles. I speared three warriors before the enemy managed to turn their shields and face us. The problem they had was that they had men attacking them from three sides, as Danner led half of our army back up the slope. It was only later that I realised the flaw in my plan. Edmund had more than half of his army with him and they could have attacked our left flank. I was happy that he did not. Instead, I heard the horn sound the retreat and King Edmund showed sense by saving half of his army. They disappeared into the woods leaving the reckless remnants of his attack to be slaughtered on the slopes of the hill. Most were the fyrd of Wessex. Without mail and armour, they had been able to charge faster. They paid the price with their deaths. We renewed our efforts, for any men who survived would join the king and we would have to fight them again. I had stuck my spear into the ground and drawn Oathsword. It was the better weapon for such combat. We had slain their best warriors and what remained were those armed with poor pole weapons and swords that bent as soon as they were struck by a better-made weapon. I rarely had to even use my shield and any blows that came through my guard were easily taken on my mail. I saw Bersi and the other boys hurling atones at such close range that even had the warriors had good helmets they would have died. The archers, too, had an easy time. By dark, it was all over and we had won.

I waved the prince forward and as he and my son climbed the slope I shouted, "Leif and Einar, find horses and follow the English. We need to know where they will stop. This is not yet over."

Looking around I saw that while we had slain more, we had lost too many men. The English had fought hard. I could not remember them fighting this hard for Edmund's father.

When the prince came close, he saw the scale of our victory. "Your plan worked. You are truly a warlord."

I nodded, "And I have seen the mettle of this king. He was not reckless and took the bulk of his men to fight another day."

We moved our camp to the shelter of the trees and our men buried our dead and scavenged the English bodies. The food that they had left would keep us supplied for many days. It was a better result than we could have expected. I wondered if Edmund Ironside had also learned lessons.

I sat with the prince and Danner. Danner had lost more men than I had but he was satisfied knowing that had we not adopted my plan then he would have lost many more. I did not ask Steana for my mail yet. He had enjoyed his moment of glory and I knew we would not be fighting the next day.

"We keep our swords in his back, eh, Sven?"

"We do, Prince Cnut, but as he headed north then he is going towards Mercia. Eadric Streona can call on more of his warriors. I believe that is why they headed north instead of heading back to Wareham or even Brycgstow."

"We are so close to victory, Sven, that I can almost taste it."

"Then rid your mind, my prince, of such thoughts. They are planted there by Loki to deceive you."

"I do not believe in Loki."

"But you believe in God and his nemesis is the devil. It is said, is it not, that within us all dwells a Christ and a Devil."

"That is blasphemy."

"And yet the Devil tempted Christ did he not? You are being tempted but from within. Be patient." I paused, "There would be no disgrace or dishonour in heading back to Lundenwic. With news of this victory, we could take Lundenwic."

Shaking his head the prince said, "Lundenwic is nothing. Edmund is all."

We ate. Danner asked, "You are a pagan, Sven. How is it that you know so much about the White Christ?"

I smiled, "My wife is not only a Christian, but she is also the daughter of a priest. Believe me, I know all the stories and their meanings."

The prince looked at me, "You know, Sven, that when I become king then the land will all become Christian, even you."

I smiled, "I can make the signs, bend the knee and mumble the words, Prince Cnut, but what no man can know is what is in here," I tapped my head, "and here," I tapped my heart. I will be true to myself and Oathsword."

"Yet Oathsword was a Christian gift."

"Given to a pagan. The Norns have spun and what King Alfred intended was not how it worked out."

I had stumped him with my logic.

The two scouts did not return until late the next evening. Their horses were almost dead and they looked exhausted beyond words, "We have found them, Lord, they are at Scorranstone, more than thirty miles north of here. He has found a fortress of hills and trees and he is building defences."

I would have gone home there and then, for he would be closer to Mercian reinforcements and we would be drawn further away from help. Cnut saw their proximity but decided that he was destined to go north and fight a final cataclysmic battle. With laden horses and men loaded down with English treasure, we headed north to Scorranstone.

It took two days to reach the new defences of King Edmund. I was learning much about the second son of King Æthelred. He was clever and he was cautious. We saw little evidence of disorder as we headed north. An army in flight often left a trail of discarded equipment behind them. That this army did not bespoke well of the control the king had. They trusted him and that meant they would fight.

We neared the hills on the second afternoon of our march. Danner's scouts had learned how to track in this land and they spotted the sentries. This time Edmund had made a series of improvised fortifications. He wished us to bleed our way to him. As I walked around them with Danner and the prince, I could not help but admire the speed with which they had been erected. We stayed well out of bow range and could not see what traps lay before the stakes.

Back at our camp, I expressed my doubts to the prince. "We can take them, Prince Cnut, but this time there can be no trick to help us. We have a wall of timber through which we have to pass. I believe our warriors are better but we will lose good men as we make our way through."

"But if we can beat him then it will be worth it." I saw then that Cnut had the same ruthless streak his father had. He was willing to sacrifice men to get what he wanted. "I trust you, Sven, and know that with you and Danner leading them then our men can win."

I picked a piece of days-old mutton and chewed it before I added my thoughts. Both Cnut and Danner were watching me, "Prince Cnut, I believe that King Edmund is waiting for reinforcements. I do not know for certain, but it is my belief that Eadric Streona has gone north to bring reinforcements and that, even now, they will be heading here to trap us against these woods."

Danner's eyes widened and then he nodded, "That makes perfect sense to me, Sven."

"And all the more reason for us to attack sooner rather than later."

Shaking my head I said, "He will flee again if he thinks he is losing."

"My mind is made up. I have listened to you, Sven Saxon Sword, and I know how your mind works. We will attack before dawn and use warbands to strike at each defensive position. I will wait at our camp with reserves. If you are right and Eadric Streona brings the Mercians then I shall sound the horn and we can fall back and return to Lundenwic. If not then we will come and add our weight to the final assault."

Despite our efforts, there was no dissuading him.

When I explained what we were doing to my men Einar the Fat made a valid point, "He is becoming his father. Do you remember the

Battle of Svolder when he hung back and allowed others to fight and die for him?"

Sweyn One Eye nodded, "Perhaps that is the way with kings."

I turned to Bersi, "You make sure you stay close to Prince Cnut. The slingers are to guard him. If he flees then follow." I saw him begin to open his mouth and I shook my head, "If Cnut flees then his hearthweru will see that he gets to Lundenwic and Thorkell the Tall. Steana and I will be easier in our minds if we know that you are safe."

"But father, it cannot come to that, surely."

"We are an island of Danes in a sea of Saxons. Heed my words for there is no time for debate. Prince Cnut has cast the bones and we must see which way they fall."

As we rose to prepare for the battle, Dreng, Snorri, Faramir, and Gandálfr all helped me to prepare. We all understood the danger we were in. If we won then all was well and good but with a Mercian army possibly on the way then we had to be ready to flee as fast as we could. When we were mailed, we put daggers and seaxes in boots and belts. I slipped one into the scabbard on the back of my shield. We each had a small satchel and we placed within it, honey, vinegar and dried meat. That done we marched to meet the others. Sweyn and I had been assigned one of the hills in the centre, Einar the Fat, the one on our left. Danner and his best men had the hill next to ours and the rest, led by Hastein the Brave, had been given the hill on the extreme left. This would be four battles for Edmund Ironside had cleverly made each of his small improvised burhs independent of the others. We would only know if we had succeeded if we all met up. Prince Cnut had fifty of our best warriors as well as the twenty slingers and the horses and pack animals. If he was called to attack it would be because we had won and he wanted to be there to capture Edmund. Cnut was showing me that he knew how to be a king. If we lost then none would know that he had tried to defeat Edmund and failed. They would all assume that the warband had been led by Thorkell, but if we won then it would be he who would garner the glory.

We moved, through the dark towards the waiting English. The greatest flaw in this plan was that only one of the warbands would achieve surprise. The rest would not. Hastein the Brave, perhaps too eager, was the one who managed surprise and we were still thirty paces from the stakes and the sentries when I heard the cries as men were roused and a hasty shield wall was formed. Edmund must have been expecting an attack for his men managed to form a shield wall very quickly and were there to greet us with bristling spears, as we made our way through the stakes. My hearthweru and I were the first and we jabbed with our spears at the first men forming a shield wall.

I shouted, "Swynfylking!" We formed up into the small wedges we had used before. It meant I was protected by my hearthweru as was Sweyn, my cousin, while the majority of the warriors I led, Steana, Leif Long Leg and the others were in two lines behind us. Holding my shield before me I jabbed Saxon Slayer at the first man. He wore mail but he had just awoken and the sight of a fully mailed warrior before him might have made him panic. Whatever the reason, although he jabbed with his own spear his shield was not high enough and Saxon Slayer drove into his left shoulder. The shield dropped even lower and allowed me to punch him in the face with the boss of my shield. He reeled but the man behind prevented him from falling too far and that was his doom for a spear came from behind me to drive up into his unprotected middle and as he slid down so I was able to strike at the next man whose shield had been lowered by his falling comrade. My spear struck his chest and I felt it grate and scrape off the breastbone.

I stepped forward and saw that there was just one rank left before me. Once we were through that then we could fall upon the flanks of the hole that we had made. I used my shield to block the thrusting spear that came at me from the dark. The third rank was proving harder than the other two. Archers behind the last row of spearmen sent arrows into the air. My men all had mail about their shoulders and good helmets. The war arrows they sent would do little harm. The third rank knew how to fight and our spears were blocked. It was the sun that gave us the edge. As it came up behind us, it flared and its beams went to the eyes and faces of the last rank. A man cannot strike if he cannot see and I used the sudden shock of the sun to punch the temporarily blinded English warrior in the face. He reeled and fell for there was no rank behind to hold him. Even as two arrows slammed into my shield, I stuck him with my spear.

My hearthweru also used the sun to their advantage and we were through. We raced to the archers. Three fled but the other four all fell to our spears. I looked for Edmund but he was not there. Instead, I saw Ælfric, the eorledman of Hampshire and his housecarls advancing towards us. Like Cnut, they were the reserve here. I had expected Edmund but he had fooled me. The eorledman and bodyguards were good warriors and this would be a harder fight.

Our formation had now changed to a traditional wedge. Sweyn and I were the tips. Had the eorledman and his men not been there then we would simply have turned and cleared the hill of the English. As it was, we became part of a struggle on the hill. We poked and jabbed with our spears but we were equally well-armed and armoured. None seemed to gain an advantage. I had cuts from spears on my arms and my legs but they were not serious. When noon came, we fell back as did the English. No one gave a command but we were all exhausted and thirsty. Without taking our eyes off each other we drank from our water and ale skins. I decided that Saxon Slayer had done all the work that it could and I stuck it in the ground. I drew Oathsword and that seemed to inspire the men I led who began banging their shields and chanting its name.

The English were not to be outdone and they used their own, strange chant. They banged their shields and chanted, "Ut!" We did so for perhaps the count of a thousand and then I decided we had endured enough and ran at the English. We caught them by surprise and I faced not Ælfric, the eorledman of Hampshire, but a thegn who had been lower down the line when we had stopped for refreshment. He may have chosen to face me, I could not say but he jabbed at my face with his spear. I used Oathsword to slice the spear in two and he tried to draw his sword. I simply backhanded the blade across his throat and he fell at my feet. It became a battle of warriors. I lost count of the number I slew but men were lost on both sides and it mattered not.

When Snorri fell, tired no doubt by the effort it needed to keep wielding a sword whilst watching my back, I renewed my efforts and we hacked and slashed through the English as I tried to get to Ælfric. Since I had slain the thegn so easily, he had kept to the rear of his men, encouraging them and stepping out only to kill warriors with weaker mail. The attack worked and he ordered his men to fall back down the other side of the hill. We halted. The day was almost gone and we were too weary to fight. I could hear the fighting to our left and right but we, it appeared, had been the only wedge to advance. Sweyn came to me and shook his head, "We have both lost hearthweru, cousin. These English fight harder for Edmund Ironside."

"Did you see him?"

He shook his head, "No, nor did I see Ulfcetel Snilling."

I turned and saw that Steana lived, "Steana take two men and return to the prince. Tell him we hold the camp of one of the English bands but know not how the rest fare. We will camp here. Fetch food and ale."

"Aye, father. And I will tell Bersi that we both live."

We had many men to bury. We had lost more than twenty warriors in the attack. Ottar, Sweyn's hearthweru and Snorri were the most serious losses. With men watching in case the English returned, we dug graves for our men. They would all be buried in their mail with their weapons and their treasure. Laid out in a long line they looked like a sleeping army ready to rise again. As we replaced the sods, I comforted myself with that thought. When we had done, I noticed that darkness had fallen and the sounds of battle had ceased. I had fires lit for comfort but ensured that the sentries I set faced outward to watch for treachery. Steana had just arrived with the food when Danner and Einar walked into my camp. Each of them was protected by just three hearthweru.

Einar smiled, "As I expected, you made the greatest advance. I am sorry we could not keep up with you but the English fought well." He saw the line of graves, "You paid the price."

I turned to my son, "What did the prince say?"

"He seemed disappointed that you had not driven the English from the hills."

Einar snorted, "They outnumbered us by two to one. He is lucky we were so resolute."

I knew that discord would help no one, "Let us eat and drink ale. Steana, take some to the other warbands."

"The prince sent little enough."

"Then we share what we have. We all fought well this day."

We naturally drank first. Fighting makes a man thirsty and drives away hunger. We would eat but only when our thirst had been slaked and we would only eat because we knew our bodies needed it.

"Did you see the king or Snilling?"

They both shook their heads. Danner added, "He did fight today, with Snilling. They slew Hastein the Brave. I think that when he attacked first, he drew the English king to him and he paid the price. His men fell back down the hill." He made a line with his bent arm, "Our line is now a little skewed. Einar, you will need to realign your men."

"You have put another in charge?"

"Thorghest Bloody Hair is a fierce warrior and will stiffen the sinews of the band."

I chewed some of the dried meat to fool my stomach into thinking I had dined well. Sweyn had his whetstone out and was sharpening his sword. I did the same. My cousin asked, "So, Sven, you have a plan?"

I smiled. My cousin always believed I had some plan in my head that would ensure victory. Shaking my head I said, "Einar is right, we are outnumbered and the best that we can hope is that we slay more of them than they do of us. If the prince brought the reserves, then we might make a breakthrough but I think that is a risk he will not take. He trusts in our blades."

"So, it will be more of the same?"

"We will attack before dawn. I do not doubt that they will be expecting it but they know not when. I will attack first and, hopefully, I will draw King Edmund to me. We attack like ferocious dogs and, it may be that in the half dark of dawn, we frighten away some of the weaker men." I shrugged, "I am sorry my plan is not better, Sweyn, but we should not have come here."

Sweyn was a thinker, "You are right. What folly was it to follow their king into the land where he has the most support? Had we stayed with Thorkell then we could have taken Lundenwic and forced their king to take it from us."

"The Norns, Sweyn, they weave and they conjure. The past is a dangerous place to visit and you cannot change what is done. It is the future where hope lies. That future will come at dawn."

My hearthweru slept close to me. I know they meant well and were protecting me but I was not comfortable and rose in the middle of the night. Gandálfr stirred and I said, "Peace, I go to make water."

After I had done so I dressed for war. I did so well away from the sleeping camp. I stood, in mail and helm, with Saxon Slayer in my hand. I looked to the east. There lay Mary and my daughter. She did not deserve to be left alone like this. I made a vow that I would finish this war sooner rather than later. As I turned, I saw the moon in the west as it began to set. It was a sign. The gods would hold me to my promise.

Chapter 12

Wessex 1016

I watched the moon start to set and then went around my men to wake them. I did so silently, just shaking them awake. They all rose, made water and then dressed. None had slept in mail. You learned when a young warrior that sleeping in mail was impossible. I had woken them deliberately early so that they could drink some ale, eat food, say a prayer to whichever god they chose and ready themselves to die. A warrior fought better if he thought he might die. The worst warriors were the ones who believed that no weapon could harm them and that they would do some great deed and earn renown. When I judged dawn to be an hour or so away, I led a double line of warriors towards the English camp. Ælfric eorledman of Hampshire had shown me that he had little appetite for war and I judged that his men would have known that. They would be less than eager to fight the Danes who had driven them from their hill. As we made our way through the trees and down the slope, it was they who would be at a disadvantage. They had no stakes to protect them.

The first men we met were slain almost silently. They were poor sentries and their lack of vigilance cost them their lives. Men rarely die silently but none screamed or roared. There was no clash of steel as they defended themselves for they did not. Spears were rammed into backs or into guts and they died. They moaned and their bodies crashed to the ground but that did not wake weary men who had fought for a whole day. These were the fyrd. They were not housecarls who were trained to fight for hours. These were farmers and labourers who had been called by their lords to fight the invader.

It was as we neared their fires that we were seen. I saw Ælfric and his housecarls eating and talking. It was a housecarl who saw us and shouted the alarm. He was on the far side of a camp of sleeping men else I could have eliminated an English leader. As it was, we had to stab and skewer men who rose and grabbed weapons to fight us.

A horn sounded from our left as Ælfric and his men fled. They abandoned their camp. I heard the clash of steel that told me that the rest of the warbands had attacked and for the briefest of moments I believed that we might have victory in our grasp. King Edmund was a better leader than his father. More, he was a warrior. He led his housecarls from our right. One of my men shouted a warning and I saw, as dawn broke to the east, that this was not the fyrd that attacked us but mailed men who knew their business. We were isolated and so I shouted, "Shield wall."

Turning to face the threat we locked shields in a double line. Edmund was a brave warrior but he was young and he made a mistake. Instead of halting and making a wedge, he allowed his men to fall upon us piecemeal. That suited us for courageous though the housecarls were and despite their obvious skills, they were faced by two or even three men as they ran up to the shield wall. When the sun broke behind us more than fifteen lay dead before us and King Edmund realised his mistake.

"Shield wall!" He had a good voice and it rang out.

His men obeyed and he was just in time for Einar the Fat and his warband, having eliminated their enemies, fell upon the flank of King Edmund. It was he who was now on the defensive and I pointed Saxon Slayer at the English king, "Men of Ribe and Agerhøne, now is our time. Let us avenge Snorri and the others and rid this land of the men of Wessex."

Edmund showed his mettle. With locked shields, he and his housecarls advanced towards us. We clashed close to the fire used by Ælfric. Spears clashed against shields. I thrust Saxon Slayer at King Edmund but a housecarl pressed his body between us and my spearhead drove into his side instead. Thanks to Einar we had the slope and we began to push them down the hill. Their feet were slipping and sliding. The slope meant that our spears were driving at faces and it is a brave man who does not flinch. The sun had risen in the sky and Edmund was about to be defeated. I heard the command to fall back and knew that Cnut had his victory.

The sound of a Danish horn, stridently recalling us told me that the Norns had spun and the treacherous Streona had struck again. Luckily for us, the English did not know what the horn meant. I shouted, "One last push and then, when they retreat, filter back to our camp." It was all that I could think to do. We roared and we charged. It was too much for the English who fled down the hill. King Edmund showed his courage for he was the last to descend, surrounded by the housecarls who had survived. I raised Saxon Slayer in salute.

"Back!"

We hurried back up the hill and when we reached the clearer ground on the other side, we saw that Cnut had mounted the horses and he and the slingers, mounted behind warriors, were fleeing. Mounted Mercians were racing after them. There were only two hundred or so, just sixty of which were mounted, but that had been enough. The prince could not have known that he had victory in his grasp. As we raced after the unsuspecting Mercians I saw that Danner, Sweyn and Einar had survived. The Mercians slowed as the horses took their prey from them. When they stopped, we hit them like a wild wall and spears were rammed into men who had thought they had won a battle. The horsemen were easy to slay as they were lightly armed and their spears were short. They fled leaving the disorganized men on foot. Struck from behind they broke and fled whence they had come. That we lost not a man was small comfort. Every man with me knew how close we had come to the victory Cnut had so desperately sought. We now had a race of ninety miles to reach the safety of our siege. I saw wounded men and knew that not all would make it. Some would be given a warrior's death before Lundewic was in sight. Had Edmund realised his opportunity then he would have rallied his men and pursued us but we had broken him and his army was fleeing west. The Mercians were routed north and so we made eighteen miles before we had to stop. Suindune was a tiny settlement on the top of a hill. When they saw the warband approach then the people wisely fled to the nearby woods. We were too weary to pursue and we settled into the palisaded village. We ate and we drank all that they had. Every animal was slaughtered and cooked. Prince Cnut had left our supplies and the English would be enjoying them.

We were all bloodied and some were wounded but we had been close to victory and so there was a good mood amongst the men. "We could raid our way east, Lord Sven. There will be many places like this." Thorghest Bloody Hair was a frightening-looking warrior. He used animal blood to make his long hair stiff and added to the cochineal with which he stained his face so he looked like a creature from hel.

I shook my head, "It will not take Edmund long to realise that we have fled. We have today gained an advantage but tomorrow we need to put as much distance between us and him as possible. He will pursue us. This will be a test of will and strength. Do we have the will to march further and faster than the English? Do we have the strength to fight them when they catch us?"

Sweyn nodded, "With you as our leader then, aye."

It was good of him to say but I would not get carried away. The Norns were spinning still and we had more than seventy miles to go. By my reckoning that might take three days.

"We sleep for three hours and then move. I want us twenty miles east of here by dawn."

Danner nodded, "You want us to disappear."

"The villagers will tell Edmund the direction we took but in the dark, there are many paths we might take. I need your scouts to be at their best."

"Aye, they will be happy to be the hounds that find the safe route."

My men made me sleep and when I woke, I felt slightly refreshed. Taking as much of the cooked food as we could carry, we followed the road east. As soon as they could the scouts would find a less well-travelled road but a warband as big as ours was hard to hide. Leif found us another small settlement, Dudecota. As with the first one, the villagers fled and we fell upon the food that they were preparing. Our scouts had done well. The men of Dudecota had not even been called to the fyrd. It was a backwater and that suited us. We rested for six hours and took turns sleeping. We left not long after the sun reached its zenith.

We were tantalisingly close to Lundenwic when we reached Mere lafan. Not far from where we camped, lay the tiny village of Windles-ore. Through it flowed the river Temese. To a Viking, the water is always a way home. We took the tiny village and ate again once the villagers had fled. It was the scouts who brought us the bad news that word had somehow reached this valley that a warband was on the loose. From their description, it was not Edmund but the local fyrd raised by the nobles of this part of Wessex. To reach the river, and therefore Lundenwic, we would need to fight again. On our flight east, we had already buried twenty men whose wounds had overcome them and I was loath to lose more but Cnut's flawed plan meant that we had no choice.

This time we could not afford to delay. The fyrd itself was not the problem, it was the thought that King Edmund was hot on our trail and to be trapped between two armies would spell disaster. We still had wounded men but we had managed to take carts from the settlements. We had twenty men to guard and tend to the wounded. The rest made a swynfylking. The Scouts had told us that the English were formed up in a shield wall astride the road to Lundenwic. The eorledman and his housecarls were in the centre. If we used a simple wedge, we had less chance of a breakthrough. This way there would be six points to our wedge and those on the flanks, led by Sweyn on one side and Thorghest on the other, would have a greater chance of breaking through the fyrd.

We marched in the wedge and banged our shields to keep the rhythm. Sweyn began to chant the saga of Bluetooth. It inspired our men. The English just heard a chant and feared the worse. Their own housecarls tried to counter with the chant of 'Ut!' but it seemed thin and reedy in comparison.

Bluetooth was a warrior strong
He used a spear stout and strong
Fighting Franks and slaying Norse
He steered the ship on a deadly course
Njörðr, Njörðr, push the dragon
Njörðr, Njörðr, push the dragon
The spear was sharp and the Norse did die
Through the air did Valkyries fly
A day of death and a day of blood
The warriors died as warriors should
Njörðr, Njörðr, push the dragon
Njörðr, Njörðr, push the dragon
When home they came with byrnies red
They toasted well our Danish dead
They sang their songs of warriors slain
And in that song, they lived again
Njörðr, Njörðr, push the dragon
Njörðr, Njörðr, push the dragon

We were just twenty paces from them and the slight slope was working against us when I shouted, "Oathsword!" and pointed my spear at the eorledman. It was my leaders at the fore of every wedge and although we ran their experience stopped it from becoming a reckless charge. I pulled back my arm and rammed Saxon Slayer towards the eorledman. He was an older warrior and his reactions were slow. Our speed of charge had taken him by surprise and my spear hit the rim of his shield as he belatedly tried to pull it up. He succeeded in helping me to drive the spearhead up under his chin and into his helmet. It was a quick death. Gandálfr, Dreng and Faramir had Snorri to avenge and even though the housecarls were well armoured, like their lord they were older men and after four or five thrusts they too, fell.

In the centre, we were doing well but it was the flanks where the victory was won. Thorghest and Sweyn simply destroyed the spearmen that they faced. None wore mail and their spears were not well made. The handful of survivors fled. I knew what they had done when the flanks began to bend in to make a circle. I had already stepped over the body of the eorledman and was duelling with a housecarl when the bulk of the fyrd broke and fell. It speaks well of the eorledman that his housecarls did not desert his body and they died to a man. Even more fortuitous was that Sweyn had managed to capture eight horses. We stripped the mail from the housecarls and the eorledman, for they were well made, and were able to take them with us. We hurried on to

Windles-ore. We had no idea if Edmund was close but we knew that Windles-ore was too small to be a burh and we needed to be by the river.

There we found a palisade. We tore it down and used it to build rafts. Even taking the whole of the perimeter did not provide us with enough for all the men but, luckily, there was a huge forest and our axes made short work of enough trees to build the number of rafts we needed. It was dark by the time we finished and so we ate, set sentries and slept. We trusted the river but sailing along a strange waterway at night invited disaster. I let Sweyn lead the flotilla of ships off and I brought up the rear. I had just boarded the raft when I heard horses. King Edmund, with a hundred mounted men, rode up. His men waved their fists impotently in the air but the king just studied me. I had seen him doing the same thing in the dawn battle. He would remember me. They followed us for a while but the current was so swift that we left the horses behind. We could then concentrate on using the poles to steer as straight a course as possible and we enjoyed a relatively peaceful journey of twenty miles. I knew that, at the front, Sweyn would be composing a saga for what we had managed to do was quite remarkable. We had extracted a Danish army from under the noses of the English. The flight east had cost us forty men and that was an acceptable number when the whole army could have been destroyed.

The rafts were all of a different size and some reached the longphort well before the others. Mine was the largest and the slowest. By the time we reached the camp, it was dark but the other leaders, along with Cnut and Thorkell were there to greet me. I had no eyes for them. Instead, I scanned the faces and only smiled when I saw Bersi whole and alive.

Cnut came over to speak to me. I had known that he would flee rather than risk capture but I was disappointed that he had not sent men back on horses to give us assistance. He clasped my arm, "I am sorry that we had to leave but," he nodded at Bersi, "we saved your son and the other ships' boys."

I said, "Thank you for that. We had King Edmund, Prince Cnut. Despite being outnumbered we had them on the run."

His face fell, "We were close to victory?"

I nodded, "Had you and the reserve been closer then we might have won a complete victory. The Mercians had numbers but nothing else."

"Then that gives us hope. We finish this siege and then we return to face Edmund."

"Prince Cnut, he was not beaten and he can take the two battles as victories now that we have fled. The fyrd at Windles-ore were brave men and they faced us. It is a sign that King Edmund has put steel back into these English and they will fight us."

My mind kept going back to Gegnesburh and Cnut's mistake. All the deaths could have been avoided had he not been so foolish. I was reminded of his youth and the need for me, despite my desire to return home, to stay at his side.

"I know and Thorkell has been less than diligent in our absence. He allowed Erik of Lade to raid up and down the river. Those men might have prosecuted the siege."

Erik of Lade and his Norsemen were excellent warriors but they were old-fashioned and preferred raiding to the kind of war that Cnut needed. Erik and his Vikings were sent by Cnut to help Thorkell make another assault on the walls. As the army that had almost defeated Edmund was exhausted, we were allowed to stay in the camp for a day. I confess that we needed the time to recover. The one hundred miles had taxed even the hardest of men. I suppose we could have marched from Windles-ore faster than we travelled by the rafts but had we marched then I think we would have been ruined as a fighting force for longer. The Norns were spinning and the thoughts that danced around my head should have been heeded but I was just happy to be reunited with Bersi.

He was animated when he spoke of the desperate ride back to Lundenwic, clinging to the back of the hearthweru, Hákon. "If I never see the back of a horse again, father, then I will be happy for I felt like a sack of grain."

Steana had also suffered during the march back and when we had camped, he had not been able to keep in his frustration at having victory snatched from us, "Tell us, brother, did the prince and his men make any attempt to fight the Mercians?"

Bersi looked at me and I nodded, "Speak, Bersi, for a warrior has to tell the truth to his shield brothers."

He shook his head, "As soon as the Mercians appeared he shouted that we were undone and the horn should be sounded to save the rest of the army. He cursed Streona."

"That man should be hanged as soon as he comes within a hundred paces of us."

Gandálfr had been listening and he said, "Now that we are back, we can end this siege quickly. They must be hungry in the walls and a determined assault on every side will see us victorious."

"Aye, tell the men that we have this night and tomorrow to rest. Tomorrow night we shall prepare to attack."

I knew that Danner and his men had also been given what might be termed leave. It was not. All that Cnut had given us was the time to recover. Tired men make mistakes and when we attacked the walls we would have to be at our best. Tomorrow would see us return to the walls facing the west gates of the city and Danner and his men relieve those East Anglians who watched the north walls.

I was not roused by my hearthweru with a beaker of ale but by a wail and the clash of arms. The hall in which we slept muffled sounds and so the noise was even more alarming. We raced from the hall and the clamour, from the north, was even louder.

"Arm! Arm!" Bersi and Steana helped me into my mail. "Go and prepare yourselves. I do not know what this clamour portends but I know that it was not planned by Prince Cnut."

My men had only had part of an afternoon and the night to recover but Einar the Fat and Sweyn brought their men to join me. One of Thorkell's men, with a blood-spattered byrnie and mounted on a horse galloped in. "My lord, we are undone. King Edmund brought an army and they attacked the northern defences. The watch that was kept was lax and the city is now reinforced. Thorkell the Tall and the prince are meeting to decide what we will do. He asks that you hold this western longphort."

Sweyn looked at me, "Once again, cuz, we have had victory snatched from us."

Einar was more cynical than my cousin, "No, my friend, we have a leader who is young. This cannot end well. We should return home, Sven."

"Perhaps but my fate is tied to the prince, you may do as you choose Einar for every man has freedom of choice, but I will stay. I cannot betray the sword."

Sweyn and my sons nodded. Sweyn said, "Sven is right. If we tried to leave then the Norns would spin once more. We trust in Sven and in Oathsword. When others have let us down, he has not."

Chapter 13

East Anglia 1016

It was a disaster. Not only were many men killed, but also others deserted and our army shrank. Thanks to our longphorts we held the south bank of the river. The English held the north. Prince Cnut held a council of war. His face showed his disappointment and his look showed where he apportioned blame, Thorkell the Tall.

"The siege is over, what do we do?" He looked at me.

I had thought about our dilemma all day and I had already worked out what we needed to do. I pointed to the bridge, "We need to destroy the bridge. We can use the longphorts to cross but we need to deny the English the ability to attack us across the bridge."

Danner said, "We should move half of our ships from the north bank. If we leave them there then there is always the danger that the English could use them to cross."

Cnut nodded, "And how do you propose to destroy the bridge, Sven? The lack of vigilance has cost us warriors both dead and deserted. We can ill afford to lose more in a bloody assault."

I smiled, "And we do not use men, my prince. We let the river destroy the bridge."

"Do not talk in riddles, Sven, I am not in the mood."

I sighed, "We made rafts to travel from Windles-ore. We simply pack them with kindling, set them alight and crew them with men who can swim. Once they hit the bridge then the crews abandon them and they will burn the bridge down. With luck, we can kill the men who watch the bridge. We could do it now, this night while the English celebrate within Lundenwic's walls. Danner is right. We should dismantle the western longphort if only to allow the rafts free access to the bridge."

Prince Cnut looked around but it was clear that not only was there no other plan but mine met with their approval. "Then, Sven, use your men to make the fire rafts. Thorkell, you move the drekar from the longphort and the rest can line the river and make them think that we are about to attack their bridge."

We hurried back to the great hall where we had tied up the rafts. There had been talk of using them to make rams. This was a better purpose. Steana and Bersi, when I told them, were interested in how it would work. As we toiled to load the oil-soaked kindling aboard, I explained. "When Alfred had the bridge constructed, he left enough space beneath the bridge and between the arches so that small boats could ply their trade. The rafts will jam between the arches so that the flames cannot be doused and the fire will lick the bottom of the bridge. Eventually, the rafts will sink but by then they will have done their work. Even if the bridge and its arches are not completely destroyed the fire will do so much damage as to make it unusable."

Einar paused in his work, "And then what?"

I too paused for the first raft was almost complete, "Einar, what is the difference between the English army and ours?"

He grinned, "We are Danes and better warriors."

"You are right but why?"

He frowned, "You are too clever for me, Sven, I do not understand the riddle."

"We are warriors all the time. Even if we were at home we would practise and prepare for war. The English are farmers. King Edmund has taken them from their fields to fight. If he keeps them here to fight us then the harvest will not be gathered and his people will starve. He has housecarls and he has thegns who can fight for him but that is not the huge army he has gathered. It is now summer. If we wait for a month or so then he will have to let his fyrd return to their fields and then we can bring him to battle."

As much as I wanted to be one of those on the rafts, for it was my plan, we all knew that the best warriors would be needed on the south bank. With Thorkell, Prince Cnut, Danner and Erik of Lade we wanted to make the English think that we were about to attack the English across the bridge. Having lost the northern siegeworks it was the logical place for us to attack. We needed their attention on us and not the river. The crews of the fire rafts were largely made up of helmsmen from the drekar and ships' boys. Bersi was one volunteer and as much as I might have wished to deny his participation, I could not. He was a member of the army and had to take his chances like the rest.

As we marched to the bridge Steana said, "He is a good swimmer, father, and he will be safe."

"I hope you are right, Steana for, if you are not, then your mother will make my life even more unbearable."

When we reached the bridge Prince Cnut had our men arrayed in four ranks. They were banging shields and chanting as we arrived. The gates of the city were open and more warriors were flooding across to make a wall of steel and iron. The bridge had stout gates and towers. Archers and slingers on the tops were sending missiles at those men in the front ranks. They did little harm for shields were held aloft and every man was well protected by a mail byrnie and a good helmet.

When the English started their chant of 'Ut!' we simply subverted it and shouted back, 'Cnut'. The effect was to make it sound as though the English were chanting the prince's name. They stopped but we did not. It was a small victory. In that small victory came the opportunity to make it a complete one for their attention was on us and they appeared not to see the glowing fires that suddenly appeared just forty paces from the bridge. The captains of the rafts had waited to ignite the fires and it was a sudden splash of flames and crackling that alerted those on the bridge to their doom. The river was bringing the rafts inexorably closer and I heard the commands to abandon ships. The sounds of splashes rippled towards us. There was nothing that the defenders could do. They could not fight an inanimate object. They had no poles to use to keep the infernos that blazed ever closer from striking and when the first raft hit it struck an arch and jammed, flames leapt up and started to burn the wooden arches. The other rafts also struck. Some did so underneath the bridge while others made a sort of combustible longphort. Within moments the western side of the bridge was on fire and men were fleeing back into the city. The sheer numbers meant that they would not all make it and the screams of men added to the roar and crackle of the fires. I saw one warrior, clothes and hair aflame who leapt from the balustrade into the river. Others tried to cross to the south bank. There they were met by a wall of spears. It would be a better death than a fiery one. The rafts had done their work and even when they sizzled and sank beneath the river the bridge burned from end to end. It could and would be rebuilt, but not this year. The only way across the river lay well to the west and that, in itself, was a small victory.

Thorkell suggested, the next day as we surveyed the charred remains of the bridge, that we ought to replace the masts of the fleet and anchor it at the south bank of the river at Grenewic. "We do not want to give the English the chance to do the same thing as we did. If we lose the fleet then we lose the war."

He was right and over the next days, the ships were refitted with their masts and sailed down the river to Grenewic. Their holds were filled with the treasures we had taken.

It was our scouts who reported that the English were preparing to march west and cross the river further upstream. Cnut ordered the bulk of the army to march to meet them. He seemed determined to try to gain a victory over the English but I knew that this was neither the time nor the place. We did not take all of our army for we had the ships to guard. Thorkell had been quite right, we had to save the ships or risk losing all.

The result was that we headed to meet King Edmund knowing that we would be outnumbered.

King Edmund was proving to be a much better foe than Cnut and Thorkell had expected. He reached the town of Breguntford before we did and he crossed the river at the bridge there. When we arrived, he was waiting for us. Despite the loops of the river he had needed to negotiate by using horses and sending men secretly before our scouts could see them, they were ready for us when we arrived. Even worse was that he had summoned the fyrd from the north and as we hastily formed a shield wall, we could see the banners approaching from the north.

Danner came to speak with me for our men, the most experienced now, had already formed and locked shields. The warriors of the Danelaw were tardier. "This Edmund is well named, Sven. He has outwitted us."

"I said before, Danner, we should wait until the fyrd are in their fields and then strike. He cannot keep such an army for long."

Danner pointed his spear at the English as more and more men reinforced their ranks. "If they defeat us this day then we will have lost our hold on the English crown. If we leave for Denmark then I know not if we will hold on to it."

I saw that King Edmund was in the front rank of his warriors. What was clear to me was that he was already revered by his men. You can tell such things when you look at how warriors stand. I saw Ulfcetel Snilling with a broad smile on his face, for he had yet to don his helmet. That told me all that I needed to know. In contrast, Prince Cnut sat on his horse, behind the fourth rank of men. He had told us when we had arrived and saw the enemy that we would fight in a shield wall four men deep. I would have used the swynfylking as that had proved more effective and allowed our better warriors to bear the brunt of the fighting.

The conversation between King Edmund, Ulfcetel and the bishops ended. Ulfcetel came forward, bareheaded and with open palms. Behind him walked a housecarl carrying King Edmund's banner. The old warrior halted twenty paces from us. I was in the centre and in his eye line. He spoke to Prince Cnut, mounted on his horse.

"Prince Cnut, I bring an offer from King Edmund." I wondered if he would be reverting to his father's methods and try to buy us off.

The prince did not move forward and I thought it was a mistake. Firstly his voice was not as powerful as the Englishman and secondly, it made him look somewhat fearful. "Speak and I will listen."

I saw Ulfcetel's eyes roll and that told me he was not impressed. He continued, "The king is anxious that men's lives are not wasted this day. He challenges you to single combat. The loser will quit this land. What say you?"

Inwardly I groaned for I knew what his answer would be but I hoped that he would answer better than he did.

"Why should I for we have yet to be beaten? If King Edmund, and I dispute the title, wishes to fight then let it be with my champion, Sven Saxon Sword. Or is he afraid to meet my champion?"

Ulfcetel's eyes lighted on me. He shook his head, "King Edmund is not afraid, Cnut." I noticed that he had dropped the title. "From your answer, I think that you are. You will not fight him?"

"No."

"Then we have tried to save lives and the deaths that will follow today will be upon your head."

The silence of our army should have told Prince Cnut that he had been outwitted. The English army cheered Ulfcetel and the king as they donned their helmets. In battle confidence is everything. The English had it in abundance and we had none.

Gandálfr said, "This will be bloody."

"Aye. The best that we can hope is that we do not lose."

Sweyn said, "Having seen the size of their army, which grows by the moment, I think that you are overly optimistic, cousin."

The English banged their shields as they advanced. In contrast, our army was silent. A few of us began to bang our shields but it was like spitting in the wind and seemed all the more pathetic.

The one advantage, for me, of our formation, was that I was flanked by my three hearthweru and I knew that my sides would be safe. If a blow came at me then it was because one of my hearthweru had died. King Edmund and Ulfcetel jointly led the army but they did not come for me. Instead, they drove at the men of East Anglia. They had been the ones who had broken at Lundenwic and the king recognised the weakness. Coincidentally, it was also the place closest to Cnut and his hearthweru. I had no time to worry about them for I saw that the men of Wessex, led by their thegns and eorledmen were coming directly for my men. I knew why. I was their bane and they wanted the honour of killing me and claiming back the sword. They marched beneath the red and gold wyvern standard and that told me that they were confident of victory.

"Men of Agerhøne, they bring a dragon to beat us. Let us show them that our beak is sharp as are our claws. No matter what happens around us we hold and we fight."

Our men all shouted, "Agerhøne!" and I felt shields pushed firmly in our backs as spears jutted over our shoulders.

Bergil the Black shouted, "Loose!" And arrows and stones flew over our heads. They clattered and cracked on shields, helmets and mail. One man at least fell, but the English had prepared well and the front ranks were all well protected.

Eager to get to us their front rank ran and it was then that the second shower of arrows and stones struck. This time they had more success for the second rank was neither as well protected nor did they have their shields held as high and at least seven fell. Then the spears were rammed at us. The shields in our back held us but that meant we had to take the spears. I felt the eorledman's spear strike my boss and then screech and slide across its front. I jabbed down with Saxon Slayer and hit his byrnie below the rim of his shield. It did not strike true for I did not take my eyes off the man but I tore links and the blade sliced across his leg. He had a wound. Neither of us had a weapon we could use for the press of men was too great and I could not move my hand. Instead, I pulled my head back and butted the warrior in the face. I used the top of my helmet, Now reinforced with the metal bird I bent the nasal on the warrior's helmet. More, his head went back and he began to overbalance. Behind me, one of the second rank seized his chance and rammed his spear into the middle of the Wessex warrior. His falling allowed me to bring my spear up and I hit the standard bearer in the shoulder. The wyvern banner began to fall and housecarls made the mistake of trying to stop it. As soon as they did then the pressure before us waned and we stepped forward to plunge our spears into distracted men. We had the weight of all my men and we took six paces forward.

"Save the banner!"

As soon as I heard the words I shouted, "Agerhøne, on!" One thing I had learned was that when you had momentum you had to use it and we did. Three of the housecarls who had tried to save the banner were easily stabbed and when they fell and the stones and arrows from our slinger and bowmen bit into the weaker rear ranks, then we began not only to push them back but drive them from the field. Men cheered as every spear thrust brought blood. Warriors fell and, unbelievably, we started to drive them further back to where they had started.

Einar the Fat's voice halted us and was like a cold shower, "Lord Sven, halt, the East Angles have broken."

As I pulled my spear from the warrior I had just slain I looked to my right and saw that King Edmund and Ulfcetel had mirrored my advance but having closed with Cnut, their advance had precipitated a flight back to Lundenwic. It was a disaster. We had no choice but to fall back too.

"On my command, we strike and kill as many as we can and then we make a wedge and fall back. We will not let the army down."

What I planned was a hard thing to do and if my men were not as well trained as they were it would be impossible.

We all stepped forward and all our spears were rammed at whoever lay before us. Wounded men were finished off. Others were slain and the rest were wounded. I stood stock still as Gandálfr and Faramir closed up behind me. I did not take my eyes off the enemy. A young warrior, seeing us fall back ran at me waving a twohanded axe around his head. He wanted glory. I timed my thrust to perfection. The axe head was just three feet away when Saxon Slayer tore into his chest and the axe fell from his lifeless hand.

"Lord Sven, back!" Leif Long Leg's voice told me the wedge was in position and as the men started our chant, we moved back.

We are the bird you cannot find
With feathers grey and black behind
Seek us if you can my friend
Our clan will beat you in the end.
Where is the bird? In the snake.
The serpent comes your gold to take.
We are the bird you cannot find
With feathers grey and black behind
Seek us if you can my friend
Our clan will beat you in the end.
Where is the bird? In the snake.
The serpent comes your gold to take.

The sides of the wedge were attacked as we fell back for the rest of the army was also retreating. Some faster than others. Danner's men along with Thorkell's and Einar the Fat were the ones protecting us. I think that we might all have been killed but for the fyrd north of the river. They saw us falling back and instead of racing for the bridge, tried to cross the Temese. I know not what they were thinking for it was not a ford. The ford was over the Bregunt river to the north of the village. As they began to drown so some of King Edmund's army tried to save them. That they did, saved us. It was just eight miles from Breguntford to Lundenwic and we fought the Saxons for all but the last three. We were tired but we had more will to fight. I think it was the initial victory we had enjoyed that kept us going. We had not lost the battle, others had but it cost us. Dreng had fallen and was slain. I did not see it but was told later. That we could not stop to save his body was distressing but we had the rest of the warband to consider. We would honour him when time allowed.

We were the last band to march to the camp and then stop. It was dark when we did so and the mood of the men was ugly. Einar the Fat had endured enough, "Sven Saxon Sword, you are the best leader I have ever followed but you do not lead this army, Prince Cnut does. Tomorrow, I take my ships and return to Denmark. I should have done so when the thought first came into my head. I have now lost three hearthweru as well as my sister's son. I will go and tell the boy what I intend."

He was not the only one. In all, we lost eight crews who simply sailed back to Denmark. Cnut was angry at the loss of so many men which, allied to our battle losses, made us far weaker than we had been.

The next morning he sent for me, "Why did you not command Einar the Fat to stay? He was your man."

I sighed, "Prince Cnut, when a warrior loses faith in his leader then it is as well to cut the threads that bind them."

"He lost faith in you?"

I shook my head, "No, Prince Cnut, in you."

It was as though I had struck him in the stomach. He had clearly not seen what the rest of the army had seen. "But why? We were so close to victory."

I held up my fingers as I spoke, "At Scorranstone it was your flight which lost us the chance to win." I held up a second finger, "Today, you refused single combat and," I held up a third finger, "you followed the men of East Anglia and fled."

He became angry, "Was I supposed to face Edmund Ironside in single combat or stay to be slaughtered by the English?"

I sighed and spoke patiently as I had done when I had first told Bersi, years earlier, that he could not go to war, "You will be a king one day, Prince Cnut, but at the moment you are making bad decisions. There is a time to be aggressive and another to be patient. Now is the time for patience,"

Thorkell nodded, "Sven is right, Prince Cnut. We should quit this river for we cannot take Lundenwic. Let us raid and hurt the English that way."

"Raid?"

"I will take my men and ships and raid Cent and use the Isle of the Sheep as a base. You take the rest of the fleet to Essex between the

Crouch and the Temese. Raid there. Sven was right when he spoke of waiting until the fyrd were gathering their harvests in. Heed his words."

The insults from the English had hurt the prince's pride but his natural good sense came back to him and as he listened to our words he nodded. It was the sensible thing to do. It was only later when we raided Essex that we discovered we had hurt King Edmund more than we had known. He had left for the west to bring reinforcements east. The war was not over.

Chapter 14

The Battle of Assandun October 1016

The fleet which headed north towards Gippeswic was a shadow of the mighty one which had landed so many warriors at Wareham. Battle losses, desertions and the action of men like Einar the Fat had depleted us. I had said nothing but I thought that Thorkell's decision was not a good one. Cent had not been touched in our raids and their farmers had been able to keep working their fields. Our single raid to the Isle of Sheep had been inconsequential for the men of Cent. The Jomsvikings would not have an easy time of it. I knew why he did this. He was proving to himself, Prince Cnut but most importantly, his men, that he was still a mighty leader. It was my name and Danner's that had been spoken around the campfires. It was our deeds that had made men smile. He wanted some of that glory.

We headed for the Orwell. The river went deep into the land of the East Angles. The small village at its mouth Felixstowe offered no resistance, and in return for the passivity, Prince Cnut allowed the people to remain. He sent a knarr back to Denmark for more warriors and with a secure base, we headed up the river towards Mercia. None of us had forgotten or forgiven the treachery of Eadric Streona. Mercia was his land and we would raid him. Once the rivers ceased to be navigable for our drekar, we sent them back to Felixstowe with just the ships' boys and helmsmen and we headed into Mercia and the upper waters of the Temese. We raided.

The men were happy to raid. The best English warriors were still with Edmund or hunting Thorkell in Cent. We chose small towns and large villages and we made the Mercians pay for their attack at Scorranstone. We spent a long month harrying the Mercians. We collected treasure from their nobles and food from their farms. No single raid yielded a fortune but we raided so often that the coins we took grew in our purses. It was the approach of autumn that drove us back to Felixstowe and Essex. When we reached it, we found a large camp and more ships. Thorkell had been driven from Cent and although he had been successful, he had lost more men than was acceptable. The extra numbers came from Denmark. Einar the Fat had returned home but he and his men had made a profit and with a poor harvest then there were men who wanted to feed their families over winter. They came not in longships but knarrs and not in clans but with brothers, uncles and cousins. They came because of Oathsword and Sven Saxon Sword of Agerhøne. Einar was a loyal man and he told of our deeds at the battles. I saw the disappointed look on the face of Prince Cnut when the newly arrived men sought me out. He was still to be accorded the title of king and I knew it rankled him. When he had spoken at Breguntford he had disputed King Edmund's use of the title. The best he achieved was when men called him prince and not all did that.

With the extra numbers, Prince Cnut decided that we had enough men to make one last attempt to take Lundenwic before winter came. There was little enthusiasm for such an attack. I think that Cnut was trying to re-establish his authority and to prove that he did not need either me or Thorkell.

"We will sail, not down the Temese but use the Crouch and head for Lundenwic from the north. We will use stealth to take the city. If we leave our ships on the Crouch and the Roach then they will not know we are approaching. We make a night attack and do not give them the opportunity to man their defences."

Thorkell knew the land better than any and he shook his head, "My prince, you would move many hundreds of men over forty miles and hope that they are not seen? The Raven Banner is a mighty emblem but even that cannot hide us. They will bring us to battle long before we reach the walls of Lundenwic."

The prince set his jaw, "I think that we can do this. Follow me and my plan. If it fails then we return to Denmark and I will find another way to claim my birthright."

I could tell that he was becoming desperate. He was risking all in one final endeavour. I should have talked him out of it but I wanted to go home. When Einar the Fat had sailed, I had envied him. Sweyn One Eye had only stayed because of me and all my men were of the same mind. I had lost half of my hearthweru as well as many good warriors and I was weary. I nodded. Danner saw my nod and added his.

Thorkell spread his arms, "Then let us cast the bones once more. I shall lead this time, Prince Cnut, for I am familiar with the waters. Half of the fleet can sail up the Crouch and half up the Roach." He smiled, "There is a bridge over the Crouch and we could sail our ships up there but I would rather we landed closer to the sea. The rivers are both wider there and allow us to flee should we be discovered."

There were many things I disliked about Thorkell and I knew that I had never truly forgiven his desertion and the attack at Gegnesburh but he was a good planner.

Prince Cnut was in a belligerent mood, "My plan, Jarl Thorkell, is to bring Lundenwic under my heel. If I can we bring the English to battle."

"And my plan, Prince Cnut, will bring that about but I want us hidden for as long as possible. When I was chased from Cent, I heard that Edmund was heading for Lundenwic and he had Eadric Streona at his side. Where is that army? I understand that you are keen to bring them to battle but let us be cunning."

Thorkell the Tall commanded the fleet that sailed up the Crouch and his deputy, Ottar, led the other half, mainly Danner's men up the Roach. We left Felixstowe at night and hoped that King Edmund would think we had sailed back to Denmark. We anchored, in the dark at the mouth of the Crouch and took down the masts and the sails. We rowed up the river in silence and Ottar took the channel that was the Roach River. Thorkell had assured us that there were just three miles between the rivers. If we left men to guard our ships then we would have a secure camp between the two of them and we would be able to use the two fleets quickly if we needed to. I leapt ashore with my men and raced to the small village of Assandun. There were barely twelve houses and they offered no resistance. We put the villagers in the largest building we could, a barn, and I placed a guard on the doors. If nothing else the villagers might prove to make good hostages.

I led my men and we headed for the bridge over the Crouch. Thorkell had told me that there was a village there and it had a palisade. It was four miles away and we reached it just as dawn was breaking behind us. However, we stopped well short of the village and the river. The smell of woodsmoke was more than would be generated by a handful of houses. King Edmund, the men of Cent and the Mercians were there. I knew not how but he had got wind of the proposed attack. We turned and ran back to the camp. Men were still disembarking when we reached it.

Thorkell, Danner and Prince Cnut were at the village I had secured and were enjoying breakfast. My words ended their enjoyment of the hot meal in an instant, "My prince, King Edmund is four miles down the road. It is now daylight and our ships will be seen. He has almost twice our numbers. We must prepare for battle."

It was Cnut who ordered us to form our shield wall and he showed that had learned a little from our campaign thus far. He chose flat ground protected by two small rises in the ground for it was clear that we were outnumbered. The fires that I had seen covered a large area. While we had raided Edmund had gathered men. The driving of Thorkell north had helped the king for he had been able to bring the men of Cent north. He must have used Ulfcetel Snilling to marshal the men from the north and he and the treacherous Eadric Streona had brought the men from the west. It was clear to me that they had converged on Lundenwic. How they had divined our plan to attack from Essex I knew not but I suppose I was not giving the young king enough credit. He would have had spies and our secret departure had failed to fool him. King Cnut had wanted a battle and now he had one.

The slingers and archers were placed before us. They were there to slow down the enemy's advance and then become the rear of our diminished army. The prince was in the rear rank. He was still unwilling to risk himself in the front. Thorkell took the right wing, Danner the left and I held the centre. The Raven Banner was in the third rank behind me and would be the lure to draw the English on. The English, when they came, formed three huge blocks. I spied the Red Dragon Banner of Wessex and the banner of Edmund Ironside. They were in the centre of the three blocks. Eadric Streona led one block and Ulfcetel Snilling the other. I noticed that the distinctive helmet of King Edmund was in the rear rank, like Cnut. He was being cautious and that caution gave me hope.

Both sides brought out priests to bless the weapons and the banners. Prayers were said but I noticed that most of those on our sides kissed their hammers and the hilts of their swords. We were fighting beneath the Raven banner and that had been carried in battle long before any Viking became a Christian. I slipped a long pointed dagger into my left hand. This day would not end quickly and victory would come to those who fought on beyond all hope of victory. I rarely did this but as the priests filtered back to the safety of the rear I stepped from the line and rammed Saxon Slayer into the earth. I drew Oathsword.

"This day we fight an English army that outnumbers us. We have done so before and we have yet to taste defeat. We have fled before now, at Gegnesburh and at Scorranstone but this day we will not." I raised my voice so that the whole army could hear me. "No matter what others do we will stand and we will fight. Sweyn One Eye will have a mighty saga to compose for we will not budge. Let Edmund Ironside and his English bleed. Let it be the treacherous Eadric Streona who flees for we will not. I have made my mark in the earth and from that point, I will not retreat." I kissed the hilt of my sword, sheathed it and withdrew Saxon Slayer from the ground, the metal head now covered in English soil. Not only my men but also the rest of the army cheered. I caught sight of Cnut, for he was mounted on a horse and, nodding to me, he dismounted. He had heard my words and understood their importance.

Back in line, I waited. Bergil the Black marshalled the missile men and, as the English advanced, they loosed their stones and arrows.

"Lock shields!" I held my shield before me and pointed Saxon Slayer at the English. Spears and shields came over our heads. The English would send arrows too and we were too few to risk lucky arrows finding flesh.

"Back." Bergil's orders were, in the main, obeyed and archers and slingers ran to race around the two flanks. Twenty slingers did not and I saw that they were led by Bersi my son. They stood their ground as the English drew nearer. I wanted to cry out to him but I knew that with the chants of the English army my words would not be heard. That their action was deliberate was clear. As the English drew closer so the stones took effect and I saw men fall. A slung stone from twenty paces could be deadly. My son and the brave ships' boys were doing their part but they were doomed to death.

Bersi's voice rang out and I knew it had been his plan and that he had planned well, "Agerhøne back. Let us fly like Alf at Svolder."

They did not run to the sides for they would have been slain but directly at us and I knew what they planned. He remembered the shield jumpers when we had trained. I shouted, "Front rank kneel." I knelt and put the spearhead on the ground, my shield was angled as were all the rest and the boys ran at the shields, jumped on them like berserkers attacking a shield wall and ran across the bridge of shields. As we rose every warrior in the army cheered. It was a small thing and the action had only killed fourteen English warriors but it was defiant and, added to my words, had put heart into the army. When the arrows and stones descended, we were ready. They clattered and crashed like hailstones but our shields afforded us good protection and, peering over the top of mine I was able to see when the three blocks of warriors began to run towards us. Edmund was using his superiority of numbers to drive us from the field.

"Brace!" The shields were lifted from over our heads and pushed into our backs. We placed our right legs behind us and levelled our spears. The English ran at us, encouraged by their thegns who were eager to finally defeat the Danes who had humiliated them for so many years. The English line was not an even one and it would be up to every warrior in our army to strike at the most opportune moment. When I saw the eyes of the Wessex warrior who approached me flicker to the ground to ascertain the footing then that was my moment to strike and my spear went into his right shoulder. The force of my blow allied with the speed of his run ensured that the spear was driven deep within the man's flesh. The force of men behind pushed him so hard that the head tore away a huge piece of flesh and he tumbled to crash his head into the boss of my shield. He fell at my feet but was not dead, not at that moment. He would die but it would be the trampling feet of the warriors behind that would kill him.

I blocked a spear and rammed with Saxon Slayer. Once again, I was rewarded by flesh and the English thegn drove himself onto my spear. The men behind pushed him so close that we were face to face when he died. I used my shield to push his body from my spearhead and awaited the next man. I saw only dead Englishmen before me. Those in our line who had been wounded had been pulled back and replaced. It was something we had practised back in Agerhøne. It ensured that fresh men faced the enemy. Clean and sharp spears found gaps in the enemy's lines and men were wounded. Such was the press of men from behind that the English could not do as we were and their weight of numbers was weakening their attack. The men of the fyrd were largely at the rear and it was they who were pushing the housecarls, thegns and armoured men onto our spears.

The initial onslaught over, the English came at us in small knots of men. Thegns led their oathsworn. I only had two hearthweru left but they flanked me and I knew that Steana had chosen to stand directly behind me. I felt cossetted and protected by their three spears. I jabbed, stabbed and thrust with Saxon Slayer. When I had fought at the battle of Svolder I had been forced to fight on the heaving deck of a ship. Ever since that time, I had fought on land and the earth did not move. I had a good eye and knew how to read an opponent's moves.

It had been midmorning when we had begun to fight and by the time noon approached the English were tiring. They began to fall back. They had not been defeated but they were wearying and I saw waterskins fetched. We did the same but ours were passed from behind us. Steana handed me a skin and said, "We hold them, when do we attack?"

I shook my head as the lukewarm and slightly stale water slipped down my throat, "We will not for they are too many. The bridge over the river is a place we could take them. When they have had enough, they will retire to their camp and it is then that we will consider an attack. By then our spears will be blunted and it will be sword against sword."

Gandálfr said, "They are changing their men. Edmund himself comes to the fore."

I looked at the English and saw that he was right. King Edmund had tired of being a spectator and was bringing his sword and spear to encourage his men. They cheered as he and his housecarls moved forward to take their place in the centre of the English line. The Mercians had suffered at the hands of Danner Liefson and his warriors. Edmund did not face me directly but was closer to Danner. I do not think it was because he feared me but he might have feared that the unreliable Mercians might choose to depart the battle early.

I knew that the English were trying to end the battle when King Edmund had the horn sounded and his warriors raced towards us, screaming wildly and swinging whatever weapon was to hand. Danner's men, in contrast, still had their spears, broken ones having been replaced and so when the English struck Danner's line it was the English who suffered more deaths. I knew it had to infuriate the king. We then had our own battle to face. A little slower than their leader the men of Dorchestershire led by their bishop, Eadnoth, charged us. The bishop was a brave man but he was no warrior. Perhaps he expected lenience and had heard that the Danes were Christian. He fought me and I knew the value of slaying a leader. I drove Saxon Slayer deep into his chest. It was a mercifully quick death but it infuriated the men of Dorchestershire that they redoubled their efforts. Their efforts were valiant but they lacked skill. To my men, who had spent many hours sparring, it was easy to deflect a wild blow and use our spears to hit unprotected legs, arms where the mail did not reach and bare necks. While my men did not forget to keep their shields up the men of Dorchestershire did and dropping a shield, even by a handspan meant a likely death.

The English line lost cohesion whilst ours retained its integrity and the battle degenerated into individual combats. We had fought so long already that when an enemy was slain you looked around for the next. Men no longer raced into battle but moved steadily and purposefully forward. It suited my hearthweru and me. As the English came forward, we looked for weaknesses, a favoured leg, a shield held too low, a slippery piece of ground over which they would have to pass and sometimes even the place they held their spear. My arm was like an adder's tongue as it darted out and caught weary warriors. I jinked my body to the side to avoid blades and used my shield as an extension of my arm. The men of Dorchestershire were done and the effort was spent. They did not flee but they pulled back to form a shield wall and to stop us from advancing. We had no intention of doing so. Had we moved then we would have created a hole into which the English would pour. It took control but my hersirs knew their business.

King Edmund saw that his line was no longer advancing and he pulled back from the fight with Danner's men. It had been an equal fight. Bodies of Danish and English warriors lay intermingled in death.

In the temporary peace, we drank ale and water. We replaced warriors in the front rank who had suffered wounds. Those with broken spears had them replaced and we waited. I looked down the enemy line and saw that Eadric Streona had chosen to wait behind his men. They had been badly handled by Thorkell the Tall and I was not sure that the Mercians would stand much more of this fight.

King Edmund turned to his warriors and shouted, "There is a sword on this field that I would have for it was made on the orders of my grandsire, the great King of England, Alfred." He turned and pointed his spear at me, "Sven Saxon Sword stole the sword and now I will take it and return it whence it belongs. I will use King Offa's Sword." I knew why he shouted as he did, he was trying to ensure that the Mercians stayed on the field. King Offa had been their greatest king.

My men began murmuring, angrily, for they knew I had not stolen the weapon. I just stared at the king. He had made a serious error of judgement. He had angered my men and made a promise I did not think he could deliver. I had seen him fight and whilst he was brave, I knew that I had more skill.

He pointed at me and shouted, "For England!"

His housecarls were equally loyal and keen. They raced ahead of him, eager to be the one to slay me and claim the sword for the king. Had the whole army been as keen then they might have knocked us back but the forty or so men who ran had bodies, blood and gore to negotiate. They arrived in groups. The five who came for me still had their spears and they thrust them as one. They met the metal of our shields and their bosses. I stabbed at the thigh of one housecarl and Saxon Slayer dug deep into his flesh. Steana's spearhead drove into the side of the head of another. It was with a lucky strike or guided by the gods for it hit below the helmet and stabbed into the ear and skull of the man. Faramir and Gandálfr easily dealt with another two and Karl Red Hair, striking from over my left shoulder speared the last of the five. Others fell to the stones and arrows sent by my archers and slingers.

King Edmund shouted, "Men of Wessex, follow me to glory."

The warriors from Wessex had been fighting the Danes and they heeded the call. The attack came between us and Danner. Danner and I had become close on the raid to the west and my friend would not let me down. His men locked shields and began to push into the flanks of the men of Wessex. While the king had reinforced his failing numbers, he had weakened his right flank. As his left flank relied upon Eadric Streona, he was gambling.

Sweyn One Eye shouted, "Oathsword! Oathsword! Oathsword!" The chant was taken up and the men in our third of the army began to bang their shields and the sound echoed and reverberated.

Edmund and a housecarl both came for me at exactly the same time. Edmund was on my left and his spear struck my shield. It was a hard blow but the tip caught on the place the boss joined the wood. It locked the spear and shield together and the housecarl thought he had an easy victory. He rammed his spear at my middle which, thanks to the locked spear, was no longer protected by my shield. I used Saxon Slayer to sweep the spearhead to the side. Such was the force he had used he began to tumble forward and my narrow-bladed dagger, which had lain in my left hand since the start of the battle. was able to drive through the mail links and into the housecarl's side. Steana's spear ended the contest as he rammed it into the middle of the housecarl.

King Edmund, frustrated by his locked spear simply let go of it to draw his sword. I used Saxon Slayer overhand and stabbed down at his shoulder while he tried to draw the sword. He lifted his shield to block the blow but Saxon Slayer still tore through links and his padded shirt. I could not tell if I had drawn blood but weakened links were as good as a wound. The advantage now lay with the king. You cannot duel a spear with a sword, the spear is too unwieldy. I lunged at his foot and he stepped back. As he did so I rammed Saxon Slayer into the ground and drew Oathsword.

The Dragon Sword was a magical sword. I never had to look for it in battle and my hand not only found it easily but the sword itself slid out as though it had been buttered in the scabbard. King Edmund struck the first blow and as our two swords, both legendary in their own way, clashed, sparks flew and it sounded like a bell ringing. Men told me after that the whole battle stopped in mid-blow when the swords struck. I had been expecting such a sound but, clearly, Edmund had not and he was taken aback. I punched with my shield and caught the back of his hand. Such blows do not win fights but they help and I knew that the boss on my sword would have hurt his hand. He had been trained well and he recovered quickly. It was clear to both of us that the battle would not be won with a few blows. Our swords, shields, helmets and armour were too good and we both had skill. Mine was greater but I did not delude myself. I would have to wear him down.

I began to swing and smash at his sword but I did not use the edge, I used the flat. King Edmund kept hacking at me with the edge of his sword and I knew that it was becoming duller with every swing. I varied the strokes so that sometimes I went for the shield, then the head, and sometimes the sword. I also let him know that he was fighting a warrior with great experience and two lunges were sent at him. The strike to his head unnerved him and his head reeled. When I lunged again, a few blows later then, he jerked his head back and the tip of my sword drew blood as my blade went through his byrnie and into his flesh. It was not a mortal strike but it would weaken him.

We were no longer fighting in a line and my hearthweru, along with Steana and my warriors were ready to protect my flanks when his housecarls saw the chance to hurt me. In such a way his bodyguards were whittled down. In trying to defeat me they were weakening the defence of their king.

It was in the late afternoon that the breakthrough came. My attention was on the king and I only had eyes for him. His sword had almost managed to strike at my body and I was only saved by my quick reactions and the rim of my shield. I was aware, however, that I could see Danes in my eye line to the left and right of the men fighting alongside the king. I knew that I was forcing the king back. He stumbled over a body and had to take longer steps to avoid falling over. He fell into the standard bearer and the wyvern dropped. It did not touch the ground but it was lowered. The voice that I heard was Eadric Streona's. Perhaps he had been waiting for such an opportunity or he might have actually believed what he said but the words must have cut the king to the quick. "The king is dead, all is lost. Flee!" He and his Mercians left so quickly that I could not help but think that this had been planned. The hole that appeared was a disaster for the English.

With Danner on one side and Thorkell on the other pushing forward, the king would be trapped and either captured or killed. Either way meant that the crown would come to Cnut. He had won.

I renewed my efforts and I caught the king again as his head involuntarily flickered to where Streona had stood. This time my sword went deeper and I knew that I had hurt him. One more strike would end the battle, win the war and give the crown to Cnut. It was his housecarls that saved him. They were loyal to death and beyond. There were just twelve of them left and while four grabbed the king and pulled him away the other eight hurled themselves at me. They did not take me by surprise but it was like an attack by berserkers. None of them tried to defend themselves but were just intent on the killing of the Dane with the Dragon Sword. Had I led any other men than my own then I would have been dead but these were my hearthweru, Steana, my cousin and the men of Agerhøne. They reacted just as quickly as the housecarls and while I fended off blows from swords, shields, daggers and even teeth, they ruthlessly killed the English warriors. Horses were brought and the king, his standards and his last four housecarls galloped off west, towards the bridge.

My men and I were too exhausted to chase them. Thorkell and Danner were in the same position but King Cnut now mounted, as were his hearthweru galloped through the fleeing English to chase down the King of England. Cnut wanted the crown. I looked around and saw that while my hearthweru, Sweyn One Eye and my sons lived, Leif Long Leg and many other warriors had fallen. They had all died well, with swords in their hands but I felt their loss. That the English had lost more than twice our numbers did not make it easier for me for I knew not the English but I had lost loyal men who had followed me for years. It was a victory and a great one but with it came great sadness.

Those that were able to, joined Prince Cnut in the pursuit but you could tell the ones who had fought all day. Most could not even raise a sword. I kissed Oathsword and sheathed it before retrieving Saxon Slayer.

I shook my head, "Once more King Edmund has proved a slippery foe. We had him and he slipped through our fingers."

Thorkell gave me a sad smile, "Treachery won the day for us. Darkness was coming and had Streona not betrayed his king then the battle would have ended at dark and the English left the field. Their army is defeated. Come the morrow we will mount horses and chase him. This time we forget Lundewic. One more push will see Edmund in our hands and then Cnut will be king."

Danner said, quietly, "Did the prince draw his sword?"

Steana snorted, "Aye, when he led his hearthweru to chase the beaten king. Until then he watched the fight from the back of his horse."

I pulled my son to me, "Steana, Cnut is of royal blood and it is different to ours. They do not think as we do. When he is king then he will carry the weight of England on his shoulders. I will take your mother and we shall move to Norton. I will hang up Oathsword and see if I can learn to be a farmer. That is the difference. My oath takes me to the throne and no further."

Thorkell said, "We shall see, we shall see."

Chapter 15

The Battle of Soudley 1016

Even if we had wanted, we could not have left to follow the prince. The autumn darkness had descended like a blanket but before we could even think about food, ale and sleep, there were wounded to be tended to and enemy warriors to be given the warrior's death. It was not kind to let men bleed to death. The English priests had left and our healers were tending to our men. All toiled to clear the field. We buried our men and had just lit the fires to cook the food when Cnut and his pursuers rode in,

We had taken off our mail but we grabbed weapons when we heard the sound of hoofbeats.

It was a despondent Cnut who dismounted and said, "We could not reach him. The press of men at the bridge over the Crouch was too great. We tried to ford the river but it was in full spate."

Olaf the Grim said, "We took one of his priests and in exchange for his life he told us that the king had fled to Wales. He has allies there."

Thorkell looked at Danner and me, "Then we have time. The men of Wessex will return to their homes. He will have to persuade the Welsh to fight for him and the men of Mercia."

Cnut brightened, "Then all is not lost?"

Thorkell looked at the prince, "If he crosses the Severn and goes into Wales then he is in exile. He is still a threat but the kingdom will be yours. He pointed to the pile of bodies that represented the leaders of the English army who had fallen, "Eadnoth, Bishop of Dorchester, Wulfsige, Abbot of Ramsay, Ælfric, Eorledman of Hampshire, Godwin eorledman of Lindsay and the slayer of my brother Hemingr, Ulfcetel Snilling. He has no leaders left and the fyrd will slink back to their farms. He has one more opportunity to throw the bones and that will be on the Severn. We have the chance to gain you the crown that you seek, Prince Cnut."

He smiled, "You all fought bravely today and none more so than you, Sven Saxon Sword. What prize would you like for your noble efforts?"

"You have promised me Norton and that is enough. If I have the valley to rule then I shall be content. I will just be happy to sheathe Oathsword."

"But what of the wars afterwards?"

I became suspicious, "What wars, my lord?"

"To have the crown is one thing, but we must be secure in the knowledge that none can steal it from us. I would have strong borders."

I shook my head, "I swore an oath to put the crown upon your head." I waved a hand at the men who stood around us, "There will be others here who still crave war. There may be warriors abed in Denmark who will join you. They can defend your land."

Danner, too, did not like the way the conversation was going and he said, with an air of finality, "Let us first catch this king and defeat him once and for all and then we can put our mind to the future. The Norns are still spinning." He looked at me, "Had the king stayed to fight me then, perhaps he might not have lost but the Norns spun and he moved to fight you. I am a warrior who is afraid of no man but Oathsword is a blade I would not face. I have seen since I came to this land the effect it has on the battlefield and there is something magical about it. It is a Dragon Sword and any warrior who is wise does not fight it."

As we ate and drank, I thought not on Danner's words for he had spoken that way to me before but of Cnut's. He was not just talking about holding what he had he was thinking of taking more. Would the crown of Denmark appeal once he had England? What of Norway? Perhaps he had desires on the Scots and the Welsh. I did not sleep well that night and it was nothing to do with the battle. It was not the spectres of the past that haunted me but the spectres of the future. A future where Bersi and Steana fought wars for Cnut's glorification. When this was over, I needed the counsel of my foster father.

We had a fleet and we could have used that fleet to sail to the Severn but that would have meant us risking the whole fleet on the teeth of the coastline of An Lysardh. The risk was too great and although Prince Cnut pressed for us to use that route the three of us, Thorkell the Tall, Danner Liefson and I all argued that we could sail back to the mighty harbour at Wareham. From there it would take a couple of days of marching to reach the Severn and we would be more refreshed than the English who would have marched all that way. We boarded our ships and were laden with the treasure we had taken. The nobles who had fallen to our swords had good mail, jewels, and fine weapons and we took from both them and their housecarls. They had left their baggage train and the gold and silver objects that they had left were ours. We fitted the masts and sailed down the river to head west along the coast of Wessex. Not all followed the prince. Sweyn One Eye was amongst many ships that decided that they had done enough and they headed east for home. Other ships had lost so many men in the battle that the heart had gone from the crews and they took their booty and headed home. Half of the ships that had sailed up the Crouch and the Roach anchored in the harbour. We used the island we had occupied in the first raid and men were left to guard it. The army that marched north to the Severn was a pale shadow of the one that had fought at Assandun. Before we had burned them, we had counted the English dead and knew that they had lost two to every one of ours. Even Prince Cnut and his oathsworn had slain many at the bridge over the Crouch when they had tried to hack and slash their way to the king. Many English fields would lie untended. Even though we had a smaller army than when we had begun, the King of England had even fewer and until he found allies, he was vulnerable; with or without Offa's Sword.

This was a familiar country to me and the men who remained with me. We had raided as far as Brycgstow and fought at Scorranstone. King Edmund had chosen his escape route wisely. He would have to cross the Severn deep into the land of Gloucestershire but so would we. Cnut grumbled all the way north, through a deserted Wessex, that we could have sailed our drekar up the Severn and landed with dry feet. This way we might have to ford the river or build rafts. Cnut had never sailed around the western side of this land. The rocks of Syllingar had claimed many ships and we were now an army pared to the bone. He may have been right but the Norns were still spinning and Thorkell, Danner and I were of one mind. The three of us knew the power of the three sisters.

Once we were twenty miles north of Scorranstone Lief and Einar led their mounted scouts north to find the trail of the English. It was the freshly dug graves that gave us the first clue. Men had marched many miles from Assandun but some had finally succumbed to their wounds. The fresh graves in the small village churchyards were worth investigating and the villagers intimidated, no doubt, by the mailed warriors who demanded answers, told them that King Edmund and the remains of his army had passed through some days before. They were heading for Gleawecastre where there was a burh and a bridge. From there it was a short march to Wales. King Edmund was so desirous of hanging on to his throne that he was willing to sup with the Welsh. I knew that our next battle, perhaps our final battle, would be in the west along that border.

I marched with fresh energy at the thought of just one more fight for Prince Cnut. Once King Edmund was defeated, and in all likelihood, killed, then there could be no opposition to Prince Cnut as king. Indeed since Assandun, the prince had received many embassies from Saxon nobles pledging allegiance to our cause. The English had pinned all of their hopes on Assandun but Streona's treachery had undone all. The next Witan, if Edmund was no longer alive, would see them demand the crowning of Cnut.

The army that approached the burh of Gleawecastre was not as large as it might have been but our victory at Assandun and the other battles meant that every warrior who stood behind Prince Cnut had good mail and a good helmet. The Saxon swords which had fought so hard were now wielded by Danes who knew how to use them. The glittering army that stood in the early afternoon with the low autumn sun glinting off mail, helmets and spears was a statement that Prince Cnut led a formidable force. Assandun and the departures of so many warriors also had an effect on Prince Cnut. He did not consult his three wise warriors but, instead, walked with the bishops who had defected to our side and stood before the gates of Gleawecastre. He spoke in English.

"Men of Gleawecastre I am Prince Cnut and a Witan has chosen me as the next King of England. Edmund Ironside was defeated by my army in Essex and now he has fled like a dog with his tail between his legs to consort with the Walhaz. Any claims he had to be king are now forfeit. Open your gates and let my army cross through your burh and your bridge so that we can stop your ancient enemies from ravaging your land. Let my army defend Gleawecastre. I will now pray with my priests whilst you debate." They all symbolically knelt and held crosses.

I stood with Thorkell and Danner and Thorkell nodded, "Clever. He appeals to their fear of the Welsh and now shows himself to be a Christian. He is defeating the men of Gleawecastre through cunning."

"Will it work?"

I smiled, "Aye, Danner. Thorkell is right and remember these are Mercians. They have been led by the most treacherous man these islands have ever seen. If they were going to fight then the banner that flies from the gate would be the Wessex wyvern and Edmund would be inside to make us bleed upon its walls. Edmund has crossed the river."

It took until the sun began to dip below the western horizon for them to agree. The only thing they asked was that we would do it at dawn. Cnut agreed. Thorkell shook his head, "They are hiding their treasures, Prince Cnut."

"They need not do that, Thorkell the Tall, for I said that we would not harm them and I meant it."

"The men of Mercia this far west have only heard of the deprivations of the Danes. They may be less suspicious after we pass through and then they may reveal their wives and their daughters but, trust me, when we pass through this burh, we will see only men."

Thorkell knew the Mercians and was proved correct. The gates opened and the streets leading to the bridge were lined with men who dutifully bowed as we passed. They would wait to see who emerged victorious before they truly accepted Cnut.

Once on the other side of the Severn, the scouts left once more. Now that Sweyn had sailed for home I spent more time on the march with my sons and my two hearthweru. Bersi Shield Jumper, as he was now called, had gained great honour by his action. The other boys had followed his orders. He was not the oldest of the slingers but he knew how to command. He had done something that no other slinger had ever done, he had changed the course of a battle. The slinging of the stones from such a close range had managed to thin the ranks of the best housecarls and had diminished the effect of their attack. There were other factors that had contributed to our victory in Essex but every man who marched with us knew that the slingers of Agerhøne had done more than many seasoned warriors. Consequently, he marched with his father and his brother and we spoke of the future.

"Will Edmund fight, father?"

"Aye, Steana. He fled with many men and there were others who followed him. He will have gathered those who hate us as he heads west but it will be the Welsh who will form the bulk of his army if they choose to join him."

"And why would they do that, lord?"

"Because of the concessions he might make. The Mercians let us through easily for they will fear that King Edmund, in return for a Welsh army, will concede Mercian land back to the Welsh. The river we have just crossed was always seen as the border between the two lands. The Mercians, led by the mighty Offa, took the land and made it theirs. I do not doubt for a moment that, thanks to Eadric Streona, he will gladly give it back to them. He wants to be king."

"And when we beat him, then we go home?"

I smiled at Bersi, "And you are so keen to leave the battlefield?"

"No, but when we are at home then I can train to be a warrior. It is not age that makes a warrior but size and skill. I will eat better in Agerhøne and practise more."

I nodded at the wisdom in one so young, "As much as I would wish to sail home my oath was to see Prince Cnut secure on the English throne. Even with Edmund defeated it will take a few weeks to see if Cnut can hold onto the crown. Then we will sail home and after that, we come back."

"Come back?"

"Remember, Steana, I have a manor in the north I have never seen. It is your mother's home and I know that she would spend the remainder of her life there. She was taken by me to Denmark against her will and at heart she is English. I am resigned to take her there."

"You do not wish to go to live in England, lord?"

"I am honour bound to take her there, Faramir. When I took her as a thrall to tend to my mother I did so with an uneasy heart for it is not in my nature to keep another as a slave. The valley in the north is, by all accounts, a pleasant place." I shook my head, "The only time I went there was as a raider. I just saw the walls and defences. I have been told that there are hills and valleys which are unlike anything we have in Denmark. It will be an adventure."

Gandálfr knew me well and he said, "But it will not be Agerhøne and you will not have your people around you."

"There you have it, Gandálfr."

Steana had been quiet for a while and he said, "You might be surprised, father, King Harald is not as popular as was King Sweyn. The land is not as fertile as it might have been. There are some younger warriors," he waved a hand behind him, "many of them have fought with you here, who would happily seek a new life in a new land."

I nodded and then advised, "Let us fight one battle at a time before we risk the wrath of the Three Sisters. Edmund is not yet done."

The scouts found the English at Soudely in the Forest of Dean. Edmund must have known that we were pursuing him and he chose Soudely for its defensive possibilities. There was a stream before the huddle of houses that rose up the bank. This time he would sit and await our attack. We arrived at the battlefield in the late afternoon. The scouts had reported their find at noon and we had hastened to pin the English before they could flee again. We made a defensive camp to the south and east of the tiny hamlet. We went with Prince Cnut to view their defences.

The stream lay parallel to the road which went northeast and southwest. The road we were on and which led to the village was fordable and hardly an obstacle but, as we stood, safely beyond bow range, Thorkell pointed out that any shield wall that attempted to cross it would become disordered. He pointed to the slopes above the houses. They were tree covered, "He has chosen his defence well. It may be, Prince Cnut, that he has Welsh allies. They are the best of bowmen and with the elevation of the slope, they could rain death upon us. We are well protected by mail but crossing a stream may well allow him to hurt us."

"But we have him pinned, Thorkell the Tall. He cannot flee. We defeat him now and the crown is ours."

I pointed to the road, "Prince Cnut, we have been lured deep into a land that the Welsh covet. He could flee north or south and disappear. Thorkell the Tall is right. He has chosen well. Remember Scorranstone?"

The prince's narrowed eyes told me that he did not like to be reminded of his flight. "I remember well, Sven Saxon Sword. Danner, I will lead your men into the battle tomorrow. Thorkell will be on the right and you, Sven, will be on the left. We advance in three warbands and we will attack just after dawn so that the sun is in the eyes of any archers."

He would not be dissuaded and we prepared our attack. I took Bersi to one side, "What you did at Assandun was brave, some might say reckless. I need you to be more cautious tomorrow. One day I would have you be a warrior in the shield wall with your brother and me and not pinned by a Welsh arrow here in the Forest of Dean."

"I will obey, father, but I am your son and the grandfather I never met whose name I bear was also a reckless man. Perhaps it is in my nature."

I found myself clutching the hammer of Thor. In naming him after my father I had thought to honour the warrior who had been much maligned. Had I, in fact, cursed my son?"

The king's banner was in the centre of their line when the sun came up. Mailed housecarls were before their king but I could see no archers. I knew then that Thorkell was right. The archers were hidden in the trees. Prince Cnut had gambled on the sun shining in their eyes. The Norns had spun and the grey and black clouds gave us no help. The prince was with Danner and his men but in the second rank. I guessed that was on the orders of Danner who was being practical. He needed his best men in the front rank for Edmund would have the best of housecarls close to him. At least the prince was finally showing that he was willing to fight for his crown.

It felt strange not to have Sweyn One Eye and his men close by. We were a smaller, more compact band that prepared to march across the stream and muddy ground. I saw that, in the night, the English had used the stream and the land before it to make water and empty their bowels. I knew why they had done so. If they could make just one warrior slip then they might profit from that fall.

The prince and his priests knelt and prayed. The Christians in the army did the same but Danner and his men did not. Danner, like me, had made a blót. We both believed in the old ways. Danner waved his spear and we marched across the stream. We held our shields above our heads. If arrows were to come then they would come from the slopes and fall upon us. There were none before us. I studied the water as I crossed for I did not want to slip on a stone. The water, for this was Gormánuður, was icy. It was deep enough to come over the tops of my boots. Fighting in soggy boots was never pleasant. The arrows fell as we stepped into the water. They struck our shields but our wisdom in holding them above us meant that we suffered no hurt. I knew that there would be flights embedded in the shield but that could not be helped. We marched just ten paces beyond the beck and then halted.

"Shield wall!"

I gingerly lowered my shield and peered over it as Steana, standing behind me, placed his shield over my head and tucked in behind me. He had fast hands but an arrow still struck my helmet. There would be a scratch but it was so well made that it would do no damage. Bersi, my slingers and my handful of archers were behind us. Bergil the Black still led them but Lief Long Leg was no longer there to marshal my reserves. I ordered the slingers and archers to take shelter behind the third rank. They would be less effective but I did not think that they would make a difference this day. The English were as we had been at Assandun. They stood behind their wall of wood and waited. We would have to endure the arrows that fell as we headed up the slight slope and this time it would be we who would have to hack our way to their banners.

It was a Mercian banner that faced us. Saxon Slayer was a well-balanced weapon and I held it perfectly. The first blow would always be the best for carrying a long spear tired a man more than wielding a sword. I looked at the eyes of the housecarl whom I faced. It was not their leader. I would have had to adjust my position to face him. The shield of the warrior had a red and white design upon it. He had a metal boss but I could not see any metal studding the shield. His byrnie came below his knees for he was not a tall man. That made me decide my attack. We did not run. The ground was slippery and a fall could be fatal. Steana and the others lowered their shields and placed them on our backs when we were twenty paces from the Mercians. We needed the strength of their shields and would have to trust in our helmets and mail. Steana's spear poked reassuringly over my right shoulder. I did not take my eyes off the Mercian. His helmet had no nasal. Some men did not like them. His spearhead was just a handspan long. I wondered if he had sharpened it. There were men who did not although I knew not why.

I heard the Mercian order, "Thrust!" when we were just three paces from them. I did not thrust Saxon Slayer, instead, I punched with my shield. The Mercian was not expecting that and the spear he jabbed at me slid up across my boss and into the air. I continued the punch and my shield hit first his hand and then his nose. The men behind were pushing but he still reeled and it was then that I thrust Saxon Slayer as Steana rammed his spear towards the Mercian's face. I do not know which of us killed him but it mattered not for he died and his body slid to the ground. I pulled back my arm and rammed blindly at the man behind. I did not hit a shield but felt the head grate through metal links and then into soft flesh. It was like the bursting of a dam as we attacked their third rank. They were not armoured and our spears were still sharp. When Faramir, Gandálfr and I slew the three men before us then there was no one left ahead of us.

I heard Welsh shouted from the woods and the distinctive noise of flight. We had destroyed the English right flank. We turned and began to spear the Mercians who suddenly found themselves attacked from the side and the front. As the third rank had no armour they fled and we began the slaughter of the Saxons.

The horn that sounded from the side was English and took us by surprise. Was this another trick? We turned as King Edmund and the men of Wessex mounted horses that had been fetched and the army that had been fighting Danner and Thorkell headed north, back to England. Edmund had outwitted us. He had lured us to battle and ensured that his route back to England was clear. I had never seen so many horses. He must have had four hundred or more. We were helpless to stop them for, unlike the Welsh who had been behind the Mercians, the rest stayed and loosed arrows at the other two warbands.

"Agerhøne, with me!" I raced with my men up into the trees. The Welsh before us had fled and once in the trees, I led my men north to attack the Welsh archers in the flank. They did not stay long but their attack had been enough to prevent pursuit. By the time we had cleared the slopes, it was over and, leaving my men to search the dead and ensure that none were feigning death I went with my sons and hearthweru to join the prince.

I spied a huddle of men over a body and I feared, for a moment, that the prince had fallen. I quickly realised that King Edmund would not have fled if the prince was dead. It was Danner who lay on the ground. His mail byrnie had been hacked open. The body of the butchered housecarl with the Danish axe still in his hand told me who his killer had been. Danner's entrails were hanging from the wound. His men parted and he gestured for me to kneel and speak with him. I handed Steana Saxon Slayer and taking off my helmet knelt.

Blood trickled from the side of his mouth, "I kept my oath. That housecarl would have had Cnut's life had I not stepped before him. He fought well, Sven." I nodded. "I have a long slow death before me. I beg you, take the Dragon Sword and while I can still feel and hold a sword, give me a warrior's death."

I nodded and drew the sword, "It has been an honour to fight alongside a great warrior. I will see you in Valhalla."

"And I will be waiting with a horn of mead, Sven Saxon Sword."

He nodded and I ended his life.

His hearthweru nodded and Oleg said, "That was well done, Sven Saxon Sword. Now we will bury him."

They lifted his body and I stood. I wiped the blood from my sword and sheathed it. Prince Cnut and Thorkell joined me. Thorkell said, "He died well."

Cnut nodded, "And he hurt Edmund before he died. Edmund Ironside will need a healer. We must follow as soon as we can."

I shook my head, "He may be wounded but this was planned. You do not keep four hundred horses so close to a battle unless you intend to use them. He is heading back to England and we are stuck here."

Thorkell the Tall shrugged, "Then we march back and we find him. Danner Liefson has ensured that he needs to find a house of healers and that helps us. We follow the road and seek him and his army where there are monasteries and priories. This is the borderlands and there will not be many of them. We have hope, Prince Cnut, and this time we have the advantage. He has but four hundred men with him. We lost few men."

He might have been right but the one we had lost was irreplaceable.

Chapter 16

The peace of Ola's Island 1016

As we headed north, I wondered just how long Danner's men would stay with us. He had been the one who had shown the greatest of loyalty. If Prince Cnut ever became king, then he would need to recruit an army and soon.

Our scouts soon found the English or rather they found where they had travelled. You cannot hide four hundred horses easily. Their dung and the grass they had grazed acted like a signpost as they headed steadily north. The king did not head across the bridge to Gleawecastre but continued north. Our army was half a day behind the mounted horsemen and when the English finally stopped, just twenty-five miles from where we had fought them, it was at a monastery. Danner had wounded the English king badly enough to need a healer.

When it became clear that we would not catch them before dark we stopped and entered the burh of Gleawecastre. It might well have been that the king had tried to enter the burh and was refused entry for we were welcomed and we enjoyed hot food. There were just three of us who gathered, after we had eaten, to discuss what we might do. None of us relished another battle. The English had shown that unlike when the weak Æthelred had led them the new king had steel for a backbone.

"Will he surrender the crown?" Cnut asked Thorkell for the Jomsviking knew the young king better than any having served King Æthelred.

"No, he will not, Prince Cnut. He has shown that he is clever and resourceful. We appear to have him but who knows? He may have another plan. I think that there might be another fight ahead of us."

He chewed his food thoughtfully as though trying to work out what was the meat he was eating. After he swallowed, he drank some ale and wiped his mouth, "We need more men. I will send word to my brother."

I shook my head, "Prince Cnut, I would not ask your brother for anything. Look at the leader he sent last time. Bloodaxe was there to undermine you. Danner was a different matter but your brother is more likely to send a Bloodaxe."

"Why?"

"It makes it less likely that you will gain the throne and makes England weak. When you become king," we had learned that Prince Cnut did not like the word if, "then you will rule a land which is richer than Denmark. He knows that you want the Danish crown too. He does not want you to be King of England."

My words struck a chord and I saw Prince Cnut reflect on them for he was silent until we retired.

The next morning we marched in line of battle towards the Benedictine monastery. Prince Cnut would not attack the abbey and we did not think that the English would use its walls for defence but we had to be prepared for an ambush. This was a fight for the crown of England and there would be men willing to sacrifice their lives if it meant killing the Danish pretender to the crown.

We were met on the road but it was by a pair of Benedictine monks. Their robes guaranteed their safety but Thorkell the Tall and I studied the woods that lined the road for signs of an ambush.

"Prince Cnut, we have been sent by King Edmund to ask you to meet with him on St Ola's Island." He pointed to the river, "It lies just two miles that way. He is there now with two advisers and he asks that you bring two." Prince Cnut frowned and the monk continued, "We two will be hostages and surety for your safety." The elder of the two smiled, "I am the prior." Whilst I might not have trusted the monks the other two were Christians and they nodded. The prior pointed to the river, "There is an island in the middle of the river, Prince Cnut and the king asks you to cross by means of a punt. He would have the river separate the armies. Whilst lords and nobles might obey the truce, he feels that some of the ordinary warriors might still fight."

Thorkell gave a wry smile, "It may mean that you two might well have a wetting."

"A man who has been baptised fears not a dousing in the water. We are Benedictines and we will endure the cold."

We marched to the island where we saw the king and two eorledmen. There was a large punt tethered on the east bank. I could see the monastery walls across the river, on the west bank. The prince turned to his hearthweru, "Guard the monks. You can see us from here although I doubt that there will be any treachery."

The prior said, "There will be no treachery."

A punt was tethered to the bank and we punted our way across. There was a table, obviously carried from the monastery and two chairs facing each other. Edmund sat on one and behind him stood the eorledmen. As we walked the few feet from the punt to the chair, which was waiting for Prince Cnut, I studied the king. He looked pained. Danner had hurt him but how much was hard to tell. I knew he bore a wound from me too. Was this the reason for peace talks? I hoped that those skills in speaking and divining men's thoughts that Cnut appeared to have in abundance would not desert him now.

The prince sat and the two men studied each other in silence. I looked at the two warriors. I smiled when I saw their eyes drop to the sword at my waist. They feared it and me more than I feared them. We had been a Saxon bane for many years. Priests, bishops, a king, princes and champions had tried to diminish its power and effect but had failed.

King Edmund began the talks and that was a sign that he still felt he had superiority over Cnut. "It is time, Prince Cnut, for us to stop fighting. We have both had victories and suffered losses. We have lost great warriors and friends. Enough blood has been shed for the crown."

The prince's voice was even as he spoke, "You concede the crown to me?"

Edmund smiled, "No, and if you are unwilling to negotiate a peace then we will resume this war and fight until men can stand no more and the land yields corpses and not crops."

"If you are not here to offer me anything then we shall leave. I can send to my brother for more men."

He nodded, "And I could send to my stepmother and have her bring her Norman kin over here. That would be a fine battle would it not? Norman and English against Dane and at the end of it the crown would be worn not by you or me but by King Harald or the Duke of Normandy."

"Then what is it that you offer?"

He winced as he waved his arm to the north and I knew that he was hurting, "We will divide England up. I will rule Wessex, Mercia and Cent. I give you Danelaw, Northumbria and Essex."

Cnut laughed, "That is good negotiating, Edmund, but only for you. I have taken Essex and Northumbria already and Danelaw has ever been Danish. You give me what I have now and yet it is you that has a handful of warriors and is clearly wounded from the battle. If that is all that you have then my men and I will return to the army and recommence the battle." He began to rise.

King Edmund put his hand out to restrain him and winced once more, "Sit, I beg you. We have just begun to speak. We fought far longer." He nodded to me, "Sven Saxon Sword and I exchanged blows for many hours. Surely you can spare a few minutes more?" Cnut did not sit. "Men say you are a Christian prince. If so, it is your duty to try to save lives when you can." Cnut sat. "I give you all that you already hold it is true but what if I offer Lundenwic too?" I saw the eyes of the two eorledmen narrow. What Edmund had said was not a surprise but it was clearly a bone of contention. "You know that to take it you would bleed away your army. It is a good prize and one you seek."

"Lundenwic, the land north of the Temese, Danelaw, Essex and Northumbria?"

Edmund nodded, "And we would jointly rule the land. We would swear never to fight each other while the other lived."

"And when one of us dies?"

"Then the other would inherit the crown." He leaned forward, "There would be hostages."

"Of course. An interesting offer King Edmund and I am tempted but…"

"And we will compensate your men for their lack of the opportunity to raid. We will pay Danegeld."

Cnut stood, "You allowed me two advisers, I will stand apart and speak to them."

As we moved closer to the river, I saw the two Saxons put their hands on their swords. They did not trust us. The peace offer was a very dangerous one. The negotiations had been spoken but the actual treaty would be written down. Killers could be hired by both sides to end the life of either of the two leaders. I realised that this did not hasten my return to Agerhøne, it extended it indefinitely.

"What say you?"

Thorkell smiled, "You have decided already Prince Cnut. You can see that Edmund is hurt and we all know that wounds that are hidden are often the most dangerous. Danner may have handed you the crown by giving Edmund Ironside a mortal wound."

"There are hostages, Prince Cnut."

He nodded, "And I have already chosen them." He gave me a strange look. "You are right, Thorkell, but I wished to make Edmund Ironside think that I debate and have doubts. I do not." He turned and headed back to the table.

"We are agreed, King Edmund, so long as I have the title of King of England alongside you."

"Of course." He nodded to one of the eorledmen who went to the bank and waved. "To ensure that all is done well we shall bring a Bible and have the monks write down the words that we have spoken. When oaths are sworn and hostages named then we shall clasp hands and be as brothers."

The priests had been prepared and they were punted across. The first order of business was the swearing of the oath. The Bible was placed between them and they put their hands upon it. The oath was spoken by the priest first in Latin and then again in English and finally in Danish. The two men swore and the oath would be binding. If I had placed my hands on the Bible, I would have felt no obligation to honour it. The Oathsword would have been a different matter. The wording of the treaty and its transcription took time. More priests were summoned with food and drink. A sign of the change in circumstances was that the priests pointedly ate and drank first to show that there was no poison. Cnut and Edmund would both need food tasters in the future. My spirits were low. We had peace but the price that I would have to pay for that peace was that I would not be able to leave Cnut's side. He would need the protection of Oathsword. The amount of Danegeld was a point of argument, King Edmund had agreed to an amount but Cnut asked for more than even Æthelred had been willing to pay. I understood Edmund's reluctance to part with so much gold. It would mean that his people endured more taxes than before and might turn some of them against him.

Eventually, a more reasonable sum was agreed and a date for its delivery was set for the spring of the next year at Lundenwic. It was agreed that both kings and their men would ride to Lundenwic to ensure that the inhabitants of the city complied with the arrangements. Then Edmund would go to the new capital of England, Oxford. It was a clever choice as it was also on the Temese and close to Lundenwic. The two men had agreed on peace but neither would let the other stray too far from his sight. If there was treachery then the battle would be joined quickly.

"And now to the matter of hostages." King Edmund spoke slowly so that the priest could write down their names. The most prominent hostages offered by King Edmund were his infant sons, Edward and Edmund. As they were so young then his wife Edith would have to be with them. That was a surety that the English would not break the treaty. The others were nobles but more dispensable.

We all looked to Cnut who reeled off the names of four minor hersirs. I saw King Edmund frown. He sought one as important as his family. Cnut said, "We know that these are not the same rank as your sons, King Edmund but I offer, as my most important hostage and surety for peace, Sven Saxon Sword."

When I saw Thorkell avoid my gaze then I knew this had been planned before the meeting. Not only was I doomed not to go home but in the event of King Edmund being killed then I would be executed too. Cnut could not hold my gaze. I had been betrayed.

Chapter 17

Oxford, Ýlir 1016

I had no chance to speak to either my sons or my hearthweru for I was closely watched, along with the other hostages, by Edmund's housecarls. I turned to Prince Cnut, "Why?"

"I had to. My son is with his mother and you are the most respected warrior in my army. Who else could I use?"

"But you are keeping me from my family."

"It will not be for long."

"However long it will be too long."

The other hostages were brought and we were exchanged on the island. The other Danish hostages appeared to be important but they were not. All were owners of large tracts of land in Denmark. If they were executed then, like Agerhøne, the land would go to Prince Cnut. I had to believe that he would not risk throwing away the Dragon Sword. We crossed the road that led to Lundenwic. We began our journey. The two kings, as Cnut now styled himself, rode behind a group made up of their hearthweru and housecarls. Ten housecarls guarded the Danish hostages and ten hearthweru the king's son and the other hostages. The mounted element of our army followed behind us. The majority of warriors, all Danish, would have to march to Lundenwic. While we might make the journey in less than a week the army, my sons included, would take almost a fortnight. The only consolation I had was that my hearthweru would not be happy about the situation and would be trying to find some way of saving me from a long exile. I knew that they would fail but the thought that they would try was comforting.

We stayed in holy houses and we were guarded. As a hostage, I had been given a choice, either hand over my sword or swear that I would not attempt to escape. I was unwilling to hand over the sword and so I gave my word. Surprisingly the housecarls were more than polite to me. They seemed to respect me as a warrior. I suppose that was because I had behaved honourably in all the battles in which I had fought. The sword fascinated them and while they did not have the courage to ask to hold it their looks were covetous. I found I could talk to them about the battles we had fought against each other and I learned much about the dissension in the English ranks. I discovered that Thurbrand the Hold was held in contempt and that Eadric Streona had managed to make enemies of every warrior in the English army. The only one who seemed able to forgive him for his treachery was Edmund himself. He seemed a very noble, Christian and honourable man. Over the fortnight I was with him I came to know him. I found that I liked him and, unlike his father, he did not seem like an enemy.

The two kings did not speak to me on the road to Lundenwic. They were busy speaking with each other. I would have loved to have been a fly on their shoulder listening to their words. They were both clever men and used words like swords. Neither wanted to share the throne and the arrangement had been forced upon them by the bloodletting. Neither had an army that was strong enough to beat the other and an alliance with Denmark, Normandy or Norway would probably have resulted in the crown being lost to both of them. I wondered what they were saying.

The presence of the king ensured that, despite so many armed Danes, we were allowed into Lundenwic. We rode to the church of St Paul, the largest church in Lundenwic. Riders had been sent ahead to warn the bishop of the king's intention and when we entered the minster, he and other senior churchmen awaited us.

It was not a coronation and I think that the ceremony had been hastily constructed by the bishop and, I do not doubt, King Edmund. Lundewic was formally handed over to King Cnut and the bishop and others swore allegiance to him. As simple as that King Cnut gained control of the greatest city in England. It was, thanks to our raids, the richest. We had the treasure of Wintan-Ceastre and Wareham already. Only the gold of Lundenwic had eluded us. Now King Cnut had it all.

King Edmund honoured his side of the treaty of Olney and we prepared to quit his former capital. He showed his affection for his family by embracing them and shedding tears as they were handed over to Cnut. Cnut spared me not a glance and that told me how he viewed me. I wondered if he was plotting.

Thorkell the Tall walked over to me and held up his hand, "I am sorry about this, Sven. I offered to be a hostage." He shrugged, "I know the English well and I have no family to speak of but Cnut wanted the most important warrior in his army to be the hostage. I suppose I know now how he views me. I am a mercenary."

I shook my head, "If this is affection, Thorkell, then Cnut can keep it."

"The English who guard you are good men, Sven, and you will be treated well."

I nodded towards my sons who were now guarded by Gandálfr and Faramir, "I know that my hearthweru will watch over my sons but I pray you do not allow the prince, sorry, the king, to put them in harm's way. They are worth more to me than he."

"There will be no fighting but I will have my oathsworn watch over them."

With that, we were done and we rode on a cold morning at the end of Gormánuður, towards Oxford, the burh chosen by King Edmund to be the place he would celebrate the Christmas feast. I resigned myself to a lonely time. The other hostages had not fought prominently in battle and I did not know them well. I suspected that they had been chosen for their lack of real importance. They had titles and lands that made them seem important but they were not. I was the hostage that would ensure that Edmund kept his word and Cnut his. Cnut did not think he needed me any longer. He was still plotting and planning, I knew that.

The hall at Oxford was a fine one and the burh, nestling by the river was well protected. As we rode through its recently improved gates, I reflected that Edmund must have prepared the defences in case Lundewic had fallen. I noticed that there were no women in the burh. It was more like a military camp than anything and I wondered at that. The king had his own chamber but the rest of us were accorded sleeping mats separated by wall hangings in the Great Hall. Ten housecarls would sleep close to us. There were two allocated to each hostage and they became our shadows.

Although it was after dark when we arrived, for the days were short, King Edmund ordered food and we sat in the Great Hall to dine. He waved me to the seat next to him, a place of honour and after prayers had been said he turned to speak to me. "I was surprised at Cnut's choice of hostage, Sven Saxon Sword. You are his most powerful warrior and your presence on a battlefield is worth five hundred men."

"Perhaps that is why, King Edmund. It guarantees he will not make war. I might say the same of you. You gave that which I would never have given, my family."

He leaned in and waved a hand around the room, "By the end of the week this hall will be filled with the nobles of England. The best that I had fell at Assandun, many by your hand. I know that my family will be safe in Lundenwic and that Cnut will ensure their safety. I picked them as hostages to keep them alive. Edith understands for her husband was murdered by those who should have been his friends. Safety for my family lies with my enemies and not my so-called friends and allies." The food was fetched and one of the servants sliced a piece of meat from the fowl to eat it. "See, I need my food tasting. The only Danes in this hall are the hostages and I do not fear them. I fear those who are English and would seek to end my life."

I ate some of the bird too, before the king, and he smiled at the gesture. I said, "I do not understand that, my lord. What would they gain from killing you, the last of Æthelred's line?"

The king ate some of the meat but, as he swallowed, I saw that it caused him to wince and he had to drink some wine to ease its passage. He shook his head, "You forget, Sven, that my father married again. Emma of Normandy bore him two sons, Edward and Alfred. They are young but old enough, some day, to be a threat. They might wish my half-brother to be king so that they could manipulate him. They are the threat and that is why I am happy that Cnut has my children and my wife. They are safe."

"I am sorry, King Edmund, but I would simply bar any who was a threat from the court."

"And if I do that, I merely encourage treachery. I will keep my enemies where I can see them. I will have my food and wine tasted and I will sleep with chamberlains across my threshold. I will smile at all and trust none." He patted the back of my hand, "You know, Sven, I trust you more than my own nobles. I allowed you to keep your sword because I know that you will never use it to harm me. You gave your word and swore an oath. Oathsword is well named."

I liked Edmund and we got on well. I had guessed he was roughly the same age as I was. He reminded me of Sweyn One Eye, my cousin. On his other side sat Edgar, the commander of his housecarls and I liked him too. Despite the circumstances that first meal was a pleasant affair and we all got on well. As the king said, when we rose to head for our beds, it would not be repeated. He would need to keep the nobles who would arrive the next day close to him when they dined, so that they all ate the same food and drank the same drink. I would be seated with the other hostages at the far end of the table. Not for the first time I was glad that I was not even close to becoming a king or an important noble. There were always others who were jealous and wanted what you had,

The burh was a new one and there were stone walls. They even had privies that were indoors. I had never seen them but, then again until now I had campaigned in England where you went to a ditch, dropped your breeks and emptied your bowels that way. Back in Agerhøne, we had a small outbuilding with a wooden seat and thralls would empty it each day. Oxford had small chambers that jutted from the walls and each had a wooden seat with a hole. You emptied your bowels and the result fell outside the walls and, as in my home would be cleaned the next day. The difference was that you did not need to wrap up in robes to endure the cold. You merely walked to the privy, closed the door and enjoyed warmth and privacy. There was even a bowl and jug to clean yourself. After I had enjoyed the facilities, I thought that, should I ever make it back to Agerhøne, I would have such a structure added to my hall. Mary would like the warmth and the privacy.

I did not enjoy the proximity of the other hostages. I did not know them. On campaign, I slept close to my hearthweru and sons. I did not feel comfortable with these men who had largely avoided having to fight. They had been in Lundenwic when we had fought King Edmund in the West and at Assandun had been with Cnut and safe from conflict. I did not have to endure the company for long but it was more than long enough.

The next day the king rose early. His pained look told me that he was not yet over his wound. I had also risen early. Æthelgar and Æthelwig, the two housecarls who were my gaolers rose with me. After using the privy and washing we went to the hall where food was fetched. Once again Edgar made the servants taste the food and then he ate too. He was a loyal captain of housecarls and took no chances.

The king turned to me, "I thought to go hunting after we had eaten and before the carrion come but I fear I cannot ride. What say, Sven, that we take my hawks and see what they can do?"

"Whatever you want, King Edmund. I am treated as a guest but we both know that you can do with me as you wish."

He nodded sadly, "Fate has placed us on opposite sides but had things been different then we might have been friends."

"Perhaps but my fate was ever tied to King Cnut. The Norns saw to that."

He looked surprised as he nibbled at the buttered bread, "You are not Christian? You still believe in the Norns?"

"I wear the cross and when I speak of God it is not hard to have him and Odin as the same deity. Thor and the White Christ also work but the Christian church has no being like the three sisters. I know that they are as powerful as God."

He shook his head and kissed the cross that hung from around his neck, "That is blasphemy."

"And how do you explain all the strange events that have led us here, King Edmund? God was on your side, you had good warriors and you are a good leader and yet you lost half your kingdom."

I knew that I had given him more than bread to digest.

We wrapped up in cloaks as we left the hall with his codger and his hawks. The shortest day of the year was less than a month away and winter was approaching rapidly. Without the mail on my back, I enjoyed more freedom than normal and I quite enjoyed striding next to the king as we headed into a nearby wood. He had good hawks and they managed to kill two pigeons and a duck. We would not eat them that night but hang them to let them become gamier and I knew that they would taste better than any domestic animal raised for food. As we headed back, he asked me about Agerhøne and the hunting there.

"Agerhøne is not just the name of my home it is also the name of a game bird that we hunt. As we are named after the bird its hunting is saved for special occasions and we enjoy the food all the more for its rarity."

He nodded, "That is good and means that you do not overhunt the bird. I like that idea. I fear that I will have fewer such days to enjoy." I saw that his eyes were ahead of us and knew what he meant. Riders were approaching. The ones he had called carrion were coming. He would not be able to enjoy himself any longer. It also meant that I would be alone once more.

The king went to greet them and I went with Æthelgar and Æthelwig to the kitchens to prepare the pigeons and ducks. There were slaves who could have done it for us but we had hunted them and we would give the birds the honour of being prepared well. We gutted them and threw the guts to the hounds who enjoyed the bloody treat. We then plucked the animals and Æthelgar fetched a brand to burn off the last of the feathers. We hung them in the larder.

Æthelgar pointed at them, "None of you touches these birds until we are ready. Do you understand? The cook nodded, clearly petrified by the fierce warrior. "We will give them a fortnight to hang and eat them on St Andrew's Day."

As we washed our hands, I reflected that the English had a longer history of being Christian. Cnut and his father had converted but we did not celebrate saints' days. The three of us went to the open ground before the hall. We had decided to spar. We were warriors and could not sit idly by and do nothing. Æthelgar fetched three swords. They were dull but well-made and would allow us to spar without much risk to us. We donned helmets but not mail. The two housecarls sparred first. They were good but well-matched and neither had an advantage.

"Now let us see how I do against you, Sven Saxon Sword. I have seen you fight but from a distance." Æthelwig had edged, slightly, Æthelgar. Without a shield, I held the sword two-handed. It was not as long as Oathsword and not as well balanced but had been a good sword in its day. Æthelwig was desperate to beat me and attacked me quickly. His blows came in a flurry which I easily deflected. The bout ended when I tired of toying with him and pirouetted to smack him in the back with my sword.

Æthelgar quickly took his place, "I can see that you have tricks, but now you will be tired. I will restore English honour."

Others, King Edmund included, had heard the clash of metal and come to watch us. I did not recognise the new arrivals but, mindful of the king's words, knew that they were untrustworthy. Æthelgar did not charge at me but tried to wear me down. He varied his blows. Some came from on high and some from below. He thought he was being clever but there was a pattern to the blows. I was enjoying the practice and lulled him into a false sense of security by just blocking them. I recognised when he would strike a high blow and my sword's tip darted in to stop a thumb's length from his throat.

Æthelwig laughed, "I am glad I never fought you at Assandun, Sven Saxon Sword, or my bones would lie there still."

I nodded and raised my sword in salute, "That was good, I enjoyed it."

We were about to depart when one of the newly arrived nobles, I learned later that his name was Godwine of Tewkesbury, shouted, "Two on one, unless, Dane, you are afraid?"

King Edmund said, "I have seen enough."

I looked at my two guards and nodded, they nodded too, "Very well for I am not yet tired."

It was not arrogance on my part but confidence and I wanted to know if I could do this. One-on-one had been easy but the two housecarls would try to attack me on two sides at once.

They marked their intent by separating and then advancing. I knew that Æthelgar would be the aggressive one and he obliged by racing at me. I could have spun and made him crash into Æthelwig but I did not want to humiliate them. Instead, I spun the other way so that I was behind them. I then took the offensive and swung my sword at Æthelgar who was slow to turn. My sword struck his helmet with a gentle tap and Æthelwig took advantage and lunged at my middle. I managed to suck in my stomach and move back so that the sword slid across my middle. I then used the same move I had used in the first bout with Æthelgar and spun around to bring my sword into his back.

The two men laughed and Æthelgar shook his head, "I think, Lord Godwine, that we have seen enough. Come, Sven Saxon Sword, while we drink some ale you can tell us how you do what you do with a borrowed sword."

I saw a wry smile from Edmund. First and foremost he was a warrior. Growing up in the shadow of his elder brother the Ætheling who had been destined to be king meant that he had been able to hone his skills as a warrior. He knew, better than the treacherous nobles who had tried to encourage bloodshed, that there was a bond between real warriors that transcended nations.

That evening, relegated to the lower table, I watched the nobles vying with each other to ingratiate themselves to Edmund. I knew that some, probably the ones who had not fought at Assandun, would be encouraging the king to make war. It would suit them for it would mean the death of his family and my death. They could only profit from that. I knew, having spent more time with him that while King Edmund wanted to rule the whole kingdom of England, he would do nothing that might jeopardise the lives of his family.

It was three days later that the king of snakes arrived. Eadric Streona rode into the burh with two of his sons, Æthelric and Æthelnoth. Both sons had the look of their father and as their mother was the daughter of Æthelred, they had a claim to the throne. I knew from my conversations with the king that he was angry with Streona for his desertion at Assundun and his absence from the subsequent battle. I was interested to see how he would deal with the meeting.

The Mercian leapt from his horse and abased himself at the king's feet, "King Edmund, you are alive! I was told at Assandun that you had been killed and I fled so that the fight could go on." He looked up, "Is that not so, Æthelric?"

"It is, King Edmund, when we discovered the truth the traitor who lied to us was executed. We came here as soon as we could for we had to avoid Danish patrols."

The king was not taken in, "Eorledman Streona, your words reek to me of conspiracy and I do not believe you." There was a collective holding in of breath for the implication of the king's words were that Eadric might be executed, along with his sons. The king waved a dismissive hand, "For the present, we will consider the punishment that might be meted out. Until then you will be kept from my presence."

The Mercian was cunning, "Whatever punishment you deem to be just we will accept, King Edmund."

I do not think that any of us were taken in by the words.

Over the next days, I ate close to the Mercian and his sons for they were relegated to our table. He was being punished by King Edmund who gathered at his table those that he would use and, in some cases, reward. The events were not feasts but more functional meals which often consisted of plain, homely fare. That Eadric Streona and his sons did not like it was clear. My two companions, for I felt that Æthelgar and Æthelwig had become more friends than guards, and I sat as far away from them as we could. The two Saxons also held the treacherous Mercian in contempt. The father and his sons were plotting. Had I been one of the English nobles with Edmund then I would have been worried. We could not hear their words but we saw their glances and their looks as they studied what was becoming King Edmund's table of counsellors. Eadric Streona wished to be part of that council.

It was during the day that I got to speak to the king. We were both early risers. King Edmund was still in pain from the wound. One morning, as he winced whilst eating, I said, "King Edmund have the healers cleansed the wound well? It is some time since you were hurt and you should be healing."

He shrugged, "They say that they have and ask me to pray to God to heal me but who knows? The outside of the wound looks to be healed but it is warm to the touch."

"At home, in Agerhøne, King Edmund, the volvas would have made a poultice to draw whatever poison lives within."

"Volvas?"

"Wise women. They heal and tend to the sick."

He held his cross and kissed it, "Witches?"

"You might call them that but they are held in great esteem by all."

"They would still be witches. I will continue to use my priests. They may not be as good as your volvas but they are close to God and if the wound your friend gave me is to result in my death, then I shall be assured of a place in heaven." He smiled, "Each night before I retire, I confess and am absolved of my sins."

The comfortable conversations always ended when the other lords rose and entered the hall. They clearly shunned me and I had no wish to be close to them. I would either walk in the woods with Æthelgar and Æthelwig or spar with them. The days were pleasant.

The feast of St Andrews was a special occasion and I was invited once more to dine with the king. The look of pure hatred from Eadric Streona made the meal even sweeter. The food was delicious. The animals that we had hunted had become gamier and had a wonderful taste. Even the king, with his troubled stomach, enjoyed it. He drank more than he normally did and laughed more than he had when dining with the nobles. He was flanked by Edgar and me. As they had hunted with me Æthelgar and Æthelwig were also on the top table. It was when Æthelgar made a pun of Agerhøne and hunting ducks that all six of us laughed so loudly that every head turned to look at us. Æthelric and Æthelnoth stood and left.

King Edmund smiled, "Our good spirits seem to leave a poor taste in Mercian mouths."

Edgar growled, "I know not why you keep that traitor so close, King Edmund. He cost us the battle of Assandun and his treachery runs deep."

"Better to keep your enemies where you can see them, Edgar."

It was a short while later that the king rose, "I need to empty my bowels. I enjoyed the birds but my wound did not. Come Edgar."

Edgar took his sword and followed the king to the toilet. The night was bitterly cold and I reflected that this English innovation was a good one.

Æthelwig said, "I think, Lord Sven, that my bowels need to be emptied. Sorry."

I nodded. The orders for the two men, despite our closeness, had been made clear by Captain Edgar. They were never to leave my side. That was not only for the protection of the king but for me. If I was killed whilst a hostage then the Treaty of Olney would be null and void. I smiled, "Then we will all three go and I will make water. At least it is not like Agerhøne and I will not need my cloak and bjorr hat."

Edgar was standing outside the door of the toilet and he smiled. There was just one unoccupied place. "Two of you will have to wait."

I gestured to Æthelwig, "His need is greater than mine."

He had barely opened the door when there was a scream that turned my blood to ice. It came from the stall occupied by King Edmund. Edgar wrenched the door open. King Edmund had been stabbed, by a spear from beneath. His dead eyes told us in an instant that he was dead or dying and the drawn entrails that hung from his buttocks confirmed it.

"Treachery! Come with me!" We raced to the door that led to the stairs. I had drawn my sword as soon as Edgar issued his orders. It was so cold that the moment we stepped outside our breath appeared before us. We saw four men running from the midden that lay below the hole they had used to kill the king.

Edgar shouted, "Guard the gates and stop those men. They have killed the king."

They were heading for the gate. The two men at the gate made the mistake of running towards the four men. They should have guarded the gate. There was a clash of steel as combat began. The two men were overpowered and killed but they delayed the assassins long enough for Æthelgar and me to reach them. They whirled to face us. It was Streona's sons and two of his housecarls. The sword wielded by the housecarl came towards my head. I did not try to block it but, ducking I dragged Oathsword across his middle. The blade tore across his stomach and he fell writhing in a puddle of guts. Æthelric and

Æthelnoth were as treacherous as their father. The two rounded on Æthelgar and although he cut Æthelnoth their blades ended his life.

Æthelgar had been English but we had become close. I became as angry as I would have been if Sweyn One Eye had been the one slain. Blocking the blow from Æthelric I drew Norse Gutter and slashed it across his brother's throat. Æthelric pushed the other housecarl towards me and I was unable to end the life of Æthelric. Æthelwig and Edgar reached us just as Æthelric began to open the gate. The housecarl was butchered but I heard the neigh of horses and knew that Æthelric would escape.

I ran as the Mercian tried to mount the horse. The other three animals had begun to gallop away as soon as he had untethered them. I ran as though my life depended on it. Æthelric swung his leg over and then made a mistake. Instead of digging his heels into the flank of his horse, he tried to end my life. The sword came down at my head and I did the only thing I could. Holding Norse Gutter above my head to block the blow I backhanded Oathsword into the leg of the killer. I heard the bone break and warm blood spurted. He tumbled from the horse's back and the animal raced off into the dark. Edgar and Æthelwig reached me when I was standing over the dying Mercian.

He looked up and gave a smile, "Now who will rule England? Cnut has already lost for you will be blamed, Saxon Sword, and the heirs of Æthelred will rule." He expired.

Æthelwig said, "What does he mean?"

Edgar shook his head, "This is the work of his father. He married the king's sister. He believes that he will get away with this. Come let us return and arrest him. He shall be tried and executed before night falls again." As we ran, he said, "And no one will blame you Sven Saxon Sword. They made a mistake. They should have brought more men and slain us all."

The eorledman had planned well. Even as we entered the gate we heard the sound of horses from the north gate as, the guards slain, Eadric Streona and his housecarls fled the scene of the murder. The king was dead and all hands would point at Cnut. What would happen next?

Chapter 18

Lundenburh Mörsugur 1017

Edgar escorted the hostages to Lundenwic. He had more than one purpose. He wanted to ensure that King Cnut, for he was clearly now king, knew that King Edmund had died but also to protect us from the wrath of the English. When we had walked into the hall with bloodied swords then there was suspicion that I had been involved. Despite Edgar's words some English nobles clearly saw their opportunity to cause dissension in the kingdom. We left the next day and reached Lundenwic by evening. King Cnut had taken up residence in the burh, Lundenburh. He was taking no chances.

King Cnut nodded, when he heard the news, "Captain Edgar, you and your housecarls shall now guard the queen and the king's sons. They are safe here but they should know that the king was murdered by an Englishman."

Æthelwig clasped my arm, "You and I are bound by the death of Æthelgar, Lord Sven. If ever you need me then I shall be at your side."

He left with Edgar and I was alone with King Cnut. "Tell me all, Sven."

I sighed. There was no apology for having sent me as a hostage. It was as though I had one duty and that was to serve King Cnut. It would always be the same. Thorkell was right, kings were made differently from mere men. I told him and he shook his head, "So he had no chance to defend himself and his death was inevitable once he sat down. A horrible way to die and, as much as he was my foe, I would have hoped for a better end."

"You have it all now, King Cnut, the crown and the country and I beg leave to return to Agerhøne and my family."

He nodded absent-mindedly, "In due course but first I need you and Thorkell here to ensure that the crown is not only placed upon my head but that I am secure. Then, and only then, can you depart. You can go to Agerhøne and if you wish, Norton, but only when I am secure." The smile appeared and he said, "Now, go to your sons. They and your men have pestered me each day demanding your return. Perhaps this will silence them."

As I left, I saw Thorkell the Tall waiting, "Is it true, Sven, King Edmund is dead?"

"Aye, he was murdered. It was Streona's sons that did the deed."

"And what happens now, I wonder?"

"The king has said that we need to be by his side until he has the crown upon his head and then…"

"We will be rewarded. He has made promises and now he will have to make good those words."

"My reward, Thorkell the Tall, will be that I shall be allowed to go home."

My sons and my men were not in the Great Hall but had been given the old hall to the west of the city, I know not if it was to keep them from him or to allow them freedom but the result was a good one for me. My ships were drawn up on the shore and now that the bridge had been destroyed, we could sail home whenever the king gave permission. The welcome from my men and my sons made me forget, albeit briefly, the loss of Æthelgar and King Edmund and the treachery of Streona. As we ate in the ancient hall, I told them of my incarceration. Bersi and Streona were surprised that I had become close to my guards but Gandálfr and Faramir understood it best of all.

"I am glad, Lord Sven, that you had two new shield brothers but now Faramir and I can return to our task and this time we shall not leave your side."

The date of the coronation was set six days before the end of Mörsugur. That was to give the English nobles the chance to get to Lundenwic. Any who did not attend would be seen as enemies. Queen Ælfgifu was already in the city and she would take, I did not doubt, great pleasure from the killers of her father being humbled.

Eadric Streona arrived four days before the coronation along with other nobles. It was noticeable that the other English nobles distanced themselves from the treacherous Mercian. Thorkell and I were used to flank the king with drawn swords. It was a clear message that any opposition to the king would be dealt with severely. Eadric Streona strode in confidently and abased himself before the king. "King Cnut, I am here to witness your coronation." The king held his hand out for the Mercian to kiss the ring and then gestured for him to rise. The king's face was impassive. "Know, King Cnut, that since I became your ally, I have worked tirelessly to ensure that the crown came to you. My feigning of support for Edmund worked well and my flight at Assandun gave you the victory. It cost me my sons but I ensured that King Edmund died."

The king nodded and gave the slightest of nods to me. My account of the murder had been confirmed. "And what is it that you wish, Eorledman Streona?"

"Why, King Cnut, a just reward. I would be raised above the other English nobles and ranked higher than any."

The king smiled and I shuddered for it was a cold cruel smile and he reminded me of his father Sweyn Forkbeard. "And that you shall have." He turned to Thorkell and me and said, "Take the eorledman from here, have his head taken and placed on the highest tower in this burh. His skull shall look down on everyone until the ravens take the flesh from his treacherous head."

"King Cnut!"

"And if he tries to speak again in my presence then take his tongue."

I took great pleasure in helping Thorkell to lift the Mercian and drag him from the hall to the courtyard outside. Streona looked up at me as the cold sunlight struck his face, "Sven Saxon Sword, mercy."

"To you? You are a snake and like all snakes, you need to have your head removed to stop your poison."

The wife and family of King Edmund were in the burh and Edgar came striding over. "He confessed?"

"He boasted and now the king wants his head."

Edgar looked not at Thorkell but at me, "Lord Sven, I beg of you the chance to end this creature's life." I looked at Thorkell who nodded.

"Noooooooo!"

We both pulled his arms so that he could not struggle. Æthelwig had come out with Edgar and he grabbed the Mercian's hair and pulled his head. Edgar stepped between Æthelwig and me. He raised his sword and the head was cut cleanly from his body.

"He had a quicker death than he deserved."

Thorkell nodded, "I have read that in Roman times they would put a traitor in a sack and fill it with poisonous snakes. That would have been a better end."

Æthelwig nodded, "Aye, but this will do." He held up the bloody skull.

I pointed to the top of the Roman tower, "The king wants it displayed there." Æthelwig took great delight in sticking the spear in the fighting platform and then planting the head of the most treacherous man I had ever met.

The coronation was not as grand an affair as I had expected but then my mind was on the journey home, back to Denmark. If I expected a quick return, I was disappointed. It took two months before the king allowed me to leave. Thorkell was given his reward sooner than I was. He was made Jarl of East Anglia. He inherited the lands of Ulfcetel Snilling. I had to wait a week beyond his departure to be allowed to sail with my sons and my ships back to Agerhøne. Everyone knew that I had been given Norton and I think all expected me to sail north to claim my manor. They clearly did not know me. My family was all.

In the greater scheme of the Norns we had not been away long but it felt like a lifetime. Steana had already been a warrior when we had left but now, he had become a man. While in Lundenwic he had bedded a woman. Bersi, too, was growing quickly. He had killed and could never go back to becoming Mary's young son. He wanted to be a warrior and I knew that would have an effect on Mary. She would blame me. As much as I was desperate to see my wife, I knew that I would have to shoulder the blame for the change in our sons.

As we crossed the sea to Agerhøne, helped by benign winds, I spoke with the men on my drekar. I had always promised Mary a return to her home and I would keep my word. I told my men my plans and gave them the freedom of choice. I did the same with my sons. My oathsworn were more than happy to follow me to Norton as was Bersi. It was Steana who looked uncomfortable.

"Father, I thought I would want to come with you to England but there are bonds and threads which tie." He nodded towards the other young men who had sailed with him to war. "I would stay in Agerhøne, at least for a while. I think that it would do me good to be with my oar and shield brothers. I know that I could learn as much with you as with my friends but if I am to leave Agerhøne I would spend another year or so there."

"I understand but I fear that your mother will not. Perhaps the Norns have spun, Steana, and planted this thought in your head for this way I can make you hersir to stand in my place."

"Hersir? But I am young."

I tapped his chest, "It is in here that counts. You have a good heart and I think that you will be a good leader. Besides, I am now getting older and one day you will lead the clan. Perhaps the weight of being a leader will make you sail to England."

In the end, half of the men on the drekar said that they would like to come with me for a new life. Surprisingly most were men with families. They had land in Agerhøne but not as much as others. I knew that they had raided with me for treasure to make a better life. Sailing to England meant a chance for better land. Mary had often told me of the fertility of the valley. The Tees, which the Romans had called the Dunum, was a larger river than any that flowed through Denmark. Even the same size farm as they had in Denmark would mean fuller bellies for the valley was fertile. I was happy for the men who chose to come with me were the ones I had first gone to war with.

My little port looked inviting as we sculled our way to the quay. We had been spied on from afar and the whole village turned out to greet us. Mary was not there but Gunhild was. She was a woman grown and I had missed my daughter blossoming from a bud to a flower.

I hugged her and said, in her ear, "Your mother?"

"She is at home. She was a little unwell." I pulled away from her and she shook her head and smiled, "Fear not, father, it is nothing. She has the sniffles and blames the damp climate of this land." She turned to Bersi who was now almost as tall as she was, "And you, little brother, what have you been eating while in England, whole boar?"

He laughed and hugged his sister back. Steana went to them and almost picked them both up. I had forgotten how strong was my son.

It took some time to reach our home for we were stopped many times on the way by my people keen to welcome me. I was touched. Gunhild was right and my wife was not lying in bed at death's door. Food was cooking and the fire made my hall welcoming. She greeted first, as I knew she would, our sons and like Gunhild could not help but notice how much they had grown. One thing we had not suffered from in England was hunger. We had been the victors and eaten of the best. Good food combined with exercise made strong muscles and my boys showed that they were both warriors. My wife saw the size but did not realise the implications. It was good to be home and to enjoy ale that, having been brewed in Agerhøne, tasted so much sweeter.

On the voyage back I had counselled the boys about the words that they would use. I told them that while we did not lie to the women, we missed out on those parts that might upset them. They had heeded my words and spoke not of slaughter and bloodshed but victories that were noble and intentions that were honourable. That was not the reality of war. The boys had wanted to join the other young men who were in the warrior hall. Mary would not hear of it and we dined, in my small hall. The mead hall would hold the feast that would celebrate the return of the clan. Until then Mary wanted all her chicks around her. I did not mind. I discovered that Gunhild, despite the fact that she was now a woman, had not yet been attracted by men.

Mary snorted, "And how could she when you took all the warriors across the sea to war? The old and the very young were left here."

Steana looked at me and I nodded. I knew my son well and he was seeking permission to bring up the splitting of the family, "And when our father returns with you, Mother, to your home in England, I shall stay here and watch this hall for the family."

Her face fell, "I thought that you would come with us to Norton."

He shook his head, "In the fullness of time I shall but there are things I need to do here in Agerhøne."

"Then I only have my family home and together for a short time."

I leaned over and took her hand, "Let us make the most of it. I thought to sail on Midsummer Day. That is three moons away. Enjoy the time, my love, we are together and do not count away the hours."

That night as we lay in each other's arms, holding the other tightly, she said, "Are we doomed to be torn apart forever?"

I did not say that would be the work of the Norns as I did not want an argument on the first night back, instead, I said, "This time the tearing is not the work of a king. You wish to return home and Steana does not. He meant what he said and he may well follow later but at the moment he wants to be a Dane in Agerhøne. You cannot blame him and we need not depart for a year or more if you…"

"I would go home to Norton on the morrow, Sven, for despite the people, this is not my home. It does not feel Christian. England does."

"Good," I told her of the men and their families who would be coming with us.

"We will not have to fight, will we?"

It was dark and she could not see my face in the dark but I would not lie to her, "I know not, but Eiríkr Hákonarson now rules that land and I will seek his advice. The manor will have enough land for me to give to those who follow me for I brought great treasure from England." The mints we had taken meant that the holds of my ships had been filled. Agerhøne and Norton would reap the benefit of the war against Æthelred and his family. When Streona had been executed his treasure had also been divided between the king, Thorkell and me. The men who came with me could buy land if they chose. Mary was right in one respect, we might have to return armed to show those who lived in the valley that we were the new rulers. The Danes had conquered England. Whether we could hold on to it was another matter.

I visited with my foster father and cousin a few days after our return. They needed to know all that had happened. They had not stayed to help Cnut gain the crown but they were Cnut's men. Both had been promised land in England. I doubted that either would take up the offer but I had to tell them that I intended to leave.

Sweyn Skull Taker nodded, "Your thread and that of the king have ever been close. The Norns have spun, Sven, and when you took Mary from England you were bound to return. I shall be sad to see you leave but here," he patted his chest, "we will still be close."

My cousin smiled, "And I may well come to visit with you. It would be good to come to England and hunt rather than fight. From what I have heard the land you have been given is fertile and teems with game. I should like to visit."

"And my son Steana stays here. I know he is young but I have made him hersir knowing that the two of you will guide him."

My foster father's face broadened into a smile, "He is like his father and you showed that your shoulders were broad enough for the weight. It will do him good and make him a better warrior. Mary will be happy."

I shook my head, "Mary will never be happy. Until Steana joins us in England she will be sad and I will be blamed for him staying in England."

"It is the Norns, Sven."

"You know that, Sweyn One Eye, and I know that but my wife is a Christian and despite all the evidence to the contrary refuses to believe in the Three Sisters."

I also gave them the news, given to me by King Cnut that my cousin and his father had both been given land in England. Sweyn had been given East Harlsey which I had been given to believe lay twenty miles or so south of Norton while Sweyn Skull Taker, being a jarl had been given Ripon which was a city with a cathedral. They had both nodded when I told them but my foster father made it quite clear that he would not be visiting any time soon. "I will trust you to collect my tithes and taxes."

Sweyn One Eye said, "I will give a year for you to make your home secure and then I will visit but like my father I have no intention of leaving Denmark." He smiled, "You will become our taxman, Sven."

To be fair to Mary, she threw herself into the preparations to leave but balanced it with ensuring that Steana, living alone in our hall would be comfortable. She was a mother through and through. I went to all the people of Agerhøne to ensure that they had all had the opportunity to decide if they wished to stay in Denmark or come to England.

I went to see Siggi the Pig. He and I rarely saw each other but our time on that first drekar had bonded us and I knew that it was unlikely that I would see him again. He had grown older and fatter but he was happy. He took me to his fields where his pigs happily grew as fat as their master.

"You remember, Sven, when you brought me those pigs from England?" I nodded, "Well I have bred from them and now have a pig that is bigger than the ones we used to raise. They have more meat and they are hardy. I would give you two, a sow and a boar, to take back with you to England."

"You need not, Siggi."

He nodded, "But I do. Sven, you are a warrior and you keep my farm safe. I am a farmer and what I do is to make what nature gives us better. I have done that. When you take these pigs back to England they will breed with the English pigs and they will change the breed. It is what farmers do." He waved a hand at his fecund fields, "You are a lean warrior and I am a fat farmer. Nature and Freyja demand that we farmers do all that we can to make the world better. Take my gift and even though we are separated by a sea and will never see each other again, the threads of the Norns will hold us tight."

He helped me to take the two animals to my farm.

I also had my ships to prepare. I would be taking my drekar and two knarr as well as four fishing boats whose captains wished to come. We would be a small fleet sailing across the sea to England.

The night before we left my wife organised a feast and invited my foster father and his family as well as those, like the priest, to whom she had become close. She did such things well and the food, as well as the ale and mead, were magnificent. Thanks were given to God for the bounty but I could not help noticing that the warriors all kissed their hammers of Thor as the priest said, 'Amen'. Warriors were still token Christians. When we went to war it was Odin and Thor were the names we used.

Sweyn One Eye ended the night with a song about Assundun.

King Edmund thought he had the chance
To end the threat of Danish blades
The English spears did advance
But we were unafraid.
We stood with spears and shields all locked
The English strode with spears held firm
To fight the Saxons who had flocked
To fight for the Wessex Wyrme.
Oathsword and Sven were brave and stout
They would stand and never rout
Oathsword and Sven were brave and stout
They would stand and never rout
The English came but the boys stood still
They used their slings with skill and speed
They hurled their stones the housecarl to kill
Then racing back they leapt the shields
As Alf had leapt on the Svolder's decks
The boys had hurt the English wall
It was Bersi the plan had wrecked

And the slingers all stood tall
Oathsword and Sven were brave and stout
They would stand and never rout
Oathsword and Sven were brave and stout
They would stand and never rout
The king now faced Saxon Slayer
The two warriors fought in the heart of the fight
Neither man gave nor did waver
With shields and spears all locked tight
The two men took their swords in hand
Oathsword and the English king
Did fight long into the day
Their fight was so great that the gods did sing
Warriors gave all and none did sway
Oathsword and Sven were brave and stout
They would stand and never rout
Oathsword and Sven were brave and stout
They would stand and never rout
Treachery ended the epic fight
The Mercians fled into the night
The English ran and the Danes held the field
Lord Sven had the victory sealed
Oathsword and Sven were brave and stout
They would stand and never rout
Oathsword and Sven were brave and stout
They would stand and never rout
Oathsword and Sven were brave and stout
They would stand and never rout
Oathsword and Sven were brave and stout
They would stand and never rout

I smiled when Bersi grew as he was named and when gods were mentioned and my wife clutched her cross. It was a typical Sweyn song and whilst not exactly true did not tell any untruths. Over the years the words might change but at its heart lay the story of Assundun.

Chapter 19

Norton 1017

Mary was not a good sailor. She had been much younger when I had taken her as a slave and that voyage must have created bad memories for she stayed by the mast for the whole voyage. Gunhild had never sailed and it was Bersi who make life easier for them both. As he scampered up the sheets and mast, he made it seem effortless and safe. I had more to concern me than my wife's discomfort for I had a small fleet to watch. We had animals on the knarr and fishing boats that were crossing a sea for the first time.

We left our home quietly and before dawn. I supposed I should have sought King Harald's permission to do so but, as I had told Jarl Sweyn Skull Taker, I suppose I did not think I owed King Harald the courtesy. He had done nothing for me. We left before dawn as both the wind and the tide were propitious. Thus it was that the only ones to see us off were Steana and a handful of relatives of those who did sail. It was only later that I realised we had rarely named Norton. We spoke of going to England and settling in King Cnut's new land.

What I did have, in the sea chest I still used was the document that King Cnut had ordered to be drawn up for me. It named me as hersir and lord of Norton and the lands within ten miles and south of the settlement. The river was the border and north was another manor, Billingham held by a Northumbrian. I was entitled to call up the fyrd and to take local taxes. My obligations were to provide men should the king need them or the Earl of Northumbria and to pay the annual taxes on the land. I knew that they were higher than they would have been in Denmark. England was used to high taxes as they had constantly to raise coins for weregeld. I had enough treasure in my hold to pay the taxes for ten years and that did not worry me. From my words with Mary, I would be able to make the taxes easily from the fertile land if I managed it well. Where I differed from my father was that I knew that while we were good warriors, for our people to prosper, we needed to be good farmers and I had learned much from Siggi. I also had Alf as one from whom I could learn. He had long ago ceased to go to war and was now like Aksel the Swede, his father-in-law. He did not need to fight to make his pile of coins grow.

Mary was excited and despite the discomfort of the sea, the voyage took years from her careworn face. I knew that she might be disappointed when we reached her former home as it could never be the home she remembered as a child. When we reached the mouth of the river with the basking seals and the fires from the folk who lived along the dunes that lined the coast. She was almost a young girl once again.

Gunhild looked at the fires which burned not in houses but on the beach and said, "Father, what are they doing?"

It was my wife who answered for she knew thus valley far better than me, "They are heating seawater to make salt and see there, on the north bank, there are women and children gathering samphire." She jabbed her finger again at the boys and their fathers wading through the mud to take the fish from the traps they had laid, "And they need not go to sea. They have a bounty each time the tide turns."

I smiled as my wife continued to instruct my two children. I had much to do. We had fewer men on the drekar than was normal and we had a tricky river to navigate. The tide would turn in an hour and the incoming tide would give us more water beneath our shallow keel but we would still need to sail in the middle of the channel of the twisting river.

"Bersi, ask your mother questions later. I need you at the prow. Watch for rocks and trees."

I knew from my previous visits up the mighty rivers of England that storms and floods in the mountains could bring down trees. Our ship was strong but a collision with a half-sunken tree could be fatal. I looked south at the sun. If the tide and the current stayed with us, along with the easterly wind, then there was a chance that we might cover the few miles from the coast to the manor before dark but I was neither reckless nor a fool and I would not risk pushing on in the dark. Even if we had to anchor within sight of the manor, I would not risk the webs of the spinning Norns.

The only other time I had sailed here I had taken an oar and faced east. I remembered twists and loops and the jarring of oars when we steered too close to the bank. I had the oars ready, not to row but to fend us off if I steered badly. I kept the longship in the centre, turning every now and then to ensure that the knarrs and fishing boats were still in close attendance. The wind was just strong enough to shift the waddling duck that was the knarr and keep her within two lengths of my ship. We were silent as we sailed and herons and ducks took flight as we disturbed their nests. The banks were devoid of any sign of habitation. The only houses we had seen thus far had been the houses close to the dunes on the north shore and the ones behind the palisades in the hills to the south. The land was flat. When Mary was learning our language many years ago we had used talk of this part of the land to help her speak Danish. She had told me that the land close to the river was swampy and inclined to inundation until the two settlements of Norton and Billingham. The curve of the river would take us close to Norton but not Billingham. There was a causeway between the two manors and becks twisted and turned over the low-lying land. The two manors were on islands raised above the land that could flood. It was used well, Mary said, as the farmers were able to grow better crops after the floodwaters had subsided, I confess that I was excited about such a land. Siggi had told me that the only fertility that came to his land was the care of his pigs and animals. Their dung was used to grow more crops. Norton sounded a better prospect. What we did not know was that the river was a living thing which had changed course over the years. The place we both remembered had changed.

We spied the wooden church spire as the sun set. I thought it further from the river than when we had raided. The river was shifting its course. We would be anchored almost a mile from the village and that meant it would take us longer to unload and we would need to build dwellings for the fishermen who needed to be close to their boats. We would not be able to go ashore. Although we had no shields strung along the side of the longship, the locals had suffered too much at the hands of Vikings for us to expect a welcome if we arrived at night. I dropped the anchor and then we made a longphort of our little fleet. We would have to endure cold fare once again but safety was all and at least we were not moving.

I woke before dawn and the reason was Mary. She had slipped from beneath the fur and was at the side of the longship staring at the shadows of the shore. I went and put my cloak about her, "I could not sleep. I am excited about my return and wonder who is left from the time I lived here."

I squeezed her tightly, "There may be no one. Last night when we anchored, I noticed two things, one was the lack of noise and the other was the absence of the smell of wood smoke. Sniff the air, Mary, there should be the smell of smoke should there not but I can just smell the river. Perhaps the wars between Northumbrians and Scots have driven them hence. They have had no lord to protect them."

My senses were well-honed and I knew how to use them. Mary did not but as she sniffed, I saw her nod. "What has happened, Sven?"

I kissed her on the top of her head and shook mine, "I know not but we will rouse the men. We can go ashore as soon as the sun appears." Even in the half-light of predawn, I could see that the river's course had changed in the time since Mary had been taken. What did that mean? Had the Norns been spinning?

I roused, first, my hearthweru who went to wake the men and then Bersi. Since he had given orders at Assundun he had been accepted as a leader amongst his peers. He roused the boys. By the time they had been awakened, there was a lighter look to the sky and with swords strapped around our waists and helmets upon our heads we untied ourselves from the other ships and I had the men scull us to the bank. The tide was on the way out and I did not mind that we might be grounded. There would always be a high tide to refloat her. As the keel ground gently against the mud I sent Bersi and the ship's boys to take ropes and secure us to the willow trees that lined the shore. We pulled the longship until it was level and then tied off the ropes. We ran out a gangplank and I led the men ashore.

"Bersi, you and the other boys make sure that the ship is secure and guard it."

He nodded. There had been a time when he might have objected and demanded to come with us. Assundun and the conquest of England had changed him. I led just fourteen men. In all thirty men had chosen to come with me. There were boys who would soon become warriors but for the moment we were a tiny band in a land where the dangers were, as yet unknown.

As soon as I stepped upon the path that wound up through the trees, I remembered that night a lifetime ago when we had raided. As we made our way up a trail that seemed neglected somewhat we passed the burnt out mill. The charring was recent and we all drew our swords as we passed it. The wooden palisade we had negotiated had long ago fallen into disrepair. The river gates were no longer there and the gaps showed where the timbers had been used for firewood. The sun came up as we passed the first building and this had not fallen into disrepair, it had been burnt. The fire looked to be weeks rather than days old. I drew my sword and the others emulated me. Scurrying from my right made my head turn suddenly and I saw rats fleeing. I went to the building they had vacated. The lower courses were made of stone but the wood and roof had been burnt. I saw where the rats had been busy. A corpse, with desiccated flesh, lay in the house. It confirmed what I already knew. This settlement had been raided. The rising sun told a sad story. Not a building remained whole and even the church had been attacked. Only the tower and the spire had survived. It had been a half-hearted attempt at burning. The wooden tower still stood but there had been an attempt to destroy it.

I waved my arm and Faramir led half of the men to investigate the north of the village. Gandálfr took the rest south. I went alone, sheathing Oathsword as I walked, to the church. The skeleton at the altar had been stripped of flesh but the vestments told me it had been the priest. All of value had been taken.

I went to the graveyard. I saw three small mounds that stood out from the rest of the cemetery as the vegetation was missing from them. A few hardy blades of grass were growing and in a year's time it would be covered but I knew that these were the freshest graves in the village. I saw the wooden shovel that had been used to bury the occupants leaning against the stone base of the church and, taking off my helmet, I began to dig.

Gandálfr joined me and said, "There is none left alive. What do you hope, hersir, that the graves will tell us what happened?"

I nodded and pointed to the grave I had half uncovered, "The villagers may have buried their own but I doubt it. These graves will, more likely than not, be three of the raiders who did this. We will see if they are Scots, Vikings or another who sought to do harm here."

With Gandálfr's help, I soon uncovered the shallow grave. It was not what I expected. The warrior had been struck about the head so that his features were unrecognisable but by his dress, he was English, a Saxon. His sword confirmed that. He held it in his dead hands along his body. He had been important, perhaps a gesithas. Certainly, his mail suggested a housecarl. I handed the shovel to Gandálfr and knelt down. Around the warrior's neck was a thong and from it hung a cross confirming that the man was a Christian but there was also a copper lozenge. I turned it over and saw the saltire, the cross. I tore it from the thong and, rising, showed it to Gandálfr.

He confirmed my suspicions, "Mercian."

I nodded, the Mercians used the saltire cross of St Alban as a symbol. It was also on one of the banners they used when going to war, "Aye and this raid did not take place in the far past. This man is fresh. Why would the Mercians raid here?"

Gandálfr took the shovel and began to clear the other grave. Faramir joined us, "What is it that you do, hersir?"

I told him. "Have the corpses cleared. Fetch them here and we will bury them. The burnt buildings will be upsetting enough for the women and children but I would not have them see rat-chewed corpses." Gandálfr gave a small shout as he cleared the soil from around the face of the next body, "I know this face. He was with Eadric Streona at Oxford." He shook his head, "I did not see him at Lundenwic."

The men arrived with the skeletons and I pointed to the three mounds. "We will make a burial mound here above the Mercian dead."

Faramir said, "Mercian?"

Gandálfr nodded, "Aye. This is one of those who came to Oxford. The gesithas may also have been there. I recognised something familiar about his mail but I cannot be certain."

"Here is a puzzle but we cannot untangle it yet. I thought to walk into a village filled with people and not a charnel house. We have more work to do before winter than I expected."

It took us a good two hours to make a burial mound. The priest my wife had brought with us could say words later on. I would tell him what we had found. The women might suspect but so long as they did not ask then they would never know. While the men went to fetch our passengers, I walked the village with Gandálfr and Faramir. There was nowhere that was whole but some of the houses could be repaired quickly. The walls too were not irredeemable. We could make good the damage and give us protection. The church and the house of the lord of this land would need to be completely rebuilt. The house in which Mary had lived was also totally destroyed. It was a blackened hole.

I heard the buzz of conversation as they ascended the path. As soon as they stepped into the open area close to the pond and before the church then silence engulfed them. The one I knew would be most affected was Mary. She was the only one who knew what Norton had been like. I saw, in her eyes, the memories. She saw not the blackened shells, she heard the laughter of the children and the faces peering from the doors. Her eyes welled up and then I saw her clutch her cross and a determined look came over her face. She strode over to me and put her arm through mine, "Well, we have much work to do but then there were always improvements to be made." Her eyes took in the least damaged buildings and she pointed, her voice imperious, "We have four women carrying babies. Those houses are theirs. For the rest, we will make shelters. Come, let us make a start. I would have a hot meal for everyone. We will work hard this day but we have a home and the Good Lord makes us work for our shelter as it will make us all better souls."

I leaned down and kissed her, "I am sorry about this, Mary."

She smiled, "Why, it is not of your doing? We make the best of it."

I sent half the men back to the ships to begin the unloading and I took the priest, John, to the mound. He had been born a Dane, Hastein, but when he had become a Christian and trained as a priest, he took the name, John. I told him what we had found. He made the sign of the cross and shook his head, "Christians did this?" He waved his hand at the church.

"Perhaps they thought to lay the blame on Vikings but it was Christians. The ones they buried wore crosses and there were no hammers of Thor."

"It is better the women do not know of this." He took out a flask, "I have here some holy water. I will use some here and some in the church. Let us make it pure once more."

Perhaps my wife was right for everyone threw themselves into the work with almost evangelical vigour. I went with my men and we hewed timbers from along the riverbank and used the willow to repair the walls. It might sprout but the trees we used would regrow. We needed the better timbers of oak, chestnut and beech for the houses. We were exhausted that first night but we had a hot meal and we had shelters rigged. After the tossing of the drekar, the women would enjoy solid ground and sleep. With the walls unfinished we kept a good watch. Until we had walls around us, we were not safe. It took a week but we had gates and walls. I sent the fishing ships to fish in the river and to explore upstream while half of the men worked on the houses. The ones who were warriors, I took with me. We crossed the causeway and headed for Billingham. We took swords but none of us wore either mail or helmets and we left our shields in Norton.

We crossed the sodden causeway. There had been recent rain. As we climbed up the slope to the wooden walls of Billingham those working in the fields fled before us. By the time we came to the gates they were barred and armed and helmeted men stood on the fighting platform of the gatehouse. Had we wished we could have taken it for the walls were little taller than a man and were really only effective against animals.

I had brought the parchment with me and I held it up, "I am Lord Sven Saxon Sword and the new King of England, Cnut, has given me Norton. I come here in peace to tell our nearest neighbours of our arrival."

One of the men on the fighting platform took off his helmet and smiled, "And I am Edward of Billingham. I saw you at Dunelm and know your reputation, Sven Saxon Sword. They say you are a good man. Open the gates and admit the Dane,"

His words told me much. He was Northumbrian and he still regarded us as invaders. He had called us Danes. King Cnut would have the same problem everywhere but the Danelaw.

By the time the gates opened, he was waiting and he held out his arm, "Welcome."

I clasped it and felt the strength in it. "We are less than sixty people, Lord Edward and we will need your advice for this land is new to us." I waved a hand in the direction of Norton, "What happened?"

He smiled, "Come to my hall and we will share a beaker of ale."

His hall was well made and I saw that his church was half stone and half wood. From the houses, I guessed there had to be more than a hundred people in Billingham. Norton had been much smaller.

In the hall, we sat apart for I could see that the Northumbrian wished for privacy. "It was at the start of the year. The month you call Þorri when they came." I worked out that was not long before we left for Agerhøne and when there was talk of me leaving the court of King Cnut. "They were Mercians. We did not know it at the time it was only later. We woke to hear the sounds of screams and battle. We saw the burning and feared retribution. I sent two of my men across the causeway to spy on them. When they returned, they told me that the village had been massacred and they recognised the dress and words of Mercians. I worried that we would share the same fate for my men did not stay to count their numbers. It was winter and cold weather descended. Our priest told me that this was the wrath of God punishing the killers. It lasted a month. When I went to the village all I found were corpses."

"Which you did not bury."

"For that I am sorry but the ground was hard and my men feared the ghosts of the dead. The days were short and…" I nodded. I understood. "I did not know there was war with Mercia."

"There is not," I told him how King Edmund had died and the punishment meted out to the eorledman.

"But why Norton?"

"Because I was given this manor by King Sweyn and his son confirmed it. The Mercians know my part in killing Streona's sons, Æthelric and Æthelnoth. Perhaps they thought I was here already."

He nodded, "You know that there was a third son?" I shook my head. "Aye, he is illegitimate but a son nonetheless." He waved a hand in the direction of Norton. "Brihtric was older than the other two and as nasty a piece of work as I have ever met."

"How do you know so much about the Mercians?"

He sighed, "I fought for King Æthelred against King Sweyn and fought alongside the Mercians. I did not like them. To be honest, Lord Sven, that is the reason I did not challenge them when they raided Norton. The deed was done and I did not wish to risk their wrath. My days of fighting are long gone. I seek peace. I pray that you do too."

I nodded, "Aye, I have fought enough but we shall need your help for we know not this land."

"Then I shall send Osgar to you. He is the captain of my housecarls and he knows this land better than any. His family were taken by pestilence a year since and the occupation will take his mind from brooding."

I stood, "It will take a week or so to organise our homes. Let us say he comes seven days from now."

As we headed back Faramir said, "Do we need local knowledge, lord? We can explore."

I shook my head, "Time is a luxury we do not have. I thought to be settled into homes before winter set in but the Norns have spun. Osgar will save us time. I need to know the lie of the land around here, my land. There may be those who do not live in Norton. I have a responsibility to them as they do to me. The Mercians were a warning. The eorl has much to watch over in Northumbria and if the Scots come raiding or Norse then we need every man that can hold a weapon to defend our new homes."

Gandálfr said as we headed up the path to what would be the new main gate to Norton, "Do you regret coming, lord?"

I shook my head, "The Three Sisters would have sent a challenge to us in Agerhøne. You cannot regret the past for it is done and that page has been written but we can learn from it and be vigilant. Osgar is part of the sisters' threads. His family were taken from him recently. It is all meant to be."

I could speak those thoughts to my hearthweru and even Bersi but not Mary.

By the time Osgar arrived, we had the gatehouse built and the only buildings to be repaired were the church and our home. Mary wanted both to have stone. We had collected as much as we could but we would have to find a quarry for the rest. Osgar was a little older than I was and his arms showed the scars of war. He had a sword hanging from his waist. None of us wore mail or helmets. It was not that I was confident we would not be attacked but I did not want to intimidate those who lived within the boundaries of my land.

"Thank you for your services, Osgar." I took out a Wessex coin, "You will be paid this for each day you serve me."

"You need not, lord, for I serve Lord Edward and he has commanded me."

"Nonetheless I will pay you for that is my way."

He nodded and took the coin. Bersi had insisted upon accompanying us and we left the village with the sound of hammers and axes ringing in our ears. Once clear he pointed to the roughly made road that headed for the causeway. "This is the road that is most used." He gestured to a smaller track heading in a roughly north-westerly direction. It was where the main gate lay, "That road leads to Dunelm." He turned and waved a hand behind us, "The river loops around us and there is a small huddle of huts close to St John's Well. We will head there."

"How many people live within this loop of the river?"

He rubbed his beard, "A good question and I have not counted. By St John's Well there may be five families. Three quarters of a mile in this direction there are another four families. Between here and there we pass four farms. Two are on the road or close to it and the other can be reached by a greenway."

"Thirteen families then, an unlucky number."

"Perhaps." He pointed to the first farm and shook his head, "Cedric the Pig lived there but I can see that they were raided too."

When we reached the farm, we saw that it was a complete ruin. The animal bones told us that they had feasted well on the pigs. The Mercians had been ruthless. We buried the farmer and his family. My spirits were sinking lower and lower.

Osgar pointed to the north side of the road, "There is a farm up that track, my lord, Rus' Worthy and as I can see smoke rising from the house it has been untouched."

The next farm had also been destroyed and I began to fear for the families at St John's Well. We buried the bodies although there appeared to be fewer than Osgar expected. He shrugged, "Perhaps they took slaves." He pointed again to the northwest, "Ragnar's Worthy lies there, my lord. He is like you a Dane and, once again there is smoke from his home."

"You have good eyes."

"I know where to look."

The small hamlet that lay north of St John's well looked untouched. It was called Akselton. It was good that we had Osgar with us as the people there were fearful.

I introduced myself to the men. The headman was Eadric and he bowed when he saw my sword and hearthweru. "The farms to the north of you were raided. What do you know of their attackers?"

He turned and said, "Wife." A woman shepherded two girls and a boy. None of them was older than seven years of age. "These three bairns arrived late at night and told us that warriors had come to their farm. Their father and elder brothers told them to run and they fled here." I nodded and looked at them. They were still terrified. "You are the new lord?" I nodded, "We have a large family, lord, and three mouths are too many for us to feed."

I understood what he said and knew that the Norns had spun again. I knelt and spoke to the eldest, a girl, "I am Lord Sven Saxon Sword. Your parents are dead, until you are old enough to choose your own path you shall live with me. "

She nodded and stared at Oathsword, "You have walls and will protect us?"

"I will, as will my warriors."

"Then we shall come." She turned and said to the headman, "We thank you for caring for us but there are no walls here."

Seara was but seven years old yet she was very practical. They had just the clothes on their backs and had nothing to carry.

As we left, I said, "Osgar, our plans will have to change. We will visit with those at St John's Well and then return. We might be able to tramp for twenty miles or more but not these bairns."

"Aye, lord."

Bersi asked, "Why do you think that the hamlet was left unharmed?"

Osgar answered that for us, "There is a bridge many miles to the west. It is at a crossing where there was a Roman fort. If you ride horses then it is the quickest route and the men had to have come by horse."

Faramir asked, "How do you know?"

"The horse dung at Cedric's farm told me. There are few horses hereabouts. The lord at Norton had two but the dung at Cedric's farm and the hoofprints told me that there were at least twenty-five mounted men."

Osgar was good. I had not looked for such signs at Norton but that could be excused by the horror that had greeted us. We needed to exorcise that image from our minds and look for clues.

St John's Well was a holy place at a narrow point in the river. Those who lived there made a living by ferrying occasional passengers across the river, fishing and farming. The headman was Alfred and he knew nothing about the attack. It confirmed Osgar's words.

"I am Lord Sven Saxon Sword and the new lord of this land."

Alfred asked, "And what does that mean for us, my lord? We are descended from Danes, like you, but we have lived here so long that we feel English."

I liked his honesty, "It means, my friend, that I am here to protect you and you, in turn, will fight in the fyrd when you are summoned."

"Norton is a few miles from here."

"I know and that is why I suggest you build a palisade around your walls for you are the furthest from us. When we have rebuilt the church, I will have a bell and it will be rung so that my people can get to the walls of Norton."

He nodded, "And we are too far to take advantage of your walls."

"You are."

"But you would still come to our aid?"

"We have a longship and we would come."

"Then we will build a palisade and come to the church if you have a priest."

"We have a priest."

"Then perhaps he will answer our prayers this time and save us from our enemies."

"Amen to that," Osgar spoke the words and I saw the cross around his neck. My warriors and I would be the only pagans in my new manor. Was this a test?"

We ended up having to carry the three children upon our shoulders for they were weary and we arrived back just an hour before dusk. I summoned the priest so that I could give our news to him as well as my wife at the same time.

Mary was a truly Christian woman and Gunhild took after her. While I spoke the two of them held the three children close to them.

"So we need a home for these three and we need the church rebuilt. The people need the church, Father John. They need God."

Mary smiled, "And I have waited a long time to hear those words, husband."

Mary thought she had changed me but she had not. This land was Christian but I was not.

The next day we visited the last farms. One was on the river and the folk who lived there at Per's track were also of Daish origin. Per had led a raid on the river and his ship had been wrecked navigating its waters. He had settled by the river and his sons had carried on the tradition. There were three families and they were happy to follow a Dane. The headman was Persson.

One of Per's men had been Ragnar and he had settled at Ragnar's Worthy. It was a large family who lived there now. They had carried on the tradition of using the name Ragnar for the eldest son and he was a warrior. The last, Rus' Worthy, had also been built by one of Per's hearthweru, a Rus warrior called Hadwin. The head of the family was Hakan. He had never fought in a battle but he looked strong and he was proud to show me his grandfather's byrnie.

When I returned to Norton, I was happier than I had been the previous day. I had another twenty warriors I could rely upon. They were untrained but I could remedy that. When they came to church on Sunday, I would start to train them while Mary got to know the women. She had learned much at Agerhøne and now she would use those skills to good effect in Norton. I was just pleased that Brihtric and his Mercians had attacked prematurely. We had the winter to make the manor secure and by spring I hoped that we would be ready to face any enemy.

Chapter 20

The Tees 1018

We worked hard in the late autumn so that by the anniversary of the death of King Edmund we had a church, I had a home and Olaf, the weaponsmith, had managed to cast a bell. On Father John's advice, we reburied the dead villagers and while the grave was open, we stripped the mail and weapons from the dead Mercians and melted it to give us the bell. It seemed right somehow. We had used stone for the bell tower and, in an emergency could be used as a last refuge. The men of the manor, even those from St John's Well, which had been renamed Stockadeton for its well-made walls, all trekked to Norton for the church and the weapon practice. Bersi had skills and he trained the archers and slingers. It would only be a year or two before he joined the shield wall. Faramir and Gandálfr became my lieutenants and it gave us more flexibility. We had forty-seven men and although only fifteen had mail everyone had a good sword. Alf had sent us a present from Ribe. One of his knarr brought swords, spearheads and arrowheads as well as food. The people of Agerhøne and Ribe did not want us to starve. I was touched by the gesture. It meant that at the Winter Solstice when we celebrated the birth of the White Christ, we did so in a more hopeful manner than when we had first stepped into the burnt and wrecked village.

It was at the end of Mörsugur when the messenger came from Dunelm and Earl Eiríkr Hákonarson. I was summoned to his stronghold. As much as I did not want to go, I knew I had to. Without horses, it would be a hard march up the road. I went with just my hearthweru. Whilst there was no snow the skies were clear and it was bitterly cold travelling along a slick and slippery road. Built by the Romans it was in need of repair. We used ash staffs to help us to keep our footing.

"You know lord, we could sail to the mouth of the river and harvest the seals. The meat would be welcome, the fat would light our homes and we could make boots and capes from the skins."

I nodded, "A good idea, Faramir."

Bersi frowned, "Hunt the seals? Do they not live in the water?"

Gandálfr chuckled, "Aye, they do, little shield jumper, but they like to bask on the rocks and you can creep up on them and batter them with staves. That way you do not damage the pelt."

I smiled, "And we could collect samphire and buy salt from the gatherers."

Bersi looked around him for the land was undulating. We had trudged up ridges and descended to dry valleys. Trees grew everywhere and we could see the berry bushes, now devoid of fruit and leaves, that lined the road. "This land is nothing like Denmark."

I waved an arm around, "I think that more people would have lived here when the Romans ruled. It would have been rich land and well-farmed but it needs protection. When we were lured north by Uhtred the Bold there was purpose in his plan for the Scots, whose land is poorer, raid here too often."

"Lord, our kin and the Norse did more damage. My grandmother was a slave taken from these lands and we have passed the remains of farms that have not been worked for two generations. You are right but King Cnut will need to guard against men such as we." Faramir had darker hair than the rest of my men as did Bersi, Steana and Gunhild.

"And I think that is why I was given this land and Thorkell the Tall, East Anglia."

Gandálfr wagged a cautionary finger, "Less than fifty men can do little, lord."

"We have made a start with the walls. They are not stone but the shifting river helps us. Until the land between us and Billingham dries out then any attacker from the north would have to travel further west. Perhaps Earl Eiríkr Hákonarson has plans to watch the road. Now that there is a palisade at St John's Well, we have two refuges."

Faramir sounded nervous as he spoke, "Some of the men asked about land, lord. We have been busy until now but soon it will be spring. There are two farms already that need just a little work. I ask not for myself, for I have no family but…"

"You are right and I am pleased that you reminded me. Farms will make Norton more secure and less crowded. When we return, I will listen to requests for land."

Being an English lord was proving to be harder than I had expected. We were not simply raiding and leaving. We had to live with the land and the people who were here. I knew, from those that I had met like Ragnar, Hakan and Persson, that I was lucky and I had no opposition. Was that the sword, the Norns or something else?

The days were short and although we did not stop for long on the road it was dark when we entered Dunelm. I was, of course, recognised and admitted directly. We were taken to the hall and Earl Eiríkr Hákonarson himself greeted me. I handed my cloak to the hovering servant. The earl said, "You and your men will sleep over there. Go and have ale while I speak with Lord Sven." His face was serious as he led me to two chairs that had been placed by the fire. A thrall brought us beakers of ale. He smiled, "They brew good ale here." He raised his beaker to toast me and then drank deeply. I did the same.

I looked over my shoulder. The hall could have been in Norway. The earl's men were Vikings through and through. I wondered if they would settle here.

"Tell me about Norton."

"You did not ask me to travel all day, on foot, my lord, just to ask me about my home."

He smiled, "No, I did not but indulge an old man, Sven, and tell me all that has happened and then I will impart my news."

I sighed and recounted everything, including the discovery of the bodies and their later desecration. Earl Eiríkr Hákonarson was a very religious man. Svolder had affected him deeply and he had converted after that monumental battle that changed our world irrevocably. When I told him about stripping the dead, he made the sign of the cross.

"From what you have told me and what I have learned the men deserved it but I am still uncomfortable. The bell, however, is a good thing and tells me that King Cnut has made a good choice for between Jorvik and Dunelm there is just you and you have a mighty weight upon your shoulders." He waved over a thrall who brought more ale and some pieces of crackling from a recently cooked pig. "Now I will tell you what I have done since we claimed back the land from Uhtred the Bold." He saw the cloud on my face and sighed, "The man deserved death. Like you, I deplore the manner of it and Thurbrand the Hold will, one day, pay for that crime but had Uhtred not been eliminated then King Cnut would not have been secure. His son, Ealdred, has not forgotten the murder and I have men close by his home to watch him. He blames Thurbrand the Hold and not us but I know that if I was less than vigilant then King Cnut might lose Northumbria for Uhtred and his family are still popular. I was tasked with stopping the Scots and men from Strathclyde making mayhem and mischief. I have used my warriors and given them lands on the borders. I often use Din Guardi as my home and there are strongholds now all along the Tweed. Chosen men, men like you, keep the populace safe and they are vigilant. I have given men land close to the old Roman wall where there is a natural defence. I use my ships to patrol the coast in case pirates decide to test our resolve. The result is, Sven Saxon Sword, that since you left none of my men have had to draw a sword or use a spear. There has been a price and Norton has paid it."

"You knew of the attack before I spoke of it?"

He shook his head, “I was warned that Thurbrand the Hold was not as watchful as he might have been in the south and that there were some disgruntled English warriors on the loose. Until you spoke, I did not know that it was Norton that was attacked. I am sorry but I have recently received intelligence which might be of more use to you.”

He leaned forward and I did too. He glanced over his shoulder to see that he was not overheard. No man was closer than twenty feet and the hubbub of the hall disguised our words. “Intelligence, my lord? From whom?”

He sighed, “This is now my home and it is a good one. The land is better than in Norway and we are comfortable here. I have brought my family here and I wish for comfort in my old age. I am a rich man and can afford to buy the best. The merchant who supplied the wall hangings comes from the land of the Five Boroughs which is close to Mercia. Mercia is now a troubled land. When the eorledman was executed then the king imposed a close watch on the land. Mercia is on the brink of rebellion. I have told the king this but I also heard that the family of Streona blames you for what happened to their father and brothers. The attack on Norton was because they thought you were already in residence. They did not know that you were in Denmark and hoped to kill you at Norton. They are not done with you.”

I felt a chill run down my spine despite the heat from the fire, “The king knows that I am in danger?”

“He does but you know the king. Until he is secure then he will expect you to look after yourself.”

“You say, family? I know of Brihtric, who is illegitimate, are there others?”

“Brihtric has two younger brothers. Eadric Streona gave their mother an estate in Cheshire. King Cnut confiscated it a month since and she is homeless. I suspect that will have added fuel to the fire burning within Brihtric’s heart. He can do little against the king but you are a different matter. He knows that you are rich. The taking of the mints gave you a fortune.” He saw my look and shrugged, “It is common knowledge and none, except men like Brihtric, disapprove. He will return when he has sufficient men.”

“And you can do nothing to aid me?”

“I told you, Sven, my men are strategically placed around Northumbria. My task is to keep the north safe from invaders. You will be on your own.”

I stood, “I thank you for this information but it could have been sent as a message, written or spoken.”

"And had I done so then word might have reached the Mercians and the man who told me this would have been in danger. I have told you now and you can prepare."

I shook my head, "And I am many miles from home and by the time I reach Norton who knows what might have happened."

"I will give you horses, Sven. I have no men to spare but we still have the horses we took from Uhtred. Take ten and you can be home by noon tomorrow."

"I thank you for the ten horses but we will be home before Lauds."

"You have not eaten and the night is freezing."

"Earl, if your family was in danger…"

He nodded, "Fetch bread and ham. Lief, have four horses saddled and another six haltered. Come I will walk you to the stables."

My hearthweru had been watching me and when the earl spoke, they and Bersi donned their cloaks and raced to my side. I said simply, "The Mercians are returned. We are leaving for home."

They never questioned me but flanked Bersi and me. The thralls hurried to our side and gave us each a small loaf which someone had filled with slices of the pig we might have eaten had we dined in the hall. Perhaps my name was remembered. I was grateful for the thought. We stepped outside as the tethered horses were brought. The four horses that needed to be saddled took longer.

As they clattered from the stable, I asked, "Are these to be returned or are they a gift?"

"A gift, Sven, for I have no men to give you. If you need anything else then send word to my steward here. I will leave orders that any request for food or weapons from Lord Sven Saxon Sword will be honoured."

I clasped his arm and then swung myself into the saddle. The others copied me. This would be hard for Bersi for he had not ridden much. "When this is over, Earl, I will return to speak further with you. If you and the king have plans for me along the river then I need to know what those plans are."

He nodded, "King Cnut comes here in the summer when the days are long. I am to arrange a meeting with King Malcolm who rules the lands north of here. I will send word."

I nodded to Faramir and Gandálfr to take the reins of the tethered horses, "And if I am still alive then I will come." I turned and said, "We ride!"

We galloped through the gates and the city. The clattering hooves warned the gatekeepers and the gates of the bridge were opened. The darkness enveloped us.

The road was broad enough for us to ride four abreast and I was able to tell Faramir and Gandálfr what I had learned.

"Lord, if he comes back with more men we will be hard-pressed to defeat him."

"Faramir, we will defeat him for he comes with murder in his heart. I cannot see Mary's god allowing evil to defeat us but I also believe that Oathsword will have something to say. The Norns have spun and when the Mercians arrive they will not find it as easy as they will have to face the Dragon Sword."

Faramir was right and on the road south, I put my mind to finding a solution. There were men abed in Agerhøne who could make the difference but would they come and, more importantly, if I sent for them would they arrive in time? I made a decision. I would send my knarr back to Agerhøne and put aboard Mary and Gunhild. They would be safe and, hopefully, Steana would send some young warriors back. The trouble was that my plan for reinforcements was flawed. It would take over a week for them to make the journey. I needed other plans too.

It was still the middle of the night when we reached the gates. Two men walked the walls each night but I now knew that would have to be increased and the men who fought the Mercians would be already tired. The thought briefly passed through my mind that we might have been better off staying in Agerhøne and just as quickly vanished. The Norns had spun and no matter what I did they would seek to test me. They had sent the sword to me in this land and I was forever tied to this land called England.

We had no stables but there was a barn with half a roof. While Bersi went to tell his mother and sister that we were home the three of us tended to the horses. "You two get some sleep. We will hold a council of war at noon."

"We can stay awake, my lord."

I shook my head, "We saw no sign of fires as we neared our home. I took that as evidence that they are not close. When they come it will be at night. I am hoping that they wait for a break in the weather."

"You are a wise man Lord Sven and we are lucky that Norton has you as its lord."

Mary looked fearful when I entered my hall. We had a roof and there was a fire but it was not yet finished. Mary had fretted about that. Now the mess seemed inconsequential. Bersi had not told them anything but the two women knew that our return in the middle of the night was not a good omen.

"Bersi, put a log on the fire and rekindle it. Come, wife, daughter, I have news to impart." The journey had given me the time to think of what I would say. I told them of the danger posed by the Mercians and that we were alone. Bersi poked the fire into life and the dried pine log quickly burst into flames as the resin ignited. "So, I shall send Lars back to Agerhøne tomorrow. You two can go with him and any others who do not wish to face the threat of the Mercians. Hopefully, Steana will be able …" I got no further.

"You think because we are women, we are weak?" I was not given the chance to answer my wife for she railed on, "This is our home and we will not squat like toads in Agerhøne while our men fight and die here. I was taken from here once and I will not leave a second time."

"But what of the other women?"

"I know them, Sven. We speak each day and we share all. I believe that they will all wish to stay. It is a good idea to send back the knarr for our son will not abandon us. What are your plans?"

She was so calm that it took me by surprise. I had expected a more tearful reaction. "The earl knew not when they would come but I believe that it will be sooner rather than later. The short days make it easier for an enemy to use darkness and they will expect us to be without defences for it was they who wrecked it. We have a week or so, I believe, to improve the ditches, towers and walls. I will ride tomorrow afternoon to visit with the others who live between us and Stockadeton. They need to know the danger."

Bersi said, "The attacks on the two farms will be motivation enough."

I saw my wife look up. The three children we had rescued now lived with us and Gunhild acted as a foster mother. She nodded firmly, "And you have had no sleep, either of you. Go to bed. Gunhild, return to the bairns and I will keep watch."

"You?"

"Husband, I do wish you would listen to me. I am a woman but this is my home too and let me do what I must."

I nodded. I was defeated.

I slept the sleep of the dead. I was no longer a young man. Bersi roused me, "Mother is speaking in the church with the women and Father John."

I frowned, I had wanted to speak to the men first. I rose and dressed. Despite the cold, the men were gathered around the fishpond. It was a natural gathering place and they were all well-wrapped against the cold with hats upon their heads. I wore my bjorr skin one and felt guilty for some had woollen ones that were not as warm. Faramir and Gandálfr were there but I knew they would not have divulged anything. As my wife was already giving out the news, I wasted no time. "I have bad news to impart. Mercians are coming to have vengeance for their dead I slew. I am sorry for bringing this upon you."

Einar Blue Eyes laughed, "Lord Sven, no matter what the priest in yonder church says we all know this is the work of the Norns and a man who tries to avoid them finds trouble in other ways. Tell us what to do and we shall do it."

There were nods and murmurs of approval.

"For the moment we improve the defences and we will need more guards on the two gates. I would have two on each gate and another two patrolling during each long and dark night. We will watch for two hours only. It means that all of us shall lose sleep but two hours is not much of a price to pay." I nodded to Lars, "I want you to sail back to Agerhøne with all speed. Tell my son of the danger and ask him for any warriors that he can spare." I paused and he nodded, "Any man who wishes to return to his family may do so."

Karl Red Hair laughed, "What, before you have given out farms? We all stay."

I smiled. I had a good clan. "Then from now on every man goes armed, aye and boys too. Bersi will command the slingers and archers. We will all be watchful and be not fearful of crying wolf."

By the time I had eaten, it was noon and Faramir, Gandálfr and Bersi joined me, "I will ride to our people and give them the news."

"And what is your plan, hersir?"

"We now have horses, Faramir. I will leave one of them at Stockadeton so that if the Mercians come by ship this time they can ride and warn us. I will leave another with Hakan at Rus' Worthy for he is also isolated."

"But you do not think that they will?"

I shook my head, "No, Gandálfr. They know that they can cross the Roman bridge and head here that way. Each day two of us will ride to the south and west to look for signs. When we know they are close we ring the bell and summon every man to the walls and we defend it. By then I hope that the weather will let us deepen the ditch. I would have men hunt every day in the woods towards Wulfstun and Thorpe. It will alert us to any danger in that direction and give us food. We will each take charge of one of the night watches. Those six hours before dawn will be the important ones." I smiled, "This is a council of war. Do you have any suggestions?"

Gandálfr nodded, "Darts, my lord. They are easy to make and even women can throw them at an enemy. Making them will occupy the boys and we can have such a store that, combined with the arrows and stones, we will make life hard for them."

"They have been here before, Gandálfr and they know the layout of the place."

Bersi piped up, "Then why do we not put obstacles where they expect them not." I looked at my son and he continued, "Let us assume that they get over the wall. They will make for our hall and the church." He pointed to the huts and homes that lay opposite the pond, church and hall. "They have to come between those houses, through the cuts. We put brambles there and attach things that will jingle. At the very least we have a warning."

Faramir nodded, "And we can put a ditch before your hall. We can use a bridge for the entrance but remove it at night."

"All are good ideas, put them in place but know this, if they are determined then they will breach our walls. From what the earl said, they seek our gold. Perhaps our treasure is a curse."

"No lord, the curse is the spawn of Streona and when these bastard sons come, we shall end the line for all time."

I nodded, "Gandálfr ride to Billingham and tell Lord Edward and Osgar of the danger. I do not expect them to help for this is our fight but they should know that they are in peril."

We talked through the specifics and then, even though they objected, I mounted a horse and led a pair of animals. I would offer a horse to Hakan for he was the most isolated. As I passed the first burnt-out farm it reminded me that I had to make decisions about the land I would give to each one who wanted it. There was an area of common farmland to the north of the church and there were some, like Alf the Smith who would like a strip of land to grow food for themselves. There were others who would wish to raise animals and they would need a farm. At the moment, all of the animals, mine included, were tended on the common. We had to husband them well and care for them should the snow come.

It was not as cold as it had been and the hard ground was slowly defrosting. It was not yet muddy but it would mean my men could work a little on deepening the ditches and planting traps. I soon reached Rus' Worthy. Hakan had a small piece of woodland and he was cutting timber to dry. He had told me, on a previous visit, that you never knew how long winter would last here in the north and even fresh wood was better than nothing. He walked over and stroked the horse.

"A fine-looking animal, my lord,"

"A gift to me from the earl. If you wish it, I can loan him to you."

"And why would I need it, my lord, not that I am disparaging the use of an animal?"

"I have had word that the Mercians intend to return."

His hands tightened on the axe handle, "The horse will only carry one, my lord."

I nodded, "You could make a cart and he could pull it and bring your family to safety. You are the most isolated of my farmers." He nodded, "And you could ride him to watch the borders of my land. When last they came, we were not warned. I would have a warning."

"Thank you for your honesty and the loan of the horse."

"We will toll the bell constantly in the church when danger is spied. Hasten to Norton."

"I will my lord."

I had no such gift for Ragnar but he was half a mile closer and could reach Norton quickly. He promised me that he would watch out for signs of Mercians. When I reached the hamlet of Akselton I saw that it could not be defended. The first time I had just been looking for evidence of a raid. I told them of the threat. "You could either try to reach me or, failing that, Stockadeton."

They nodded, "We would not be caught out in the open. I think we will head to Stockadeton but that will leave you with fewer warriors, lord."

"I know but it cannot be helped."

The people of Stockadeton said the same thing although they knew that, as a last resort, they had the river and as we were downstream from them then they had a way to escape. They appreciated the horse although the way that they looked at it I doubted that any would risk riding the animal.

Persson at Pers Track was my last visit and he pointed to the river. "We live by fishing and using the water. If we hear the bell then we will come by water."

As I returned home alone, I reflected that I was lucky that I had such resilient people.

It was as I neared the burnt farm that lay close to Ragnar's Worthy that the horse I was riding pricked up his ears. He had not done so on the way out. I looked at the sky, it was an hour or so before dusk. I stopped and stroked him to calm him. I did not dismount but walked him slowly towards the burnt-out farm. I had not left the road on the way to the river and I saw now fresh hoofprints on the ground. It could have been Hakan, trying out his horse but I guessed he would have ridden north. Either way, it was worth investigating, especially as the tracks headed to the farm but did not return. I drew Oathsword and walked my calmer horse to follow them. I sniffed the air and there was a smell I did not recognise. I had learned long ago that a man smelled of the food he ate, his own body and, if he rode a horse, horse sweat. I could smell horse sweat amongst the other strange smells. If Hakan had ridden the horse then he would not have acquired that smell. There was a strange horse here and a rider who was not one of my people. That made him an enemy. I could not see any danger but that did not mean it was not there. My horse's warning and the feeling in my gut were enough. Better to look foolish than end up lying dead and alone.

The farm had been a reasonably large one and apart from the house, there was a hogbog, cow byre and a barn. The raiders had eaten the cow and left its bones as evidence. The tracks led to the barn and I walked the horse cautiously. My feet gripped the horse's middle. I had heard that the Vikings who lived in Normandy used something called stiraps to keep themselves secure. I did not want that, I wanted to be able to leap from the horse's back if danger loomed.

The Mercian burst from behind the cow byre when I was less than six feet from him. He must have realised that had I continued on my path I would have seen him and he took the initiative. He was mounted on a small horse and he charged at me with a spear in his hand. Had I not been armed then I would have been a dead man. As it was, I let go of the reins and grabbed the spear's shaft whilst sweeping my sword horizontally. The Mercian wore neither mail nor leather byrnie, he was clearly a scout and my sword sliced across his middle and made him fall. As his horse ran off, I swung my legs over and landed next to the dying scout. His hands held not a weapon but his stomach as he tried to control the writhing snakes there.

I stood over him, "Where is Brihtric?"

"He is coming, you Danish devil." He tried to imbue the words with power and it was a mistake for the effort proved too much and he expired.

I put my hand to his neck but felt no life and I searched his body. He had Mercian coins in his purse. That confirmed his identity if confirmation was needed. He had a cloak and his boots were well-worn. He had a seax and a short sword. I took both and then walked over to his skittish horse. At first, it would not come close. I had taken with me the last couple of gnarly old apples from the apple store in case one of the two horses proved uncooperative. I took one out and held it on the palm of my left hand.

I spoke Saxon in a gentle sing-song manner, "Here boy. I mean you no harm." I moved slowly and the temptation of the apple proved too much. He began to eat it and I took his reins. While he ate and grew used to my smell, I examined the saddle. There was a blanket, a large waterskin and a bag with food. The man was a scout and was not close to Brihtric and the rest of the warband. He expected to sleep rough. Night was falling and the man had sought somewhere he knew he would be able to rest before scouting out the defences of Norton.

I led the animal back to the body and tied the reins to a convenient post. I slung the body over the back as well as the belt holding the sword and seax. I mounted my horse and headed back to the road. I stroked my horse's neck. Until now I had not named him but I knew his name now, "Today, you saved, I think, our settlement. I shall name you, Verðandi, for you can see into the future." I knew I was risking the wrath of the Norns by naming my horse after one of the three sisters but it was *wyrd* and when the horse neighed, I knew I had chosen well.

Chapter 21

Norton 1018

When I rode into my stronghold all work stopped and I saw Faramir frown at the body and the new horse. "I knew one of us should have gone with you, hersir."

I stroked my horse, "Verðandi here warned me." I dismounted and Karl Red Hair pulled the body from the saddle. "We will bury him." Karl nodded, "The Mercians are coming but this one was just their scout. He did not plan on returning to the others this day for he was planning on camping close by. He will not be missed until tomorrow. That means the earliest that any can reach us will be the day after. On that day I want you Faramir to ride with another warrior and try to find the Mercians. They will be within half a day of us and so I want you to travel no further than Sadbergh."

When we had sought the Mercians we heard that a warband had been spotted by the villagers of Sadbergh. If they had not been seen then that gave us an extra day.

"For the rest keep working. Tomorrow, Gandálfr, you can ride to warn those I spoke with today. They may well choose to come within the walls now. Tell them exactly what I found."

In many ways, it was a relief to know that we would meet our enemies within a day or so. It would be better to get it over with rather than wait, living in fear and dread.

The women had been busy. They had not only cleaned and prepared the freshly caught fish and small animals and birds that had been hunted, but they had also used the feathers from the ducks, chickens and partridges to put flights on the simple darts that had been made. Bone needles had been put in small wooden darts. They were quickly made and disposable. When we hunted and fished the bones, even the small ones, were never discarded. My news merely added urgency to their task.

That night I had my first watch and I used Saxon Slayer rather than Oathsword. A sentry could rest and lean on a spear. It kept a weapon close to hand and if any tried to climb the palisade it was the best weapon to use. As I walked the walls for my two hour stint, I spoke with all the men. They were in good heart. We might be outnumbered but we would give a good account of ourselves.

When I woke, I felt more refreshed than I had for a few days. Breakfast was a simple affair of porridge followed by rye bread smeared in butter but it would set me up for a day of hard work. My three men had left before dawn and I was working in the ditch when Osgar strode over. He had with him a helmet, shield, byrnie and sword. I looked up at him, "What brings you here, Osgar of Billingham?"

He leaned his spear and helmet against the wall, "My master fears to spare more men but I asked if I could fight here alongside Sven Saxon Sword and Oathsword. The last time the Mercians came they killed men I had fought alongside. Call it vengeance."

I smiled and took his arm as he pulled me from the ditch, "I care not for the reason I am just glad that you are here. I have news." I told him of my encounter.

"I think you are right. I would guess that this Mercian warband crossed the river and are somewhere close to Barton, Croft or Hurworth and near to the River Skerne. We have work to do."

We barely stopped to eat at noon such was the determination of everyone that we make life as hard for the warband as we could.

Gandálfr rode in during the early afternoon. "Those in Akselton will join the men of Stockadeton. Persson, Ragnar and Hakan will be here tomorrow shortly after dawn. They will be driving their animals."

"Then I hope we have time. It all depends now on what Faramir discovers."

It was after dark when they rode in on weary, sweaty horses. The triumphant look on Faramir's face told me that he had good news. "We found their camp at Hurworth. There are sixty or more of them. We did not get too close. They are not all Mercians. I saw Danes, Norse and Irishmen there. He has gathered a band of bandits and mercenaries. I think, Lord Sven, that the lure of gold was too great. We warned the men of Sadbergh as we passed through and they have raised the fyrd. If nothing else it means that the warband will have a longer journey than the thirteen miles we made."

Gandálfr, Bersi and Osgar were with me and I nodded, "Then our plans are made and the defences will have to stay as they are. Tomorrow, we wait for our allies and keep watch for the Mercians."

"Your battle plan, lord?"

"The way I see it they will not risk the river. If they do then the recent thaw will make their progress too slow. The mill has yet to be repaired and will afford them little cover. We have six men on the river gate with women on the rest of the north walls. Let us see if their darts can hurt the enemy. The rest of us will be on the other three walls. If nothing else I now see the weaknesses of our walls. We need small towers at the corners."

Osgar nodded, "And the two gates whilst that makes us strong can also trap us."

Gandálfr said, "And the drekar and the fishing boats?"

"Anchor them in the river and have the captains and just six men aboard the drekar. It can be a floating fort. I know it takes men from the walls but that cannot be helped." I turned to Faramir, "You will watch for the Mercians." He nodded. "Until we know whence they come then we are in the dark. You will enlighten us."

"I will take Haraldr again, lord, he has good eyes and rides well."

"Leave before dawn for you may have far to travel."

None seemed dismayed at the prospect and we ate in two shifts. One shift ate while the other watched and worked on the defences.

That night as my wife lay in my arms, I told her the plans. "Do not worry, husband, the women will not let you down. We know what the Mercians did here the first time."

"How?"

"Father John and Bersi bowed to my torrent of words and told me of the bodies you found. You need not protect me from such images, my husband. I know that the world in which we live is not a perfect one but you are doing your best to make it better. God will help us."

I did not say it but to my mind it would be Oathsword and my warriors that would stop them.

When my scout left, the next day, I walked around the perimeter with Osgar and Bersi. Osgar had never seen our defences close up and Bersi was young enough ask searching questions.

Osgar pointed out the stand of trees that lay just eighty feet from the south wall, "If they have archers there or men with crossbows then they could send missiles down into the village."

I nodded, "I know and we do little about it now. Bersi, you command the archers and slingers, place the best bowmen facing this wood."

"We have slingers who can reach this distance too."

When we reached the river side of the walls Osgar shook his head, "What is to stop them ascending here? They have cover from the trees and by your own admission there are just women and a couple of defenders here."

I pointed to the seemingly deserted ships at anchor, a small longphort of vessels. "They have a horn and if this side is the point of attack, then the horn will summon my men to defend it."

By the time we returned to the main gate, the one we called Dunelm gate, I had seen the flaws in the defence and knew that this was not the time to try to remedy them. That would have to wait until we had either defeated the Mercians or our corpses littered the ground.

Osgar made me feel better for he said, "It is better defended than Billingham, lord, but then again, we do not have a Viking horde of gold to attract an enemy. If they attacked us, it would not be worth the arrows."

I looked at Bersi who showed he had been observant, "I will have the boys collect more stones for their slings. We need them on every wall."

The farmers began to arrive soon after the sun had risen. Ragnar and his family were first followed by Hakan and his family. Mary was in her element, greeting the new women of the clan and arranging for their sleeping arrangements. It was Persson who arrived last and he surprised us all by arriving along the river. The women, children and most of the fishermen landed on the south shore of the river while two of his sons took the boats and moored them alongside ours. I went to the river gate to meet them. There had been rain during the night and they slid and slipped up the increasingly greasy track.

Persson gave an apologetic shrug, "We have made, it seems, a mess of your path, Lord Sven."

I clapped him around the shoulders, "Quite the contrary, you have improved the defences for an attacker will struggle even more to ascend the slope. Come, bring your folk inside. Your brother and sons are a welcome addition."

While the women were settled, I took the men to the walls and showed them where they would fight. I was not a fool and knew a man fought better amongst either friends or relatives. The farmers and fishermen who had joined us were placed on the north, east and west walls. Gandálfr would command the west wall, Faramir the east and I would be at the north wall and the gate. Osgar would be with me. Mary had organised food and at noon our guests and half of our men ate. I stood at the Dunelm gate with Osgar and Bersi. The gate was locked and we were the only sentries on the wall.

The men who had eaten returned to the walls to become accustomed to the land in daylight. Less than four hours after sext the land would become dark. The new men were not warriors as such but they had lived with danger and knew the things that they ought to do. Bersi showed that he had good eyes when he was the first to spot my two scouts as they came, not down the Dunelm Road but through the copse of trees that led to swampy ground and the causeway from Billingham. They led a third horse.

Osgar rubbed his beard, "Now why from that direction?"

It had me puzzled too, "This Mercian must be as cunning as his father. We will soon discover the reason."

Faramir and Haraldr were admitted and the gates slammed behind them. The bars were placed across them and I descended. I cupped my hands, "Heads of families, to me. You should hear this news."

I had already decided that no matter how bad was the news I would let all of those within my walls hear it. Haraldr led the horses off as Gandálfr handed an ale skin to Faramir. He drank deeply and pointed to the third horse, "Like you, Lord Sven, we found a scout. We were lucky or perhaps the Norns spun for we ambushed him and captured him. With the aid of my knife he told us where the enemy were and their purpose."

Gunhild had brought some food for Faramir and Haraldr and had heard the last words, "And where is he now?"

Faramir looked at me and I nodded. My daughter needed to know the reality of living where we did. "He is dead."

Her eyes widened and she handed over the food and then fled.

"Where are they?"

"They were clever and came nowhere near Sadbergh. They passed Thorpe and camped, last night at the farm of Fulthorpe." He looked to see if any women overheard his words, "The family was slain and their animals butchered."

"A strange route." I looked at Osgar who shrugged, "It means they have added a couple of miles to their journey for no purpose that I can see,"

Faramir nodded, "Oh, there was a purpose. They met up with a band of Scots at the farm. They now have an extra twenty men,"

"Scots?"

"I left Haraldr with the horses and crept close to their camp. The scout told us, before he died, that the Scots had arrived in the middle of the night and were on foot. They have just four or so miles to travel to reach us here. I crept close for there are many woods there and they kept not a good watch. I knew they were Scots by their weapons and their garb. Many of them have the blue tattooed faces of wild warriors. Some had bones plaited in their hair."

"You have done well, now tell us the number we face."

He looked at the faces of the men he did not know, Ragnar, Persson and Hakan. He knew the reaction of the others but not these new men. The words were intended for me but he sought the reaction of the new men. “Twenty or more Scots and more than sixty Mercians.” My face told him that I needed more information and he continued, “Most of the Mercians ride ponies. Just six wore mail. They are well armed but they looked to me to be the sweepings of the gutter. It is not an army.”

Osgar shook his head, “It is worse, it is a band of killers.”

Hakan nodded, “I knew Edwin of Fulthorpe. He was a good man. His wife was kind and fed strangers who passed down the road from Segges Field. When these killers come, none shall leave. What are your orders, lord?”

I was less sure now of their intentions. I did not answer immediately. “They have lost two scouts and I doubt that they will risk a third. They might well know now that we expect them. When they came the last time, it seemed to me that they used the track from the river. They destroyed the mill and slew the miller first. I think that they might risk the river route but I cannot be certain. I want half of the men to watch until midnight and I will watch with the other half after that.”

Osgar nodded, “I will take the first watch.”

It was not a well thought out plan but it was a plan and I had learned, serving Cnut, that men just wanted to know in their minds what was expected of them. If they believed their leader knew what he was doing then that gave them more confidence. We just had to wait.

Gunhild had told my wife of the scout and his death. I saw her speaking with Father John. I went over to them, “Father John, I know not when the enemy will come but when they do, they will try all that they can to gain the walls. Men will be hurt. I would use your church as a place of sanctuary and healing.” I looked at Mary, “Have some of the younger girls and older women help Father John.”

She nodded, “Was the death of the scout necessary?”

I shook my head, “No, he could have stayed in Mercia but he came raiding. It is not a pleasant thought but in such raids men die. They seek vengeance and gold. This is not a war such as King Cnut or King Edmund might have fought, it is more basic than that. These men seek to destroy us and take all that we have, including our lives. Had Faramir spared the scout then there would be a greater chance of that happening. Keep a knife about you always. That includes you, Father, your robes will not save you from such men.”

I took over and Osgar said that while he had seen nothing, noises in the night from the causeway had him worried, “I know that Lord Edward knows of the danger but Billingham is not as well defended as Norton. He could easily take that first.”

"And we would be alerted. No, Osgar, if Norton falls then so will Billingham. Their best defence is us. Now get some food and rest. Tomorrow will be a long day."

It was a cold night and the sky was clear. There was no cloud but also no moon. I was grateful for my cloak. Bersi had joined me. I was mailed from top to toe. Bersi, like my slingers, had no mail but he had a leather vest studded with metal and he wore Steana's first helmet. He would be better protected than most of the slingers but he would only be in danger if they breached our walls. We had to stop that.

I walked the whole perimeter. When I reached the river wall I spied the ships, tied together. There were fifteen men in all, guarding the boats and had they been in the village then our defence would have been stronger but we needed the ships to be protected. It was as I passed the mill that I heard noises that were not the noises of the night. I hissed to the men who stood watch on the east and south walls, "Stand to and shout if you hear anything." There was no point in rousing the men who had only recently retired but I feared that an attack was about to begin.

Gandálfr was on the west wall and I hurried around to him, "I heard noises from the river. It could be scouts but, equally, it could be a ruse to make us move men. Be alert."

"From what Faramir told us they only have four miles to walk. They could have been in place since the sun slipped below the western sky. They will have seen the sentries." I nodded. He continued, "If that was us, we would count on the sentries being tired and make a dawn attack."

"You are right. I will watch the sky and rouse the rest before dawn. Better that they lose an hour of sleep than their lives."

As I walked around the walls to tell Faramir I found myself gripping Oathsword tightly. It comforted me. When I reached the east wall, I studied the sky. Was that dawn or false dawn?

I spoke to Faramir and he nodded, "Osgar and the others have had more than three hours of sleep. It is not enough but it will have to do. That looks like the sun to the east."

I was about to descend the ladder when a horn from the river made me turn. Those watching from the river had seen what we had not. Men were moving along the riverbank. I hurled myself down the ladder and ran through the village shouting, "Stand to! Stand to!" I ran to the river gate as men emerged from where they had slept.

I clambered up the ladder. Karl Red Hair was on watch, "I can hear men, Lord Sven, but I cannot see them."

I looked down as the sky lightened a little. He was right. Men could be heard. Persson and his folk had done us a favour in making the trail muddy. I heard a shout as a Mercian slid down the slippery bank and another voice belatedly ordered silence. Karl would have to command this wall and I turned to him as the women defenders, clutching their darts and improvised spears joined us, "I think that the mud may defeat them but no heroics, Karl, you have the women with you. If they near the gates or the walls then shout for me. Do you understand?"

"I do, my lord, and as my Anna will be with us, I will not be tardy in my cry!"

I ran around the fighting platform as men climbed up to take their positions. There was no confusion as they had done this in daylight and each man knew where they would stand. The day before had been overcast and damp. This one would be brighter and those on the east wall would have the sun in their eyes. As I passed each man, I patted them on the back or gave them encouragement. They each had a determined look about them. The sun suddenly flared from my left and glinted off helmets. There were warriors to the east and to the north. The roar from the south told me that they were trying to attack there. At the same time a horn sounded and the Mercians and their allies began their attack. Even as I hefted my spear, I saw that the Norns had spun. If we had not put ships and men to watch from the river then the sneak attack on the river gate might have worked. Had Persson and his people not made the path from the river impassable then they might have made the gate.

Turning to my left I cupped my hand and shouted, Gandálfr, reinforce the river wall!"

"Aye, lord."

Bersi shouted, "Loose arrows and stones." His experience fighting Edmund Ironside helped him and I saw men sheltering in the copse fall, their arrows and bows dropping at their feet as they were struck by Bersi's bowmen. My son could not yet draw a warbow but he knew how to command. His grandfather's blood coursed through his veins.

I heard the banging of spears on shields as a warrior, I took it to be Brihtric, for he had a full face helmet with small wings at the side, rose from a fold in the ground and led a shield wall of thirty men towards us. It was half of the Mercians. His plan was clear. Attack the river wall and draw off defenders from the other walls and then breach the Dunelm gate. There were just twelve of us, along with the slingers and archers to defend this wall. Their shields made them impervious to stones and arrows. The ditch would narrow their attack and force them to take the bridge.

Osgar tightened the strap on his helmet, "This Mercian is clever and uses his men well. We cannot hurt them so long as they keep their shields high. Where are their spears I wonder?"

I did not get the chance to respond as I heard a blood curdling war cry to my right and knew where the Scottish mercenaries were attacking. Faramir and his twelve men would have a hard battle. The Scots were fierce and wild men. They could fight on even when wounded. I found myself in an uncomfortable position. Usually, when I fought, I was at the heart of the battle and could see everything. I could only see one third of the enemy. I guessed that the Scots were attacking the east wall but that left the rest of the Mercians unaccounted for.

"This will be a test of our new walls, Osgar." He said nothing for, like me he feared that they would fail and fall.

As they neared the gate the Mercians changed formation. They did it so well that not one warrior was hit by either a stone or an arrow. What I had forgotten to have on the fighting platform was a pile of rocks to drop onto their shields. Would my mistake come to haunt us? The formation was four men wide and five men deep. They made their way over the bridge and it was only then I saw that they carried not shields but axes and swords. When I heard the sound of axes on wood then I knew that they were hacking through the two bars on the gates. I took a decision, "Bersi, keep the slingers and archers loosing to deter the enemy, the rest with me."

"Aye, father."

I led my twelve men down the steps. Osgar and I were the only two with mail. I shouted, when we reached the gates, "Osgar and I will be the top of the wedge. The rest lock in behind us." I felt a shield in my back. This time it would not be a hearthweru. For the first time in a long time I would be reliant on men I did not know.

Osgar and I levelled our spears as I saw chips of wood flying from the bars on the gate. Their axmen were hitting between the gates to great effect. I heard a scream from beyond the gates and a cheer from the walls. One of the men attacking had been hit. I was not a fool. One dead man did not get us victory and I knew that the gates would not hold. When they were burst asunder then more than twenty warriors would charge my twelve.

A clash of steel above me told me that the Scots had used ladders or shields to ascend the walls and had made the fighting platform. If Faramir could not hold them then all was lost.

Gandálfr's voice came from my left, "You three men stay here, you other two, follow me." Our west wall was about to be held by three men and my north wall by boys. The Norns had, indeed, spun a strange spell. I saw Gandálfr run along the fighting platform to aid his shield brother. As he passed us the first bar was split and they began to hack at the other. I heard the bang as men hurled their shields at the gate. The wood we had used was young. Had we seasoned it enough? The answer came as Gandálfr led his two men to go to the aid of a beleaguered Faramir. The gates burst open and the Mercians flooded in, "Brace and thrust!"

Only half the men with me were from Agerhøne. Ragnar and his folk made up the other half. I hoped they knew that my command meant to lock shields and thrust our spears at the same time. The first two men wore no mail. They had been axemen whose shields were around their backs. Their success had gone to their heads and cost them their lives as they hurled themselves at us. Saxon Slayer found the neck of one and Osgar drove his deep within the second.

I heard Brihtric shout, "The Viking is mine. No one touch him but me."

That suited me for it meant others would not have to face the one who was clearly the most dangerous. He wore good mail and had a fine sword.

Bersi shouted, "Loose at their backs!" His slingers and archers had easy targets.

I levelled Saxon Slayer and thrust at Brihtric. Even as it neared him a Mercian hacked his axe at the ash shaft and the spear I had carried for so many years was cut in twain. I hurled the stump at Brihtric and drew Oathsword. The Mercian was fast and his sword came at me like a serpent's fangs. My left hand just reacted and my shield blocked the blow but such was the force that I was forced back and there was no comforting shield to bolster me. Our shield wall was shattered and we had to fight as individuals. I forced myself to be calm and did not waste effort in blows that might be wasted. I was helped by my opponent who could not resist taunting me.

"I am here to have vengeance for my brothers and my father. I will kill you and then slaughter every man, woman and child in this village. With your gold I will build an army and show Cnut that Mercia is mightier than Wessex ever was." Even as he spoke, I was thrusting Oathsword over his shield and into his right arm. My blade slid through some links and made a cut on his arm. It was first blood to me and although did little or no damage it angered him and he reacted, "You have no honour, you Danish dog!"

He punched with his shield and slashed with his sword. I knew there was no one behind me and I simply stepped back. He almost tumbled forward such was his angry momentum. His helmet looked like a good one but while the bird on my helmet was there for extra protection, his bird's wings, small though they were, actually made the helmet weaker. I raised Oathsword and brought it down, using the flat of the blade at the wing on the left of the helmet. I hit it hard and not only did it ring like a bell but the wing fell leaving a hole where it had been attached. He swung a mighty blow at my side that I easily held with my shield and I lunged at his face. He had thought to knock me from my feet with the blow and his shield was slow to come around. He jerked his head back and Oathsword sliced through the leather strap and tore a wound across his neck. The unbalanced helmet fell to the floor. The wound was not deep but having blood drip down your neck is discomfiting to say the least. Without his helmet I saw fear in his eyes. He had not expected to die and I could see he was unprepared for his death. He tried to step back as I swung Oathsword again and he slipped. The Dragon Sword split his skull open and he fell dead.

A cry from Osgar told the Mercians that their leader was dead, "Brihtric is dead! The Oathsword is victorious."

While the Mercians looked in horror at the dead man, Bersi and the slingers rained death upon the others. Darts were hurled and a Mercian voice screamed, "All is lost! Flee,"

Ragnar and his men were in no mood to hold back and they raced after the Mercians. Others left the walls and hurried about them.

Osgar raised my right arm and shouted, "Today I fought with a hero." Thank you, Lord Sven, you have made an old warrior remember his youth. We won and against the odds too."

As I nodded and sheathed Oathsword, I looked to the east wall and saw Gandálfr cradling the body of Faramir. We had won but, as in all battles, there was a cost.

Epilogue

Every family had lost someone but the loss of Faramir hurt me more than any other. He had been the most loyal of men and saved my life on more than one occasion. It had been his news that had warned us of the attack and he had saved us. For Gandálfr it was even worse as he was now the last of the hearthweru and I knew that it weighed heavily with him. The Scots had fought ferociously and died to a man. Our heaviest losses were on that wall. For my wife it had been a chastening experience. The Mercians had not threatened the walls too much but she had witnessed death as the other women and warriors had slain men with darts and spears. In the end we had thirty dead Mercians and twenty dead Scots to strip and then burn. Ragnar, Persson and Hakan had mounted captured horses and pursued the survivors as far as Thorpe. There they had stopped their hunt and buried the dead family slaughtered by the Mercians. I think that barely fifteen men escaped and I doubted that they would make it back to Mercia. Streona's family was punished for his treachery. We gained thirty horses which were equitably shared amongst the defenders. I received no more than any other warrior. We had all fought equally well. The dead were buried and the families returned to their homes.

Karl Red Hair asked for and was given one of the farms and the other went to Beorn the Grim and his family. The whole clan went to help rebuild their homes and I felt better knowing that the two men were rewarded for their heroism. Another eight chose plots of land that lay closer to Norton. We worked on those as well.

It was a fortnight after the battle and three days after we finished work on the two farms when Steana sailed his drekar next to the river along with the knarr.

He was relieved to see that we were all alive but angry that they had not made it faster than they had. He growled, "I am sorry, father, but the drekar was not ready for sea. I shouted at Olaf but it was my fault. I had forgotten that we are sailors and our ships should be ready to sail."

I shook my head, "The Norns, Steana, you would not have been in time even had you sailed back on the knarr but it is good that we see you."

He nodded, "Lars told us of your situation and another two families have come, including Haaken who heard there was a mill."

I smiled, "Then all is well. When time allows, I will show you the manor and we will hunt. The Mercians are no longer a threat and the battle has made us all one. Now that our service to Cnut is over, we can live our lives."

The wind changed a little and even as we headed to my hall, I knew that the Norns were spinning and Oathsword would be needed again.

The End

Norse Calendar

Gormánuður October 14th - November 13th
Ýlir November 14th - December 13th
Mörsugur December 14th - January 12th
Þorri - January 13th - February 11th
Gói - February 12th - March 13th
Einmánuður - March 14th - April 13th
Harpa April 14th - May 13th
Skerpla - May 14th - June 12th
Sólmánuður - June 13th - July 12th
Heyannir - July 13th - August 14th
Tvímánuður - August 15th - September 14th
Haustmánuður September 15th-October 13th

Canonical Hours

Matins (nighttime)
Lauds (early morning)
Prime (first hour of daylight)
Terce (third hour)
Sext (noon)
Nones (ninth hour)
Vespers (sunset evening)
Compline (end of the day)

Glossary

Acemannesceastre- Bath (aching men's city- a reference to the springs.)
Bagsheta - Bagshot
Beardestapol – Barnstaple
Beck- a stream
Blót – a blood sacrifice made by a jarl
Bondi- Viking farmers who fight
Bjorr – Beaver
Breguntford - Brentford
Brycgstow - Bristol
Burgh/Burh-King Alfred's defences. The largest was Winchester
Byrnie- a mail or leather shirt reaching down to the knees
Cantwareburh- Canterbury
Cent – Kent
Chape- the tip of a scabbard
Corebricg – Corbridge
Dorchestershire- Devon
Deoraby – Derby
Din Guardi - Bamburgh
Drekar- a Dragon ship (a Viking warship) pl. drekar
Dudecota - Didcot
Dunelm- Durham
Dyflin- Old Norse for Dublin
Eoforwic- Saxon for York
Føroyar- Faroe Islands
Fey- having second sight
Ferneberga – Farnborough (Hants)
Firkin- a barrel containing eight gallons (usually beer)
Fret - a sea mist
Fyrd-the Saxon levy
Galdramenn- wizard
Gegnesburh – Gainsborough (Lincolnshire)
Gesithas – a Saxon bodyguard, hearthweru
Gighesbore – Guisborough
Gippeswic- Ipswich
Gleawecastre – Gloucester
Hamtunscīr -Hampshire
Hamwic- Southampton

Heiða-býr – Hedeby in Schleswig- destroyed in 1066
Herepath- the military roads connecting the burghs of King Alfred
Herkumbl- a badge on a helmet denoting the clan
Hersir- a Viking landowner and minor noble. It ranks below a jarl
Herterpol – Hartlepool
Hnefatafl – a Viking game a little like chess
Hoggs or Hogging- when the pressure of the wind causes the stern or the bow to droop
Hremmesgeat – Ramsgate
Hringmaraheior – Ringmere
Hrofescester- Rochester, Kent
Hundred- Saxon military organization. (One hundred men from an area led by a thegn or gesith)
Isle of Greon- Isle of Grain (Thames Estuary)
Jarl- Norse earl or lord
Joro-goddess of the earth
kjerringa - Old Woman- the solid block in which the mast rested
Knarr- a merchant ship or a coastal vessel
Kyrtle-woven top
Ligera caestre – Leicester
Lincylene – Lincoln
Lydwicnaesse- Breton Point, Exmouth
Mast fish- two large racks on a ship designed to store the mast when not required.
Meðune –River Medina in the Isle of Wight
Mere lafan – Marlow Bucks
Midden- a place where they dumped human waste
Miklagård - Constantinople
Northwic-Norwich
Njörðr- God of the sea
Nithing- A man without honour (Saxon)
Northantone, - Northampton
Ocmundtune- Oakhampton
Odin- The 'All Father' God of war, also associated with wisdom, poetry, and magic (The Ruler of the gods).
Østersøen – The Baltic Sea
Otorbrunna – Otterburn
Oxnaford - Oxford
Ran- Goddess of the sea
Roof rock- slate
Saami - the people who live in what is now Northern Norway/Sweden

Sabrina - The River Severn
Sandwic – Sandwich (Kent)
Scorranstone - Sherston (Wilts)
Scree - loose rocks in a glacial valley
Seax – short sword
Sennight - seven nights- a week
Shamblord - Cowes, Isle of Wight
Sheerstrake - the uppermost strake in the hull
Sheet - a rope fastened to the lower corner of a sail
Shroud - a rope from the masthead to the hull amidships
Skald - a Viking poet and singer of songs
Skeggox – an axe with a shorter beard on one side of the blade
Skumasþorp- Scunthorpe
Skreið- stockfish (any fish which is preserved)
Skjalborg- shield wall
Snekke- a small warship
Snotingaham - Nottingham
Stanford - Stamford
Stad- Norse settlement
Stays- ropes running from the masthead to the bow
Strake- the wood on the side of a drekar
Suindune - Swindon
Swynfylking – a series of small wedges.
Tarn - small lake (Norse)
Teignton - Kingsteignton
The Norns - The three sisters who weave webs of intrigue for men
Thing - Norse for a parliament or a debate (Tynwald in the Isle of Man)
Thor's day - Thursday
Threttanessa- a drekar with 13 oars on each side.
Thrall- slave
Trenail- a round wooden peg used to secure strakes
Úlfarrberg- Helvellyn
Ullr-Norse God of Hunting
Ulfheonar-an elite Norse warrior who wore a wolf skin over his armour
Verðandi -the Norn who sees the future
Volva- a witch or healing woman in Norse culture
Walhaz -Norse for the Welsh (foreigners)
Waite- a Viking word for farm
Wiht -The Isle of Wight
Windles-ore - Windsor

Witan- Saxon Parliament
Withy- the mechanism connecting the steering board to the ship
Wintan-ceastre -Winchester
Woden's day- Wednesday
Wyrd- Fate
Wyrme- Norse for Dragon
Yard- a timber from which the sail is suspended

Historical Notes

The Dragon Sword is a blade of my own imagination although King Alfred did give a sword to the illegitimate son of Prince Edward, the king's son. Æthelstan became the first king accorded the title King of England. As readers of my books will know swords are always important. This series will reflect that.

A word about Denmark, the maps and the place names. If you look at a map of modern Denmark, you will see that Ribe is not where I place it. Names change over the years and you will see, as the series progresses, the reason for some of the changes. The Heiða-býr of King Sweyn is also no longer there. It was destroyed sometime after King Sweyn died. There are some ruins where it once was but as the Danes built using wood they are not as substantial as the Roman ones would have been.

The names of the places around Norton are based on the names I found on the 1866 map. Rus' Worthy is Roseworth and Ragnar's Worthy is Ragworth. Pers' Track is Portrack and Stockadeton is Stockton. Fulthorpe is the name of a farm close to Thorpe Thewles.

The treachery of the period beggars belief. Eadric Streona changed sides as often as a weathervane turns yet Cnut, Æthelred and Edmund continued to believe him. The challenge from Edmund to Cnut was real. At Assundun Cnut stayed in the rear while Edmund fought in the front rank.

The death of Edmund has four reported versions. One suggested that he died of wounds received at Assundun. The other three all have similar threads. One was that when he was on the privy a hook was inserted into his bowels and that his how he died. I dismissed that one as clearly improbable. A second was that a crossbow was fired into him. That too seemed unlikely as it did not guarantee death. The one I took was a spear. Streona claimed it was he who did the deed but he seems to me to be too cowardly to do such a thing and I used the evidence that it was his sons. He did admit to the deed to Cnut and was executed as I said. There were rumours that Cnut put Streona up to it. He may have done. He was a far more ruthless man than history suggests.

Sven Saxon Sword is an invention of mine. He helps to put flesh on the historical bones. The story will continue.

- **King Cnut- W B Bartlett**
- **Vikings- Life and Legends -British Museum**

- **Saxon, Norman and Viking by Terence Wise (Osprey)**
- **The Vikings (Osprey) -Ian Heath**
- **Byzantine Armies 668-1118 (Osprey)-Ian Heath**
- **Romano-Byzantine Armies 4th- 9th Century (Osprey) -David Nicholle**
- **The Walls of Constantinople AD 324-1453 (Osprey) -Stephen Turnbull**
- **Viking Longship (Osprey) - Keith Durham**
- **The Vikings- David Wernick (Time-Life)**
- **The Vikings in England Anglo-Danish Project**
- **Anglo Saxon Thegn AD 449-1066- Mark Harrison (Osprey)**
- **Viking Hersir- 793-1066 AD - Mark Harrison (Osprey)**
- **National Geographic- March 2017**
- **British Kings and Queens- Mike Ashley**

Griff Hosker January 2023

Other books by Griff Hosker

If you enjoyed reading this book, then why not read another one by the author?

Ancient History

The Sword of Cartimandua Series
(Germania and Britannia 50 A.D. – 128 A.D.)
Ulpius Felix- Roman Warrior (prequel)
The Sword of Cartimandua
The Horse Warriors
Invasion Caledonia
Roman Retreat
Revolt of the Red Witch
Druid's Gold
Trajan's Hunters
The Last Frontier
Hero of Rome
Roman Hawk
Roman Treachery
Roman Wall
Roman Courage

The Wolf Warrior series
(Britain in the late 6th Century)
Saxon Dawn
Saxon Revenge
Saxon England
Saxon Blood
Saxon Slayer
Saxon Slaughter
Saxon Bane
Saxon Fall: Rise of the Warlord
Saxon Throne
Saxon Sword

Medieval History

Danish Sword

The Dragon Heart Series
Viking Slave
Viking Warrior
Viking Jarl
Viking Kingdom
Viking Wolf
Viking War
Viking Sword
Viking Wrath
Viking Raid
Viking Legend
Viking Vengeance
Viking Dragon
Viking Treasure
Viking Enemy
Viking Witch
Viking Blood
Viking Weregeld
Viking Storm
Viking Warband
Viking Shadow
Viking Legacy
Viking Clan
Viking Bravery

The Norman Genesis Series
Hrolf the Viking
Horseman
The Battle for a Home
Revenge of the Franks
The Land of the Northmen
Ragnvald Hrolfsson
Brothers in Blood
Lord of Rouen
Drekar in the Seine
Duke of Normandy
The Duke and the King

Danelaw
(England and Denmark in the 11th Century)
The Dragon Sword
Oathsword

Danish Sword

Blood Sword
Danish Sword

New World Series
Blood on the Blade
Across the Seas
The Savage Wilderness
The Bear and the Wolf
Erik The Navigator
Erik's Clan

The Vengeance Trail

The Reconquista Chronicles
Castilian Knight
El Campeador
The Lord of Valencia

The Aelfraed Series
(Britain and Byzantium 1050 A.D. - 1085 A.D.)
Housecarl
Outlaw
Varangian

The Anarchy Series England 1120-1180
English Knight
Knight of the Empress
Northern Knight
Baron of the North
Earl
King Henry's Champion
The King is Dead
Warlord of the North
Enemy at the Gate
The Fallen Crown
Warlord's War
Kingmaker
Henry II
Crusader
The Welsh Marches
Irish War

Danish Sword

Poisonous Plots
The Princes' Revolt
Earl Marshal
The Perfect Knight

Border Knight
1182-1300
Sword for Hire
Return of the Knight
Baron's War
Magna Carta
Welsh Wars
Henry III
The Bloody Border
Baron's Crusade
Sentinel of the North
War in the West
Debt of Honour
The Blood of the Warlord
The Fettered King

Sir John Hawkwood Series
France and Italy 1339- 1387
Crécy: The Age of the Archer
Man At Arms
The White Company
Leader of Men
Tuscan Warlord

Lord Edward's Archer
Lord Edward's Archer
King in Waiting
An Archer's Crusade
Targets of Treachery
The Great Cause
Wallace's War

Struggle for a Crown
1360- 1485
Blood on the Crown
To Murder a King
The Throne

Danish Sword

King Henry IV
The Road to Agincourt
St Crispin's Day
The Battle for France
The Last Knight
Queen's Knight

Tales from the Sword I
(Short stories from the Medieval period)

Tudor Warrior series
England and Scotland in the late 14th and early 15th century
Tudor Warrior
Tudor Spy

Conquistador
England and America in the 16th Century
Conquistador
The English Adventurer

Modern History

The Napoleonic Horseman Series
Chasseur à Cheval
Napoleon's Guard
British Light Dragoon
Soldier Spy
1808: The Road to Coruña
Talavera
The Lines of Torres Vedras
Bloody Badajoz
The Road to France
Waterloo

The Lucky Jack American Civil War series
Rebel Raiders
Confederate Rangers
The Road to Gettysburg

The Soldier of the Queen Series
Soldier of the Queen

Danish Sword

Redcoat's Rifle

The British Ace Series

1914

1915 Fokker Scourge

1916 Angels over the Somme

1917 Eagles Fall

1918 We will remember them

From Arctic Snow to Desert Sand

Wings over Persia

Combined Operations series
1940-1945

Commando

Raider

Behind Enemy Lines

Dieppe

Toehold in Europe

Sword Beach

Breakout

The Battle for Antwerp

King Tiger

Beyond the Rhine

Korea

Korean Winter

Tales from the Sword II
(Short stories from the Modern period)

Other Books

Great Granny's Ghost (Aimed at 9-14-year-old young people)

For more information on all of the books then please visit the author's website at www.griffhosker.com where there is a link to contact him or visit his Facebook page: GriffHosker at Sword Books

Printed in Great Britain
by Amazon

20313470R00132